SPELLBOUND

"Do you need help, Miss Wakefield?" A man's deep voice drifted up from the base of the tree.

Quickly, Lauren pulled her skirt around her legs. "Good afternoon, Mr. Hawkes," she said, schooling her voice to calmness, "I was just . . . rescuing my cat."

"So I see." The picture of those shapely legs, exposed nearly to the thighs, would stay with him forever.

"Will you . . . go away so I can come down?" Just then her foot slipped, and she slid several feet downward.

"Jump," he called. "I'll catch you. Send the cat down first."

He braced himself as she launched herself toward him. A moment later a luscious, violet-scented bundle of womanhood dropped into his arms.

Lauren gazed at him, spellbound. Although his hand was barely touching her, she could feel it like a hot brand on her flesh.

"Lauren!" he muttered hoarsely. His hand moved up to clasp her neck; he could feel her racing pulse. His world narrowed to her full, red mouth. Bending his head, he caught her lips with his. She whimpered against his mouth, fighting the passion that buffeted her, but he merely sank one hand into her thick chignon and deepened the kiss until she almost swooned with desire.

Wendy Garrett
Love's Magic Spell

ZEBRA BOOKS
KENSINGTON PUBLISHING CORP.

To Sam,
who had to leave much too soon,
and to Michael and George,
who must carry the torch.

Special thanks
to my agent, Eugenia Panettieri,
and to Ann LaFarge
for making it all possible.

ZEBRA BOOKS

are published by

Kensington Publishing Corp.
475 Park Avenue South
New York, NY 10016

First printing: February, 1992

Printed in the United States of America

Chapter One

London 1870

Lauren gently drew the covers up over her mother's frail, sleeping form, then retrieved her sewing from the nearby table and settled in the chair beside the bed. Instead of working, however, she watched her mother sleep. Four months ago Alanna Stanton had been one of the most beautiful women in England. But illness had wasted her once-lovely face and taken the luster from her honey blond hair. Now she was merely a sick, middle-aged woman. Her skin, once flawless, had become papery, almost transparent, the veins making a dark tracery beneath it. A tear traced a slow path down Lauren's cheek. Absently, she wiped it away, then leaned forward to stroke a lock of hair away from her mother's face.

There was a peremptory knock at the front door. Setting the sewing aside, Lauren rose and slipped quietly away from the bed.

"Lauren."

Her mother's voice, however faint, stopped Lauren in mid-stride. "Mother, you should be asleep," she chided softly, turning back towards the bed.

"I heard a knock. Sebastian has come." Alanna's

head rolled from side to side fretfully. "He cannot see me like this. Help me, child. I must dress."

Lauren doubted very much that the visitor was Lord Parry; the man hadn't been to the house since her mother had become ill. "I'll go see," she said. "Try to rest."

"Of course, it is him," Alanna murmured, closing her eyes again. "I can't imagine what has kept him away all this time." Her voice trailed away as sleep claimed her.

Lauren took a deep, shuddering breath. Then, regaining her composure with an effort, she tiptoed from the room and hurried towards the front of the house.

The maid was just closing the double door leading into the parlor. When Lauren came into sight, she called, "It's Mr. Gill."

Anxiety knotted Lauren's stomach. "Thank you, Mary. Will you stay with Mother while I see him?"

"Yes, Miss." Mary tucked a lock of gray-streaked brown hair up into her starched cap. "What's 'e doing 'ere?"

"I don't know." Again Lauren's stomach twisted. John Gill was his lordship's man of business. Whatever his reason for coming here might be, she was certain it boded ill for her mother. For a moment she faltered, her fingers twining nervously in the dark blue woolen fabric of her dress. Then she called on the iron control she had learned by being the daughter of a kept woman, reviled and disdained merely because of what her mother was. Holding her head up proudly, she flung the doors open and went in.

Mr. Gill rose from his seat. "Good afternoon, Miss Stanton."

"Good afternoon, Mr. Gill." Absently, she noted that the room was rather cool and dark. She walked past the visitor to open the heavy velvet draperies that shrouded the windows. The soft morning light flooded in, picking up the reddish tones of the mahogany tables and making the gold silk damask of the two matching sofas gleam richly, as though Midas himself had placed his hand upon them.

"How is your mother? Better, I trust?" the visitor asked.

"The doctors say that the illness seems to have run its course, but that she will be a very long time in recovering, if ever." If Lord Parry had arranged this visit to show his concern for his mistress's health, she thought, it was a very poor way of going about it. And far too late to fool anyone. Disgusted, she said, "Forgive my bluntness, Mr. Gill, but I am extremely busy just now. Why don't you just tell me why you've come?"

He flushed, surprising himself. He hadn't been embarrassed in years. Although his lordship paid him an excellent salary to take care of delicate matters such as the one he had come here to discuss, this tall young woman's poise threw him off balance. With her bright auburn hair drawn tightly back into a knot and the prim, high-necked gown she wore, she might be a governess. She might be his own daughter.

"Mr. Gill?" she prompted.

He recovered his composure with an effort. "I'm sorry to be the bearer of such unfortunate tidings, Miss Stanton, but I've come to tell you that his lordship will, er, require the use of this house."

"I see." Lauren's chin went up a fraction of an inch. She had expected this. But expecting it didn't make it hurt any less. "We have lived here nearly ten years, Mr. Gill."

"I'm sorry." Again surprising himself, he found that he meant it.

"Has he replaced her already?" she asked, anger goading her out of her normal reticence.

"Perhaps," he said, sympathy prompting him to reply to a question he would never have answered at another time.

Lauren turned to stare out of the window. Her mother had given Lord Parry ten years of her life. She had settled for less than marriage, and would now have to settle for what his lordship would be willing to give a mistress he no longer wanted. And that, Lauren thought bitterly, was nothing. Worse than nothing. Now that Alanna was ill, unable to share his idle, extravagant fancies any longer, he was casting her off like an old cloak. He didn't even have the courage to tell her himself, but sent a lackey to do it for him.

Tears stung Lauren's eyelids. Nothing she had endured in her twenty years—not the shame of being the illegitimate child of a woman whose name was a scandal in two countries, not the lack of friends, or the warmth of a real family—was as awful as having to face her mother with this. Foolish, lovely Alanna Stanton—daughter of one of the foremost families in New York—had given up her home, her reputation, even her child's happiness, for two selfish men who had cared nothing for her sacrifice. Both had forsaken her when she needed them most; Piero Cavalli, when she became pregnant, and Lord Parry, when she became ill. Now she was to learn the price of mistaking passion for love. God grant the lesson didn't kill her.

Pride stiffened Lauren's back. *She* loved her mother. Somehow she would find a way to support her. A decent way. Never again would they depend on a man for anything. Fiercely, she blinked the tears away and forced coolness into her voice. "Tell his lordship that I'll begin packing immediately. We *will* be allowed to take our personal belongings, I trust?"

8

"Of course. But there is the matter of the emerald necklace and earrings his lordship let Mrs. Stanton use."

Lauren turned away from the window and went to stand beside one of the graceful Queen Anne chairs that flanked the fireplace. Her hands gripping its back for support, she said, "It was my understanding that the jewels were a gift." A love gift, she added silently, lightly given and as lightly taken away.

"You must understand that they belonged to his lordship's wife's mother—"

"I understand, Mr. Gill. The jewelry is in my mother's room. Shall I tell her that you want to take it with you, or will you trust me to have it sent to Lord Parry's residence?"

"By all means, have it sent," he agreed hastily. "And now I have one more piece of business to discuss with you before I go."

She stood, outwardly composed, and waited for him to make the next move. Inwardly, however, her thoughts churned in confusion. By casting her mother off, Lord Parry had already taken everything the poor woman held dear. What else could he possibly want from them?

"I think I can arrange for you to stay here," Gill said. "His lordship would be willing—"

"He'll rent the house to us?" she asked, surprised but very pleased by the unexpected generosity. "I'm quite good with a needle, you know. I could easily find work as a seamstress. It shouldn't take me long to obtain a steady clientele."

"I'm afraid you've misunderstood me. His lordship is not at all interested in renting the house. He would . . . he prefers . . ." Gill cleared his throat. Her expression, so innocently expectant, shamed him, taking away the facile words he'd planned to use. Finally he

9

blurted, "Surely, Miss Stanton, you realize that you are a very lovely young woman. His lordship thinks highly of you. Most highly."

Lauren felt herself go hot and cold and hot again as she realized what he meant. She swallowed convulsively, the thought of what he was suggesting making her physically ill. "And my mother . . ." she couldn't finish the sentence.

"I'm afraid that his lordship prefers, ah, freshness in his companions, Miss Stanton." Oh, yes, he thought, Lord Parry had long admired Lauren Stanton. How could he resist her stunning auburn hair and thick-lashed Latin eyes, her white, perfect skin, the challenge of her innocence. Gill was surprised the man had waited this long. Alanna Stanton's illness was merely an excuse for what his lordship had wanted to do for years.

He waited for her to speak, but the silence went on for an uncomfortably long time. "Miss Stanton?" he asked, unable to bear the tense stillness any longer.

"Yes?"

"Have you an answer for his lordship?"

Her dark gaze was unwavering. "Tell him no."

"London can be a terrible place for a woman alone," he said, indicating the expensively furnished room in which they stood. "His lordship can be very generous, as you know. There are worse things than being under his protection."

"Are there?" Abruptly becoming aware of the rich fabric under her hands, she jerked them away as if they'd been burned. Put herself under Parry's protection? Oh, no. Never, never, *never* would she allow him—or any man, for that matter—to use her as her mother had been used.

"Mr. Gill, I'd rather drown myself in the Thames,"

10

she said. Although she kept her voice calm, she wanted to scream, to curse, to break things. But passion was for Alanna, not her daughter.

"But what will you do, Miss Stanton?"

"Anything but . . . that. I'll work in a factory if I have to."

"A factory! Life with his lordship would be easier, surely," he said.

She looked past him, towards the back of the house where her mother lay. "I assure you that it would not be easier. Goodbye, Mr. Gill."

Silently he took his leave. As the door closed behind him, Lauren let her breath out in a long sigh. A moment later Mary opened the door and peered into the room.

"What did 'e say?" she demanded in a whisper.

"His lordship needs the house."

Mary's eyes widened. "Cor! Just like that?"

"Just like that."

" 'E didn't even offer to send you back home?"

"No." Lauren knew that gentlemen were expected to give a generous parting gift as compensation to their former mistresses. It galled her that Lord Parry hadn't given her the chance to cast his money back in his face.

"May 'is nose rot off 'is face, the scoundrelly 'ound!" Mary cried.

Lauren moved forward to take the woman's hands in hers. "Mary, I don't know how much money we'll have. It's only fair to give you a chance to find another situation—"

"D'you think I'm goin' to leave after all you've done for me?" Mary demanded in outrage. "Miss Alanna needs me, she does. I'm staying."

"Mary . . ." Lauren looked into the older woman's eyes, read the loyalty and determination there, and

11

dropped the protest she had intended to make. "Thank you."

Mary twisted her apron in her hands. "Poor Miss Alanna. She's got the softest, gentlest 'eart I ever seen, and this is just goin' to break it into pieces."

"You're right, I'm afraid," Lauren said. She tapped her foot fretfully, her mind going in several directions at once. Then she nodded in decision. The first thing she must do was to visit her mother's solicitor and find out exactly what their financial situation was. "I have to go out, Mary. I'll be several hours. Will you be all right alone with mother?"

" 'Course." Mary brought Lauren's cloak and helped her into it. "I'll send for the coach."

"No, Mary. I'll walk."

"Walk!" The maid stared at her uncomprehendingly.

For the first time, Lauren allowed her seething anger to show. "I'll be damned if I'll use anything that belongs to his bloody lordship!" With that, she stalked out of the house, slamming the door behind her.

Lauren left the solicitor's office in a grim mood, for the state of her mother's finances was worse than she'd expected. In fact, she was deeply in debt. Lauren's throat ached with unshed tears. She had hoped that there was enough money to take them back to America. Away from the fog, away from the shame, where they could have a modest little home in a city where no one had ever heard of Alanna Stanton. But as things were, they'd be lucky to have enough money for food.

There was a crash from the street, then a woman's frightened scream. Lauren whirled to see a carriage go over onto its side. A horse reared, fighting its traces, then broke free and trotted away. Several bystanders rushed in pursuit of the animal.

Spying a woman struggling to climb out of the over-turned vehicle, Lauren dashed into the street. "Here, let me help you," she cried, putting her arm around the woman and lifting her to her feet. They stood together in the lee of the carriage as the traffic swirled around them. "Are you hurt?"

"I don't think so," the woman replied a bit shakily, patting ineffectually at the wisps of white hair that had escaped her chignon. Her accent was American, and gave Lauren a pang of homesickness. Glancing around, the woman exclaimed, "Good heavens, my driver! Chambers, are you all right?"

The driver appeared on the other side of the carriage. "I believe so, Ma'am." He brushed himself off, muttering under his breath, then sighed with relief when he saw two men returning with his horse. "It don't look too bad, Ma'am. I'll get some of these blokes to help me right the carriage."

"Come, let's get out of the street," Lauren urged, holding out her hand. "I'll help you."

"Why, you're American!" The woman took Lauren's slim, graceful hand in her tiny, plump one and held it as they walked.

"Yes." Lauren glanced at the woman beside her. She was short and rather stout, with a round, placid face and blue eyes whose innocent friendliness belonged in a child's face, not that of a woman in her sixties. She was expensively and tastefully dressed in widow's weeds. Rich and respectable, Lauren thought, the sort of woman who would recoil in disgust if she knew the history of the girl whose hand she held so familiarly.

"I'm Portia Danforth, from New York," the widow said, smiling up at her rescuer. "And you?"

New York, her mother's home! Oh, this was terri-ble! Lauren smoothed her hair back with her free hand. "I'm Lauren—" A dray, painted with the 'Wake-

13

field Crackers' went by. "I'm Lauren Wakefield, from . . . from Philadelphia." It was mad to give a false name, but she couldn't bear to see the friendship on Mrs. Danforth's pleasant face turn into cold hauteur. A simple lie to ease the few minutes' association they would have.

"Why, we're practically neighbors," Mrs. Danforth said. "I can't tell you what a pleasure it is to hear an American voice."

Part of Lauren wanted to get away as soon as possible, but another part of her, hungry for companionship from home, made her stay. While the driver and some of the bystanders worked to right the carriage, she chatted with the widow. She found Mrs. Danforth to be a charming, amiable person, completely without pretense, and wished with all her heart that a friendship between them was possible.

As though reading her thoughts, Mrs. Danforth said, "It's a shame to let such a pleasant conversation end. Please, won't you dine with me?"

Before Lauren could reply, the driver joined them.

"We're ready to go, Ma'am," he said, tipping his hat.

Mrs. Danforth nodded, then turned back to Lauren. "Please come, Miss Wakefield."

Lauren stared at her, confused by the pleading in those soft blue eyes. Could it be possible that this rich, respectable woman was as lonely as she? Instead of making her excuses and leaving, as she'd intended, she asked, "Are you alone here?"

"Yes." Mrs. Danforth patted her hair again. "I thought a change of surroundings might bring some . . . excitement to my life. But I discovered that traveling alone is just as dreary as living alone."

"Excuse me for asking, but your husband—did he pass away recently?"

"Nearly twenty-five years ago." Mrs. Danforth's eyes grew sad. "It seems like yesterday." Then she smiled again. "Listen to me, maundering on like a fool. I'm sure you have better things to do than listen to a silly old woman."

Lauren thought about her mother, safe at home with Mary. Surely telling her about Lord Parry could wait a few more hours. "Of course, I'll come," she said.

"Oh, I'm glad!" Mrs. Danforth allowed the driver to help her into the carriage, then indicated that Lauren join her. "We must tell your parents where you'll be."

"Oh, that won't be necessary. My parents . . ." Lauren hesitated, hating the deception she was playing, then said, "My parents aren't here."

"Your guardian or chaperone, then." The widow looked at Lauren quizzically, as the younger woman shook her head.

Lauren folded her hands in her lap. "I'm quite alone, Mrs. Danforth. I work for my living."

"I see." The widow was silent for a moment. Then she reached out to take Lauren's hand in both of hers. "Thaddeus—my husband always said that although I might be a twit about some things, I'm very good at judging people. Lauren—I *may* call you Lauren? Good. Well, as I was saying, I know people. I need a companion, and I haven't met anyone I think would do as well as you."

"But you don't know a thing about me!" Lauren protested.

"I know that you've been raised properly, no matter how your circumstances might have changed. I know that you're kind to strange old women, and I suspect you're as homesick as I am."

"But—"

"Every one of my friends was once a stranger,

15

Lauren," Mrs. Danforth said. "If it would make you feel better, why don't we have a week's trial here in London? If we suit, I'd like for you to come back home to New York with me."

Home! Lauren thought wistfully. The offer was tempting, oh, so tempting! She wanted work; here it was for the taking. Decent work. If she sold her mother's jewelry, she could pay for Mary and Alanna's passage to America. She'd save every cent she could of her wages, and one day that simple little home she'd dreamed about would be theirs. Yes, New York was her mother's home. But, wasted with illness as she was, no one was likely to recognize Alanna Stanton.

Lauren hesitated. Although she shrank from the thought of living a lie, she knew that Lauren Wakefield could afford the doctors and treatments Alanna needed if she was ever to get well. Lauren Wakefield could take her mother home. Lauren Stanton, illegitimate child of a notorious fallen woman, could do none of those things.

"What do you say, Lauren?" the widow asked. "I'm willing to take a chance on you. Will you take a chance on me?"

"Yes, I will." Lauren looked into the old woman's kind blue eyes. "And I promise you, Mrs. Danforth, that I will do my very best for you."

Chapter Two

New York City
October 1872

Lauren stepped onto the granite stoop of Mrs. Danforth's house amid a wind-tossed scattering of bright autumn leaves. Their colors echoed the glow in her heart; today her mother had taken her first steps in more than two years. Oh, how wonderful that it had happened while she was visiting! She wished she had the money to get her mother and Mary out of that dreary apartment on Bleeker Street, and into a house with a garden.

The front door opened suddenly, startling her out of her reverie. Fanny, the downstairs maid, peered out at her.

"Miss Wakefield, I'm so glad you're back!" she said breathlessly.

Lauren stepped inside. "What has you in such a flutter, Fanny?"

"There's a gentleman here to see Mrs. Danforth, Miss. He's most insistent. Since she's unavailable, I thought you might be able to talk to him."

"Unavailable?" Lauren took her cloak off and placed it in the maid's outstretched arms. "That's

17

strange. I thought she was going to be in all afternoon."

"She *is* in, Miss." Fanny pushed the door open and came into the room. "She's with Mr. Eldridge."

"Good heavens, not again!" Lauren muttered under her breath. Raising her voice so the maid could hear, she asked, "Are they . . . communing with the spirits again?"

The maid rolled her eyes upward. "Yes, Miss."

Lauren's full lips thinned in disapproval. Ever since Edward Eldridge, the so-called psychic expert, had come into their lives, the household had been in complete chaos. Although Portia thought he was the most wonderful person she'd ever met, it was obvious to Lauren and the servants that he was only interested in getting as much money from the credulous widow as possible. Charlatan, scoundrel, and a great many other things Lauren was too polite to say, even to herself, he was preying upon the old woman's desire to contact the spirit of her beloved — and many years deceased — husband. And now the man had actually moved into the house! Lauren had seen much of human folly in her twenty-two years, but nothing had ever matched this situation for sheer absurdity.

"What am I to do with the gentleman?" Fanny asked, breaking into Lauren's reverie. "You know Mrs. Danforth's order about being disturbed when they're . . . communicating."

Lauren nodded. But the order was Eldridge's, not the widow's, testament to the amount of power the fraudulent medium held in this house. "I'll see him," she said, holding her hand out for the man's card. She examined the small rectangle curiously. It was of the finest stock, thick and creamy, and said only -

18

Stephen Hawkes. This was no tradesman's card. But in the two years she had lived with the widow, Lauren had never heard his name mentioned.

"Do you know him, Fanny?" she asked.

"No, Miss." The maid smoothed her apron. "But he's ever so refined. And ever so handsome," she added.

Lauren smiled. "So, that is what has you in such a dither. Well, I'll just have to see this handsome Mr. Hawkes for myself."

After smoothing her wind-ruffled hair, she opened the library door and went in. Her gaze swept over the room, scanning the two Chippendale sofas with their elegant brocade upholstery and the graceful Queen Anne chairs that were clustered in front of the Italian marble fireplace. But there was no sign of the visitor. Had she misunderstood Fanny? she wondered, glancing towards the doorway. Perhaps Mr. Hawkes was in the parlor.

"Good afternoon." The deep voice came from the depths of the battered Morris chair that was tucked into the far corner, where tall windows let a flood of golden afternoon light into the room.

"Oh!" Lauren gasped in surprise.

"I'm sorry if I startled you," the visitor said.

He set the book he'd been reading aside, then rose to his feet. With the light behind him, all Lauren could tell was that he was broad-shouldered and quite tall.

"You didn't . . . it's just that guests don't usually choose that chair." She waved her hand, silently comparing the well-used Morris chair to the other furniture.

"But it's the most comfortable," he said.

He came towards her, his footsteps silent on the

thick Aubusson carpet. When she got a good look at him, Lauren had to resist the impulse to smooth her hair in sheer, feminine flutter. He was in his early to mid thirties, she guessed, a man of experience. The muted gray of his sack coat and trousers complemented his thick, black hair with its sprinkling of silver strands at his temples, and his starched turn-over collar emphasized the bold sweep of his jaw. Stephen Hawkes wasn't handsome in the strict sense of the word; his face was a shade too rugged, his chin too determined and his eyes — deep gray eyes just the color of a storm-tossed sky, she noted — a bit too observant and clever. But his was the most vital, most arresting face she had ever seen, and she was uncomfortably aware of the racing of her heart as she looked at him. The faint scent of a spicy, masculine cologne drifted to her, and her nostrils flared as she savored it.

Admonishing herself sternly, she shook off the disturbing feelings surging through her body. "I'm afraid Mrs. Danforth is . . . occupied at the moment, Mr. Hawkes," she said, relieved to hear that her voice was cool and composed.

He raised one flaring black eyebrow, intrigued by her hesitation before choosing the word occupied. Interesting. Interesting in more ways than one, he thought, admiring her vivid auburn hair and the smooth, silken skin that was so pale it almost seemed to glow from within. Fire and ice and — if he didn't mistake the import of her ardent dark eyes and the lovely double curve of her mouth — a great deal of passion. With her oval face and delicate features, she might have stepped from a Botticelli painting. Most intriguing of all was the air of innocence about her.

Lauren felt heat rise into her face. That too-penetrating gaze of his was unnerving, as if he could see through her flesh into her soul. "May I be of help to you?" she asked, anxious to end his silent appraisal.

"Perhaps. It depends on who you are."

"Oh, forgive me. I'm Lauren Wakefield, Mrs. Danforth's . . . cousin." Lauren still cringed inwardly whenever she said that. Although it was Portia who insisted on presenting Lauren as a member of her family, it seemed a bit dishonest.

His other eyebrow went up. Again that most interesting hesitation, he thought. Absently, he noted that there was a tiny cleft in her chin and a most alluring dimple near the left corner of her mouth. "How closely related are you?" he asked.

"Not closely at all, in anything but affection." Lauren drew herself up in sudden indignation. What business was it of his? And why in heaven had she answered his impertinent question? What was it about his boldly appraising gaze that made her heart pound like this?

"Then you can hardly speak for her in business matters," he said.

"No, I can't speak for her," she retorted, struggling to maintain her composure, "nor did I intend to. As a courtesy, I merely offered to give her your message so that you wouldn't have to wait."

Laughter leaped into his eyes. "Why, thank you. But I prefer to wait."

"Mr. Hawkes, she will most likely be occupied for the rest of the afternoon."

"I have no other engagements today," he said.

"Very well." Lauren resisted the impulse to smooth her hair again. "Please make yourself comfortable. I'll have some tea sent in for you."

21

"Won't you join me?" he asked.

"Thank you, but no." She wanted nothing more than to escape this disturbing man who had the ability to pull her emotions about so strongly. He was compelling and attractive, obviously used to getting what he wanted. After a lifetime of watching such men work their wiles on her mother, Lauren had thought herself immune. But her reaction to Stephen Hawkes proved her wrong. Fortunately, her facade of composure—hard-won from years of holding her feelings inside where none could see them—kept her from revealing her confusion. Coolly, she nodded to him and turned towards the door.

Stephen appraised her with interest. Tall, slender and graceful, her head held proudly and her back straight, she was as regal as a princess. He was fascinated by the contradiction of her chill manner and her sensual mouth. And he didn't want her to go.

"Is Mrs. Danforth with Eldridge?" he asked, seeking a way to keep her with him a while longer.

Lauren whirled. "What do you know of Mr. Eldridge?" she demanded, surprised out of her composure for a moment.

"Edward Eldridge, spiritualist extraordinaire?" he asked with a flash of white, even teeth. "Why, Miss Wakefield, Mr. Eldridge and I are members of the same profession, although I'm much better at it than he is."

Lauren's brows contracted in a frown. So, that was it! He was just another unscrupulous rogue come to steal Portia's money! Word must have gotten ten 'round that the widow was ripe for the plucking, and Hawkes was here to try to get a share of the spoils. "A better medium?" she asked, her voice seething with contempt, "or a better thief?"

22

"Thief? That's a very harsh word, Miss Wakefield."

"That is not a denial, Mr. Hawkes."

"Then I deny it," he said, smiling. Inwardly he winced at the distaste on her face. There were many reactions he would like to have from lovely Lauren Wakefield, and contempt was not one of them. Then the professional part of his mind took over, insulating him from his emotions. He was here to do a job, and if that meant gaining her dislike, then so be it. But he couldn't quite shake the regret that came over him; she was a very lovely woman, and one of the most intriguing he'd ever met.

"I assure you that we won't be needing your services, Mr. Hawkes," Lauren said, her chin going up another disdainful inch. "I'll have Fanny show you out."

"I haven't seen Mrs. Danforth yet." Stephen sat down in the chair Lauren had used, and stretched his long legs out comfortably in front of him. "As I said before, I'll wait for her."

Lauren clenched her fists, hiding this evidence of her anger in the folds of her skirt. "You're wasting your time."

"Perhaps. But since my business *is* with Mrs. Danforth, I believe I'll let her tell me that." Aha! he thought, watching Lauren's face with amused interest, that remark had gotten her temper flaring. Which aspect would come out now—the icy, refined gentlewoman or the fire-haired beauty with the passionate dark eyes?

"I can have you thrown out of this house," she said stiffly, staring down her nose at him.

Stephen grinned. So, it was to be ice. "I happen to know there are only female servants in this house,

23

Miss Wakefield." He crossed his arms over his chest. "How many maids do you think it will take to carry me out to the street?"

"Who told you—" she pressed her lips together, determined not to let him bait her into continuing this absurd conversation. No doubt whoever had told him about Portia's involvement with spiritualism had also told him a great deal about the widow's preference for an all-female household.

She drew herself up, offended by the very notion of Mrs. Danforth's mild eccentricities being bandied about the streets. "Mr. Hawkes, I think—Oh!" she gasped as the widow's fat white Persian cat bounded into the room, nearly coming to rest beneath her skirts.

She bent to pick him up, but he stalked across the room to Stephen. With a graceful spring, the big cat launched himself into the visitor's lap.

"Nero, come away," she ordered. "Mr. Hawkes doesn't want you."

"He's not bothering me," Stephen said, reaching to scratch behind the animal's ears.

"But he doesn't like men," she protested. "He'll—"

Nero began to purr, a loud rattle that fairly echoed in the room. He stared at Lauren unblinkingly, his golden eyes full of triumph. She watched, fascinated, as Stephen's big hand stroked slowly along the cat's back, smoothing the long white fur. It was a tender, unconscious gesture, the action of a man accustomed to animals. Nero's eyes slitted almost closed, and he began to knead the fabric of Stephen's pants.

"Nero! Where are you, you naughty animal?" Portia appeared in the doorway, breathless from running. "Oh! I didn't know we had company!"

24

Stephen set Nero on the floor and rose to his feet as the old woman bustled into the library. The widow was small and stout, her fine silver hair drawn into a simple chignon at the back of her head. Although her face was covered with a network of wrinkles, her clear blue eyes were undimmed by time.

"Mr. Hawkes is just leaving," Lauren said.

The widow glanced at Lauren, noting the disapproval on the younger woman's face, then tilted her head to one side and inspected Stephen thoughtfully. "*Are* you leaving, Mr. Hawkes?" she asked.

Stephen chuckled. "Not quite yet, Mrs. Danforth. I came to see you, after all."

"Such wonderful luck! There are not many handsome young men who seek my company any longer." Portia held out her plump little hand in welcome.

Stephen strode forward. With a flourish, he raised the offered hand to his lips. "Then they're fools," he said. "Such beauty should be admired."

The widow laughed delightedly. "Such beauty should be forty years younger, if it is to listen to such arrant flattery."

"Then perhaps I should compliment you on your wit and charm," Stephen grinned down at her. Mrs. Danforth was a lady in the truest sense of the word, and it was a damned shame that Eldridge had gotten his hooks into her.

"Come sit down, Mr. Hawkes," Portia said, plumping herself down onto the sofa and waving Stephen into a nearby chair. Nero jumped into the widow's lap and made himself comfortable.

Lauren hovered near the door, wishing she could leave, but not daring to leave Portia alone with

Stephen Hawkes. The man was already charming his way into the widow's good graces. This whole thing had gone too far. Séances, spirit rappings—good heavens, what was next? Somehow she had to find a way to save Portia from her own folly.

"Lauren, dear, come sit down," Portia called, reaching to tug on the bellpull.

Shooting a glare at Stephen from under her lashes, Lauren perched on the edge of the chair beside his. Before she could say anything, however, the maid appeared in the doorway.

"Fanny, bring us some tea," Portia said. As the girl turned to obey, the widow turned back to Stephen. "Now, Mr. Hawkes, suppose you tell us what brings you to Danforth House."

"I've come to help you reach your husband, Mrs. Danforth."

Portia's eyes widened. "Do you really think you can?"

"This is ridiculous!" Lauren went to Portia and took the older woman's hands in hers. "Portia dear, you can't possibly believe any of this. This man is—"

"One of the best," Stephen interposed smoothly. "Mrs. Danforth, I can give you any number of recommendations from people who have benefited from my skill."

"Who?" Lauren demanded.

He stood up and walked to the fireplace and leaned against the cool marble, putting his arm across the mantel in a gesture that was both indolent and possessive. "For instance, there are the Babcocks and Fowlers, in Albany—"

"We don't know them, or anything about them." Lauren said. "And we only have your word that they even exist." The look of disdain on her face was am-

26

ple evidence of what she thought his word was worth.

He smiled, but a shaft of anger speared through him. A few moments ago she had accused him of being a thief, and now she was calling him a liar. If she were a man, he'd . . . but she wasn't. And, he reminded himself, he was here to do a job. "Would you believe your own eyes?"

She looked down her nose at him. "Eyes! Your sort works in the dark."

"Lauren, you're being unfair," Portia said. "You can't expect spirits to function in daylight." She scratched Nero's chin, eliciting another of those loud, buzzing purrs. "We must let Mr. Hawkes hold a séance."

"You can't be serious!"

"Yes!" Portia clapped her hands delightedly. "What do you say, Mr. Hawkes?"

He grinned. "I'd be delighted, Mrs. Danforth."

The man had no shame at all! Lauren thought, clenching her fists. Then, realizing that Hawkes was looking at her whitened knuckles, she relaxed her hands and took a deep, calming breath. "I think—"

"Ah, here you are, my dear Mrs. Danforth!" Edward Eldridge's resonant British voice sounded from the doorway.

He swept regally into the room, as though expecting a fanfare of trumpets to announce him. His dark jacket and pants, relieved only by a stiff, white winged collar, were as theatrically somber as his black hair and whiskers. Although he never actually claimed to be of titled lineage, he didn't deny it, either. Rumor had him the son of a lord, a duke, sometimes even a descendant of the royal family.

Lauren, however, knew that he was lazy, selfish,

and utterly without conscience. That resonant bass voice of his must surely have been cultivated on the stage, as was, she suspected, the distinguished British accent with which he thrilled credulous American women. Although some of those ladies touted Eldridge's slightly protuberant hazel eyes as "mesmerizing," Lauren read in them only his own self-awareness.

She glanced at Stephen Hawkes. He was a different caliber of man entirely, she realized, comparing his long-limbed, feral grace to Eldridge's overly dramatic gestures. Hawkes was much more intelligent and determined. Much more dangerous.

Eldridge sank onto the sofa beside Portia. Crossing his legs languidly, he laid his arm across the back of the seat, nearly touching the widow's shoulder. Nero gave a low, threatening growl, and the spiritualist quickly dropped his arm back to his side.

Lauren noted that there were four long, bloody scratches on the back of Eldridge's hand. So, that was the little contretemps that had brought the afternoon's séance to such an early end. Good for you, Nero, she thought.

"Do I know you, sir?" Eldridge asked, turning to look assessingly at Stephen.

"We've never met," Stephen replied. His gray eyes had darkened to charcoal, and were as cold as the sky in winter.

"Oh, please excuse me! Really, my manners!" Portia pulled out a lace-edged handkerchief and fanned herself with it. "Mr. Hawkes, this is Edward Eldridge, the famous spiritualist. Edward, Mr. Hawkes is a member of your profession."

"Indeed?" Eldridge's eyebrows rose in surprised

disdain. "Forgive me, but I have never heard of you, Mr. Hawkes."

Stephen smiled. "I expect not. You've only been in this country a short time, from what I've heard." He ran his thumbnail over his chin thoughtfully. "Why *did* you leave England, Mr. Eldridge?"

"I was . . . told that my work was here." With a beatific look on his weak, handsome face, the medium added, "And once I met this dear lady, I knew it was true."

"Oh, yes!" Portia clasped her hands together and pressed them to her bosom. "If only you could convince Thaddeus to communicate with us!"

Surprised, Stephen abandoned his indolent pose. "What? Do you mean you haven't actually contacted Mr. Danforth?"

"No," Eldridge said shortly.

Lauren knew Eldridge was furious, although he hid it well. With intense satisfaction, she realized that Hawkes's presence was even more unwelcome to him than it was to her.

"You see, Mr. Hawkes," Portia murmured, "my Thaddeus was a very stubborn man. And it seems that he just isn't interested in returning to this . . . plane." She glanced at Eldridge, who nodded in confirmation.

Lauren spoke up then, relishing the chance to put a spike in Stephen Hawkes's plans. "Mrs. Danforth insists that her husband will identify himself by revealing something only he and his wife could possibly know. So far, Mr. Eldridge has not succeeded in producing a spirit with the requisite knowledge."

Eldridge shook his head regretfully. "My dear Miss Wakefield, with the negative influences that abound in this house, it's a miracle that I've been able to summon any spirit entities at all."

"What negative influences can you possibly mean, *dear* Mr. Eldridge?" Lauren asked.

"There are several unbelievers in this house." Eldridge stroked his whiskers with his fingertips, adding, "As you very well know. Such disharmonious thoughts make spirits reluctant to visit."

"I'm sure they do." Lauren looked at Stephen and smiled. "Do you see what you would have to work against, Mr. Hawkes? Disharmonious thoughts. Reluctant spirits. Negative influences. Perhaps you ought to reconsider your offer of . . . help."

"Not at all," Stephen said, meeting her challenging dark gaze. Now that he'd met her, now that he'd gotten an idea of the fascinating things going on in this house, no power on earth was going to make him leave.

"What sort of help?" Eldridge demanded, sitting forward abruptly.

"Mrs. Danforth has decided to let someone else try to contact her husband," Stephen said.

The spiritualist's astonished gaze turned to Portia. "My dear Mrs. Danforth, you cannot be serious!"

"Edward, what harm could there be for Mr. Hawkes to try?" Portia's handkerchief fluttered nervously. "You said yourself that it might take a long time to reach Thaddeus—"

"I forbid it!" Eldridge thundered.

Portia's handkerchief stilled.

Lauren stared at Eldridge incredulously for a moment, then sprang to her feet. "How dare you use that tone to her!" she cried, her reserve shattered by outrage.

"I am only trying to protect her!" he shot back.

"Edward, please!" Mrs. Danforth said with uncharacteristic sharpness. "I've agreed to give Mr. Hawkes a chance to prove his talents, and that, I hope, will be the end of this discussion." She smiled when Fanny came into the room, pushing a tea cart ahead of her. "Ah, here's our tea! Lauren, dear, will you?"

"Yes, Mrs. Danforth." Lauren picked up the graceful Limoges teapot, proud that her hands didn't shake. The homely act of serving calmed her, allowing her fury to abate. By the time the cups were filled, she had retreated behind her customary mask of serenity.

Stephen studied her profile, enjoying the gentle curve of her cheek, the dark sable sweep of her long lashes against her creamy skin. At last he'd glimpsed the fire she kept hidden from the world. When she leaped from her chair, anger blazing in her dark eyes, she had revealed the passion that smoldered beneath the cool facade. The sight of it had hit him almost like a physical blow, making his blood hammer in his veins. He wanted to see more of that fire. He wanted to find out if her desire burned as hot as her anger.

Lauren abruptly became aware that Stephen Hawkes was staring at her. Turning to meet his gaze, she was stunned by the raw hunger on his face. It was frightening, compelling, and all too dangerous. Shaking from an emotion far different from anger, she turned away from it.

Chapter Three

Lauren settled into her chair with a steaming cup of tea, content merely to listen to the conversation. But no matter who happened to be speaking, her gaze somehow seemed to seek Hawkes's rugged face. There was such vitality in him, such bold self-assurance, she mused. What strange quirk of character had prompted such a man to embrace the fakery of spiritualism?

Hawkes glanced up, catching her staring at him, and the corners of his mouth curved upward. Lauren felt heat rise into her face. Hurriedly, she returned her attention to Portia, although she was still aware of Hawkes's gaze on her. That awareness pulled at her, almost making her look at him again before she damped it down sternly. She was a newly betrothed woman, after all, and ought to have enough control to keep her eyes to herself.

Then Portia laughed at something Eldridge said, and Lauren's wandering attention focused. She'd seen that giddy excitement on Portia's pleasant face all too often lately. It meant that no amount of pleading, no amount of carefully laid-out logic was going to make the widow see reason. And now she had not one, but two charming men to dance attendance on her. It made no difference that those handsome faces masked devious hearts, or that their charm was given in trade for something far more valuable. Lauren sighed; how could she possibly protect Portia if she wouldn't listen to common sense?

"You're very quiet, Miss Wakefield," Stephen said.

"I'm always quiet, Mr. Hawkes."

"Perhaps if you didn't have to listen to me chatter all the time, you'd talk more yourself," Portia said with a grin.

"Nonsense!" Lauren poured herself another cup of tea. "I was dull company long before I came to live with you."

"How *did* you come to live here?" Stephen asked with apparent casualness.

Lauren's cup rattled in the saucer as she set it down. "I—"

"Lauren is a distant relation of my husband's," Portia interposed. "We met by accident in London. Since we were both alone in the world, it seemed to be a good idea to join forces." The widow reached across the table to grasp Lauren's hand. "It has been a wonderful two years. I couldn't love her more if she were my own daughter."

Lauren blushed, embarrassed by the widow's declaration of affection. Her mother had never been physically demonstrative, and it was hard to become accustomed to Portia's openness, her instant loyalty, and unself-conscious embraces. Despite her discomfiture, however, Lauren was pleased, and gave Portia's hand a squeeze in return.

Stephen watched the exchange with interest. Again, there was that intriguing contrast between Lauren's outward coolness and the genuine warmth he saw in her eyes. What a contradiction she was! With that face and fiery hair and those liquid dark eyes, she'd be more at home in opulent Renaissance dress than in that prim mousegray gown she wore. What sort of person was she behind the cool facade, and how did a man go about finding out who she really was?

Suddenly he noticed that Eldridge was staring at her with an all-too-easily read expression on his face. The thought that the other man wanted her made the blood pound in Stephen's veins. It gave him another reason to pry the spiritualist's strangle-hold away from this house, and the sooner the better. Well, son, he said to himself, you'd better get started.

He pulled out his watch and flipped it open. "It's nearly five o'clock. As much as I've enjoyed myself, I'd better be going." He stood up and bent over Portia's hand. "Thank you for your hospitality, Mrs. Danforth. When will you want me back?"

"The Talmadges are to have dinner with us Thursday, Mrs. Danforth," Lauren said quickly. "I'm sure they'd be interested to see Mr. Hawkes's ah, performance."

Portia hesitated. "You know how Jane feels about—"

"But that's just my point," Lauren persisted. "Surely Mr. Hawkes won't mind a few impartial witnesses."

"By impartial, I assume you mean that these

34

friends of yours are rather skeptical about spiritualism?" Stephen asked.

Lauren looked into his eyes and smiled. "Rather."

"I accept," he said. How could he not? The challenge and insolence in her face was irresistibly provocative. "Thursday it is."

"Wonderful!" Portia said. "Dinner is at seven, but you'll want to be early to acquaint yourself with the room you'll use for the séance. Shall we say five o'clock?" At his nod, she held out her hand. "Lauren, will you see Mr. Hawkes out?"

"Of course." She rose and waited while Stephen kissed Portia's hand again.

Irritated by his blatant fawning, Lauren turned on her heel and headed towards the door. Stephen grinned, reading her mood in the indignant sway of her bustle. He nodded a farewell to Eldridge, receiving a frigid stare in return, then went after her. Catching up with her in a few long strides, he took her by the elbow and steered her out into the marble-floored foyer. His gaze swept over the rich mahogany paneling, the antique gilt mirrors, and the wide marble stairs and carved rosewood bannister of the graceful staircase. This wasn't the blatant luxury of those who were building their elaborate mansions on Fifth Avenue, but the elegant taste of old money.

"It won't be as easy as you think," Lauren said, startling him out of his reverie.

"What?"

"Putting your hand into Mrs. Danforth's purse."

He turned to look at her. A light scent of violets came to him, a heady fragrance for all its faintness. The gaslights had been lit, their radiance muted by frosted glass globes. Her hair caught the soft light, seeming to distribute it among the silken auburn strands, and making her look as though she were crowned with molten copper.

He resisted the urge to run his fingers through those bright tresses. "I might simply be here to help her, as I said."

"By offering to bring back her husband's ghost?" she asked scornfully.

"Doing so might remove Eldridge from his position of trust."

"Only to put *you* in his place. I doubt that would be an improvement." Suddenly realizing that he was still holding her arm, she tried to pull away. His grip tightened, then shifted from her elbow to her upper arm. She looked down at his hand, dark against the pale gray fabric of her sleeve, and noted its strength, the long, sensitive fingers, the sprinkling of dark hairs that disappeared beneath his cuff. Her heartbeat quickened, and a strange weakness crept into her limbs.

Then common sense flooded back into her, and she pulled out of his grasp. Her skin felt hot where his hand had been and now, bereft somehow. She reached up to rub her elbow, then, realizing how revealing her action was, dropped her hands to her sides. What was wrong with her? *You're engaged, for heaven's sake!* she reminded herself again, wielding that fact like a talisman against her churning feelings. Even though it was an arranged marriage settled between Portia and her fiance's father, her betrothed deserved her loyalty and respect. Marriage meant children, family, a respectable name—those things she had craved all her life. She was not going to allow this disturbing stranger to confuse her.

Anger—at Hawkes, but more at herself—brought her chin up. "If you had a shred of decency, you'd walk out that door and never come back."

"But then I'd never see you again," he murmured.

Lauren stiffened. "I'll get your coat," she said, her voice shaking with fury and yes, she had to admit it—fear. Fear of the way her blood rushed through her veins in response to his deep, caressing voice, the way her legs trembled. Sternly, she pushed those feelings deep inside, securing them behind the wall she kept between herself and anyone who might hurt her. She knew Hawkes's sort; once he discovered her weakness, he'd use it against her.

Stephen knew he'd found a chink in her armor. "Anxious to see the last of me?" he asked, hoping to provoke her into still more response.

Lauren inspected him coldly. "Yes." Controlling her voice with an effort, she added, "I find you despicable."

"Such honesty! And such distaste!" Although he raised his eyebrows, outwardly feigning indifference, he found that her chilly disdain annoyed him far more than it should have. Why the hell should her opinion matter, anyway? *He* knew what kind of man he was.

"My distaste stems from an afternoon of watching you play your nasty little game with Mrs.

Danforth, and as for honesty . . ." She put her hands on her hips. "I'm surprised you know the word exists."

He wrestled his annoyance down again. Damn, but she knew just how to goad him! And why? Was it mere dislike for his profession, or did she have another motive? Perhaps she wasn't as averse to Eldridge as she seemed. Now *that* was a notion that really scalded. Looking at her from under half-closed lids, he said, "Maybe you prefer Eldridge's brand of the truth."

Somehow she managed to keep her voice cool and her tone impersonally sardonic. "Mr. Hawkes, the only thing worse than having to endure Mr. Eldridge is the thought of having to endure him *and* you."

His temper, held in abeyance until now, flared into life. He took a step closer. "You've got the tongue of an adder, Miss Wakefield."

"Indeed?" She held her ground, refusing to be intimidated by his looming height and broad shoulders. "And you've got the morals of a gutter-snipe, Mr. Hawkes."

His eyes narrowed. "Then you'll be expecting this," he growled, his big hands snaking out to circle her waist and pull her against him.

His mouth covered hers, hard, punishing. Lauren was so astonished that for a moment she couldn't react. Then hot outrage flooded in, and she opened her mouth to cry for help. That was her undoing; his tongue stabbed into her mouth with aggressive possession, tasting her, exploring her, and even through her anger she was aware of that frightening weakness flooding through her

38

body again. And then her fear, her fury, was submerged in a flaming wave of sensation—the feel of his firm lips slanting across hers, gently now, and the warmth of his hands, which had somehow moved without her noticing to spread out across her ribs just under her breasts. The raw shock of her response to him made her tremble, made her open her clenched fists so that she could feel the strong, rapid beat of his heart beneath her palms.

Stephen lifted his head so he could look at her. His gaze traveled over her smooth oval face, her full, red mouth, slightly swollen now from his kisses, the astonishment in her eyes. And there was something more in those fathomless sable depths, a smoldering heat that revealed the sensuality held deep inside her.

"You're beautiful," he breathed.

His words—those empty, useless words she'd heard men say to her mother over and over—brought her abruptly out of her state of bewilderment. How dare he do this to her? How dare he make her feel like this? Of its own volition, her hand lashed out, catching him on the cheek with a crack that echoed in the quiet foyer.

Stepping back, he touched the spot where she had struck him. "I suppose you think I deserved that."

"You did."

His smoky gray gaze warred with her dark one. He'd intended to provoke her out of her icy control, but he'd been the one who had succumbed. The fact that it was his own doing didn't make him any less angry, however. "I'll allow you that one," he said, his voice a soft, dangerous growl.

"But if you ever hit me again, you'll regret it."

"It's you who'll be sorry if you dare put your hands on me again," she hissed.

There was a loud knock at the front door, making them both jump in surprise. Lauren glared at Stephen for a moment, then went to open the door. A man stood outside, his hand upraised as though to knock again.

"Why, Richard!" she exclaimed, opening the portal wider. "I wasn't expecting you today."

"But you don't mind, do you?" he teased.

"Of course, I don't."

Richard stepped inside and leaned forward to kiss her on the cheek, then, noticing the other man standing near the staircase, straightened in surprise. "I didn't know you had company, my dear."

"This is Stephen Hawkes." She lifted her chin defiantly. "And this is Richard Farleigh, my fiancé."

Fiancé! Stephen felt as though someone had punched him in the chest. He looked the other man over, gauging his expensive, stylish clothes, curly brown hair that tumbled over his high forehead, his pale, almost colorless eyes. Clever, but not intelligent, Stephen guessed. Charming, but shallow. A boy, for all that he must be nearing thirty. And with that slightly petulant droop to his lower lip, a spoiled boy. What the hell did Lauren see in him?

"Pleasure to meet you," Stephen lied, striding forward to offer his hand to the younger man. He found Farleigh's palm to be as cold as his eyes, his grip disinterested.

"Mr. Hawkes is going to try to reach Thaddeus Danforth's ghost for us," Lauren said. Her full lips curved in a smile that held more contempt than humor.

Watching the other man's expression change, Stephen knew he'd been classed as a person of no importance whatsoever—a hireling, and thus below Farleigh's consideration.

"Old Thaddeus, indeed!" Richard laughed. "How jolly! May I watch?"

"That will be up to Mrs. Danforth, I'm afraid," Stephen replied. "You might ask her."

"I will," Richard said, still chuckling. "You spiritualist fellows are more entertaining than a whole troupe of jugglers and clowns. I can hardly wait."

Lauren saw Stephen's eyes turn iron gray with anger. Knowing that an argument was soon to begin if she didn't get him out of the house quickly, she rushed into the cloakroom to retrieve his coat. As she hurried back to the foyer with it, his faint, musky cologne rose from the garment. Unconsciously, her hand smoothed the fabric as she reentered the foyer.

She noted that although Stephen Hawkes and Richard were standing only a few feet apart, they were studiously ignoring one another. Both were tall, dark-haired men, both handsome. But Hawkes was taller, his shoulders wider, his vitality a sharp contrast to Richard's languid demeanor. Hawkes was . . . nothing but a charlatan! she told herself savagely. You're doing Richard an injustice by comparing him to such a man. Realizing at last that she was stroking Hawkes's coat, she thrust it at him brusquely.

41

"Your coat, sir," she said.

He took the garment from her, then raised her hand to his lips and whispered, "Until we meet again, beautiful lady."

Pulling her hand out of his grasp, she went to stand beside Farleigh. Again Stephen felt that jolt deep in his gut. Turning away abruptly, he strode to the door.

Lauren sighed with relief. Then Stephen stopped, his hand on the knob, and turned to look at her. For one frozen moment, his gaze locked with hers as though he could pull her away from Farleigh's side with the intensity of his stare.

"Goodbye, Miss Wakefield," he said. His voice was rough-edged with anger and desire, and as caressing as his hands had been a short time ago.

Lauren's thick lashes dipped downward, hiding her eyes from his too-perceptive gaze, lest he see the jumble he'd made of her emotions. "Goodbye, Mr. Hawkes." The door closed behind him, and the foyer suddenly felt very empty.

"Come, Richard," she murmured, taking her fiancé's arm and turning him towards the library. "Mrs. Danforth will want to see you."

Outside, Stephen stood and stared up at the towering front of Portia Danforth's mansion. But he wasn't seeing the brown stone of the exterior or the carved granite moldings above the windows. He was seeing Lauren's face as she looked up at the man she was to marry. Was Farleigh kissing her now? he wondered savagely. Was she responding to the fellow, gazing up at him with the same stunned wonder in her beautiful eyes?

"Damn it to hell!" he muttered under his

breath, jamming his hands into his coat pockets and striding down the street. "Damn it to hell!"

Stephen strode alongside the tall iron fence that surrounded Gramercy Park—an exquisite small park that belonged to the residents who lived around it. Reaching the Talmadge house, he stood upon the carved granite stoop and surveyed the moonlit street behind him. It was empty, save for the fallen leaves that skittered before the unseasonably warm wind. He could see the back of Portia Danforth's mansion through the winter-bared branches of the trees. There was a single light showing, and he wondered if that third-floor window belonged to Lauren's room.

Pushing thoughts of her away, he turned and knocked on the Talmadges' door. A stiffly polite butler answered immediately. As Stephen followed the man towards the parlor, he noted that the furnishings, like Mrs. Danforth's, hearkened back to an earlier era.

Three people turned to look at him when he entered the room: Jane Talmadge, her son Martin, and Victor Padgett, the Police Commissioner.

The Commissioner beckoned Stephen closer. "Mrs. Talmadge, Mr. Talmadge, I'd like you to meet Detective Stephen Hawkes, one of our best men."

Stephen bowed to Jane Talmadge. She was well into her seventies, tiny and so thin she looked as though she'd break in a stiff wind. Her hands, spotted and curled with age, resembled the talons of a bird against the black silk of her dress. Intelligent blue eyes peered at him from a network of deeply etched wrinkles. They, and a large, slightly bent nose, dominated her face.

"Thank you for coming, Mr. Hawkes." Martin Talmadge, a square, blunt-featured man in his late forties, came forward to shake hands.

Stephen immediately liked him; his grip was firm and honest, and there was considerable good humor in his brown eyes. "Was it you who brought Mr. Eldridge to our attention?" he asked.

"No, my mother was the one who contacted Commissioner Padgett." Martin went to stand behind the old woman's chair. He patted her bony shoulders affectionately. "She knew what Eldridge was the moment she met him."

"Can you do anything about that bounder, Mr. Hawkes?" she asked. Her voice was a lovely deep contralto, still young, still full of life. "I would dearly hate to see him hurt Portia in any way."

"I'll do my best." Stephen studied them, weighing their personalities, then said, "I could use your help."

"What sort of help?" Martin asked.

"I'm to hold a séance there after dinner Thursday night—"

"A séance!" Jane's thin white eyebrows went up. "Where did you come by that particular expertise, Mr. Hawkes?"

The Commissioner cleared his throat. "Our detectives acquire a surprising variety of skills in their work, Mrs. Talmadge."

"I asked *him*," she snapped.

Stephen grinned at her impudently. "Sleight of hand happens to be a hobby of mine. I collect tricks—those that work against the mind as well as the eye."

"Do you know many?" Martin asked.

"A few." At Jane's sniff of disbelief, he amended, "Well, more than a few, actually. But I doubt I'm quite in Eldridge's league."

"So that's why you'll need our help." A roguish smile spread over Martin's face. "I'd make a thumping good ghost."

"I don't think you'll have to go quite that far," Stephen said with a chuckle. "But I promise you'll have fun."

"What shall I do?" Jane asked, the imperious hauteur of her expression daring them to protest.

Stephen ran his thumbnail over his chin. "Can you faint?"

She smiled. "Most excellently."

"Good," he said with a nod of satisfaction. "You'll faint, and Martin will do tricks with hooks and things. I'll come back tomorrow to show you what to do."

Jane motioned him into a nearby chair. "I just don't understand why Portia has allowed the man to so totally take control. It's like he holds some sort of spell over her. She won't even listen to Lauren."

"Ah, yes, the charming Miss Wakefield," Stephen said, his relaxed pose hiding the sudden tension in his body. "What can you tell me about her?"

Jane lifted her shoulder in a delicate shrug. "She's a distant relative of some kind. Thaddeus's side, I believe; his people came from Shropshire. Portia found her in London and brought her here, oh, about two years ago."

"Is that all you know?" the Commissioner asked.

Jane nodded. "Besides being rather a love, Lauren has been wonderful for Portia."

"Rather a love," Stephen repeated to himself. Yes, Lauren Wakefield could be called that, and more. A man could drown in her dark eyes, in her fragrance, and the auburn glory of her hair.

"How has Miss Wakefield been good for her, exactly?" the Commissioner asked.

"Well, running her household, arranging her social engagements — that sort of thing," Jane said. "Portia has never been a very organized person, you know."

"I see." Commissioner Padgett exchanged a glance with Stephen, then rose from his chair. "It's very late. We'd better be going."

With a nod to Martin, the Commissioner took his leave. Stephen bent over Jane's tiny claw of a hand before following his superior out into the street.

"Damn stupid mess!" Padgett growled, plopping his hat on his head in disgust. "This is going to be a difficult job, Hawkes."

"Yes, sir," Stephen agreed, thinking of Lauren. Keeping his hands off her was going to be a great deal more difficult than stopping Eldridge's tricks. He knew better — or at least he ought to know better, after nearly ten years as a detective — than to become involved with someone he was investigating. It was foolish and dangerous. And oh, so tempting!

"We'll ask Scotland Yard to look into the Wakefield girl's past as well as Eldridge's," the Commissioner said.

"I'll wager the Yard is well acquainted with Eldridge; I got the impression he left England rather suddenly." Stephen cocked his head to one side and regarded his superior. "It wouldn't hurt to find out what Richard Farleigh's part is in this."

The Commissioner grunted. "What the devil are you talking about?"

"He's betrothed to Lauren Wakefield."

Padgett put his hands behind his back and began walking rapidly down the quiet street. Stephen followed, taking one stride to the shorter man's two.

"Betrothed, eh?" the Commissioner said at last. "Y'know, young Farleigh's a bit wild, but I don't think he'd stoop to swindling an old woman. His family is swimming in money, for one thing."

"He might do it for fun," Stephen pointed out. "You never know with these bored society people."

"Damn it, Hawkes, don't even say it unless you've got clean proof. William Farleigh practically runs this city. It's bad enough with the Talmadges putting their fingers in this case, but if the Farleighs' youngest son is involved—" Padgett gave an explosive hiss of exasperation. "One hint of scandal, and half the bluebloods in the city will be screaming for our heads. We'll have to tread softly on this."

Stephen grinned. *"You* have to tread softly; you're the one who has to toady to the aristocrats. I just have to do my job."

47

"Get out of my sight," Padgett growled good-naturedly.

"Yes, sir." Whistling under his breath, Stephen strode towards his home. He was considerably pleased with the day's events; despite its complications, this case was turning out to be a very interesting one. Damn, but he could hardly wait until Thursday. What a show he was going to give them!

His thoughts again turned to Lauren, but he repressed them sternly, telling himself that his impatience had nothing to do with seeing her again.

Chapter Four

Clouds hung low over Gramercy Park, spitting light rain over the land below. Lauren stood bareheaded in the drizzle, looking up into the bare, glistening branches of an oak tree. Nero crouched on one of the highest limbs, his ears laid flat against his head. A piteous yowl came from his mouth.

"Nero!" Lauren called, holding her arms up encouragingly. "Come on, boy! Don't be afraid!"

Another, louder yowl was her only answer.

Lauren chewed her bottom lip in indecision. Nero was obviously not going to come down. The cat was considerably overweight and getting along in years, and she didn't dare leave him alone to get help. Well, she decided, she was just going to have to go up after him. It wouldn't be the first time she'd climbed a tree. It was, however, the first time since she'd graduated to long skirts.

After taking a quick look around to make sure that no one was watching, she shrugged out of her cloak, tucked the excess material of her skirt into her waistband, and began to climb the tree. In moments, her pale blue plaid dress—her favorite—was soiled. She hoped the cat would be properly appreciative.

Deciding that Nero's branch was too fragile to hold her, Lauren chose one a few feet below. Settling herself carefully into the crook between the branch and the trunk of the tree, she looked up at the cat and crooned, "Come on now, Nero. Come to Lauren."

The Persian suddenly stopped yowling. His great golden eyes opened wide, and he began to back downward towards her, his claws scrabbling against the bark. When he was close enough, she reached up and gathered him in, cradling him against her chest. "There, sweetheart. You're safe." He began to purr, kneading her bodice with his muddy paws.

"Do you need some help, Miss Wakefield?" A man's deep voice drifted up from the base of the tree.

Lauren knew that voice, although she'd met its owner only once. Stephen Hawkes. Swiftly she pulled her skirt around her legs while the rain, surprisingly warm for this time of year, spattered gently upon her face.

"Good afternoon, Mr. Hawkes," she said, schooling her voice to calmness. The only way to get through this was to pretend that it was perfectly normal for young ladies to climb trees in the rain. "I was just trying to coax Nero down. He was stuck."

"So I see." Stephen kept his voice solemn, but it was a hell of an effort. The picture of cool, collected Miss Wakefield sitting high in an oak tree, her shapely legs exposed nearly to the thighs, would stay with him forever. He'd even caught a glimpse of pale garters, which his mind turned into a very erotic daydream of peeling them slowly down her legs.

"What are you doing here?" she asked.

50

Reluctantly, he forced the wanton picture to fade from his mind. "It's Thursday. Have you forgotten our engagement?"

"No, I hadn't forgotten. I hoped *you* had."

He laughed. With her cheeks pink from embarrassment and her coppery hair mussed from her climb, she was as alluring as some forest sprite. He was tempted to tease her more, but decided he ought to get her down from her precarious seat first. "I suppose you'd better drop Nero down to me."

"Do you think that's a good idea?" she asked doubtfully.

"It's as good as any." He moved closer to the trunk of the tree.

"Well . . . all right." Lauren held Nero at arm's length. He howled in fright and extended the claws of all four feet as far as they would go.

Stephen, looking up in alarm at those sharp claws suspended overhead, quickly changed his mind. "On second thought, perhaps this isn't the best way to go about it."

Relieved, Lauren tucked Nero against her shoulder. He immediately sank his claws into her dress and hung on, determined not to be separated from her again. After one halfhearted attempt to dislodge him, Lauren knew she was going to have to carry him down. But she wasn't about to move an inch with Stephen Hawkes standing directly below. "Mr. Hawkes, will you go away so I can come down?"

"If you call me Stephen, I might consider it."

Lauren gritted her teeth, but kept her tone pleasant. If she irritated him, he'd never move. And although calling him by his first name shouldn't be such a terrible thing, she had the feeling that by giv-

51

ing in to that seemingly small demand, she was opening herself to a great deal of trouble.

But there was nothing to do but humor him, for she had no doubt that he was capable of standing there far longer than she was capable of sitting on this branch. "Will you please leave . . . Stephen?"

"Certainly, lovely lady." He moved, but to a spot just a few feet away.

Lauren stared down at him with slitted eyes. Although he wouldn't be able to see up her dress — quite — he was near enough to make the climb a most embarrassing one. He was expecting her to demand that he leave before climbing down. And then he'd laugh, and congratulate himself on having made her angry again. Well, she wasn't going to make a fool of herself for any man. Or, she amended silently, she'd make her own sort of fool, rather than his. So, serene as a queen going to her coronation, she patted Nero reassuringly and began climbing down.

Stephen nearly whistled in admiration for her aplomb; a lesser woman would have lost her temper and ordered him away, or resorted to tears. Or encouraged him to come up after her.

Although she would have died before admitting it, Lauren was afraid. Going down was much worse than going up, for her skirt interfered with her movements to the point of danger. Drat Stephen Hawkes! she snarled to herself. If he would just remove his uninvited and unwanted person from the area, she could hoist her skirt again. Just then her foot slipped. With a cry of alarm, she slid a few feet downward before catching hold of a branch and steadying herself.

Stephen strode forward, his heart pounding in reaction. Hurriedly, she pressed against the bole of the tree and clutched her skirts with her free hand. Nero balanced easily on her shoulder, glaring balefully at Stephen as though it was the man who had caused all the trouble.

"Will you go away?" Lauren cried.

"Don't be ridiculous," he snapped. "As fascinating as your legs are, keeping them covered isn't worth breaking your neck." He held his arms up towards her. "Now come here."

Lauren hesitated.

"Jump," he ordered. "I'll catch you."

"It's too far! We'll both end up in the mud!"

He took off his derby and hung it on a nearby branch. "Don't you trust me?"

"Not for an instant."

With a muttered curse, he began unbuttoning his coat. "All right, I'm coming up after you."

"No! I'll come to you," she said hurriedly.

She felt below her with her foot, found purchase on another branch, and edged downward. When she was within a few feet of Stephen's upraised arms, she put her back against the trunk of the tree. "Ready?" she asked, her heart racing with apprehension.

"Ready."

He braced himself as she launched herself towards him. A moment later a luscious, violet- and rainwater-scented bundle of womanhood dropped into his arms.

Unfortunately, so did Nero. The cat squalled and bit, and Stephen staggered and swore, trying to fend him away without dropping Lauren into the mud. Finally Nero set his hind feet against her chest and kicked off. With a hiss of disgust, he loped towards home, his white tail held upward like a plume.

"Ouch!" Lauren cried, her hands going to her chest. They came away spotted with blood.

Stephen set her upright. Her bodice was torn diagonally, revealing a glimpse of white corset and pale, creamy flesh, bisected by four parallel red lines. She reached up to cover herself, but he pushed her hands away. "Don't be an idiot," he growled. "Let me see that."

"It's nothing, really, just a scratch," she protested. "Mr. Hawkes—"

"Stephen," he corrected absently, pulling the edges of the torn fabric apart. The cat's claws had scored her from her left collarbone to the spot where her corset ended above her right breast. They *were* only scratches, as she'd said, but the sight of those raised, red marks on her tender skin made his chest tighten. He wanted to kiss them away, to heal them with his touch. Lightly, he ran his fingertips along the wounds.

Lauren gazed at him, spellbound. Although his hand was barely touching her, she could feel it like a hot brand on her flesh. He was gentle, so infinitely gentle! His fingers had come to rest a scant inch above the cleft between her breasts, and for a moment she wanted to move so they'd slide downward. Her nipples hardened, and the fabric of her corset felt uncomfortably rough against them.

Fascinated, she saw his gray eyes darken to the color of the clouds overhead, and a smoldering flame of desire spring to life in their depths. Something in her responded to that sight, making her chest heave with some strange emotion she could neither name nor resist.

"Lauren!" he muttered hoarsely, rocked by the emotions she raised in him—desire, frustration, sheer male possessiveness. His hand flattened upon her chest, moving up to clasp her neck so he could feel her racing pulse.

His voice broke the spell that held Lauren in thrall. Dropping her gaze, she turned away and pulled her bodice together with shaking hands. Waves of self-disgust washed over her. What hold did this man have over her, that the simplest touch turned her will to jelly? Oh, she knew what it was. Carnal desire. Flesh calling to flesh, urging voluptuous pleasure that had nothing to do with love. It was just this sort of madness that had made her mother abandon home, friends, and family. Well, it wouldn't happen to her. She pulled her hard-earned facade of serenity over herself like a blanket, shutting herself in, shutting him out.

Stephen watched her withdrawal with mingled regret and relief. Regret because he had loved touching her, feeling her response, relief because that response had drawn him in like a whirlpool, submerging rational thought in a sweeping tide of desire. God, how he wanted her! His body clamored for him to pull her back, to kiss her, make love to her until she abandoned that damned icy demeanor forever.

There was moisture on her cheeks, whether tears or rain, he didn't know. Cursing himself under his breath, he pulled his handkerchief out and handed it to her. "Here," he said, his voice rough with frustration.

She shook her head, her expression so cool and composed that he decided that the wetness was rain,

55

after all. Without a word, she turned and headed back to the house. Stephen scooped her cloak up off the ground, retrieved his hat, and hurried after her. Catching up with her easily, he wrapped the cloak around her shoulders.

"You forgot this," he said.

She didn't look at him. "Thank you."

"You're welcome." He put his hands behind his back, whistling a tune under his breath as he walked beside her.

Lauren was confused by the sudden change in his manner. Surely she had misinterpreted the scene earlier, she told herself. He hadn't actually touched . . . well, his hand hadn't strayed to anything but her throat. Perhaps the emotion had been all on her part, and he had merely been concerned for her injury. She fastened on that thought, wanting it to be true.

"Have you known Richard Farleigh long?" he asked, breaking into her reverie.

"Not very." She glanced up at him, then away, blushing because for a moment she'd almost forgotten Richard.

"Then you haven't been betrothed long."

"No, not long." Without intending to, she added, "A week."

"Why did you accept his proposal?"

The bluntness of his question took her by surprise. Before she could recover, she blurted, "It was his father who . . ." Furious at her own thoughtless tongue, she pressed her lips together to keep from saying anything more. She wanted this marriage—arranged or not! Many couples knew as little about one another as she and Richard, and managed to build good, solid lives together. Mutual respect—not passion, not the fickle emotion called love—was what made a successful marriage. No thoughtless rogue with overbold eyes and roaming hands was going to convince her otherwise.

An arranged marriage! Stephen thought in relieved triumph. She didn't love Farleigh after all. The extent of his happiness at that news surprised him. "And when is the happy event to take place?"

"I don't see what business it is of yours, Mr. Hawkes." Reaching the park gate, she unlocked it and pushed it open, resisting the impulse to lock him in.

"Stephen," he admonished. He grabbed her by the arm and spun her around, using his greater weight to pin her against the fence. "And I'm making it my business. I'm making everything you do my business, Lauren Wakefield."

Her hope that he hadn't been affected by the scene beneath the tree shriveled and died. Lauren stared up at him with wide eyes, the iron bars at her back no harder than the male chest pressing against her breasts. She was afraid, afraid of what he might make her feel. And yet there was triumph lurking beneath her fear, and a reckless heat coiling deep in her body. He wanted her!

"Don't be afraid of me," he muttered, his voice harsh with desire. His world narrowed to her full, red mouth. He couldn't let her go in the house—to let her go to Farleigh—without kissing her.

Bending his head, he caught her lips with his. Lauren whimpered against his mouth, fighting the passion that buffeted her. She twisted frantically, but he merely sank one hand into her thick chignon and deepened the kiss still more. His body was hot against hers, and she could feel the hard evidence of his desire pressing against her abdomen. Heat, a consuming, liquid fire, settled in her lower body. Slowly, her head fell back against his arm as she succumbed to the sweet torment of it.

He raised his head. His hand left her hair to trace her lips, her cheek, the graceful dark line of her brows. "You don't love Farleigh," he said. His chest was rising and falling like a bellows. "You couldn't kiss me like that if you did."

A great tide of mingled fury, outrage, and humiliation flooded through her, stiffening her spine. "I was not kissing you, you conceited ass," she retorted. "I was trying to get away."

"Is that what you call it?"

"Let go of me," she said, willing her voice to be as cold as she wished her body could be. She must have succeeded, for he released her, stepping back to run his hand through his silver-streaked hair.

"You don't love him," he said again.

She stalked past him, her head held high. Suddenly she paused, turned. "Of course, I love him. I'm going to marry him, aren't I?"

His eyebrows went up. "Is it his money that you want?" he asked, anger making him cruel.

Regarding him as though he were some particularly offensive species of rodent, she replied, "If answering yes will make you leave me alone, then yes it is." Judging by the way his jaw tightened, she knew she had hit a soft spot. She ought to walk away, now that she had the upper hand. She wanted to, even started to, but she couldn't stop herself from adding, "Of course *you'd* think money would be reason enough for *anything*."

"We're two of a kind then, aren't we?" he asked, suddenly recovering his good humor. That peevish last statement of hers proved that she was neither as cool nor as indifferent as she'd like him to think. Besides, how could he be angry with her when there were rain-jewels beading her hair and long eyelashes, again making her look like some fey forest sprite?

Taking her by the elbow, he steered her into the house. The moment they stepped inside, Portia bore down on them like a ship under full sail.

"Lauren, dear, where on earth have you been?" At the sight of Lauren's disheveled state, the widow came to an abrupt halt. "Whatever happened to you?"

"A slight disagreement with Nero," Stephen said, striding forward to kiss Portia's hand.

"Did he hurt you?" the old woman asked in concern. She rushed forward to peer nearsightedly at Lauren's bodice. "Oh, I'm so sorry. That cat . . . Oh, you're bleeding—"

"Who's bleeding?" Richard Farleigh strolled into the foyer. "Not my future bride?" His footsteps quickened.

He slid adroitly between Stephen and Lauren and put his arm around her waist. His gaze was drawn to the glimpse of creamy flesh revealed by the rent in her bodice.

Lauren blushed and put her hands up to cover her chest. Oddly, she was very embarrassed by his intent stare, although Stephen had seen—and done—much more. Stupid girl, she chided herself. Richard is your fiancé! If anyone has the right to look at you, he does.

59

"Shall we send for a doctor?" Richard asked, still staring at her bosom.

"Certainly not! It's only a scratch, Richard. I'll just go upstairs and wash it, and I'll be as good as new." Although Lauren didn't dare glance at Stephen, she knew he was looking at her. Anxious to get away from that too-penetrating regard, she tried unsuccessfully to step out from Richard's encircling arm.

Stephen's gaze shifted from Lauren to the back of the smaller man's neck. He barely resisted the urge to throttle the fellow. How dare he touch her! Farleigh's her fiancé, he reminded himself harshly. He has the right, if anyone does. But when Stephen looked at Farleigh's arm wrapped so possessively around her, saw those white, impeccably manicured fingers spread out along her narrow waist, it was all he could do to control himself.

Although Lauren had tried to be subtle about getting away, he noticed her surreptitious attempt to free herself. It gave him an excuse to take action. "Why don't you go upstairs and freshen up, Miss Wakefield," he said, letting his hand fall heavily on Farleigh's shoulder. "We've got less than an hour until dinner."

A young woman with blond hair and an indolent, swaying walk came out of the parlor. "Richard, Mother wants you. Where have you . . . Oh, there you are!"

Her dress was of green silk, exactly matching her eyes, and was heavily encrusted with lace and seed pearls. A rather formal and expensive gown to wear to an intimate dinner at a friend's house, in Stephen's opinion.

Spying Lauren's wet hair and wrinkled, muddy clothing, the woman gave a trill of laughter. "You really ought to learn to use an umbrella, Lauren."

"Yes, I know." Lauren stepped backward, out of the circle of Richard's arm. She noticed that Stephen took his hand from the other man's shoulder at the same moment. "Mr. Hawkes, this is Clarissa Farleigh, Richard's sister."

Clarissa's attention focused on Stephen. Brazenly, her gaze traveled the long length of him, noting the width of his powerful shoulders, his ruggedly handsome features, the sensuality of his hard mouth. "This is our medium? Mmmm, how interesting," she murmured, smiling seductively. Her teeth were chalk white against her red lips. "No wonder Edward Eldridge is furious."

She reminded Stephen of a sleek, spoiled cat. There were razor-sharp claws hidden beneath that pampered, powdered exterior, he was sure. Grinning, he strode forward and raised her hand to his lips. "A pleasure to meet you, Miss Farleigh."

"I hope so. Come, Mr. Hawkes, let's get to know one another better." Looping her arm around his, she led him towards the parlor.

Portia stared at the retreating pair, astonished by Clarissa's bold appropriation of her guest. "But . . . but . . ." she stammered.

"Oh, that's just Clarissa's way of being the first to hear any gossip Mr. Hawkes might happen to have. She'll have wrung a whole arsenal of news from him before the evening's over, even if he doesn't think he knows anything." Richard said, chuckling. He held out his arm to Portia. "While we're waiting for my lovely bride-to-be to fix her toilette, why don't we try to get in a rubber of bridge?"

Portia glanced over at Lauren. "Will you need any help, dear?"

"I'll do fine by myself," she said. "Go enjoy your game."

The sound of Clarissa's high, trilling laugh floated from the parlor, followed by Stephen's deep-toned chuckle. Well, they certainly seemed to be having fun, Lauren thought sourly. They seemed to have become quite friendly in just a few minutes.

As she headed upstairs, it occurred to her that she didn't like her future sister-in-law very much.

Chapter Five

Stephen chose the library for his séance. Servants brought a table and chairs in, moving Portia's writing desk and one of the sofas into the parlor to make room, then drawing the heavy velvet draperies against the rainy night. To ensure that the room would be totally dark during the séance, no fire had been lit. Edward Eldridge prowled the room restlessly.

"Looking for something, Mr. Eldridge?" Stephen asked. He knew full well that the spiritualist was searching for any devices his rival might have planted.

"No." Surreptitiously, Eldridge ran his finger along the edge of the nearest curtain. Finding nothing there, he moved to the table and peered down at its glossy top.

Grinning maliciously at his opponent's discomfiture, Stephen turned the gaslights to a minimum. The soft illumination made a fanciful play of light and shadow in the room, gleaming mellowly on the polished wood of the table, yet leaving mysterious shadows in the corners and behind the furniture. That, and the drumming of the rain against the windows, created just the mood he wanted.

Richard, cradling a brandy snifter in his cupped hand, came to stand beside Stephen. "Are you going to allow Mr. Eldridge to attend your little, ah, performance?" he asked, loudly enough for everyone to hear. The others turned to look at him.

"Will you, Mr. Hawkes?" Eldridge's sonorous voice dominated the room.

"Only if you allow me to attend yours," Stephen replied.

"Mine!" Eldridge's voice fairly quivered with indignation, as though Stephen had offered to serve High Mass. With dramatic effect, Eldridge tipped his head back so he could look down his nose at the taller man. "That would be quite impossible, sir. My spirits would hardly countenance such an antagonistic presence."

Stephen showed the edges of his teeth in a humorless smile. "My spirits are fully as discriminating as yours, Mr. Eldridge."

"A masterful riposte!" Richard said, his curls bobbing as he looked avidly from one spiritualist to the other. This was going to furnish the most delicious gossip! "Mr. Eldridge, have you a reply?"

Eldridge ignored him, turning to appeal to Portia. "Mrs. Danforth, surely you want me to make sure this fellow doesn't play any tricks!"

"But my dear Edward, you wouldn't want to adversely affect the conditions of this séance, would you?" Portia said in her fluttery voice. "You've told me so many times how important it is to have a proper atmosphere for the spirits, and we have accommodated *your* every request to create that atmosphere. Surely we can allow Mr. Hawkes the same consideration."

"If you insist, Madam." Eldridge bowed stiffly, gave Stephen one burning glare of hatred, then left the room. A few moments later they heard the outer door slam closed.

"Well, well!" Richard laughed in delight. "Mr. Eldridge is in rather a snit. You seem to have upset the fellow's digestion, Mr. Hawkes."

"Dickie, you *are* bad," his mother said fondly, adjusting her bulk on the sofa. She was a physically imposing woman, tall and stout, with an enormous, jutting bosom. Her beautifully coiffed blond head sat upon a thick white pillar of a neck, giving her the look of an overweight swan.

Stephen restrained a grimace. The woman was coldly haughty, except when she spoke to her children. Then her face took on such an insipid look of doting maternal affection that he wanted to laugh. Her blatantly displayed wealth sat poorly with him; her lace alone would cost several years of a policeman's salary. And the son! It was all he could do not to grab the man by his jiggling curls and shear him down to the scalp. Surely the only thing the fellow had to offer was money. Was that what Lauren wanted? Would she marry that prancing fop so that she could have jewels and silk dresses with lace trains?

He swung around to look at her. She was sitting with Martin Talmadge, Clarissa Farleigh, and the two elderly widows, looking like a governess in her plain blue muslin gown with its high neck and long, close-fitting sleeves. Prim, proper, and—superficially compared to Clarissa's studied, expensive beauty— plain. But he was not a superficial man; in his opinion, Lauren was stunning, alluring—and most compelling, perhaps—an enigma.

Richard moved to stand behind her chair. Stephen watched him trail his fingers over the rich brocade upholstery just behind her shoulder, languidly, sensually, as though he were caressing Lauren herself. The man couldn't wait to get his hands on her! he thought savagely. He watched her expression closely, searching for any sign that she responded in kind.

Martin Talmadge stood up and offered his arm to his mother. "Are you ready, Mr. Hawkes?"

"Yes," Stephen said hurriedly, mentally giving himself a shake. Damn, but that fire-haired woman had him rattled! Bringing this séance off was going to take all his concentration and skill, and if he didn't keep his mind on business, the whole investigation was going to come a cropper.

The Talmadges swept past him, wearing identical expressions of scornful dislike, although Jane winked as she went by. Martin seated his mother, then stood behind the chair at the foot of the table, opposite the one Stephen was to take. Stephen congratulated himself on picking them as accomplices. "Be sure you take that particular seat," he'd told Martin earlier, "and damn good manners, even if you have to chuck someone out of it."

"Stephen, dear, where do you want me?" Clarissa asked, tucking her hand into his. Her voice and eyes conveyed a more complex meaning to her question.

"Where I can see you best, lovely Clarissa," he replied. Seeing a tiny frown appear on Lauren's brow, he smiled. Could the cool Miss Wakefield be a bit jealous?

Still smiling, he led Clarissa to the table and

placed her at Martin's left, as far from his own seat as possible; her feet and hands had an alarming tendency to stray in his direction, as he had learned at dinner. Before she had a chance to think of a reason to change her seat, he levered Mrs. Farleigh up from the sofa and escorted her to the chair beside her daughter's. Then he went to bow before Portia.

"Will you honor me, lovely lady?" he murmured, holding out his arm.

"Certainly, gallant sir," she teased back, placing her small plump hand on his forearm.

He seated her at his right, leaving two unoccupied chairs for Lauren and Farleigh, one on either side of the table. Pulling out the chair immediately to his left, he called, "Miss Wakefield, will you please take your place?"

She shot him a challenging glance from under her eyelashes, as she slipped in front of him to take her place at the table. The rogue has already managed to separate Richard and me, she thought. Irritation warred with amusement at his impudence.

She watched Richard as he took the seat between Jane Talmadge and Portia. His lips were pressed tightly together with displeasure, making him look for a moment like a younger, thinner version of his mother. Lauren shot a glance at the corpulent woman beside her. Drusilla Farleigh was a haughty, intolerant woman, contemptuous of anyone who had less money or more education than she did. *Nouveau riche,* her own mother would have said with pity and amusement.

Sternly, Lauren banished that disloyal notion from her mind. Richard was her betrothed, Drusilla and Clarissa her future in-laws. She would adjust to their

67

ways, in time. Then Stephen's fingertips brushed across the back of her neck, bringing a trail of delicious shivers up her spine, and all her thoughts about marrying Richard Farleigh faded before the fear of what would happen if she did not. Would she end up with a will-o'-the-wisp like Stephen Hawkes, who would enjoy her for a time, wring her heart out, then leave her to pursue the next adventure?

Oh, no, she thought, hitching her chair forward to get away from that caressing hand, I'll not throw my life away like my mother did. Marriage to Richard would be respectable — and safe. What did love and passion have to do with marriage, anyway? She'd have a good name, one that didn't make decent people turn from her, and children who would know their father.

She clasped her hands on the table in front of her, keeping her gaze upon them as Stephen moved away to turn out the gaslights one by one. Soon there was just one left, the one nearest the table.

Richard brushed his hair back from his forehead and fixed his cold, pale gaze on Stephen. "Can't you fellows ever do anything in the light?" he asked.

"Some things," Stephen said, a smile deepening the creases at the corner of his mouth. "I can give a demonstration, if you like. But the spirits prefer candlelight. Do you have an objection to candles, Mr. Farleigh?"

"Not at all." There was a sour look on Richard's face that belied his words, however.

Stephen took a six-armed silver candelabra from the mantel and brought it to the table. He lit the candles, then turned the last remaining gaslight off. The tapers cast a pale, flickering circle of light around the table. The rest of the room was cloaked in darkness. It created a wonderfully eerie atmosphere, Stephen thought with satisfaction, and had to have an effect on those who had come here ready to disbelieve everything they saw. As if on cue, the wind died and the rain stopped, leaving the world in sudden silence.

"Mr. Talmadge." Although Stephen spoke softly, his deep voice seemed to roll through the room.

Martin started. "Yes?" He shook his head; even he, expecting this, was falling into bemusement.

"Choose a book," Stephen said. "Don't open it. Slip one of your cards into it—anywhere you choose."

Martin rose from his chair to grope along the nearest bookcase. He grabbed a book seemingly at random, although he had marked its location earlier. It was the one he and Stephen had agreed on earlier—Milton's *Paradise Lost*. Bringing it back to the table, he slid his card into it, leaving about a third protruding.

"Thank you." Stephen took the book from him and handed it to Richard. "Since you requested this demonstration, you will be our control, Mr. Farleigh."

"Excellent." Richard put the book in front of him, angling it so the others could see the card sticking out from between the pages.

Stephen took his place at the head of the table and spread his big hands out on the polished wood. He swept his audience with an intense stare, then bent his head and allowed his eyes to drift closed. Behind his closed lids, however, he was acutely aware of everything around him—the nervous shuffle of someone's feet beneath the table, the sound of the rain beginning to fall softly again, the faint, compelling aura of Lauren's violet scent.

He pushed the distractions aside. He slowed his breathing, letting the atmosphere seep into his mind, submerging the persona of Hawkes the policeman beneath that of Hawkes the spiritualist. He must make them believe. He *would* make them believe.

Lauren watched him from beneath lowered lashes, noting how the candlelight delineated his straight nose and the bold planes of his face. His high cheekbones cast twin wedges of sepia shadow along his jaw, and his eyes were hidden by his brows. He seemed remote, mysterious, almost a different person. It was as though he had doffed one identity to take on another. The change in him was so abrupt, so chilling, that it made her shiver.

His head came up slowly, but his eyes didn't open. His voice was hoarse, strained. "I see . . . I am told . . . Ahhh, I cannot . . ."

Richard's face twisted with disgust. He rolled his eyes upward, then glanced at Lauren as if to say, "See, I told you he couldn't do it!"

Although Lauren had hoped he'd fail miserably, she felt cheated, somehow. Charlatan, thief, liar — she'd called him all those things. Somehow, she'd held the mad hope that he'd prove her wrong. Her shoulders slumped.

"Now it begins," Stephen said, bringing her upright with a jerk. " 'By night . . . By night he fled, and at midnight . . .' " He broke off momentarily, muttering, "Hard to see . . . Ah!" His voice strengthened.

" '. . . at midnight returned
From encompassing the Earth—cautious of day
Since Uriel, regent of the sun, descried
His entrance, and forewarned the Cherubim . . .' "

Hurriedly, Richard flipped the book open to the marked place and began to read. Astonishment spread over his face as Stephen continued to quote, speaking faster and faster.

Richard looked around the table at the others. Helplessly, he waved his hand over the pages before him. Lauren, her patience at an end, reached to snatch the book from him, only to have Jane Talmadge do it first.

The old woman peered at the open pages. "Good heavens, he's doing it!" she cried.

Stephen's breath went out in a sharp gasp.

"There, Jane, you've ruined his concentration!" Portia cried.

"Well, how was I supposed to know—"

"Don't get upset, Mrs. Talmadge," Lauren soothed. "You couldn't help—"

"Order, please!" Martin pounded the table with his open hand. When he had everyone's attention, he said, "Mr. Hawkes, I don't know what it was that you did, but I can honestly say that I am impressed."

Stephen nodded. "Now, shall we get on with the business that brought us all together tonight?"

"Yes," Portia said, her blue eyes sparkling with eagerness. "Go on, Mr. Hawkes."

He leaned forward and blew out the candles, leaving the room in total darkness. "This contact will be more difficult than the last," he told them. "Breathe slowly, deeply, and empty your minds of everything but welcoming our ethereal visitor. Until I tell you, do not speak, do not rise from your chairs."

Lauren sat in the darkness, smelling the acrid smoke that hung in the still air. No one spoke, no one moved. She was conscious of the floor under her feet and the hard smoothness of the table under her hands, but the rest of the world seemed to have disappeared. She closed her eyes and opened them again, but there was no difference in what she saw. She strained to hear something, anything, but there was only the sound of her own breathing.

Only a few minutes passed, but the short time seemed like hours. She tried counting her own heartbeats, the breaths she took. It started raining again, and she welcomed the new sound eagerly, savoring it. But it soon faded into the background as had her breathing, only intensifying the velvet shrouding of the darkness. Feeling as though she might float away like a wraith herself, she clutched the edge of the table with both hands, fighting the disorientation that had her in thrall.

Suddenly she became aware that there was something in the room that hadn't been there before—a small, glowing shape that seemed to hover at the edge of her vision for an instant before disappearing. At first she thought she'd imagined it, but then it appeared again, this time in another spot. Still clutching the table, she turned her head to get a better view of it. But it was teasingly elusive, appearing now on one side of the table, now on the other. Then Stephen began to speak, his voice so startling after the prolonged silence that Lauren nearly cried out.

"I am . . . I was James," he said in a harsh, strained voice. I seek — "

"My brother!" Mrs. Farleigh cried. "Show me a sign if you can hear me, James!"

Lauren gasped as the heavy table shuddered. Slowly, almost hesitantly, it rose a few inches into the air.

"It *is* you, James!" Mrs. Farleigh moaned. "Oh, James, are you happy? I've missed you so much!"

The table sank back to the floor. Stephen murmured, "I am content. There are many here to . . . keep me company."

"Mother? Is she there?" Mrs. Farleigh's voice shook. "Can she speak with me?"

"I will try . . ." Stephen's voice took on a different tone, rougher, less cultured. "I once was George Lee, I killed a man and hung for it."

"Where is Mother?" Mrs. Farleigh wailed. "I want to talk with Mother!"

"*I* want to talk," the spirit answered with Stephen's voice.

"Do you know the spirit of Thaddeus Danforth?" Portia asked. Her voice was commanding and confident, courtesy of Edward Eldridge's training.

"Yes." Stephen's tone was sullen, uncooperative.

"Can you bring him here?" the widow asked.

"Don't want to."

"You must!" Portia commanded.

Thunder rolled nearby, suddenly, startlingly. Lauren, whose attention had been riveted on the conversation, half-rose from her chair with a startled gasp. Her heart beating as if to pound its way out of her chest, she sank down again.

"George Lee, you've been asked to contact Thaddeus Danforth," Portia said, her voice shaking a little. "Do as you are bid, or relinquish your place to another."

There was a moment of silence, then Stephen muttered, "He don't want to come. "Says it's a fat lot of horse manure."

"That's Thaddeus exactly!" Portia shrieked. "He—"

Lightning flared outside, limning the room in platinum radiance for one brief, vision-searing instant as thunder rattled the windows. Then the darkness wrapped around them once more, seeming to be even denser than before, almost suffocating. Mrs. Farliegh's voice rose in a quavering moan.

Stephen paused for a moment, the rapid pant of his breathing clearly audible. "He says . . . he says to tell his wife that there is someone close to her who is false." He took a deep breath and began to speak rapidly, his deep tones echoing the thunder's dying rumble. "Lies upon lies . . . feeding on her kindness." His voice became stronger, hoarser, grating on the nerves like fingernails upon a slate. "If she knew what sort of serpent she has held to her bosom, she would cast it away in disgust. She would—"

Lightning flared again, followed by a tremendous crash of thunder. A woman screamed, shrill and frightened, and as the darkness fell again there was the sound of a chair—and a body—crashing heavily to the floor.

Stephen leaped for the nearest light, envisioning, what could have happened if Jane, fragile as she was, had fallen with force. To his surprise, he saw that it was Mrs. Farleigh who was sprawled unconscious upon the carpet. Martin and Richard rushed to aid her, while Jane Talmadge pouted with disgust at this usurping of her much-anticipated performance. In a few moments, Mrs. Farleigh groaned and sat up. The others hovered over her, talking excitedly.

The corner of Stephen's mouth turned up in a sardonic grin. Then he turned to look at Lauren, and his awareness of the babble of voices faded. She was staring at him, her eyes wide with astonishment and fear. Her face was white, her lips bloodless. Sure that she was about to faint, he took a step towards her. Then he saw her grope for the back of the chair and grip it with such force that the fine tendons in the back of her hand stood out like wires. Color rushed back into her face, and the wild emotion drained from her eyes.

Such control she has! he thought in admiration. But what had prompted that devastating, revealing moment? He'd meant the warning to be pointed towards Edward Eldridge; what guilty secret did Lauren harbor beneath her icy facade that would make her react so dramatically to those particular words? His chest tightened with the knot of anticipation he'd felt many times before—whenever his policeman's instincts told him that a case was going to turn ugly!

"I think we could all use some refreshment," Portia said, her clear voice rising over the rapidly retreating noise of the storm. She poured a tiny glass of sherry for each of the ladies. "Martin, will you pour brandy for the gentlemen?"

"Gladly." Martin obeyed, then took his own snifter and raised it to Stephen. "My compliments, Mr. Hawkes, for a most, er, enervating demonstration."

"Thank you, Mr. Talmadge," Stephen said, adding silently, And thank *you* for giving me the name of Mrs. Farleigh's brother, and most especially the bit about the horse manure. It gave a most authentic touch.

Numbly, Lauren sank back into her chair and closed her hand over the glass Portia offered her. Setting it aside, untasted, she silently pondered the statement that had startled her so. That warning had been about her, no one else. She had lied to obtain her place here, and continued to lie to keep it; the widow, despite her kind nature, was very proper, almost prudish. If Portia knew that Lauren was the daughter of the notorious Alanna Stanton — whose behavior had scandalized New York society not once, but twice — she would be terribly shocked. And, as Stephen had so vividly said, she would cast the sneaking serpent from her house and from her heart. No, not serpent, but bastard — go on, say it, she told herself brutally. Bastard. Whore's bastard. It has been said so many times by others, that you should be used to it by now.

But how had Stephen known? It couldn't have been spirits — she wasn't so gullible as to believe *that,* despite his admittedly impressive performance. More importantly, was he going to reveal what he knew? Perhaps she should just leave now, disappear while Portia still had some regard for her. She'd managed to save a little money. Her mother was getting well, slowly but steadily, and her medical bills weren't quite so staggering as they once were. Somehow, they'd manage.

She lifted her head in alarm, abruptly becoming aware of the conversation between Portia and Stephen Hawkes.

". . . Sorry I couldn't reach your husband," Stephen said.

Portia put her hand on his arm. "My dear Mr. Hawkes, you came so very close. I have great hopes that you will soon be able to persuade him to speak to me."

"I'll be pleased to try again," he said.

"You'll stay here, won't you?" Portia nodded, as though to reply to her own question. "Mr. Eldridge tells me that the more time a medium spends at the place of possible contact, the more likely it is that the contact will occur."

Stephen smiled. "I would say it more simply, but yes, I must agree with Mr. Eldridge in this case." He'd done it! he thought triumphantly. He'd matched Eldridge at his own game. And now he'd obtained a place in the widow's home, where he could keep an eye on things.

"Then you'll bring your things tomorrow?" Portia asked.

"Tomorrow will be fine."

All desire of leaving drained from Lauren, to be replaced by outrage. How could she walk away, leaving Portia in the clutches of two unscrupulous rogues? No, oh, no! She had to stay here to protect the woman whose friendship had come to mean so much. If Portia learned her secret and ordered her from the house, Lauren would live in the street outside, until she found a way to get rid of the two charlatans!

She pushed her chair back and stood up, ready to

protest Stephen's invitation into the household. But before she could speak, Richard came up behind her and put his arm around her waist. Instinctively, she stiffened at the unexpected touch. Richard had become increasingly demonstrative during the last few days, and it made her uncomfortable. Good heavens, she chided herself, the man is your betrothed! You'd better get used to it.

"I hate to break up this entertaining little party," he said. "But we ought to take Mother home."

Portia pressed her hand to her bosom. "Oh, I'm so sorry we made her faint."

"Mother faints all the time," he said, waving his hand negligently. "Lauren, my dear, remember that we're to attend the party at the Ganton's on Saturday. Clarissa and I will call for you at nine o'clock."

"You mean that you, Clarissa, and your mother will pick her up, don't you?" Portia asked.

He laughed. "Oh, yes. We'll be strenuously chaperoned, my dear lady."

Clarissa abandoned her mother for Stephen. She linked her arm in his, pressing flirtatiously against his side. "It just so happens that I'm without an escort for Saturday."

Stephen smiled down at her, extremely pleased by her implied invitation. Going to that party would give him the opportunity to keep his eye on Lauren's overeager fiancé. *Most strenuously chaperoned,* he repeated silently to himself. Oh, yes. "In need of an escort, lovely lady?" he asked. "Will I do?"

"You'll do," she murmured, gazing up at him with eyes that promised everything. To her chagrin, she found that he wasn't looking at her, but at Lauren. Irritated, she squeezed his arm against her breast.

"Nine o'clock, then?"

"Yes." Stephen glanced at her briefly, then returned his gaze to Lauren. He was barely aware of Clarissa leaving his side to return to her mother.

Richard released Lauren's waist, only to grasp both her hands and raise them to his mouth. He kissed one, then the other. "Until Saturday, darling."

"Yes." Her face scarlet with embarrassment, Lauren pulled her hands away and took a step backward.

As the Farleighs turned towards the door, Martin Talmadge and his mother also rose.

"It's time for us to go, too," Jane Talmadge said. "Thank you for a most interesting evening." As she walked past Stephen, she closed one eye in a wink. "Perhaps you might visit, Mr. Hawkes. I have many questions to ask you about your profession."

He bowed. "I'm at your disposal, Mrs. Talmadge."

Portia followed her guests out into the foyer. When Stephen would have followed, however, Lauren closed the library door and put her back against it.

"You are contemptible," she said coldly.

His eyebrows rose in dark, flaring arcs. "Oh, really? Why do you say that?"

"You know why." Icy rage coursed through her veins—rage, and fear of what he might say next. He knew—or suspected—her secret. Would he offer a blackmailer's bargain for his silence?

"Because I tried to contact Mrs. Danforth's husband—as she requested, may I add?"

Lauren was taken aback; she had expected another answer entirely. "I—"

"Is it so hard for you to believe that I might genuinely want to help her?" he demanded, taking a long stride towards her.

"I'll tell you what I believe!" Her chin lifted defiantly. "I believe that you and Eldridge are human vultures, come to pick the bones of an old woman's grief."

"And you hate us for it."

She looked down her nose at him, putting every shred of her cold rage into her gaze. "Hate is much too strong an emotion, Mr. Hawkes. Despise is far more accurate. I despise everything you do, everything you are."

His hands snaked out suddenly, grasping her by the shoulders with a grip that made her gasp. "You don't despise *everything* I do."

His body, taut with anger, was pressed tightly against her. His mouth was poised over hers. Lauren knew he was about to kiss her, and that it would hurt. Still, she faced him defiantly. "Yes, everything!"

"You shouldn't have said that," he growled. "Now I'm going to have to prove you wrong."

She tried to turn her face aside, but his fingers caught her chin and held her motionless. His mouth came down on hers, his tongue probing between her lips. It was an angry kiss, meant to punish. Humiliating, hurtful. And yet she couldn't stop herself from responding to it, the now-familiar flooding warmth rushing through her loins, the weakness in her limbs. She tried to shake her head in denial of what was happening, but his iron grip anchored her while he plundered her mouth and her emotions. Tears leaked out from under her closed lids to run down over her cheeks and onto their tightly locked mouths.

Stephen tasted the salt of her tears, felt the trembling of her body. Filled with disgust at his own lack of control, he released her so suddenly that she staggered. He raked his hand through his hair, stunned that he'd let her push him that far. Why the hell hadn't he just walked away?

Lauren stood staring at him, unable to move, unable to speak. She reached up, feeling her lips with shaking fingers.

"Go on, get out of here," he rasped.

As though released by his words, she whirled. Flinging the door open, she fled up the stairs.

After taking his mother and sister back to their mansion on Fifth Avenue, Richard directed the driver to hurry towards his own house. Tonight, as most nights, a prostitute would be waiting there for him, procured by his ever so resourceful manservant. This one was to have red hair.

Red hair, like Lauren Wakefield's. With a sigh, Richard settled back against the upholstered seat. A little shy, his fiancée, but she had potential. Oh, he'd set up a proper howl when his father—hoping that responsibility would settle his scapegrace son down—insisted that he marry her. But the widow was offering a twenty-thousand-dollar dowry, and that amount would just about cover his gambling losses at Morrissey's. And as the old woman's only living relative, Lauren would surely inherit the whole bundle.

He chuckled. The widow had insisted that he not tell Lauren about the dowry, lest he injure the girl's pride. Portia Danforth, closeted in that stuffy monstrosity of a house all these years, was surely the most naive woman in New York. It would be easy to wheedle more money out of her, especially when he got Lauren pregnant.

He ruminated on the pleasures of bedding Lauren. At first he'd thought her plain and stupid, but he'd soon revised that opinion. With that marvelous hair and the sweetly curved breasts he'd glimpsed earlier today, she might prove to be entertaining. And the prospect of training her to his carnal tastes was nearly as exciting as the twenty thousand. Such innocence! It was rare in the world he frequented, so rare that it was intriguing.

When the carriage reached his house, Richard bolted from the vehicle and ran up the white stone steps. His manservant opened the door as he approached.

"Did you find one, Garvin?" Richard asked breathlessly, striding into the elaborate foyer.

"Yes, sir." The servant took Richard's coat and hat. "She's upstairs, waiting for you."

"Red hair?"

Garvey nodded. "I think you'll be pleased, sir. And surprised."

Richard, who had turned away, whirled to face him again. "What do you mean, surprised?"

"Why don't you go see, sir?" The manservant's face showed no emotion, but his eyes glittered with amusement.

Richard ran upstairs to his room. What the devil did the man mean? he wondered, pushing the door open.

The prostitute stood before the tall cheval mirror,

brushing her hair. She was wearing nothing but a sheer lawn nightgown, her small feet bare against the thick Persian carpet. Hearing him come in, she turned to look at him.

Richard was speechless as his astonished gaze took in the fiery wealth of her hair, the creamy oval of her face, her liquid dark eyes. The image of Lauren Wakefield, he thought incredulously.

"Somethin' wrong?" she asked.

"No, nothing's wrong," he said, coming into the room and closing the door behind him. He must remember to give Garvey a bonus for this night's work. Oh, yes, he was pleased.

The prostitute strolled towards him. Despite the experienced seductiveness of her manner, he realized with a shiver of pleasure that she was still in her teens. When she finally stood before him, he saw that her resemblance to Lauren was not as pronounced as he'd thought; the whore was shorter and much more voluptuous, her features coarser. But the hair, the glorious, flaming hair, and the eyes were the same.

A thrill of delight went through him at the thought of sharing a wife and a mistress who looked so much alike. He'd keep them both; Lauren to please his father, the whore to please *him*. The best of both situations would be his: enjoying what was already corrupt, corrupting what was innocent.

Aroused by the very thought, he reached out and untied the ribbons on the prostitute's bodice, freeing her heavy breasts. She laughed lustily, shaking those overlarge mounds until he grabbed them, one in each hand. Truly, he couldn't decide which he preferred — Lauren's slim, graceful curves, or this whore's fleshy abundance.

He bent to run his tongue over the woman's big, dark nipples. "What's your name?" he asked between licks.

"Bianca Cavalli," she said, reaching down to run her hands over his manhood.

Gently, he put her from him. Going to the bedside table where a decanter of brandy sat in its accustomed place, he poured two snifters of brandy and held one out to her.

"Come, Bianca Cavalli," he said.

She took the glass from him and downed it without a cough. He grinned in approval, sipping his own brandy while he played with her breasts with one hand.

"Do you like money?" he asked.

She laughed. " 'Course I like it. Who don't?"

"How would you like to have me as a regular customer?" he asked, his hips thrusting upward to meet her hands.

Grinning, she pulled her nightgown up over her head and tossed it aside, exposing her rounded belly and the thatch of auburn hair between her thighs. "Will you pay 'nuff for me to quit my other men?"

He pulled her against him, his hands going to her buttocks to clench and unclench on the soft flesh. "I'll pay you more than you ever dreamed you could earn walking the streets. But as long as you're available when I want you, I don't give a damn how many other men you have."

She rubbed herself against him. "Maybe if you're good 'nuff, my fine gentleman, I won't need anybody else."

"I don't have to be good, *you* do," he said,

squeezing the flesh of her buttocks with brutal strength.

She didn't flinch. "Like this?" she asked, reaching between them to caress his groin. "I know lots of ways to please men. Want me to please you?"

"Yes," he muttered, shifting so that she could unfasten his trousers. He was incredibly aroused, whether from her ministrations or from the thought of possessing both her and Lauren, he didn't know. What miracle had produced two women who looked so much alike, and who had come so fortuitously into his life? It was just too delicious! The prospect of bedding them both was nearly as pleasurable as what Bianca was doing with her hands. Then she sank to her knees in front of him. As her mouth closed over him, narrowing his world to a single, blazing tunnel of sensuality, he gave up thinking altogether.

Chapter Six

Lauren woke to a sullen, gray morning. Yawning, she pushed herself up on her elbows and peered at the clock upon the mantel. "Only six-thirty!" she groaned, rolling onto her stomach and burying her face in the soft feather pillow. A moment later, she turned on her right side, then, restless, changed positions yet again. She squeezed her eyes closed and willed herself to sleep, but to no avail. The clock downstairs chimed seven, then half-past.

Giving up at last, she climbed out of bed and padded barefoot to the window, opening the blue velvet curtains so she could look outside. Low-hanging clouds spat a steady, soaking rain upon the already sodden world below. It was a depressing sight, nearly as depressing as her dreams had been.

With a sigh, she settled into the comfortable nest of pillows that cushioned the window seat. Her sleep had been haunted by Stephen Hawkes—his deep laugh, his too-perceptive gray eyes, and most especially the touch of his hands, his mouth, the feel of his hard male body against hers. Her dreams had been feverish, full of aching need and heated, trembling desire—dreams no honorable woman should have. She had wakened from each one to find the bedclothes twined around her like a lover's arms, her body aflame, her heart pounding.

What sort of bewitchment had Hawkes cast over her? He had invaded her senses and her emotions in a way she wouldn't have thought possible. She drew her feet up onto the seat and laid her cheek upon her upraised knees. Cool, composed Lauren Stanton, she mused bitterly, the girl who'd thought herself above the weakness of desire. She'd been so sure—so arrogantly, wrongly sure—that no man would ever affect her the way Piero Cavalli and Lord Parry had affected her mother.

"No, no, no!" she muttered, pounding her fists on the cushions. Then she raised her head, her chin firming with determination. So, she was human after all, subject to the same weakness that had been the ruin of her mother's life. But she didn't have to give in to that weakness. She *would not* give in. She had seen the cost, and it was a price she wasn't willing to pay. Stephen Hawkes could go straight to . . .

There was a woman's scream, then a muffled crash from downstairs. Lauren leaped to her feet with a gasp, then snatched her dressing gown from the foot of her bed and ran from her room. As she reached the top of the stairs, she heard Kate, the cook, calling out in a frightened, urgent voice.

"Miss Wakefield! Mrs. Danforth!" the woman cried. "Come quick!"

Picking up her voluminous skirts, Lauren rushed downstairs, her bare feet silent and sure on the cool marble steps.

"Where are you, Kate?" she cried as she reached the foyer.

"Oh, Miss Wakefield!" The cook appeared in the doorway of the parlor, her broad, middle-aged face creased with worry. "Hurry! Fanny's been hurt!"

Lauren hurried into the parlor to find Fanny unconscious upon the floor. There was no visible wound on the girl, but a heavy Sevres urn lay a short distance from her limp, outstretched hand.

Lauren sank to her knees beside the girl. To her relief, the maid groaned and began to stir. She glanced over her shoulder at the cook. "Kate, did you see what happened?"

"N-no." the woman's lower lip quivered. "I heard her cry out, and then I come in here an' find her like this. Oh, Miss Wakefield! Is she hurt bad?"

"I don't know if she's hurt at all or just fainted," Lauren said.

There was a peremptory knock at the front door, and Kate looked up. "That must be Mr. Hawkes. He was s'posed to be here at eight."

Lauren frowned. Drat the man! Of all the times for him to show up! If Fanny wasn't more important than getting rid of him, she'd get up right now and answer the door herself.

"Kate, why don't you fetch me a wet cloth?" she asked.

"What about Mr. Hawkes?"

Mr. Hawkes can go straight to the devil, for all I care, Lauren thought. But aloud, she only said, "I hear Mrs. Danforth coming. She'll let him in."

As the cook went to do her bidding, Lauren heard Portia calling from the hallway upstairs, demanding to know what was going on. Stephen Hawkes knocked again, louder this time, and the widow's agitated voice moved down the stairs and to the door.

A moment later the widow and Stephen appeared in the doorway. At the sight of the prostrate girl, Portia clutched his arm, and the voluminous folds of her dressing gown swirled absurdly around his black-clad legs.

Stephen took in the room with one encompassing glance, then disengaged himself from the widow's grasp and knelt beside Lauren. He lightly touched Fanny's cheek. "How long has she been unconscious?"

Lauren glanced at the clock, surprised to see that only a few minutes had passed since she'd heard Fanny scream. "Only five minutes or so. I really don't know what's wrong with her. She's already stirred a bit, and as you can see, her breathing and color are good."

"Well, let's see what we can find." He removed the maid's starched white cap and tossed it aside so he could examine her head for any other injury. He drew in his breath. "There's a lump the size of a goose egg back here. She must have hit her head when she fell. But I can't find anything else."

Lauren watched his long fingers move through the girl's dark hair. Such gentleness, such care! she thought. And he seemed to know what he was doing. For the first time, she was glad that he'd come when he had.

Fanny's eyelids fluttered, then opened, and she looked about vaguely. Then her gaze focused on

Lauren's face. "Oh, Miss Wakefield!"

"Shhh, Fanny. Don't upset yourself," Lauren soothed, taking the girl's groping hand and holding it. "Can you tell us what happened?"

The maid's gaze went to the urn that lay nearby. "It just . . . flew at me!"

"It fell?" Lauren asked in confusion.

"No!" Fanny shook her head from side to side, then winced at the pain the movement caused. "It jumped up from the table and flew right at my face, I tell you!"

Mrs. Danforth came forward to stand behind Lauren. "But Fanny, dear, urns don't leap up and attack people."

"Apparently this one did," Stephen said, catching the widow's gaze and shaking his head slightly to warn her against upsetting the maid.

"The spirits are angry." Edward Eldridge's resonant voice came from the doorway, startling them all.

Fanny whimpered. "It was spirits what threw that thing at me! Oh, oh!"

"Fanny, don't. There's a perfectly rational explanation for it, I'm sure," Lauren said, stroking the distraught girl's cheek before returning her attention to Eldridge. Although she wanted to scream her frustration to the sky, she used her calmest and most reasonable voice. "Mr. Eldridge, this is hardly the time—"

"The spirits are angry," Eldridge intoned, "because you have allowed this man to interfere with the delicate balances between this plane and theirs." He came forward into the room, his arms

90

outstretched, his head thrown back in an eerie, trancelike ecstasy. With his long, midnight-dark dressing gown flaring around him, he looked like the Angel of Death himself. "And there will be further displays of their outrage, each more dangerous than the last, until this . . . interloper is gone!"

Fanny moaned and tried to sit up, but Stephen gently urged her back down. His gray eyes smoldering with fury, he turned to look at Lauren.

"Shall I knock his teeth out now?" he gritted.

A rush of emotions went through her—amusement, admiration, and a giddy sort of recklessness that almost made her want to say yes. Before she could open her mouth to reply, however, Portia reached out to prevent Stephen from getting up.

"Now, Stephen, don't get upset," the widow urged. "Mr. Eldridge is just going upstairs to dress. Aren't you, Edward?"

The spiritualist began to shake his head, but then he glanced at Stephen's outthrust chin and glittering, smoky eyes, and hastily changed his mind. Drawing himself up with injured dignity, he swept out of the room so fast that Kate, who was returning with a basin of water and several clean cloths, was forced to step hurriedly out of his way.

Lauren rose gracefully to her feet to take the basin and cloths, then knelt down again beside Fanny. Dipping a cloth into the water, she wrung it nearly dry and held the cool compress against the lump on Fanny's head.

Portia bent solicitously over the maid. "Fanny, did the urn actually try to hit you?"

"N-no, but you have no idea what it's like to see

something like that floating in the air—"

"Floating?" Kate squealed.

"Floating, all by itself!" Fanny insisted. "It was evil spirits, just like Mr. Eldridge said!"

The cook twisted her apron into a tangled mess. "Spirits! I knew something would happen, with all the crazy goings-on around here!"

"Now, Kate, that's enough of that kind of talk," Portia said firmly, her round little chin held high. "I think we should tend to the most important thing first, which is Fanny's injury." She turned to Stephen. "Shall I send for a doctor?"

"It couldn't hurt," he said. "I *think* she's only gotten a bad bump, but we want to be sure." Gently, he gathered Fanny into his arms, then rose to his feet. "Where do you want her?"

With a swish of skirts, Portia bustled towards the doorway. "Lauren, show him to Fanny's room. Kate, you go for Dr. Janus while I fetch the medicine chest. What a terrible thing to happen to the poor . . ." her voice faded as she moved away.

Stephen looked down at Lauren. She was still kneeling on the floor, her head bent in thought. Her bright hair was bound in a thick, coppery braid that fell nearly to her waist, and her slim, bare feet peeped out from under the tumbled folds of her dark green woolen dressing gown. She looked young and vulnerable—and utterly desirable.

Lauren looked up, catching him staring at her. Despite her loose, enveloping garments, she felt as though he'd stripped her naked. It embarrassed her, and more—it brought a treacherous warmth creeping through her body.

"Where shall I take her?" he prompted.

Lauren rose to her feet, gathering her composure about her like a cloak, shielding herself. "Come with me, Mr. Hawkes," she said, turning towards the door.

Stephen wanted to shake her, kiss her, anything to shatter that cocoon of icy imperturbability with which she shielded herself. But he only shifted Fanny to a more comfortable position in his arms and followed Lauren's tall, graceful figure towards the back stairs. But just wait, Miss Wakefield, he promised silently. Just wait.

After the doctor left, Lauren ran up the back stairs to her room and dressed, then hurried back to the parlor. The Sevres urn had been replaced on the table from which it had come. She picked it up and examined it, noting that there was a chip in the base and also a hairline crack in one of its curved handles. She pursed her lips thoughtfully. Eldridge had staged that cruel trick, she was sure. But how? How had he managed to hurl that urn without letting Fanny see him?

Suddenly she whirled, grabbing one of the nearby chairs and dragging it into the center of the room. She stood on its seat and inspected the chandelier, even going so far as to run her hands over each of the four brass arms that supported the etched glass globes.

"There's nothing there. I've already checked,"

Stephen Hawkes said from behind her.

She turned to look over her shoulder at him. He'd taken his coat off and rolled up the sleeves of his shirt, exposing his wrists and part of his muscular forearms. He leaned against the doorjamb, looking like some big, graceful cat, languid now, but ready to burst into motion without warning.

"Not only are you beautiful, but you're clever as well," he said, grinning at her in a most infuriating and arrogant manner.

Heat rose into her cheeks at the thought that she'd actually been glad to see him! *"You* should know how it was done, shouldn't you, Mr. Hawkes?" she asked, schooling her voice to calmness.

"Yes," he agreed good-naturedly, coming to stand before her chair. "What did the doctor say about Fanny?"

"She's had a bad knock and an even worse scare, but she'll be as good as new after a day's rest. Portia is with her now."

"I'm glad to hear it." His gaze swept over her gown, which was another of that mouse-gray hue that was so at odds with her coloring. It was plain of fabric and design, and completely devoid of ornamentation. Why did she insist on hiding behind the unflattering clothing? Did she think that a man—that he—would fail to look beyond the covering to see the woman beneath? Especially after seeing her in a dressing gown, he added silently. Those soft folds of green fabric had revealed a most alluring side of her—feminine, unfettered, seductive. That glimpse had touched him deeply,

94

making him want to see more. Much more.

"Is there anything else, Mr. Hawkes?" she inquired.

"Yes. No one has yet offered to show me to my room," he said. "I was hoping you would."

She damped down a surge of anger. He will not bait me into another of those absurd exchanges he seems to like so well, she told herself firmly. If only he weren't standing so close, so that to step from the chair would be to step right into his arms.

"Well?" he prompted.

She wanted to show him the door, not his room. But he was an invited guest in Portia's house, and Lauren knew it was not her place to interfere. Openly, at least. "Very well," she said, promising herself ample revenge for everything he was forcing upon her now.

Without warning, he reached forward to swing her into his arms. Lauren, instead of struggling or protesting—which she knew would do no good, anyway—merely held herself stiffly and tried to ignore him. But even through her clothes she could feel his warmth, the hard strength of the arms that cradled her shoulders and beneath her knees. His face was so near hers that she could see the variegations of gray in his irises, and pick out each individual silver hair at his temples. Her heart beat a staccato pace in her chest, and for a moment she almost allowed herself to relax against him. Then she got her wayward emotions under control again, and shifted her gaze to a point on the wall behind him.

"Fanny was much more cooperative about being carried," he said, his warm breath tickling the hair at her temple.

"Fanny was very nearly unconscious," she pointed out, "and in no position to protest."

"And you are?" His breath shifted to her other temple.

It took every shred of her control not to look at him. If she did, he'd kiss her. "I am not protesting, Mr. Hawkes. I am merely enduring this until you decide to abandon your childish behavior."

"Are we back to Mr. Hawkes? Yesterday, I was Stephen."

"Yesterday, you hadn't schemed your way into this house."

"I see." He set her on her feet, transferring his grasp to her wrists. Her pulse was hammering as fast as his, he noted. Why the hell was it so important that he get a response from her? Why, when it was stupid and dangerous and a threat to the case, did he keep pursuing her? He knew the answer, although he didn't like it. He wanted to be the man—the only man—who could break her unnatural reserve. He wanted to know her secrets as badly as he wanted to bed her. Damn, but he was a fool! He released her abruptly.

She stepped back, nearly upsetting the chair, then turned and stalked towards the foyer. "Coming, Mr. Hawkes?" she asked with a coolness she didn't feel inside at all.

Stephen retrieved his case and followed her upstairs, admiring the graceful sway of her bustle as she walked up the steps ahead of him. As they reached the hallway beyond, Nero appeared seemingly out of nowhere to join them. The cat strutted a few inches in front of Lauren's skirts, his tail held straight up like a fluffy banner.

Lauren reached the room that had been prepared for Stephen's use and pushed the door open. She stepped aside to let him in, but didn't enter. Nero, however, had no such qualms; he wove a path between Stephen's feet, then jumped up onto the bed and settled himself with his paws before him, sphinxlike.

Stephen set his case down and turned in a circle to inspect the room. Floor-to-ceiling draperies of burgundy velvet shrouded the window, the rug was a pattern of cream, burgundy, and black, as were the counterpane and curtains of the massive antique bed.

"Let me guess," he said. "This is the Red Room."

"Of course." Lauren moved to the window and opened the draperies. The clouds were beginning to break up, and the warm, golden disk of the sun was a welcome sight. "Mr. Eldridge has the Green Room, Mrs. Danforth the Gold—"

"And you?"

"The Blue Room."

"Which one is it?" He grinned at her. "I wouldn't want to miss it in the dark."

She turned to face him. "Then you'll also want to know that it has a very good lock on the door."

"A pity." He sat down on the edge of the bed and began to stroke Nero, but kept his gaze on her.

"Why don't you leave?" she asked.

"I'm an invited guest. I'm wanted here."

"You forget Mr. Eldridge's spirits," she retorted. *"They* don't want you here."

He shrugged, dismissing both Eldridge and his spirits. Nero clambered into his lap, closing his golden cat eyes in ecstasy as Stephen scratched behind his ears.

Lauren let out a sigh of exasperation. "I don't understand why he likes you."

"You've a less than flattering way with words, my lovely Lauren." He laughed, but there was a note of irritation below his mirth. "Are you like this with all your swains?"

"I have no swains. Just a fiancé." Her words were as much a reminder to herself as to him. She clutched the fact of her betrothal to her heart like a shield, hoping to keep her wayward emotions in check.

"You don't love Richard Farleigh."

Her chin went up defiantly. "My relationship with Richard is no concern of yours."

Stephen gazed at her from under half-closed lids. She was right. The only business he should be tending to was the case he'd been sent here to investigate. But she looked so damned beautiful standing there, her dark eyes flashing with exasperation, and the sun turning her hair into a fiery aureole! How could flesh and blood resist the challenge and mystery she posed? God knows, *he* hadn't been able to.

Feeling as though he'd been caught in a whirlpool, he set Nero aside gently, then rose from the bed and strode towards her. "What are you afraid of, Lauren?" he asked.

"I'm not afraid." As he came closer, she began to tremble. He was so tall, so arrogantly masculine, and her heart was beating much too fast for comfort. She wanted to run. She told her feet to run, but they wouldn't move.

He stopped a scant foot in front of her, his wide shoulders blocking her view of the room. Taking her hand, he raised it to his lips, then turned it over and ran his open mouth across her palm. His tongue darted out to trace the base of her thumb.

A shaft of desire went through her from that contact point, a hot, coiling need deep in her body. Unable to move, unable to speak, she could only watch helplessly as he kissed his way from her palm to her wrist. Pull away! a small, sane part of her mind screamed. But still she stood motionless, her gaze fixed on the hard line of his cheek, his lips, the faint shadow of the beard on his clean-shaven chin. She barely had the strength to keep herself from reaching out with her free hand to caress that bold jaw, to run her fingers through the silver-streaked thickness of his hair.

"If you're not frightened, then why is your pulse racing?" he asked, watching her expression narrowly. "Are you afraid I'll discover that guilty secret you've been keeping?"

Shocked into motion by his words, Lauren jerked her hand away from him. So now it comes out! she thought furiously, wishing she'd never agreed to attend his ridiculous séance. He'd guessed her lie; what price was he going to demand for his silence? Well, whatever it was, she wouldn't pay it. "You can—"

"My, my, what an interesting little scene!" Eldridge's drawling voice came from the doorway behind her. "I wonder what your fiancé would think of it."

Lauren glanced at him over her shoulder, then returned her attention to Stephen. "Probably as little as I do, Mr. Eldridge." She met Stephen's gaze challengingly for a moment, then whirled and swept out of the room.

Eldridge watched her until she disappeared around the corner, then turned back to Stephen. "You're wasting your time with that one, Hawkes. She's as cold as the North Sea in winter."

Stephen shrugged with feigned indifference. Always make the other man lose control, he'd learned, and it was a lesson that had never yet failed him. But it was hard—damned hard—not to take Eldridge by the neck and throttle an answer out of him. The thought of Lauren in another man's arms, even unwillingly, made the blood pound in his veins. "How do *you* know whether she's cold or not?" he asked, his tone dangerously soft.

"A gentleman never tells." Eldridge inspected his nails.

Stephen forced himself to relax. "She probably slapped your face," he said. A red flush stained Eldridge's cheeks, and Stephen showed his teeth in a humorless smile. "Hit it on the first try, didn't I?"

"You have an excellent imagination, Mr. Hawkes," Eldridge snapped.

Stephen leaned back against the pillows, cradling Nero against his chest, and looked at the spiritualist with narrowed eyes. "She's figured out how you worked that trick with the urn," he said.

Apprehension crossed Eldridge's face, but was quickly suppressed. "There was no trick," he retorted stiffly. "Miss Wakefield's imagination is even better than yours."

"Indeed?" Stephen's hand stroked slowly along the length of Nero's back, and the cat arched to meet his touch. "What do you think, Nero?" he asked. "Is he telling the truth?"

Nero fixed Eldridge with a baleful yellow glare. A low growl rumbled deep in his chest. Stephen showed the edges of his teeth in a grin that held nothing of humor, and for a moment his expression was identical to Nero's. With a curse, Eldridge whirled and stalked away.

"Dickie, I do believe you're falling asleep," Drusilla Farleigh said, bracing herself as the carriage turned the corner and headed up Fifty-ninth Street towards Central Park.

"Sorry, Mother." Richard straightened in his seat, wishing he were anywhere but in this carriage with her and Neda Barfield, who was the fattest and stupidest of all Mother's fat, stupid friends. But the hope of charming a little money out of his mother forced him to endure.

Mrs. Farleigh turned to her companion. "I hardly ever see him any longer, Neda. Don't you think the least he can do is keep his eyes open?"

Richard stifled another yawn. He'd spent half the night gambling away the betrothal money he planned to get from Mrs. Danforth, and the other half wrapped in Bianca Cavalli's steamy embrace. The whore was delightful, truly delightful. She was willing—no, eager—to accommodate his slightest whim, no matter how strange. She was waiting at home for him at this minute. If only he could find a way to shake free of the old biddies early and go back to Bianca—he'd thought of something new, something marvelously sinful . . .

"Good heavens!" Neda cried. "No, it couldn't be. Yes! Yes, it is!"

"What? What is it?" Mrs. Farleigh demanded.

"Driver, stop!" the other woman ordered. "Drusilla, look in that carriage—the one parked just over there."

Richard's eyelids began to droop. More gossip. He'd already heard enough to float a frigate, and none of it interesting in the least.

"That's Alanna Stanton, I'm sure of it!" Neda said.

Mrs. Farleigh gasped. "You're right! Why, it's been twenty years since I've seen her, if it's a day! And she's with a man, as would be expected. But she's terribly ravaged."

"I shouldn't wonder, after the life she's led. One man after another, and each worse than the last. I wonder who that one is." Neda leaned over the side of the carriage vehicle to peer at Alanna and her companion. "He doesn't look like much."

Mrs. Farleigh laughed, her face twisted with malice. "To a woman like that, any man is better than

102

none. I wonder what old Caldwell would think if he knew his wayward daughter had come back to New York?"

Richard's eyes popped open. "Caldwell Stanton, the industrialist?" He turned to look at Alanna Stanton. Yes, he thought, she must really have been a beauty at one time.

"Yes, indeed," Neda said avidly. "Oh, Alanna's story is just too delicious! Who was that Italian dancing master who got her, ah, in a delicate way?"

Mrs. Farleigh waved her hands in agitation. "It's been such a long time. Let's see . . . Cardosa, Capelli? No—"

"Cavalli! That's it! Piero Cavalli." Neda said. "Don't you remember him, Drusilla? He taught in most of the better homes, until that incident with Alanna."

Richard sat up with a jolt. "Cavalli? Did you say Cavalli?"

His mother nodded. "Oh, he was a dream of a man. Tall, handsome, incredibly graceful. And the most marvelous Titian hair, so unusual in an Italian. The younger girls were all terribly infatuated with him, but only Alanna was foolish enough to . . . well, take him seriously. Then her father cut her off without a cent, and Cavalli dropped her. And Alanna, poor, romantic girl! She didn't have sense enough to visit a doctor to get rid of her, ah, encumbrance before it was born. I heard it was a girl. Really too bad, for I think Caldwell might have accepted a bastard, if it were male."

"How old would the child be today?" Richard

asked.

"Oh, twenty-one, perhaps twenty-two," his mother said, raising her eyebrows for confirmation. Neda nodded.

Excitement washed over Richard, making him tremble. Could Bianca be the one? She hadn't seemed as old as twenty, but he'd never actually asked her age. He turned to stare at Alanna again. Her features were finer than Bianca's, and her coloring was much lighter—honey-blond hair and pale, pale skin. But imagine her with auburn hair, and there could definitely be a resemblance between them. "What happened to the child? Did she give it up?" he asked.

"She must have," Mrs. Farleigh shrugged. "After Cavalli left her, she went to England. If I remember my gossip correctly," a simper creased her face, "which you know I do, she eventually became some nobleman's mistress. I can't imagine him tolerating another man's illegitimate child."

"I have to go!" Richard said, jumping down from the carriage.

"Dickie!" Mrs. Farleigh gasped. "Our ride! Where—"

"Urgent business," he called over his shoulder. Ignoring her cries, he hailed a carriage-for-hire and climbed in. Giving his address to the driver, he added, "And as quick as you can!" before settling back into the cushions.

As soon as the carriage pulled up in front of his house, he flung some money to the driver without even counting it, and rushed into the house.

"Bianca!" he shouted.

His manservant hurried out of the library. "Is something wrong, sir?"

"Garvin! Is Bianca still here?"

"She's upstairs, sir," the man said. "Shall I fetch her?"

"No." Richard took the stairs two at a time. Flinging his door open, he rushed into the room.

Bianca sat up in bed, blinking sleepily. She pushed her tumbled hair back from her face, making her large, naked breasts swing. "Richard? Is somethin' wrong?"

He strode to the bed and took her by the shoulders in a brutal grip. "How old are you?"

"Seventeen."

"Are you sure?" He shook her.

"Yes! Ow! You're hurtin' me!" she wailed.

He released her, cursing under his breath. Seventeen! So, she couldn't be the one. Raking his hand through his hair, he asked, "What is your father's name?"

"Piero Cavalli," she said, her eyes wide with confusion and alarm. "Why? Has he done somethin' again?

"He's still alive?"

She knelt before him, reaching up to run her hands along his arms. "Sure. But I never know where he is, honey. He's got him a couple of women for fun, an' only comes back to me and Mama when he's in trouble. Why else do you think I'm out peddlin' this?" She put her hand over the wedge of auburn hair between her legs. "But you don' mind that, do you, honey?" Smiling, she ground her pelvis against his.

Richard wiped his brow. It wasn't carnal desire that caused his sudden perspiration, but the thought of Caldwell Stanton's money. Millions. Stanton was old now, and old men tended to become maudlin about their loved ones. They want to correct old wrongs, to make peace with the world before they die. If I can get enough details from Piero Cavalli, Richard thought, I can pass Bianca off as Stanton's long-lost granddaughter. And if Alanna Stanton gave her child away, as surely she must have, even she couldn't know for sure.

"I want to talk to your father, Bianca."

She lay on her side, her legs drawn up in a seductive pose. "Come to bed, honey. We'll talk about Papa later."

"Can you find him?" he asked, his pulse beginning to pound. Truly an insatiable woman, he thought. "It might mean a great deal of money to you."

"I'll find him." She licked her lips slowly, lasciviously. "Isn't there somethin' you want me to do first?"

Richard began unbuttoning his shirt. "Lie on your stomach, my sweet. I've got a surprise for you."

Chapter Seven

Lauren took a stage to Madison Street, then climbed into one of the noisy streetcars that abounded in the city. It was unusually crowded for a Saturday; the weather had remained unseasonably warm, and it seemed that everyone in New York was out to enjoy the springlike weather. She endured the jostling without complaint, drawing no attention to herself. When the vehicle reached Fourteenth Street, she got off and walked the rest of the way to Bleeker Street.

She didn't stop to speak to anyone. She never did. Like the inhabitants of Bleeker Street, she was interested in minding her own business and expected everyone else to do the same. No one cared who she was or what she did, as long as she didn't attract the attention of the police.

Entering a red brick building that had passed its prime a good twenty years before, she ran up the first flight of steps and down the hallway to her mother's apartment.

"Mary," she called through the door, rapping once with her knuckles.

The door opened, and Mary Brodie enveloped

her in a hug. "It's so good to see you! Come in, come in!"

"How are you?" Lauren asked, kissing the older woman's cheek fondly. "Is Mother well?"

"Better and better."

Mary closed the door and led the way into the single room that served as kitchen, living and dining area. It was small and cramped, but there were pretty curtains on the window, a flowered carpet covering most of the worn floorboards, and the furniture was the best Lauren could afford.

Alanna Stanton sat upon the chintz cushions of the sofa, a soft yellow blanket over her legs. A man sat beside her, laughing at something she'd said. He looked up, startled, then rose hastily to his feet. He was in his early fifties, with a head of curly gray hair and a stocky, still-powerful body.

"Why, hello, Alex," Lauren said, coming forward to take his hands in hers. She was always pleased to see this American cousin of Mary's. He'd been so kind to them, finding this apartment, and leasing it in his own name when the owner balked at renting to a young woman new to town. Although she'd never met his wife or three grown children, she'd always envied his obvious happiness with his family.

"Come, sit by me, Lauren." Alanna patted the seat beside her. She peered closely at her daughter's face. "Why, there's something wrong, isn't there?"

"I just have something to tell you," Lauren said, her hands pleating the front of her skirt nervously. She glanced up at Mary.

Nodding, Mary took Alex's arm and pulled him

towards the door. "I got to go down to the market for somethin'. You can 'elp carry, Alex."

Alanna waited until they were gone, then asked, "What is it, dear?"

"I'm betrothed."

"Betrothed?" Alanna let out a sudden breath, as though she'd been struck.

Lauren nodded. "Mrs. Danforth arranged it." She reached towards her mother, wanting to hold her, then dropped her hands back into her lap.

"As Lauren Wakefield."

"Of course," Lauren said. What decent family would accept Lauren Stanton? Illegitimate. Bastard. Whore's get. Those names had followed her all her life, ugly, hurtful words that had been hurled at her by the children whose games she had sought to join.

Alanna averted her face. Guilt consumed her, guilt for what her actions had cost her daughter. Lauren had always defended her with pride and with grace, taking abuse that rightfully belonged to her mother. It's time, Alanna told herself, to give the same unquestioning loyalty she's always given you. Taking a deep breath, she said, "Well, that's wonderful, dear. Who is he?"

"Richard Farleigh."

"I've heard the name." Alanna's thin white hand smoothed a fold of the blanket. "Do you love him?"

"I'll learn to love him." A vision of Stephen Hawkes's rugged face swam into Lauren's mind, bringing with it a sharp stab of remembered heat. She tried to force it away by concentrating on

109

Richard. But for some reason she couldn't quite bring a picture of her fiancé's face into focus.

Alanna sighed. "But are you sure, absolutely sure, that this is what you want?"

"Yes," Lauren said. But Stephen Hawkes' face drifted into her mind again. Why couldn't she forget him? Why did he haunt her like this, even coming into her dreams to torment her with feelings she'd never thought to have?

"Then I'm very happy for you," Alanna said.

Lauren reached over and took Alanna's hands in hers. "I'll always love you. I'll always take care of you. You know that."

"Yes, I know." Forcing a bright smile to her lips, Alanna gently disengaged her hands from Lauren's grasp. Deftly, she turned the conversation to the subject of trousseaus.

Mary and Alex returned a short time later. In addition to an armload of paper-wrapped parcels, Alex carried a large bouquet of red roses. With a flourish, he presented them to Alanna.

Stunned, Lauren looked from him to her mother, then back again. A horrible suspicion went through her like a tidal wave.

"They're lovely, Alex," Alanna said, gazing up at him with all her heart shining in her eyes. Regally, she held out her free hand so he could steady her while she climbed slowly to her feet. Holding the roses against her chest, she said, "Actually, Lauren, I have an announcement of my own to make. You see, Alex and I—"

"No! Not again!" Lauren cried, jumping to her feet. "Oh, Mother, how could you do this to me!"

She whirled and ran from the apartment, slamming the door behind her.

"I'll go after her and explain," Alex said, his face creased with concern.

Alanna held him back, shaking her head. Her eyes glittered with unshed tears. "No, Alex. She'll come around. She always does."

Lauren stood before the full-length mirror, inspecting her reflection critically. Cold water had removed most of the traces of crying from her face, but her cheeks were still pale and her eyelids felt as heavy as her heart. Richard was due to call for her in just a few minutes. After the day she'd had, she felt as much like attending a society party as another séance.

Her mother and Alex Brodie! She wouldn't have believed it if she hadn't seen it with her own eyes. Alex had seemed like such a devoted family man, such a *nice* man. A married man. How could he do this to his wife—and to Alanna? Lauren had seen the love in her mother's eyes when she'd looked up at him, the tender way she had held the bouquet against her breast. Once again Alanna Stanton was ready to risk everything for a man who could give her nothing but heartache in return. And once again Lauren would have to pick up the pieces when it was all over.

Someone knocked on the door, startling Lauren out of her reverie. "Who is it?" she called.

"Stephen. Open the door, Lauren. I'll walk downstairs with you."

111

She grimaced at herself in the mirror, hating the way her pulse accelerated at the mere sound of his voice. She felt off balance, jumbled up inside and out, and the last person she wanted to see just now was Stephen Hawkes.

"I'm not ready," she said.

There was a moment of silence, then he said, "Of course, you are. I heard you tell Fanny so not two minutes ago." There was considerable amusement in his voice.

"Do you peep through keyholes as well as eavesdrop, Mr. Hawkes?"

He laughed. "If necessary."

Lauren tucked a white satin rose into her elaborately coiled chignon, thinking about the roses Alex Brodie had given her mother. Red roses, for love. Love! Lust, rather. Poor, foolish Alanna, who could no more do without a man than she could stop breathing.

"Well, I'm not my mother!" Lauren whispered fiercely. Raising her voice, she called, "Go away, Mr. Hawkes."

He knocked again, louder. What did she have to do to get rid of the man? Her teeth clenched in fury, she swept her train out of the way and stalked to the door.

She flung it open. "Mr. Hawkes, if you don't —" her voice trailed off in surprise when she saw Portia standing beside Stephen Hawkes.

"Do you see how she treats me?" Stephen asked, grinning down at the widow.

"Indeed I do," Portia said with a laugh. Then she sobered, a fleeting expression of displeasure crossing her usually placid countenance. "Lauren, dear, I came to tell you that Mr. Farleigh is waiting downstairs for you."

"Oh, I'd better hurry, then." She retrieved her gloves from the bureau and slipped them on. "I don't want to be late."

"A punctual woman!" Stephen exclaimed. "Isn't it just my luck that she's already spoken for?" He shook his head, not in amused regret as he pretended, but from a need to clear it. He'd been stunned—actually stunned—by Lauren's sudden appearance in the doorway. The lines of her dress were deceivingly simple; the bodice and overskirt were of shimmering ivory silk, drawn back over a fringed and pleated underskirt of pale bronze silk. The neckline was a smooth, graceful curve that just skimmed the tops of her breasts, revealing just a hint of cleavage, and tiny, puffed sleeves accented her slim white arms. It was perfect for her, showing off the woman rather than the dressmaker's skill. Fire-haired sprite, he mused, more alluring than he'd thought a woman could be. He wanted her. Wanted her with an intensity that was devastating to a man who had always prided himself on his detachment, his calm, inquisitive mind, and his devotion to his duty.

"Don't rush, Lauren. I want to speak to Mr. Farleigh privately for a moment," Portia said. Reaching into her pocket, she pulled out something that glittered with green fire. "Before I go, I want to give you something. Hold out your hands."

Lauren obeyed, and the widow placed a necklace across her outstretched palms. The smooth, lumi-

113

nescent whiteness of the looped triple strands of pearls contrasted sharply with the beauty of the seven emeralds that held them together. The stones were a deep, pure green, and were the size of a man's thumbnail.

"But I can't take this!" Lauren protested. "It was Mr. Danforth's betrothal gift to you! Oh, Mrs. Danforth—"

"I know you'll take good care of it," Portia said, closing Lauren's fingers over the lovely piece of jewelry. "I love you as much as if you were my own daughter, Lauren. Please, take it. Make an old woman happy."

Lauren opened her mouth to protest again, then closed it again. To refuse the necklace was to refuse the love that was being offered with it, and that was something she couldn't do. So, ducking her head to hide the sudden tears that sprang into her eyes, she began fumbling with the catch.

"Allow me," Stephen said, taking it from her. He held it up against her throat, admiring how the emeralds complemented her vivid hair, the pearls her pale satin skin. Lovely, just like the woman who would wear them.

Lauren stared at him numbly, and he finally took her by the shoulders and turned her so that her back was to him. He fastened the necklace around her throat, his hands lingering for a moment on the tender skin at the back of her neck. A rushing warmth went through her at that touch, making her eyelids flutter nearly closed, and it was all she could do not to let her head fall back against him.

"Well, go look at yourself, silly," Portia ordered.

Lauren's eyes jerked open as the lovely spell shattered under the widow's words. Obediently, she went to the mirror. But she didn't look at herself; her gaze was for the man behind her. Ruggedly handsome in day wear, in evening dress he was devastating—dark and dangerous-looking, with that feral grace of his only accentuated by the stiffly formal clothing. Surely no man had ever looked so untameable in a black tailcoat and trousers.

"Well?" Portia demanded. "What do you think?"

"It . . . it's the loveliest thing I've ever had," Lauren said. Impulsively, she went to Portia and took the old woman into her arms in a quick, hard hug.

Portia took out her handkerchief and dabbed at the corners of her eyes. "Well, I suppose I'd better go talk to Mr. Farleigh, or you'll be fearfully late. Here, put these on," she said, reaching into her pocket to draw out a pair of earrings that matched the necklace. "Stephen, bring her down in a moment, will you?"

The earrings lay forgotten in Lauren's hand for a moment. "Why does she want to talk to Richard, I wonder?"

"Your fiancé came without either his mother or sister, and Mrs. Danforth has some concern about your chaperonage." With a grin, Stephen added, "Young Farleigh's got some fancy talking to do, I expect."

Lauren turned back to the mirror to replace her plain gold earrings with the emerald and pearl pendants. They swung deliciously against her neck, sending green sparks dancing upon her skin. "Isn't

115

Clarissa coming?" she asked.

"Do you think she'd miss it?" He grinned at her reflection.

"No." It was hard to keep the acid out of her voice. And although she struggled against saying it, she couldn't stop herself from adding, "I doubt she's the kind of woman who would pass up—" Horrified at her own shrewish words, she clamped her lips together.

Stephen came up silently behind her and put his hands on her shoulders, sending a frisson of mingled dread and pleasure shooting through her body. His right hand made a slow, searing path to her throat, where his long fingers spread out over her skin possessively. Although she tried to control it, her chest rose and fell with her suddenly ragged breathing.

"Are you jealous?" he asked.

"Certainly not!" She closed her eyes, embarrassed by the sight of his strong hands clasping her. Then, unable to resist, she opened them again to watch, as his fingertips moved lower to lightly caress the beginning swell of her breasts.

Stephen brushed his cheek against her hair, lost in her fragrance and the feel of her silken skin beneath his hands. A powerful wave of desire surged through him. He wanted to kiss her, to explore every inch of her body, to bury himself in her sweet, hot depths over and over, until he'd purged this strange madness from his heart.

"You're beautiful, Lauren," he murmured in her ear.

She stiffened. Those words again! Those empty,

116

hateful, meaningless words! Women loved to hear them, foolishly mistaking admiration for true caring, passion for love. Well, if her mother hadn't learned that lesson, *she* certainly had. Forcing a coldness into her eyes that she didn't feel, she looked at him in the mirror. "Are you quite finished pawing me, Mr. Hawkes? If you remember, my fiancé is waiting downstairs."

He met her gaze, reading the icy calmness there. But the skin under his hand was hot, and the pulse in her throat was beating as fast as his. So, he thought, we're still playing that little game. He turned her, pinning her against the throbbing hardness of his manhood. Triumphantly, he saw the awareness of it in her eyes.

"You don't want Farleigh," he murmured. "I can prove it to you."

"The only thing you can prove to me is how dishonorable *you* can be," she said, pleased that her voice remained calm despite the frantic beating of her heart. Her body was one leaping flame of sensation, searing, insistent, shameful. "Now, let me go. I hear Portia calling us."

Reluctantly, he released her. Damn it, he was tempted to kiss her anyway, to somehow force her to admit what she really felt for him. If only she hadn't referred to his honor! Of all the arguments she might have used against him, that was the most effective.

Raking his hand through his hair, he strove to keep his voice as cool as hers. "Come, Miss Wakefield," he said, holding out his arm.

Portia and Richard were waiting in the foyer,

Richard tapping his hand on the bannister impatiently. Hearing their footsteps, he whirled and looked up at them.

"Lauren, you're beautiful!" he said, coming up to take her from Stephen.

Lauren's lashes swept downward in confusion. Why didn't it bother her for Richard to give her that meaningless compliment, when she had reacted so profoundly to Stephen speaking the very same words?

Richard's gaze moved over her face and bosom, coming to rest on the emerald necklace. Without glancing at Stephen, he said, "Mr. Hawkes, my sister is running rather late. We'll pick her up on the way." Then, tucking Lauren's hand into the crook of his arm, he led her down the stairs.

Stephen followed them, his hands clenching and unclenching in fury. How many times was he going to have to give Lauren up to that prancing booby? Just let him catch the fellow trying to kiss her, just once. It would be all the excuse he'd need to knock Farleigh across the room.

Portia came to take his arm, murmuring archly, "My, Stephen, you ought to see the look on your face. Such violent thoughts you must be having!" Before he could recover from his surprise, she added in a low voice, "It seems that Mrs. Farleigh is indisposed and cannot go to the party. And Clarissa, I fear, is a less than adequate chaperone."

"Less than adequate chaperone" was not exactly how Stephen would have described Clarissa's behavior. She was one of the most brazen females he'd ever met. And if Richard's morals were anything like his sister's, Lauren's betrothal was a very poor bargain indeed.

I'd better not let her out of my sight! Stephen thought, watching the way Farleigh's hands lingered on Lauren's shoulders as he helped her into her cloak. Damn, but this was going to be an awkward night! He knew he wasn't going to be able to stand by and watch Lauren spend the entire evening with another man. Hell, he was flesh and blood, after all. How was he going to keep his hands off Farleigh's skinny neck, and how was he going to avoid Clarissa's clutches long enough to slip Lauren away from the other man? You're a detective, son, he told himself. You've tricked some of the best. Somehow, you'll find a way.

Portia tapped Stephen's arm to regain his attention. "I truly hate to admit this, but Mr. Farleigh strikes me as a rather ah, frivolous young man," she whispered. "Watch over Lauren for me, Stephen. I'm counting on you."

He looked over at Richard, his gray eyes darkening to the color of a stormy winter sky. "You can be assured, Mrs. Danforth, that he will do nothing to harm her in any way."

"Thank you." She squeezed his arm, then turned and went upstairs.

119

Chapter Eight

Richard paused in the doorway of the ballroom. "This is the newest, the biggest, and the best," he said. "Well, what do you think?"

"It . . . it certainly is interesting," Lauren said, staring in amazement. Like the rest of what she had seen in the Gantons' enormous, turreted mansion, this room was of the most ornate construction that money could buy. Three huge crystal chandeliers hung from the intricately coiled whorls of the plaster ceiling, casting shards of rainbow hues upon the people below, and the ranks of towering windows were covered with elegant gold brocade draperies. The far walls of the room were dominated by two huge fireplaces, massive edifices of black, white, and pink marble, carved into a dizzying array of columns, fretwork, and figures from mythology.

The people were even more elegant than their surroundings, a swirling, glittering mass of well-fed humanity that rivaled the chandeliers in brilliance. These are the people who cast Mother out, Lauren mused. She'd expected to feel triumph at this moment; she, Alanna Stanton's illegitimate daughter, had fooled them all. But all she felt now was uncertainty. Strangers all, even the man she was going to marry. A most unnerving thought.

She stole a glance over her shoulder at Stephen. He was looking, not at the ballroom, but at her. His gray eyes were the color of smoke, as full of warmth as though a fire had been lit in their depths. She recognized it for what it was: passion, sheer masculine desire. The sight of it turned her uncertainty into stubborn determination. These people were no more judgmental than those with less money; she and her mother had been shunned by "decent" people from every class.

Leaning closer to Richard, she whispered, "We seem to be the last ones here. Are we very late?"

"Late!" He chuckled. "My dear, these affairs hardly get going until after midnight. The real fun doesn't start until the wee hours."

Lauren stared at him in surprise. "But I told Mrs. Danforth I'd be home by midnight or soon after!"

With a grin, Richard glanced over his shoulder at Stephen and Clarissa. "My lovely bride-to-be thought she'd be home by midnight. Now tell me, hasn't she been buried alive in that house?"

Clarissa laughed. "Well, being married to you will certainly, ah, broaden her experience, Dickie."

Lauren turned to look at Clarissa. Coarse as that statement was, it wasn't the actual words that bothered her so much. But there was a gloating, secretive tone underlying the humor in Clarissa's voice, that made Lauren's instincts cry caution. But before she could focus that thought, Richard drew her forward, swinging her into his arms to join the

121

waltzing couples that thronged the room.

Stephen watched them go, his chest tight with fury. Damn it, he raged inwardly, get a hold on yourself! But he knew he wasn't going to make it through an entire night of watching Lauren with another man. With sudden, devastating clarity, he realized what had happened to him: Stephen Hawkes, the aloof, logical detective, was feeling the bite of jealousy at last.

"You belong to me, Lauren Wakefield," he muttered under his breath. "And the sooner you learn it, the better."

He started after her, but Clarissa tucked her hand in the crook of his arm and accompanied him. Irritated, he nearly jerked out of her grasp. But then he regained a measure of control, realizing that he couldn't very well drag Lauren away from her fiancé in the middle of a society party. Not that he gave a damn what the bluebloods thought, but such a drastic action wasn't going to convince Lauren to listen to him calmly and courteously. No, he'd better wait until he could get her alone.

"Are you ready for me?" Clarissa asked archly.

Stephen looked down at her in surprise; for a moment he'd actually forgotten she was there. "I'm always ready to dance with a beautiful woman," he said with absent courtesy, thinking that the rich crimson color of Clarissa's dress would look stunning on Lauren, just the color of that fiery hair. He'd buy her a gown like that some day. No, not a gown, a nightgown. And then he'd take it off her, slowly, kissing every delightful, silken inch of her as it was exposed. She'd hold him close, wanting him, drowning him with that searing passion he'd only tasted as yet, and then . . .

"I'm not talking about dancing," Clarissa breathed, smiling seductively up at him.

"What?" His mind wrapped up in the sensuous vision of Lauren naked and responding to him, Stephen had completely lost track of the conversation he was supposed to be having.

Clarissa pressed her breast against his arm. "Let's go somewhere else. Somewhere private, where we can really have fun."

A wave of distaste went through him. He'd seen streetwalkers with less brazenness than this elegant daughter of a rich man.

"Come on, Stephen," she murmured. "I promise it will be more fun than this silly party."

"Tempting," he said, feigning regret, "but I promised Mrs. Danforth that I'd watch over Miss Wakefield."

She pouted. "Oh, don't be like that, Stephen. Dickie will take care of her."

That's what I'm afraid of, Stephen thought. Aloud, he said, "Sorry, but I gave my word." Shifting her weight back onto her own feet, he swung her into the twirling rhythm of the waltz. Although he kept up an appearance of listening to Clarissa's chatter, most of his attention was directed towards maneuvering closer to a flame-haired woman in ivory silk.

Lauren saw him coming. She also saw how closely Clarissa was pressed against him and how interested he seemed in what the woman was saying. Maybe he'd found just what he wanted. If he could charm Clarissa's father the way he'd charmed Mrs. Danforth, he might even marry into the Farleigh money. And then he won't need to bother us any longer, Lauren thought, surprised at the pang that caused her. The man is a charlatan and a thief! she told herself savagely. You ought to be glad at the thought of being rid of him! But she wasn't.

"You're a lovely dancer," Richard murmured in her ear. "We move well together, darling."

"You would make anyone seem to be a good dancer, Richard," she replied, determinedly fixing her gaze on his face. Stephen Hawkes was *not* going to bother her. Even if he was laughing down at Clarissa, whose bodice was cut so low that nearly all her breasts were exposed. From his height, he could probably see straight down to the hussy's knees!

Richard pulled her a little closer, his hand moving up her back possessively. Such grace, he mused, and such marvelous skin. She excited him. And Bianca Cavalli, with her likeness to Lauren and her own lusty coarseness, was waiting at home for him. It was going to be a very pleasant evening, indeed.

"I could announce our betrothal tonight," he said, his breath tickling Lauren's ear.

"Mrs. Danforth is so looking forward to having the banns read in Grace Church next Sunday. Why take her pleasure from her?" Inwardly, however, Lauren wondered if she had refused for Mrs. Danforth's sake, or because she couldn't bear to have

Richard claim her with Stephen Hawkes looking on.

Richard's hand drifted up to caress the exposed skin of her shoulders. She was as smooth and fine as spun silk, he thought, cool and slim and graceful. If only he could get rid of her too-watchful guardian! With a little persuasion and some champagne, he might be able to convince her to let him taste the joys of the conjugal bed a bit early. The thought of having her and Bianca in one night nearly made his head swim. He caressed the delicate skin at the nape of her neck, trying to think of a way to shed Stephen Hawkes.

Lauren glanced away from Richard's intent gaze, resisting the impulse to shrug his hand away. There was something about his look and touch that bothered her. Both were too eager, too . . . greedy, that was the word. How was she ever going to get through her wedding night, if this simple caress disturbed her so?

"You're trembling, darling," Richard said. "Come. I'll get you something to drink."

He led her to one of the chairs that lined the walls, then disappeared into the supper room. She scanned the crowd, searching for a man who was taller than most, a man with gray eyes and dark hair lightly touched with silver.

"Looking for me?" Stephen's voice came from the chair beside her.

"No." She kept her face turned forward, refusing to look at him. Before she could stop herself, she added, "Where is your . . . friend?"

"My . . . friend went to fix her toilette." He'd

125

gotten rid of Clarissa by telling her that her hair was coming down. If it *was* hers; he suspected that a great deal of that blond chignon was false. Not like Lauren's, he thought, gazing at her wealth of fiery tresses admiringly. What wouldn't he give to see that silken hair down, to be able to run his hands through it!

"What are you doing here?" she asked peevishly.

"What's got you so snappish all of a sudden?" He grinned, pleased by the thought that she might be jealous. "Is it my . . . friend?"

"Certainly not." She turned to face him. "In fact, I think you ought to devote all your attention to her. Her father is much richer than Mrs. Danforth. And I assure you that Clarissa is far more cooperative than Thaddeus Danforth's ghost will ever be."

Jealousy, indeed! he thought in triumph. "There are other things besides money to consider." He ran his fingertip along the top of her glove, tickling the sensitive skin of her arm.

"I'm sure Clarissa would be happy to give you those things as well," she said coldly.

He just smiled, his hand sliding her glove down to her wrist, then moving back up her bare skin to clasp her upper arm. His knuckles brushed the side of her breast.

A shiver went through her, part cold, part heat, part dread. How did he make her body obey him like this, responding so powerfully to the lightest touch? It was a dangerous weakness, this raging passion coursing through her. But she knew the price of passion, and it was much too high. She must reject it — and him.

She pulled free of him and jerked her glove back into place, then rose to her feet. "Truly, Mr. Hawkes, your arrogance is remarkable. If you think that I would find pleasure in being fondled in a public place, you must be accustomed to a very different sort of woman."

"You're a liar if you . . . Damn!" That expletive was torn from him as he saw Clarissa coming towards him from one direction, Richard from another.

Richard reached them first, coming to a stop in front of Lauren's chair and holding out a glass of champagne. "I'm back at last, darling."

That "darling" brought Stephen to his feet. He'd controlled himself as he'd watched Farleigh touching her, whispering in her ear, acting as though he owned her, but he wasn't about to take anymore. With a muttered curse, Stephen reached out to pull Lauren out of the way, but Clarissa slid between them.

"Stephen, love, I've been looking everywhere for you," she chided, pressing herself against his outstretched arm.

"I'm just seeing to my duties as chaperone." He dropped his hand to Clarissa's waist, gratified when he saw Lauren's shoulders stiffen. Aha, he thought, now *that* really gets a reaction from the ice princess! Tit for tat, then. At least we'll both be miserable. He bowed curtly. "Now that your fiancé is back, Miss Wakefield, I'll turn my attentions to more interesting pursuits."

"Please do." Lauren spoke calmly, her voice

schooled by years of hiding her emotions. Inwardly, however, she seethed with jealousy. More interesting indeed! If brazenness was what he was looking for, then he'd certainly found the right woman in Clarissa Farleigh.

Richard offered Lauren the glass he was holding. "Have some champagne, my dear. It's very good."

"I don't drink champagne, I'm afraid," Lauren said.

"Oh, well." Richard downed the champagne, then tucked her hand into the crook of his arm. "Come along, my love. We'll get you something else."

Lauren didn't dare glance over her shoulder at Stephen. She was afraid he might be looking at her—and even more afraid he might not. Perhaps he had already dismissed her from his mind, preferring, as he'd said, Clarissa's more interesting talents.

Richard led her into the supper room, where long tables fairly groaned under the weight of the food they held. Huge arrangements of hothouse flowers made bright splotches of color against the white damask tablecloths. Instead of going towards the food, however, he headed directly towards the table where three servants were pouring champagne. A crowd was gathered around this table, emptying the bottles almost as soon as they were opened. Richard managed to scoop two full glasses from the table without spilling a drop. He offered one to Lauren.

"I don't drink champagne," she reminded him.

"Oh, yes, that's right. Well, we can't let good

champagne go to waste, can we?" He drank both, then held one out to be refilled.

Lauren had never seen anyone drink so much in so short a time. And Richard wasn't the only one; many other gentlemen, and even a number of ladies, were downing an appalling amount of liquor. "Richard, why don't we get something to eat before—"

"In a moment, darling," he said. "I'm parched."

A gentleman, obviously having been at the champagne table a bit too long, stumbled past them, and Lauren whisked her train out of his way just in time. Now this is quite enough, she thought. I refuse to stand here and be trampled.

"I'm going to go sit down," she said, turning away.

Richard grasped her arm, sensing her irritation. "No, darling, I'll come with you." Truly, I'm going to have to take her in hand once we're married, he thought. But it was obvious he'd have to ease her into his way of life slowly. Once he'd bedded her, she was bound to be more amenable.

Solicitously, he led her through the crowd and found an unoccupied table. He seated her, then pulled a chair around so that he was sitting beside her. "I suppose this must be a bit overwhelming when you're not used to it."

"Yes, it is," Lauren said, taking a deep breath. "Richard, does everyone drink this much at these affairs?"

"Is that what's bothering you?" He took her gloved hand in both of his and, putting a solemn expression on his face, said, "A few people some-

129

times go a bit too far with the liquor, mostly the younger, unmarried set. I'll even admit to a bit of indulgence myself. But now that I've met you," he raised her hand to his lips and kissed it lingeringly, "I find that my interests have changed."

"Then you're not unhappy with our arrangement?"

"Oh, no. Since I hadn't met anyone who interested me, I saw no reason to object when Father proposed an arranged marriage." His arm went around her shoulders, and his hand toyed with her sleeve. "And when I met you, I realized that Fate had chosen the perfect woman for me."

She ducked her head, her cheeks flaming. So, she was the perfect woman! What would he think, she wondered, if he knew who and what she was? Guilt clenched her stomach. Guilt, and anger at the unfairness of the world. Wasn't she the same person inside, no matter what her parentage? Couldn't a woman of illegitimate birth care as well for her husband, bear his children, honor his name and his house, as well as any other woman?

"Ahhh, don't be shy, darling," Richard murmured, misinterpreting her blush.

"I just don't know you very well," she said. "And you certainly don't know me."

He kissed her hand again, then pressed her palm to his cheek. "I know what I need to know for now. And think how wonderful it will be for us to discover the rest."

His gentleness only intensified her guilt. For a moment she wished she could tell him her secret. But if she revealed who she was, she would expose her mother as well. The whole story would come out again, as well as a storm of renewed gossip. Brutal, lascivious gossip, and Alanna was not strong enough to bear it.

"Lauren, my beautiful Lauren, can't you tell how I feel?" Richard whispered, leaning to kiss the tempting bare skin where her neck joined her shoulder.

His lips were hot and wet, and Lauren had to resist the urge to push him away. "Richard, please!"

"No one's looking," he chuckled, nibbling her earlobe. "So sweet," he breathed. "So very, very sweet!"

She forced herself to endure his caresses. This was her fiancé. He had the right, if anyone did. And in a few months, he'd have the right to do a great deal more. A shudder of distaste went through her. And with it, a shaft of anger at Stephen. If he hadn't forced his way into her life, if he hadn't taught her what real passion felt like, she would never have known that there was something other than what she was feeling now.

"You're trembling, darling," Richard murmured in her ear. "This bodes well for our future."

She pulled away, clasping her hands in her lap and fixing her gaze on them. Oh, she was a cheat! A cheat and a liar. But I'll treat him with all honor, she told herself firmly. I'll learn to love him. He's kind and gentle, and seems to care for me. That is all I ever expected, and all I should ever want.

He traced the curve of her ear with his forefinger. "Think of how it will be, darling. Just the two of us at home in front of the fire. And then when we have children, we'll be such a great, sprawling happy family!" Aha, he thought, seeing the look of wonder come into her eyes at the mention of children, that's got her! "I think we'll make beautiful children, don't you?"

"Yes," Lauren agreed. But she couldn't shake the vision of a child with black hair and smoky gray eyes, and a man with the same hair and eyes looking at her with love. Oh, God, are you going to steal even that from Richard? she asked herself. With a voice that shook with self-hatred, she said, "Please, could you get me something to eat?"

"Of course, darling." Smiling in pleased triumph, he planted a parting kiss on her shoulder and rose to his feet.

Lauren sighed, watching him move away. If only she could feel the way he wanted her to. If only she'd never met Stephen Hawkes! Although she would do the sensible thing and marry Richard, the memory of the passion she had tasted in Stephen's arms would haunt her all her life.

Someone put a plate of food down on the table in front of her. Startled, Lauren looked up. Stephen grinned at her and put his own plate down on the table.

"I thought you might want something to eat," he said. "Especially as your fiancé has made a detour."

Her gaze followed his pointing finger, and she saw that Richard was deep in conversation with another man. She was tempted to get up from the table and go to him, but the look on Stephen's face warned her that this wouldn't be allowed.

"This seat is taken," she said, hoping rudeness would drive him away.

"Now it is," Stephen replied calmly, sliding into the chair beside hers. Despite his outward composure, he was near the edge of his control; he'd seen enough of that little tête-á-tête to set his blood boiling. Richard, Clarissa, and all the rest of the bluebloods be damned, he wasn't going to allow it! He was going to stick to Lauren like a burr for the rest of the evening, even if he had to be pleasant to Farleigh to do it.

"Mr. Hawkes—"

"Eat your food, Lauren." He buttered a roll and handed it to her.

Startled, she took the bread from him and bit into it, watching from the corner of her eye as he ate with neat, economical movements. Outwardly, he seemed so trustworthy! Such a handsome, forceful man, a man whose drive and intelligence ought to be turned to better pursuits than bilking elderly women. It was a shame—and more, a waste.

"Where is Clarissa?" she asked, and instantly blushed with mortification for asking.

"Attending to her toilette. Again," he replied.

She toyed with the roll, nervously tearing little pieces from it and dropping them into her plate. Stephen watched her, a tender smile curving his lips. So beautiful, so nervous, and so aware of him as a man, despite her pose of indifference.

"You've got butter on your lip," he murmured.

"Where?" She dabbed nervously at her mouth with her napkin. "Here?"

133

"No, you've missed it." He touched his thumb to her lower lip. The butter melted from his body heat, and he smoothed it over the lovely double curve of her mouth. His thumb moved slickly over her lips, back and forth, over and around, spreading heat wherever he touched.

Lauren knew she should stop him. She wanted to stop him. But her eyes closed at the sheer pleasure of his touch, and it was all she could do not to lean forward in encouragement.

He dropped his hand abruptly. He'd seen her response in the way her lips had softened and nearly parted, and he'd felt an answering jolt right through his body. Another minute of this, and he'd kiss her right here in front of everyone.

"You've got a beautiful mouth," he murmured.

Her eyes snapped open. He'd done it to her again! Mesmerized her with his touch, taking her will and her self-respect. With an indignant gasp, she pushed her chair back and jumped to her feet.

He grabbed her wrist. "Where do you think you're going?"

"I find *my* toilette in need of repair." She twisted away from him. "I can only hope that the ladies' dressing room will be the one spot where you won't bother me."

"I want to bother you," he growled, infuriated by her rejection. "And I intend to keep bothering you, until you admit that I'm the only man for you."

"What?" Her mouth dropped open in astonishment. "Have you taken leave of your senses?"

"No, just my patience." Controlling his temper with an effort, he leaned back in his chair and regarded her with narrowed eyes. "I give you fair warning, Lauren. I'm not about to let you throw yourself away on that spoiled fop. You belong to me."

"Belong . . . ? Ohhh!" she gasped, clutching her outrage to push aside the treacherous, powerful surge of elation his words caused. She should hate him! Conceited, deceitful . . . Unable to deal with either him or her own emotions just now, she turned away.

"Where are you going?" he snapped.

She looked at him over her shoulder, her dark eyes blazing with resentment. "I'm going to find my fiancé, Mr. Hawkes."

"Fine. As long as you lose him later." He grinned. "And call me Stephen. You might as well get used to it, you know."

She fled, her cheeks burning.

Chapter Nine

Dressed for bed but unable to sleep, Lauren stared out her window at the moonlit expanse of Gramercy Park. Guilt weighed her down, in body and spirit. Richard had been attentive and oh, so charming, promising her how wonderful their life together would be. He had taken every opportunity to show her how much he cared for her—touching her hand, her waist, leaning close to whisper in her ear. And instead of responding to her fiancé, she was completely, sensually aware of Stephen's storm-gray gaze on her—hot, knowing, holding a infinite promise of passion.

"Oh, Mother, I never really understood before," she murmured, leaning her forehead against the cool glass. "But now I do." With Stephen Hawkes, she tasted the same soaring passion that had cost Alanna so much. It was the reckless desire to hold a man who could not be held, to touch him, to explore the limits of the sensuality he engendered in her. It was a powerful, compelling force, one that could very easily seem like love to the unwary. Her mother hadn't known the dangers of that seductive force, but *she* did, and somehow Lauren had to find a way to resist it.

Her head came up in surprise as she heard quick, stealthy footsteps going down the corridor towards the back stairs. She tiptoed to her door, opening it a crack, and peered out to see a figure silhouetted against the window at the end of the hall. The sly movement of that dark shape bespoke its malevolent purpose. More "spiritual manifestations," she thought. A shaft of hope went through her; if that skulking figure was Stephen, and if she could catch him in the act, she might be able to get rid of him for good!

"Wait for me!" she muttered to herself, grabbing up her dressing gown and putting it on as she slipped out of the room. Her bare feet silent and sure upon the floorboards, she followed that mysterious figure.

It disappeared around the corner. She picked up the skirts of her dressing gown and hurried after it. But just as she reached the corner, a hard male hand clamped over her mouth, stifling the cry she'd been about to make.

"Who—Lauren!" Stephen Hawkes' voice was a harsh whisper.

Still holding his hand over her mouth, he opened the nearest door and hauled her roughly inside. He closed the door behind him with his heel, then thrust her against the wall beside it, pinning her in place with his forearm.

Lauren pushed at his chest. Her fingers came in contact with bare skin and silky hair. Shocked, she jerked her hands back abruptly. Not daring to touch him again, she held her arms stiffly at her sides.

"What the hell are you doing?" he whispered.

"I was following someone!" she hissed back.

"Who?"

"I thought it was you." Her eyes were growing accustomed to the darkness now; she could see the outline of his face, the dark, flaring line of his brows.

He chuckled. "Honey, if you wanted me, why didn't you just knock on my door?"

"Wanted you!" She gasped in outrage. "I thought you were skulking around tending to your charlatan's tricks!"

Stephen went to the window and opened the drapes halfway, letting the moonlight flood into the room. This must be one of the spare bedrooms, he noted; the furniture was shrouded with cloths, and the air had a faint, musty taint to it.

He turned back to her, watching her breasts heave beneath her dressing gown. "Obviously you misjudged me," he said.

"My judgement of you is sound," she snapped. "It was just my timing that was bad."

"Timing?" His eyebrows went up.

She nodded. "It was my misfortune to choose one of the few times when you *weren't* up to something. And if I *had* been lucky enough to catch you, you would have been out of this house so fast your head would spin."

"Would that please you?"

"Beyond measure!" Then she'd be safe. Safe from him, safe from herself.

"Liar," he murmured. He strolled across the room and stopped in front of her, so close that he

138

could smell the faint violet scent of her perfume. He had never felt like this about a woman before— part aching tenderness, part exasperation, part desire so strong he had to force himself not to tremble with it.

Lauren stared up at him, hardly breathing. Dread made her pulse race—or was it the sight of him with nothing on but his trousers? His shoulders seemed even wider without clothing, his chest and arms leanly muscled. A dusting of black hair covered his chest, arrowing down to disappear beneath his waistband. His belly was hard-ridged with muscle, his hips narrow. The moonlight limned his taut body with silver and outlined the bold planes of his face. His arousal was a palpable force in the room, and her treacherous body responded to it.

"Please, leave me alone," she whispered.

"I can't," he sighed, his gaze dropping to her unconfined breasts again. To his amazement, he saw that her nipples had risen into taut points and were clearly visible beneath the fabric of her dressing gown. Whatever she might say, she wanted him. And God knows, I want her! he thought. I want her more than I've ever wanted another woman. Tonight I'm claiming her for my own, and damn the rest of the world!

Lauren saw the raw passion come into his face, read his decision. She had to get out of here, or she was lost! Whirling, she grabbed for the doorknob. But his arm came over her shoulder, holding the door closed no matter how hard she pulled.

Finally she gave up and stood, panting, with her back to him. She was trembling, her chest heaving

139

as though she'd run a race. "Let go of the door," she said, her voice barely above a whisper. "I-I'll scream."

"Go on, then," he said. "Scream."

Still she stood, mute. Her limbs felt molten, her skin overly sensitive. When his hands came down on her arms, she closed her eyes in unconscious response. Oh, God, he felt so good!

Gently, he turned her to face him. "Look at me, Lauren."

She obeyed, and was shaken by the depth of the passion that blazed in his gray eyes. Deliberately, he untied the sash of her dressing gown and pushed it off her shoulders. She felt his hands tremble slightly, and there was something incredibly stirring in the knowledge that she had such a powerful effect on him.

"Stephen," she began, unsure what she really wanted to say.

He framed her face with his hands, a tender, gentle gesture that made her heart tighten. "Say my name again," he breathed. "Just like that."

Mindlessly, held by the emotions in his darkened eyes, she said his name again. And when he kissed her, his lips claiming hers with driving passion, she repeated it again and yet again, sighing it into the hot depths of his mouth.

"You feel so good," he groaned, his mouth moving to the wildly throbbing pulsepoint beneath her ear. She felt so right. *This* felt so right, so perfect. And he was going to see that it was perfect for her, too.

He reached behind her, untying the ribbon that

140

secured her braid, then unwound her fiery hair. Like silken flames, he thought, running his fingers through the bright tresses. Then, slowly, gently, he slid his palm down over her collarbone to her breast. Feeling her nipple harden even more, he drew in his breath in wonderment.

Lauren stared at him, helpless to do anything but watch the planes of his face tighten with passion. Hot, incredibly powerful desire, the kind that could immolate them both. She waited for her conscience to tell her to stop this, but there was nothing. Nothing, that is, but him—no consequences, no world but the one they were creating here in this room. This was beyond thought, beyond restraint, beyond anything she had ever believed she could feel.

He leaned towards her. Lost in a haze of desire, she raised her head to meet him. His lips slanted across hers, opening them for his tongue, and his strong arms went around her to draw her body against his. Feeling the hard length of his manhood through her thin clothing, she gasped. But it wasn't shock that drew that gasp from her, but passion, and her body instinctively arched to bring still more contact between them.

"Sweet, sweet," he muttered, pressing tiny, nibbling kisses on her mouth. Then his tongue darted back inside, exploring the sensitive skin inside her lips, the edges of her teeth, then delving deeper to play a sensual game with her tongue. His hands moved over her feverishly, gliding over her sides and hips, cupping her buttocks to pull her even more tightly against him.

Suddenly he lifted her away from him, and she felt her nightgown sliding away from her. Tumbling as she was in a vortex of desire, she didn't care. Naked, wanton, she stood before him, her hair cascading around her in a bright auburn flood.

His breath going out in a sharp hiss, he surveyed her high, full breasts, curving hips, and the incredibly long, graceful legs with the triangle of auburn curls at their juncture. Her nipples were hard little nubs, begging for him. Dropping to his knees in front of her, he drew her towards him and took one of those eager peaks into his mouth. His tongue rasped over one turgid nipple, then the other, while his hands caressed the silken weight of her breasts.

"Oh, oh!" Lauren gasped, her eyes closing in ecstasy. Sharp, sweet sensation, too powerful to do anything but enjoy. She was mad with it, burning with it. Her head bent forward, encasing Stephen in a shining, violet-scented curtain of hair.

The feel of those silken tresses nearly drove him over the edge. He was so hard inside his trousers that it was painful, and it was only with an effort of will that he kept from taking her right there. Slowly, he cautioned himself, slowly. Think of her innocence. To control his raging need, he concentrated on her, wanting to make her as crazy with passion as he was.

He suckled her, tugging on her nipples until she moaned in pleasure, then soothing them with his tongue. His fingers traced the cleft of her buttocks, coming close to the moist, beckoning heat below, then retreating in exquisite restraint. Tormenting her, tormenting himself even more. His hand caressed the smooth skin of her waist, her inner thighs, then moved at last to the core of her. Gently, he parted her flesh. Gently, he sought and found the source of her heat.

As his finger dipped into her wet warmth, then moved upward to stroke the tiny nub that was the center of her desire, Lauren arched her back in almost unbearable pleasure. She whimpered, looking down at him with beautiful, dazed eyes, and he nearly lost control right then. Sweat broke out on his forehead as he struggled to restrain himself. She was so sweet, so responsive, so completely desirable! But he wanted this to be for her, to bind her to him fully and irrevocably, so he put his own need aside. Feverishly, he kissed her smooth flat belly, his tongue dipping into her navel, then moved up to suck her nipples again. And always, his fingers moved over the silken wetness of her woman's flesh with devastating intent. He heard her moan, felt her quiver under his hand, and realized she was nearing her crisis.

"Ahhh, Lauren!" he rasped against her breasts.

As the pace of his caresses increased, Lauren felt a strange tightening sensation in her lower body. She writhed, tormented by the spiraling tension. She ached. She wanted, she needed . . . Her hands clenched in the thick darkness of his hair. Oh, it was too much! Surely she was about to die from the sheer pleasure of what he was doing!

"Please, oh, please!" she moaned, not knowing what she was begging for, but sure he could give it to her.

"Let yourself go, honey," he rasped. "I'll take care of you."

As though his words were the release, the first tiny tremors began, deep in her body, and then a tremendous wave of shuddering, clenching sensation washed through her. She cried out, her fingers tightening in his hair.

He groaned, burying his face against the smooth, fragrant skin of her belly as he felt her climax. It was wonderful, he thought dazedly, supporting her while she recovered. *She* was wonderful—lovely, generous, more passionate than he'd believed a woman could be. She was his. His woman. And he was going to take her now, to put his claim on her so thoroughly that she'd never be able to deny it.

"You're beautiful, Lauren," he murmured. "So beautiful."

At the sound of those words, reality crashed in on her, cold, hard, horrible reality. Dear God, what had she done? Tears welled into her eyes and spilled over, and a tortured sob escaped her.

"What the hell . . . ?" Completely confused, Stephen leaped to his feet. "Lauren, what's wrong?"

"Wrong? You ask me what's wrong? Oh, God!" She covered her face with her hands. In allowing Stephen to touch her, she had dishonored her betrothal, dishonored herself. And she'd known better! She had known the dangers of the sort of passion Stephen offered, and had still allowed herself to fall under his spell. Great, gasping sobs were torn from her, and she slid down the door to fall in a crumpled heap on the floor.

144

Stephen stared down at her, his hands clenched into fists, his chest heaving like a bellows. For a moment, he thought he was surely going to die of frustration. What the devil could be wrong with her? One moment she'd been passionate, completely, delightfully wanton, the next, weeping as though her whole world had collapsed! Then concern for her overcame the demands of his body, and he sank to his knees beside her, watching her slim back heave with the force of her misery. God, he'd never heard anyone cry like that — deep, wracking sobs, as though her very heart had been shredded.

"Honey, what's wrong?" he asked, reaching out to stroke her tumbled hair.

She flinched away from his hand. "Don't touch me! Please, don't touch me!"

Her rejection hurt more than he would have believed. "Is this virginal shock?" he asked, anger and frustrated desire making his voice harsh, "or is it something else?"

His words gave her the strength to pull the ragged shreds of her control together. With an effort, she pushed herself to a sitting position, then grabbed her clothing and dragged it on with shaking hands. Virginal, he'd said. Oh, yes, she was still a virgin. But her innocence was gone, burned away by his hands, his lips, by the searing passion he had made her feel.

"I hope you're satisfied with what you've done to me," she said. Her long lashes were spiked with moisture, and there was accusation in her glare.

He chose to misunderstand her words. *"You* were

145

the one satisfied, as I recall."

She flushed scarlet. "I never wanted—"

"What the hell is the matter with you?" he hissed, grabbing her by the shoulders.

"I'm betrothed to another man," she said, averting her face.

He shook her. Not hard, but enough to shock her into looking at him. "Not anymore. After what just happened, you must surely have learned that you belong to me, not him."

"If I were to break off with Richard tomorrow, that would not lessen my dishonor."

He released her abruptly and surged to his feet. Thoroughly annoyed now, and even more thoroughly frustrated, he growled, "Then you should have thought about your damned honor a little sooner. I was ready to make love to you. From your response, I had every reason to expect to make love to you. Don't you know what it cost me to stop?" Seeing her head bow under the lash of his words, he raked his hands through his hair. "Do you have any idea what that does to a man? You're damned lucky I've got some scruples; another man would have taken you right here on the floor, tears notwithstanding."

Lauren's heart flinched beneath his words, and she felt even more ashamed. He was right. This was all her fault. If she had been strong enough to walk out of this room before he'd kissed her, before he'd driven her half-mad with desire, none of this would have happened.

She climbed to her feet and faced his anger squarely. "I'm very sorry," she said. "I was wrong to have allowed things to go this far, and not . . ." Tears stung her eyes again. She swallowed convulsively, unable to finish the sentence, and turned away. "It won't happen again."

He grasped her by the wrist. "It *will* happen again," he promised.

"Please, Stephen, let me go." Her voice was a whisper, barely audible.

He was tempted to draw her back, to kiss away her fears and her misgivings and arouse her all over again. He knew he could do it. But, seeing the tears spill out over her cheeks and her bottom lip quiver as she struggled to repress her sobs, he reluctantly let her go. Yes, he wanted her. His body ached for her. But he also wanted her to come to him willingly, in joy. He wanted their joining to be a mutual sharing, not a taking, not a seduction. And when they finished making love, he wanted her to laugh with him and then begin all over again.

He sighed, feeling his deprivation down to his toes. If he pressed her now, he could only hurt her. And despite the clamoring of his frustrated desire, he found he couldn't face that prospect. There would be another time. And when it came, there would be no fiancé to interfere, and no more excuses. She was his, body and soul, whether she believed it or not. Either she broke her engagement, or he'd do it for her.

"Go on," he said roughly. "While I still have my wits about me."

With a muffled sob, she fled.

147

Chapter Ten

Lauren stumbled down the hall towards her room. She knew Stephen was not at all finished with her. If only she could be as sure that she wouldn't succumb to him! After what happened tonight, she realized that she could trust herself even less than she could trust him. And since she couldn't marry one man while feeling this towering passion for another, she would have to let Richard go. In allowing Stephen to take such liberties, she had thrown her future away. Marrying Richard now would be completely dishonest, and she was no cheat. Wanton, foolish, incredibly gullible, yes — but no cheat. But what made it hurt the most was the fact that Stephen would never understand what he had cost her.

As Lauren walked past Portia's room, the widow opened her door and peered out into the hall. Oh, no! Lauren thought. Not now!

"Lauren, what on earth are you doing up at this hour?" the widow demanded, fussily adjusting her lace-trimmed nightcap. Then, becoming aware of the tears that glistened on Lauren's cheeks, she opened her door wider. "Come in, dear."

Lauren shook her head, not trusting herself to speak.

The old woman beckoned her in imperiously. "This instant, young lady."

Numbly, Lauren obeyed. The widow led her to the nearest chair and pushed her into it, then plumped down on the footstool.

"Now, tell me what's wrong," Portia said.

Lauren blotted her eyes on the sleeve of her dressing gown, then clasped her hands in her lap. "I-I'm just confused. Terribly confused." She bent her head, a hot blush of shame stinging her cheeks.

"About your betrothal?"

With a start of surprise, Lauren raised her head and stared at the old woman. "Yes. How did you know?"

"I've seen it coming, dear."

Lauren was appalled. Good heavens, was her desire for Stephen Hawkes written on her face for all to see? But there was no condemnation on the old woman's face, only concern, so Lauren forced herself to continue. "I think it best if I break the engagement."

"I think that's —" Portia began.

"I know you were terribly pleased to have made such a match for me, but . . . but I just don't think I can go through with it!"

"Lauren, please let me finish!" Portia took a deep breath. "I think you've made a very wise decision."

"You do?" Lauren stared at her in astonishment.

The widow clasped Lauren's hands in hers. "I made the arrangement because I wanted to see you settled and safe, especially after I'm gone. But I

149

hadn't actually met young Mr. Farleigh. Once I did, however, it didn't take long for me to realize that he isn't at all the man for you."

"But—"

"I was just waiting for you to come to the same conclusion." Portia nodded her head, as though confirming Lauren's agreement. "I knew you would; you're a sensible girl."

Lauren stared at her wide-eyed, dazed by her acceptance. "I thought you'd be upset."

"I just want you to be happy, dear." Portia exhaled in gusty relief. "Try to get a little sleep. Later, we'll send for Richard. Do you want me to talk to him?"

"I'll do it. I owe him that much," Lauren said. Oh, God, what was she going to tell him? He honestly seemed to care for her. She had never hurt anyone before, never! Feeling as though the whole world was sitting on her shoulders, she rose, helping the old woman up as she did.

Lauren chewed nervously at the inside of her lip. There was something she wanted to know, but asking it might reveal more about her feelings than she wanted to show anyone. But she *had* to know. "Portia?" she asked hesitantly.

"Yes, dear?"

"You said that Richard is not the man for me." Lauren stared down at her feet. "What sort of man is, then?"

"What sort? Well . . ." The widow paused and smiled, a winsome, knowing smile that made Lauren gulp in guilty reaction.

Does she know, or doesn't she? Lauren thought,

frantically wishing she could retract her question. If she brings up Stephen Hawkes, what on earth am I going to tell her?

Portia folded her small, plump hands over her stomach. "I expect you'll know when you meet him."

Lauren sighed. That was worse than no answer at all, for the man who appealed to her was absolutely the least suitable candidate for a husband. "But what if—"

Someone screamed downstairs, a full-throated shriek of terror. After a moment's startlement Lauren whirled, flung the door open, then dashed out into the hall, and headed for the stairs.

"Lauren, wait!" Portia cried, grabbing her dressing gown and pulling it on with fumbling hands. "Stephen! Steeeephen!"

Stephen, who had just come charging around the corner in response to the first scream, skidded to a halt in the widow's doorway. She waved her arms at him, shouting, "Lauren's gone down alone!"

With a muttered curse, he whirled and ran towards the stairs. His bare feet making no sound on the polished oak floor, he hurtled after Lauren. Damn her! Damn her for rushing into God knows what kind of danger without waiting for him! His heart pounded as he took the stairs two at a time.

Upon reaching the first floor, he heard frenzied sobbing, then Lauren's voice speaking in a soothing tone. "Where are you?" he called, his voice harsh with concern.

"Down here," she answered. "Kate's room."

He took the stairs to the basement at a reckless

151

pace, sliding part of the way in his haste. The door to the cook's room was open, and a candle had been lit inside. Kate was crouched on the floor, keening, her face buried in her arms. Lauren knelt beside her, stroking her heaving back, while Fanny cowered in the corner.

Stephen grabbed Lauren by the shoulders and pulled her to her feet. "Are you all right?"

"Yes, yes!" she cried impatiently. "Let me go. She needs me!"

He released her, pushing her to one side to bend over Kate. Gently, he raised the distraught woman from the floor and sat her on the bed. Lauren sat down beside the cook and put her arm around her waist. Stephen beckoned Fanny to join them, but the girl shook her head, her eyes wide with fright. He let his breath out in a sigh of exasperation and turned back to the cook.

"What happened, Kate?" he asked.

A wail was his only answer. "Tell me what happened!" he snapped, his voice harsh and commanding.

"It touched me!" the woman sobbed. "It touched me!"

"What?" Stephen and Lauren asked in unison.

"Cold. Cold like the grave." Kate wrapped her arms around herself and rocked back and forth. "One of them horrible spirits! It came for me, ran its fingers over my face!"

"Good heavens!" Portia gasped from the doorway.

Edward Eldridge, his dark hair standing up around his head in sleep-spikes, stood behind her.

"What the devil is going on?" he demanded.

Stephen made a sharp gesture with his hand to silence them. "What did this spirit look like, Kate?"

"It glowed, it did, an' its eyes was big, dark holes." Kate drew in a deep, shuddering breath in an effort to calm herself.

Portia, her face creased with concern, said, "Kate, I'm sure it must have been a nightmare—"

"I saw what I saw," the cook insisted.

"I told you there would be more manifestations," Eldridge said, pushing past Portia to enter the room. "Yes, yes. A spirit was here, an angry spirit. I feel the psychic residue."

Not trusting herself to respond to that statement, Lauren turned to Portia. "Hasn't this gone far enough? Make those two charlatans," she jabbed her forefinger angrily at Stephen and Eldridge, "leave now, tonight, and this nonsense will stop."

"It will not stop. It will get worse." Eldridge looked down his nose at her. "The spirits, once aroused, are not easily pacified. If you weren't such a fool, Miss Wakefield, you'd realize that I am the only protection you've got against them."

With a curse, Stephen grabbed Eldridge by the velvet lapels of his dressing gown and lifted the smaller man clear off the floor. Fanny screamed, backing even farther into her corner.

"Stop!" Lauren leaped from the bed and clutched Stephen's arm, trying to use her weight to pull it down. She might have been trying to drag the house itself down, for all the good it did her.

"I ought to tear his throat out," Stephen

153

growled, giving Eldridge a shake.

Portia put her plump hand on his iron-hard bicep. "Put him down, Stephen," she said.

Reluctantly, he obeyed. Eldridge snatched free, his hands going up to smooth his rumpled collar with sharp, angry movements. His face was so pale that his black whiskers looked as though they'd been painted on, and his lips were drawn back over his teeth in a grimace of frustrated rage.

"You'll pay for this, Hawkes," he hissed. "Some day I'm going to—"

"Anytime you like," Stephen replied, his narrowed eyes as hard and cold as pewter.

"Are you *gentlemen* quite finished?" Portia asked, putting her hands on her hips.

"For now, Mrs. Danforth. For now." Eldridge smoothed his rumpled hair. "If you were wise, you would eject this bounder from your house, before he completely ruins your chances of contacting your husband."

Portia's plump chin lifted. "Perhaps, as Lauren suggests, I should eject both of you."

"That would be most reckless, dear lady," the spiritualist said. "Remember: these attacks will likely get worse. And I am the only one who can help you."

"Is that true, Mr. Hawkes?" Portia turned to Stephen, her brows raised inquiringly.

"No. But I wouldn't presume to make your decision for you." He looked at Eldridge with narrowed eyes. "But when you're awakened at night by another of these alarms, wouldn't you rather have two mediums at your disposal instead of just one?"

154

She nodded. "I'm sure you're right. Very well, you will both stay."

Eldridge bowed. "I defer to your decision, of course. But I sincerely hope you don't regret it: the longer this man stays, the angrier the spirits are going to become." With a haughty toss of his head, he turned and stalked from the room.

"I've heard enough," Kate said. "There's goin' to be more hauntin's." She rose to her feet and began taking clothes out of the armoire.

"What are you doing?" Portia asked in alarm.

"I'm not stayin' in this house another minute!" Kate glanced over her shoulder at Fanny. "I'm leaving. And if you know what's good for you, Fanny, you'll do the same."

Fanny looked from her to Portia in indecision. Then she nodded. "I'm going, too."

"Oh, this is terrible!" Portia cried.

"I'm sorry, Mrs. Danforth," the cook said. "You been awful good to me, but there's only so much a body can take."

Portia twisted her hands together in agitation. "I don't want to lose you, Kate, or Fanny, either. Why don't you both take a paid holiday—say, two weeks—and we'll talk about this again. Please?"

"Well . . ." Kate hesitated, then glanced at Fanny, who nodded. The cook sighed. "I s'pose I could visit my sister in Rhode Island. Then, if—*if*, mind you—all these spirits an' things are gone, I'll come back."

Portia beamed. "Good. I think it might be a good idea for the rest of us to spend a week or so at the house in Peekskill. It might give things here

155

a chance to settle down, mightn't it, Stephen?"

"It might," Stephen said doubtfully. Eldridge had promised to increase the severity of the "hauntings," and the man had probably gotten a copy of every key to every door in the house by now.

"We'll leave tomorrow," Portia said. "All of us."

"What?" Lauren cried in horror. "I can't believe you're going to bring them with us!"

"Why, Lauren!" The widow's blue eyes widened in surprise. "You heard what Edward said about the visitations. They *will* get worse. Edward and Stephen are the experts in this matter; under the circumstances, how can we possibly go without them?"

Lauren threw her hands up in despair and turned to Stephen. He couldn't be such a cad as to let this go on another moment, he just couldn't! But he only smiled and studied her leisurely, that bold, caressing warmth returning to his gray eyes.

God help her, her body was already responding to that heated look, that treacherous weakness returning to her limbs. Like a mouse cornered by a hunting cat, Lauren stared at him in fascinated dread. A charlatan, a thief, a man obviously without conscience, or he'd stop this deception now. And still she wanted him. Wanted to feel his lips on hers, his hands on her body. Shame coursed through her, cold, heart-clenching shame.

"May I have a word with you in private, Mr. Hawkes?" she asked from between clenched teeth.

"Certainly, Miss Wakefield." He swept his arm to indicate the open doorway. "After you."

Her back ramrod-stiff, she walked a short way

156

down the hall, then whirled to face him. "Why don't you stop this farce now?"

"What farce?" he asked with mock innocence. He couldn't tell her who and what he really was, not yet. The caution and training that had saved his life countless times forbade it. When the case was over, he'd explain everything.

"This spiritualist nonsense! Can't you see it's gone much too far?"

"Unlike other things," he murmured. With his finger, he lifted a shining auburn curl to his mouth and kissed it, breathing in its faint violet scent.

She snatched her hair away. "If you had any scruples at all, you'd leave this house and never come back."

"But then I wouldn't be with you," he said. "And that's a pleasure I don't intend to give up." He moved closer, backing her against the wall. He wasn't about to let her out of his sight, until she realized that she belonged in his arms.

"Leave me alone," she whispered.

"No." His finger traced the graceful curve of her cheek with gentle, but potent sensuality.

Lauren struggled to control her suddenly ragged breathing. His broad, naked chest was much too close, and it was all she could do not to reach out for him. She wanted to stroke her fingers over that leanly muscled expanse, to feel the strength of him, and then to let her hands drift down over that intriguing arrow of hair that disappeared beneath the waistband of his trousers. Oh, God, she was never going to get away! He'd continue to stalk her like some great, hungry cat. And when he'd finished

157

playing with her, he'd toss her aside.

She shook her head wildly, denying him, denying herself. "How could you?" she asked brokenly, her distress partly for herself, partly for Portia. "How could you!" So quickly that she took him by surprise, she slid out of his reach and ran upstairs.

Richard stood on the massive stone wall that protected the harbor side of the Battery and took a drink out of the bottle of absinthe, shuddering with delicious pleasure at the strong licorice taste. Then he turned and passed the bottle to Piero Cavalli.

The Italian tipped his head back and finished the liqueur, his throat working with each swallow. "Ahhh. Good stuff, eh, young fellow?" He jabbed his elbow into Richard's ribs.

"Indeed." Richard repressed his distaste. Cavalli was a shell of a man—balding, emaciated, his hands constantly trembling from a lifetime of drinking. But shrewd enough, it seemed, to extract money for each bit of information he gave out. Richard grimaced; a hundred dollars so far, and all he'd gotten was a rambling account of the man's pathetic life.

"Tell me about Alanna Stanton," he urged.

"Ahhh, such a lovely girl," Cavalli murmured, making expressive hourglass gestures in the air. Then he shrugged. "But her papa, he was impossible. When he disowned her, I simply could not afford her any longer."

"There was a child, wasn't there?" Richard tried

158

to control the eagerness in his voice.

"Yesss . . ." Cavalli held his hand out.

Richard pressed a folded bill into the out-stretched palm. The money disappeared, but the palm did not. With a muttered curse, Richard handed over another bill.

"Thank you." Cavalli whisked the money away before continuing. "The child was a girl. Red-haired, like me. I wanted to name her Maria, but Alanna insisted on a stupid American name . . . what was it now?" He puckered his brow thought-fully. "My mind, it does not work so well some-times . . ."

"Here," Richard growled, handing over a handful of notes. "The name!"

Cavalli licked his fingers and counted the money. Nodding in satisfaction, he put it in his pocket. "It was Lauren. Alanna loved her—took her to En-gland after I moved on."

Richard was dumbstruck. Then the effects of the revelation and the absinthe coursed through him in a wild rush, and he began to laugh. Lauren! Red-haired Lauren, so recently come to America from London. Twenty-two years old, and so reticent about her past. If her name was really Wakefield, he'd . . . he'd give up gambling and women and . . . He clutched his ribs, staggering with un-holy joy.

"You got some scheme to get money from Stan-ton?" Cavalli demanded shrewdly. "If you do, I want in."

"Of course, of course," Richard said, hiccuping with laughter. The absinthe coursed through him in a flood of burning heat, almost better than a woman. He felt invincible.

Cavalli scowled, his affability disappearing. "You tell me now. What're you planning?" he growled, giving the younger man a shove that sent him to his knees.

Richard's hands closed on a loose stone. Still laughing, he surged to his feet and smashed the rock against Cavalli's temple. The Italian crumpled. Richard went through the unconscious man's pockets, retrieved his money, then pushed the inert body over the seawall. There was a gentle splash, then all was quiet.

Richard counted the money. Three hundred dollars, enough for a fling at Nadine's. He'd have a good meal, some more absinthe, then he'd pick out a woman for the night. What the hell, two women! he thought. As long as they had red hair.

"Lauren," he murmured, laughter bubbling up into his throat again. "Lauren, my sweet!"

Chapter Eleven

Stephen sat in Commissioner Padgett's parlor and gave his report.

"Nothing useful there, if you ask me," Padgett growled. "I suppose *you're* having fun playing spiritualist, while the rest of us are doing your work for you."

Stephen grinned. "Yes, sir."

"Do you think it will be worth your while to go with them to Peekskill?"

"Yes, sir." Anything that kept him near Lauren was worth his while. His body tightened at the memory of what had happened last night. From the moment he'd met her, he had wanted to spark the deeply hidden passion he sensed in her. But he'd had no idea that her fire burned so hot.

The Commissioner drew a piece of paper from his pocket and waved it under Stephen's nose. "We received this cable from Scotland Yard yesterday. They found nothing on Eldridge but rumors; it seems that his victims are too embarrassed to admit that he fleeced them. Hmmph! Not unusual in these cases. But there's some interesting information about Miss Wakefield."

Every muscle in Stephen's body tensed, and he barely resisted the urge to snatch the paper from Padgett's fingers. "What information?"

"It seems the Shropsire Danforths are a tight-knit group — know their fourth cousins twice removed, that sort of thing." Padgett leaned back in his chair and crossed his arms over his chest. "And none of them have ever married a Wakefield. None have ever *known* a Wakefield."

The news hit Stephen like a physical blow. "Then Lauren can't be related to Mrs. Danforth."

"Very doubtful. Scotland Yard even checked out the London Wakefields — the girl says she came from London — and all the Wakefield women are right where they're supposed to be, with their families. And none of them are named Lauren."

Stephen's hands tightened into fists. She had lied. If her identity was a lie, then everything he thought he knew about her was false, too. She'd drawn him in so damned skillfully! Damn it to hell, he'd fallen in love with a lie, fooled by her act of innocence. He, Stephen Hawkes, who had played against the best of them and won, had been sucked into her sticky little net like the rawest bumpkin from the country. It hurt. It twisted in his guts like a white-hot sword.

"It's time we found out the status of Mrs. Danforth's will, don't you think, Commissioner?" he asked.

Padgett nodded. "Think the girl's gotten her to change it yet?"

"I wouldn't be surprised," Stephen growled. She'd already managed to get her hands on the widow's emerald necklace. What an act she'd put on that

162

night, protesting the gift, then allowing herself to be persuaded—oh, so graciously!—into accepting it. Portia had been completely taken in. And so were you, he told himself disgustedly. No wonder Lauren had been so upset when you invaded her tidy little set-up!

Stephen's eyes narrowed. All right, my lovely, fire-haired deceiver, he promised silently, now the game begins in earnest!

Lauren, Portia, and Edward Eldridge sat in the comfortable gilt and velvet luxury of their Pullman car, staring out the windows at the echoing vastness of Grand Central Station. The train smoked and grumbled like some huge mythological beast. There were six other people in the car, all well-to-do, all occupied with their own private pursuits.

"Where could Stephen be?" Portia asked, taking her handkerchief out and fanning herself with it.

Lauren looked up in surprise. "Didn't you send him to the Talmadges with Nero?"

"Well, yes, but he was supposed to be here at eleven, and it's nearly eleven-thirty now."

"Perhaps he's decided not to come at all," Eldridge offered hopefully.

Lauren stared down at her hands, which were clasped so tightly in her lap that her knuckles were white. She knew he would come. After what had happened last night, she knew no power on earth would keep him from following her—at least until he'd gotten what he wanted.

Portia leaned closer. "Did you reach Richard?" she whispered.

"I sent a note to his house, but he was out, and not expected back all day," Lauren whispered back. "I'll have to see him when we get back. I wish—"

"Good morning, ladies," Stephen said from the doorway of the car.

His deep voice washed over Lauren like a caress, and she was astonished by the blinding happiness that swelled her heart at the sound of it. She looked up. There was a flaring of desire in the smoky depths of his eyes, that brought an answering surge of liquid warmth deep in her body. With an effort, she tore her gaze away.

He sat down on one of the enormous, padded chairs that occupied the car. "Sorry to be so late, Mrs. Danforth, but Mrs. Talmadge had a great many questions to ask. She promised to take good care of Nero for you, and also to see that someone watches the house while we're gone. She sends her love and . . ." he grinned, pausing for dramatic effect, "her fondest hope that you will soon regain your sanity. Her words, exactly."

Portia laughed. "Dear Jane, always so tactful."

The train gave a mighty belch, then shuddered into motion. Slowly, inch by inch at first, then with increasing swiftness, it made its way forward.

Lauren stared out the window, fascinated by the vast space, the tangled web of gleaming silver track, and the teeming, noisy crowd of humanity that was Grand Central Station. Then they passed out of the building, and soon after, the city.

For nearly an hour Lauren managed not to look at Stephen. But she was completely, uncomfortably aware of him, as though he'd been branded into her flesh. No, into her soul. There could be no other ex-

164

planation for this compelling urge to look at him. Unable to resist any longer, she turned towards him. He was staring at her, a half-mocking, half-apprecia-tive smile on his lips.

After glancing at Portia and Eldridge to make sure they were engrossed in their own conversation, Stephen leaned closer and whispered, "Did you miss me?"

"Of course not." She forced her voice to calmness.

"I think you did," he growled, angry that he couldn't keep his emotions in check. He knew her for what she was, but he still wanted her so badly he could taste it. "I couldn't sleep at all last night from wanting you. You're mine, Lauren Wakefield. The sooner you realize it, the better off you'll be."

Lauren looked deeply into his eyes, as though the intensity of her gaze would give her the power to delve beneath those smoky gray pupils and see the thoughts below. Want, he'd said. Desire, not love. But there had been such grim savagery in his voice when he'd said that! If he were another sort of man, she'd think she was truly important to him.

"You're going to break your engagement to Far-leigh. I don't intend to share you with anyone," he said. It was true, and not part of the game he was playing. She belonged to him until he decided other-wise.

She gasped in outrage. "How dare you—"

His hand darted out to fasten on her wrist with a force that brought a gasp to her lips. She stared at him with wide, shocked eyes, surprised and a little frightened at his sudden violence.

"You heard what I said," he growled.

Her courage came flooding back, and she twisted

her wrist out of his grasp. "Yes, I heard you!" she hissed through clenched teeth. "And I'll tell you one thing: *if* I decide to break my betrothal, it will be because *I* want to, not because some arrogant, beastly man has given me orders!"

Stephen sat back, satisfied. Very well, he'd make her want to break with Farleigh. He'd do the man a favor by prying her away from him. After all, it was his duty to protect the citizens of New York. The thought cheered him immensely; he couldn't think of a more enjoyable way to spend his working hours than to fan Lauren's fire to white-hot intensity, then to bask in the heat. He ran his finger idly along the tassels that trimmed the arms of his chair, planning just how he was going to do it.

Lauren's gaze followed that slow, playful movement of his finger, and her wayward memory strayed to last night, when he had caressed her breast just that way, his sensitive, knowing fingertips teasing her nipple into taut fullness. Desire curled up through her body, making her blood pound in her veins, and a sultry, aching warmth settle between her legs.

Stephen watched it happen to her, and his own body reacted powerfully, his manhood springing to instant, throbbing attention. God, what a woman! he thought. She might be a liar and a cheat and other things he'd yet to discover, but she packed a hell of a lot of passion in that beautiful body of hers. He wanted her so badly that it shook him. And that made him angry. Made him want to hurt her, to make her as angry as he was.

"Want to find a nice, quiet place?" he murmured. "I'll scratch your itch, and you can scratch mine."

Lauren gasped. Shock banished the sensuous spell that gripped her, to be replaced by humiliation at his crudeness. How dare he talk to her like that! And what was wrong with her that she blindly allowed herself to be snared by his blandishments again! Giving him a withering glare, she turned away to stare determinedly out of the window. Behind her, she heard him chuckle softly.

Stephen studied the soft curve of her cheek, noting the flush that stained her perfect skin. She played the innocent so well! Truly, he'd never seen better. Eldridge couldn't hold a candle to her, for she had beauty and brains, and those dark ardent eyes that could turn any man's head. Even, he reminded himself bitterly, a policeman's. He wanted to pick her up and shake her, punish her for being a lie.

His hands clenched on the armrests of his chair. If he didn't get out of here, he'd give himself away. "I'm for the club car," he said, rising abruptly to his feet. "Mr. Eldridge, will you join me for a drink?"

"Later, perhaps," the spiritualist said. There was hatred in his protuberant eyes, and a slow, smoldering anger.

Stephen met that burning gaze levelly before bowing to Portia. "I'll be back in an hour or so. Adieu, Miss Wakefield."

Lauren glanced at him over her shoulder. Regally, she inclined her head. "Goodbye, Mr. Hawkes."

It took every ounce of her control not to watch him walk out, but she managed it somehow. Without his presence to disturb her, she was finally able to relax. She leaned her head against the cushioned softness of the seat behind her and listened to the drone of conversation around her, and beneath it, the soothing, rhythmic clacking of the wheels. Her eyes drifted closed, and then all awareness faded.

She woke with a start, hours later, to see someone bending over her. It was getting dark already, aided by a heavy, slashing downpour that created wide rivulets of water on the windows. Numb with sleep, she spoke without thinking. "Stephen?"

"He's still in the club car." Portia's voice quivered with amusement. "Were you dreaming?"

"No, I was just . . ." her voice trailed off as heat rushed into her face. Yes, she had been dreaming about Stephen. Would she never be free of him, even in her sleep?

"Never mind." Portia reached out and patted her hand. "I was just teasing you. Why don't we go along to the dining car? The others have already gone, and it's long past dinnertime."

"Oh, of course." Hurriedly, she rose to her feet and began smoothing the wrinkles out of her dress. "I must look a sight!"

"You look lovely, as always," Portia said.

"Liar," Lauren teased. "You just want to hurry me along so you can start in on all the wonderful food they—"

The car lurched sickeningly. Lauren flung her arms around the old woman and held her as they were hurled into one of the seats. There was a nerve-wrenching screeching of brakes, then a tremendous crash as their car leaped into the air with a scream of tearing metal. Portia was ripped from Lauren's grasp.

"Portia!" she shrieked. A mass of shattered wood and broken glass hurtled towards her. She just had time to get her arms in front of her face before it hit. There was an instant of pain, and then blackness closed in around her.

As soon as the club car ground to a shuddering, bouncing halt, Stephen and the other occupants jumped down and headed towards the front of the train. Or rather, what was left of it.

"What happened?" a nearby man demanded.

Stephen peered into the rain-frosted darkness. "Looks like some cars jumped the track . . . Christ Almighty!" That was torn from him as he got a glimpse of what lay ahead. "The bridge collapsed!" *Lauren!* he thought in panic.

Slowly, he told himself. You can't help her—or anyone—if you lose your head. Pulling his companion to a halt, he turned and held out his hands to stop the men who were coming swiftly up behind him.

"Hold it!" he shouted. "Let's organize ourselves!" One man tried to run past, but Stephen grabbed him by the shoulder and stopped him.

"My wife is up there!" the man cried.

Stephen held on. "You'll do her more good by taking a moment to plan what you're going to do."

The other men crowded close, obviously happy to have someone take control. Stephen noted that the brakeman and several porters were among them, and he chose them as the most likely to keep their wits. "Brakeman, is there a town nearby where we can get help?"

"Yes, sir, about seven or eight miles north of here. I think it's called Centerville. No station, they're a few miles off the tracks." He jabbed his thumb towards one of the porters. "Franklin here's got a nose like a bloodhound. He'll find it if anyone can."

"Go on, Franklin," Stephen said. "Tell them we need everything they've got—wagons, a winch, if possible."

The porter took off at a run, and Stephen turned back to the other men. He pointed to the brakeman and the porters. "Each of you take three men and check the nearest cars for survivors. I'm going up to the bridge. Someone may have survived down there."

"It's nearly sixty feet to the bottom of that gorge!" the brakeman whispered, putting his hand on Stephen's shoulder. "You're not going to find anything but crow bait down there."

Not Lauren! Stephen's mind shouted. He shook the man's hand off. "I've got to try."

He left the others behind quickly, jumping scattered piles of debris in his haste. With a stab of fear deep in his gut, he realized that only a few cars hadn't followed the engine in its deadly plunge into the gorge ahead. That meant that the dining car, full at this hour, had gone over. Had Lauren and Portia gone there to eat? Damn it to hell, why hadn't he been with them, instead of nursing a whiskey and his resentment in the club car?

Then a small, bedraggled figure came staggering out of the darkness. "Portia!" he shouted. He leaped towards her, sweeping her into his arms.

"I'm fine," she said, pushing at him. "Truly, just bumps and bruises. But I can't find Lauren!"

"Did she go to the dining car?" he demanded, his heart pounding heavily with dread.

"No, she was with me." Portia pointed towards the

overturned Pullman car, which looked like a great, broken-backed beast in the dimness.

He set the widow down and rushed to the mass of shattered wood and twisted metal. "Lauren! Lauren, are you in there?"

A low moan answered him. Lauren's voice. He began to work frenziedly, hurling massive timbers aside as though they weighed nothing. A few moments later he found her lying beneath one of the seats, her eyes closed, her face as white as chalk. Tossing the heavy chair aside, he bent over her. Please, God, he prayed frantically, let her be all right!

He resisted the urge to snatch her into his arms. Instead, he ran his hands along her arms and legs, searching for any sign of broken bones.

"Lauren, honey, answer me," he murmured.

She moaned and began to stir. A moment later, she opened her eyes. He sank to one knee beside her.

"Are you all right?" he asked. He couldn't stop touching her, as though his hands could convince his mind that she wasn't injured. "Answer me! Are you hurt?"

"Ahh, no. No, I seem to have escaped without . . . Portia!" She struggled to sit up, pulling on his arms with a grip strengthened by concern. "Dear God, is she—"

"She's fine. I saw her not two minutes ago," he soothed. Relief shot through him, a wild surge of emotion that shocked him with its intensity. If Lauren had died . . . The thought was too terrible to bear, and he pushed it away hurriedly.

There was a crashing of timbers behind him. "I've got to go," he said urgently. "Can you manage?"

"Yes, yes!" She pushed at him. "Go on!"

171

He kissed her hard, then surged to his feet with a lithe coiling of muscles. A moment later he had disappeared into the darkness. With a hiss of pain, she pulled a sliver of glass out of her arm, then rose shakily to her feet. There was the sound of hammering from the darkness nearby, as men struggled to free people from the wreckage of the next car. Forgetting her own discomfort, Lauren groped her way towards the sounds. A moment later she made out the dim shapes of the workers.

"What can I do to help?" she asked.

"We got two women out, but they're hurt," one of the men panted. "Over there, by those bushes."

She rushed to the spot he indicated, and found the victims. One seemed to have only a broken arm, but the other was unconscious, a trickle of blood coming from her mouth. After checking her, Lauren shook her head sadly. The woman was dying, and fast.

"She's not going to make it, is she?" the other woman asked.

"No, I'm afraid not," Lauren said honestly, tearing off a strip of her petticoat to make a makeshift sling for the broken arm. "Is she a relative of yours?"

"Never met her." She glanced down at the dying woman. "I'll stay with her 'til the end. You go on to where you might do someone else some good."

Lauren patted her on the uninjured shoulder, then went back to the spot where the men were working. "Have you found anyone else?"

He kept working, his breath rasping in his throat. "Not any that need *our* help. Do us a favor, Miss, and see if you can find us some lanterns back in the

172

club car. We've got to have light."

"I'll be back as soon as I can." Lauren stumbled towards the rear of the train. Fortunately, the rain had slowed to a drizzle, and she could see a few feet in front of her.

A group of men rushed past, led by a strong-looking fellow in the garb of a brakeman. She grabbed his coat as he went by, dragging him to a halt.

"Miss, unless you're hurt—"

"Some of the men are asking for lanterns," she interrupted.

He laughed humorlessly. "We've got exactly three lanterns. Everyone needs light, especially down in the gorge, where a man can't see his hand in front of his face."

"The gorge? The train went . . ." She swallowed convulsively, realizing at last the scale of the disaster. "You could make some torches. We ladies will be glad to contribute our petticoats."

His grin was a flash of white, in the dripping dimness. "You've got a head on you, Miss. All right, collect us some petticoats while I find some wood." Cupping his hands over his mouth, he roared after the retreating men. "Jake! Go get that can of kerosene from the caboose! You, Harry! Tell Hawkes we've got torches coming down to him!"

"Hawkes? Stephen?" she cried, a wave of fear crashing over her. "He's gone down into the gorge?"

"Somebody's got to. Might be people trapped in the wreckage down there." The brakeman gave her a push. "Go on, girl. Get those petticoats!"

Chapter Twelve

"Look, Lauren! The moon is coming out," Portia said, brushing her tangled hair back from her forehead with the back of her hand.

"Thank God!" Lauren spared a brief glance to the bright, welcome orb in the sky, then bent once more to the soiled bandages she was rinsing in a bucket of rainwater. The clouds had moved away just in time, for they were running out of torches—and petticoats. It was a good thing women wore so many layers of clothing nowadays, she reflected. Even so, they were tearing their corsets apart to make bandages now.

"Look, here comes another injured man from the gorge. Oh, dear, it looks bad this time," Portia said, as she bent and grabbed a handful of bandages.

"Wait for me!" Lauren rose to her feet and started after the widow's retreating form, but someone caught at her arm.

"I'm hurt," Edward Eldridge croaked.

Lauren put her arm around him and helped him to sit. "Where are you injured?" she asked.

"My head," he moaned. "I was unconscious for hours, and no one came for me! And my hand! Look at my hand!"

174

Lauren checked his hand, but there was only a single cut across the palm, and that not even deep. She then inspected his head with gentle fingers, but found nothing—no cuts, no blood, not even a lump. If he'd been unconscious for hours, it certainly hadn't been from a blow on the head. "Does anything else hurt?" she asked.

"Everything. I was beaten about most severely," he groaned.

She pulled up his shirt to examine his ribs and back. Again, nothing. Not a single bruise. He wasn't even dirty! Oh, there was the cut on his hand, admittedly, but hardly enough to warrant that volume of complaint.

Chiding herself for her lack of sympathy, she ran her hands over his head again. Perhaps she'd missed something the first time. But no, there was nothing at all to indicate he'd been injured in any way. Her lips thinned in disapproval as she realized that he was lying about being unconscious. More than likely, he'd been hiding, afraid someone might make him do something dangerous. And Stephen had willingly gone down into the gorge, the most perilous job of all! Even now he might be lying hurt, needing her, while this pompous booby wailed about a cut hand.

"Well, aren't you going to bandage me?" Eldridge demanded.

Gritting her teeth against making a remark she was sure she'd regret later, she wrapped a piece of cloth around his hand.

"Ouch!" the spiritualist cried. "That hurt!"

"Sorry." Lauren wasn't sorry at all. What she really wanted to do was slap his face. He sat here, whining, while men with far more severe hurts were working to save others. She tied the bandage, eliciting another wail from her patient. Too bad Portia wasn't able to hear how her dear Edward reacted to a crisis; she might reconsider how useful he'd be if there really *was* an attack by an angry spirit.

Turning away from him, she snatched up some bandages and headed towards Portia as fast as she could, forcing one foot after the other with stubborn determination. She was tired, bone-tired. And in addition to her weariness, she harbored a deep, grinding fear for Stephen, who was crawling through the dangerous mass of twisted steel and splintered wood that littered the bottom of the gorge.

She joined Portia, who was still tending the newly arrived casualty. Lauren knelt beside her, helping her splint his broken legs. One arm was broken as well, and there was a long gash along the left side of his face. Gently, Lauren laid a pad of cloth over that wound, then bound it into place.

"Thank you," he muttered. "Pile of metal shifted, came down on top of my legs. Stupid of me to be caught like that."

"No, brave of you," Lauren said. "You didn't have to go down there." And neither had Stephen. But he had, and he might be the next broken and bloody casualty brought up here. Please, God, she prayed. Keep him safe!

"Bodies everywhere," the injured man muttered. "Pieces of bodies." He rolled his head from side to side in agony. Lauren took his uninjured hand and held it, thinking of Eldridge and his paltry wound, and the way he'd whined about them.

"You'll be all right," she said. "Just hold on. I'm sure help will be here soon."

He nodded, his eyes bright with pain. She gave his hand a squeeze before climbing to her feet. She couldn't go another minute without seeing if Stephen was all right. Just one glimpse of him, and she'd have the strength to go on a little longer.

"Portia, I'm going to the bridge."

"You don't want to see that!" Portia cried.

Lauren looked down at her. "I've already seen the worst a person could imagine," she said wearily. This night was going to haunt her for the rest of her life. She'd seen people cruelly broken and twisted: the lucky ones were dead. She'd heard screams of agony that echoed in her ears even now, and she had held the hands of people to ease their passage into death. More people than she cared to count.

Hearing a commotion from the direction of the club car, she whirled to see a group of perhaps fifty men walking towards her along the track. Behind them were wagons and mules and a cart, with a strong-looking winch mounted on it.

"Look!" she cried, her weariness dropping away in a great flood of relief. "Oh, look!"

A ragged cheer went up from the crowd. The group of men nearest the gorge turned to look, then one of them came running to meet the newcomers.

"Bring that winch, and hurry!" he shouted. "They've found someone alive down there!"

The newcomers put their shoulders to the winch and soon had it poised at the edge of the gorge. Lauren hovered at the fringe of the seething throng of men, trying to see down into the chasm. The crowd shifted, and she looked down into the chaos below. Railcars lay in an enormous stack, shattered into matchwood. Even the massive steel engine had been broken by the force of its fall onto the rocks. And down amid the shards of steel and splintered wood, she saw men toiling to hook the cable onto the overturned car that lay atop the pile, teetering perilously on its roof.

Then she spotted Stephen. Bare-chested, his arms and back smeared with blood—his or someone else's, she didn't know—he climbed onto that rocking car to finish hooking the cable.

"Oh, please, God, don't let him fall!" she whispered, her hand coming up to clasp her throat. "Just let him get down from there alive!"

He jumped down, then pumped his arm to indicate that the men above should start cranking the winch. The overturned car creaked and groaned, audible even up here, then came up with grudging slowness. As soon as there was room, Stephen flung himself on his belly and wriggled beneath it.

Lauren's breath came in quick pants. If she'd known fear when he'd climbed atop the teetering car, then what she felt now was abject terror. What if the cable slipped? He'd be trapped in that dark cavern of death, crushed, or perhaps worse, to lie in blackness waiting for a much slower end.

Portia came up beside her and put her arm around Lauren's waist. "Did you see Stephen?"

"He . . . He . . ." Lauren took a deep breath in an attempt to calm herself. "He went under there." Needing the comfort of human contact, she put her arm around Portia's plump shoulders.

Holding each other tightly, they stared at the spot where Stephen had disappeared. It felt as though an eternity passed, although some small, rational part of Lauren's mind knew it was only minutes. Then there was a flicker of movement in the inky darkness beneath the car.

"Look!" Portia breathed, straining forward. "Look!"

The men below rushed forward on their hands and knees. A small form was passed up into their hands, then another. Children. A moment later Stephen crawled out of the tangled metal, dragging a woman's limp form after him. His companions grabbed him and his burden and hauled them out into the moonlight. For a moment he crouched, every line of his body revealing his exhaustion. Then he rose to his feet and signalled the workers above to release the winch.

"He's very brave, isn't he?" Portia asked.

"Yes," Lauren whispered. She watched the railcar settle slowly over what would have been the graves of a woman and two children, but for him. Him, Lauren thought, Stephen Hawkes—spurious medium, trickster, liar, courageous rescuer, lover. The worst and the best all rolled into one devastating man. And she was in love with him. She'd refused to see it until now. But she couldn't fool herself any longer. She loved him. That was why her betrothal to Richard had seemed so wrong, and why her body was consumed with desire whenever Stephen touched her, whenever he looked at her.

She was lost. Lost, because she would love him forever, and he was the kind of man who would soon move on to other things. Just like her mother, she couldn't stop herself from loving him anyway. And just like her mother, she would be left behind one day, blaming herself for not being woman enough to hold him. She swayed, and the world

179

seemed to tilt around her.

"Lauren, you're terribly pale," Portia said in alarm, tightening her grip on Lauren's waist. "You're not going to faint, are you?"

Lauren bit the inside of her lip until the blood came. Slowly the world steadied. "No," she said. "I'm not going to faint." Stepping away from Portia's encircling arm, she pointed towards the bridge. "Look, they're bringing the injured up now. We'd better go see if we're needed."

As they went to offer their services, however, a man from town pushed through the crowd. "Let me through!" he cried. "I'm a doctor."

As he expertly tended the woman and children, Lauren realized that she and Portia were not needed. *Go back to the club car,* the rational portion of her mind urged, *you can't face Stephen, not now.* But even that prompting couldn't move her from this spot. She loved him. When he came up over the edge of the precipice, she wanted him to see her waiting for him.

So she and Portia stood at the edge of the workers who crowded around the winch, waiting as the men were brought up one by one. Stephen was the last, and several men rushed forward to shake his hand and thump him on the back.

He looked over their heads at the two women who waited for him. After glancing at Portia, his gaze fastened on Lauren's face. He'd spent the night in hell itself, and the memory of what he'd seen and heard there hung over him like a shroud. If only Lauren would touch him, hold him, it would be a re-affirmation of life and joy. Disengaging himself from the congratulatory crowd, he walked towards

180

her. Damn the lies, damn the game! he thought. Right now I just need to hold her.

Lauren watched him come. She yearned to run to him, but she was rooted to the spot by the force of her own feelings. His arms and chest were a patchwork of cuts and bruises, and there was a nasty-looking gash on his right arm. His trousers were so torn they were hardly decent, and he was covered from head to foot with soot and dried blood. He was the most beautiful human being she had ever seen. Please, God, she thought frantically, make Portia do something before I make a complete fool of myself!

As though hearing that silent plea, Portia stepped forward to take Stephen's hands in hers. Lauren merely stared at him, trying to regain some control of her shaking legs.

"Waiting for me, ladies?" he asked, trying to put some humor into his tired voice and failing completely.

"Yes, indeed." Portia reached up to put her hands on his scratched and stubbled cheeks. "You are quite a man, Mr. Hawkes," she murmured, drawing him down to kiss him full on the mouth. Then, blushing furiously, she backed away.

He smiled down at the old woman, a tender warmth in his eyes. Then he glanced at Lauren, and his eyes darkened to the color of charcoal. She read hunger there, not carnal hunger, but a need of human warmth and comfort. More than that—*her* warmth, *her* comfort. It was irresistibly stirring to know that no one else could give him what he needed.

Drawn like a fly to a spider's web, she stepped forward. His arms went around her waist, and he brought her against his chest in a hug that nearly took the breath from her. She didn't care. Squeezing her eyes shut, she clung to him, feeling his heartbeat against her cheek. He laid his cheek against her hair, and his sigh was that of a man coming home after a long absence.

Her hands slid around his neck and into his thick hair. Ignoring the crowd of grinning men, she pulled his head down and pressed her lips to his. His hard arm came around her waist, lifting her against him as his mouth slanted over hers. Lauren's fingers clenched in his hair as her body responded even now. Exhausted, dirty, under the eyes of at least twenty laughing men, she held him as though she'd never have to let go.

For a moment Stephen allowed himself the luxury of her touch. Then, becoming aware of the chuckles behind him, he put her from him gently.

"The warrior's reward, Miss Wakefield: a kiss from a beautiful woman," he said, hiding his tumultuous emotions beneath a sardonic grin.

The watching men cheered his remark, then headed down the slope to help lift the wounded into the wagons that were to take them to town.

Portia linked her arm with Stephen's. "Come with me, young man. I'll wash those cuts for you."

"Thank you." He held out his other hand to Lauren. "Miss Wakefield?"

Stephen soon discovered that the widow, despite her dithery manner, was a most efficient nurse. In a very few minutes he found himself washed, bandaged, and set out to dry. Lauren sat a short distance away, once more cool and composed, her hands folded in her lap, as though she sat in Portia's elegant drawing room. What was she hiding beneath that lovely face of hers? he wondered. For a moment, up there at the edge of the gorge, he'd felt as though his very soul was entwined with hers. With her clasped so willingly in his arms, he'd gotten a taste of what might have been. Damn, why did she have to be false? Sometimes the world seemed to be a hell of an ugly place, when such beauty, such outward innocence and caring was only a disguise for a greedy, grasping soul. He wanted to love her, gently and without reservation, and he couldn't.

He climbed stiffly to his feet when he saw the brakeman, who had been supervising the loading of the injured into the wagons, toiling up the slope towards him.

"Stephen, they're all loaded," the man panted. "There's room for you and the ladies in the last wagon."

"It's going to be a hell of a rough ride for some of those people. Did anyone think to cable the railroad to send another train up here?" Stephen asked.

The brakeman shook his head. "The storm blew the telegraph lines down. It'll be tomorrow before word gets out, and we can't leave the injured out here in the open."

With a sigh, Stephen raised Lauren to her feet, then held out his arm to Portia.

The brakeman took the widow's other arm to help her across the churned, muddy ground. "These two ladies of yours have been a godsend to us," he said. "Those torches were Miss Wakefield's idea, you know. Petticoats."

"Oh?" Stephen's eyebrows went up. "I *had* noticed

the ladies were less, ah, encumbered than usual." A most gratifying sight, at least in Lauren's case.

Portia blushed. "Stephen, you're terrible."

As they neared the wagon, Edward Eldridge stood up to hold out his hands to Portia. "My dear lady! Let me help you up!"

To Lauren's disgust, she saw that he had acquired more bandages. His dramatic air was heightened by the white cloth wrapped around his head, nearly obscuring his left eye.

"Edward, how wonderful to see you," Portia said, holding up her arms so he could lift her into the crowded wagon. "I was so worried about you. Are you terribly hurt?"

"I'll survive," he murmured bravely, helping her sit in the space he had just vacated.

"I think I'm going to be sick," Lauren whispered to Stephen. "Why, the man has nothing but a cut on his hand!"

He laughed at the disgusted look on her face, then swept her into his arms and set her gently into the wagon bed. Seeing that Eldridge had turned to give the driver a few orders, which were studiously being ignored, Stephen climbed nimbly into the wagon. He slid into the place beside Portia and pulled Lauren down on his other side. Not surprisingly, he found that Eldridge had managed to acquire one of the best places in the wagon, where a man could lean his back against the wooden slats of the side. Stephen settled himself comfortably, making sure he and Lauren occupied all the remaining space.

When Eldridge turned to take his seat again, he found it occupied. He opened his mouth to protest, but, after glancing at Portia, closed it and took a less favored place in the center of the wagon. Still unwilling to give up, he managed to squirm as close as possible to the widow. He glared at Stephen resentfully, but it was hard to take the older man seriously when he was crouched at Portia's feet like a puppy dog. Lauren felt Stephen's sturdy frame shake with silent laughter, and she had to duck her head to hide her own smile.

A moment later the wagon lurched into motion. Lauren leaned back against the wall behind her and closed her eyes. She was tired, so tired. At another time, the jolting motion of the wagon would have kept her awake, but just now it was like the gentle rocking of a baby's cradle. Then all sensation faded as she fell into a deep, dreamless sleep.

It was the sun that woke her, welcome, golden warmth that penetrated to her very bones. She opened her eyes to find herself in Stephen's lap, her head pillowed against his hard chest. His arm was curved around her, holding her in place. His body was lax beneath her, his breathing deep and regular. She looked around at her companions, but they, too, seemed to be asleep. So she shut her eyes again, allowing herself to enjoy this closeness. For a few precious minutes, she could pretend that Stephen was her betrothed, that she could love him, trust him, and freely give him everything a woman could give her lover.

Stephen, however, was not asleep. He watched her from beneath his lashes, enjoying the way her unconfined breasts rested against him, and most especially the way they bounced with the motion of the

185

wagon. There were several buttons missing from the bodice of her dress, giving him a most enticing glimpse of creamy white curves and the shadowed cleft between. He shifted her slightly, giving himself an even better view, and felt his manhood swell in response. No corset, he thought, nothing between them but the fabric of her dress. It was too bad there were twenty other people with them, or he'd take swift advantage of the situation. Damn, but he wanted her! He moved her downward so that her bottom rested upon his throbbing erection.

Lauren's eyes flew open as she realized the extent of his arousal. And she'd thought he was asleep! The rogue never missed an opportunity to show her exactly what he was really interested in! So much for love and trust and uncomplicated embraces. She stiffened, but before she could move off his lap, his arm tightened, pinning her where she was.

"Don't go," he murmured.

What was she going to do? she thought frantically. If she tried to wriggle free, it would only incite him further. But she couldn't possibly stay here like this, with his hardened manhood like a searing brand beneath her buttocks? Even worse, she was responding to him, that now-familiar, coiling warmth settling between her legs. There was such strength in him, such promise! And after the searing pleasure he'd given her, she knew just how devastating that promise was. That thought caused her to shift restlessly, disturbed by the memory of what had happened between them. Her breasts became sensitive, her nipples rising up in turgid peaks.

Stephen nearly groaned. Without the corset to conceal her, he could clearly see those hardened points through the fabric of her gown. God, it was almost more than a man could take! He was shaking with the desire to peel that dress away from her, to take those sweetly beckoning nipples into his mouth until she moaned with desire the way he remembered. And then he'd taste the rest of her, every hot, beautiful inch. His chest heaved with frustration. Unable to do what he really wanted, he pressed her down more firmly against his aching shaft.

"We're almost there," the driver called over his shoulder.

Lauren stiffened and pushed away from Stephen's chest, withdrawing as far from him as the confined space allowed. Harlot! she berated herself savagely. Have you no shame?

Stephen raised his knees to hide his arousal from the others, who had begun to stir. His chest rose and fell raggedly as he strove to regain control. In a moment he was able to speak calmly enough. "How much farther?"

"A mile or so," the driver said.

People sat up and began to straighten their clothing as best they could. All in all, Stephen thought, we're a sorry sight. And these were the least battered of the lot, the worst of the injured having gone on ahead.

As they entered the outskirts of town, a man on horseback cantered up to the wagon and conferred with the driver. A moment later, they changed direction, heading away from town.

"What's the problem here?" Eldridge demanded in a loud, peremptory voice.

The driver glanced at him over his shoulder, then leaned over the side of the wagon to spit. "There

187

ain't any more room in town. Rich feller 'bout six miles out of town offered to put up enny who didn't need too much nursin'. Now don't you worry none, it's only an hour or so drive from here."

"Oh, how kind of him!" Portia exclaimed.

"Now, I don't know if I'd call him kind, exactly," the driver said. "He's a hel—heck of a strange feller. You never kin tell what he's goin' to do next, or why. He built that place more'n twenty years ago, but he don't spend but a couple of months of the year there. He comes an' he goes, an' nobody knows when he's plannin' to do either one."

"Well, who is he?" Eldridge demanded.

"You ever heerd the name Stanton?" the driver asked. "Caldwell Stanton?"

Lauren fought for breath, for control. *This can't be happening!* she screamed inwardly. *Oh, please, God, don't let it be true!* Then, with an effort of will, she managed to force her panic away. Why should she be frightened of one old man after what she'd been through?

She lifted her chin defiantly, gathering her courage around herself like a cloak. But her heart was beating a rapid tattoo of fear inside her chest. Caldwell Stanton. Her grandfather.

Chapter Thirteen

"Ohhh, what time is it?" the woman on Lauren's right asked, bracing herself against the movement of the wagon.

Stephen sighed. She had asked the same question over and over, approximately every fifteen minutes. But just as he'd done every other time she had asked, he pulled his watch out and flipped it open. "A quarter to ten, ma'am."

"I'm awful hungry," the woman said. "We haven't had anything to eat since yesterday afternoon. And I think it's — getting colder. Don't the rest of you think it's getting colder? I wish . . . Good heavens, will you look at that?"

Her exclamation came as the wagon topped a rise and Caldwell Stanton's enormous house came into view. The mansion sprawled across the center of the valley below, its numerous turrets and gracefully arched windows reminiscent of a French Renaissance chateau.

The wagon turned from the rutted track it had been following, and crunched slowly along the curving gravel drive that led to the house.

"Is all that just for one man?" one of the women asked incredulously.

The driver glanced over his shoulder at his passengers. "Yep. Old Stanton's one of the richest men in America."

"Then what's he doing buried way out here?" the man directly across from Lauren demanded.

"Who knows?" The driver shrugged. "When you're as rich as he is, you be as dotty as you want."

Stephen chuckled. "Well, dotty or not, I'm not complaining. I'd much rather spend the night in the lap of luxury than in someone's barn."

The wagon lurched to a halt outside the great double doors, and a number of servants hurried outside to help the passengers down. A regal butler stood on the top step, directing the activity with efficient aplomb, and in only a few minutes everyone had been whisked into the house.

They stood in a group just inside the doors, staring in awe at the enormous foyer. A vast sea of marble spread out before them, a pristine white expanse that led the eye to a magnificent double stairway. An intricately carved marble balustrade enclosed the upper landing, and graceful, curving pillars supported the lofty ceiling. Lauren shivered; despite its beauty, it was an enormous, cold, almost oppressive space.

"This way, please," the butler murmured, indicating a door to their right. "I understand you have not yet eaten. An informal meal will be served in the comfort of the drawing room."

They followed him into the drawing room which, although nearly as large as the foyer, was a much more welcoming chamber. A fire crackled cheerfully in the fireplace, and the walls were softened by green velvet hangings. The polished oak floor was covered by a very old and very beautiful Persian rug, the colors of which gleamed jewel-rich in the sunlight that streamed through the tall windows.

Sofas and chairs were interspersed throughout the room in small, intimate groups. At the butler's gesture of invitation, the tired travelers took their seats. Maids bustled in to set small tables before each chair, then brought a tray of sandwiches and steaming vegetables to each visitor.

Portia inhaled the delicious aroma of freshly-baked bread, then looked up at the butler. "Your name?" she asked.

"Reed, Madam."

"Thank you, Reed. This is most welcome."

He inclined his head. "I hope you enjoy your meal. Mr. Stanton will be down shortly to greet all of you."

Lauren lost her appetite. She pushed her uneaten sandwich around her plate listlessly, while her stomach churned with dread. In a few minutes she'd meet her grandfather. She knew what he looked like, for although her mother hadn't kept any portraits of the father who had cast her out, Lauren had read every newspaper account of him, poring over the sketches that accompanied those stories. Caldwell Stanton the financial genius. Caldwell Stanton the mercantile prince, who had fought his way to supremacy over the ruin of lesser men. Caldwell Stanton—cold, calculating, ruthless, even with his own daughter. Lauren's hands shook so hard that she clenched them in her lap.

Stephen studied her closely, realizing that she was controlling herself with an effort of will. Exhaustion had left dark smudges beneath her eyes, making them look even larger than usual against the pallor of her face. She looked as though she was walking the edge, and that the smallest push would send her over.

He clenched his teeth. Part of him wanted to give

her that push, but another part of him wanted to take her in his arms and comfort her, to take away whatever it was that was troubling her. His sandwich, held too tightly, crumbled in his hand. Damn! She had him so twisted up inside, that he wasn't sure if he'd know the truth about her if it were staring him in the face.

"You're not eating, Lauren," Portia said. "Is something wrong, dear?"

She shook her head. "I'm just not hungry."

"You must eat if you're going to regain your strength," Portia insisted. "Now go on, try."

Lauren took a bite of sandwich, but it was like eating sawdust. Seeing that Portia was watching her, she forced herself to swallow and take another unwanted bite. Stephen was looking at her, too, but there was nothing of solicitousness in his gaze; he was studying her with disturbing intensity, as though he'd like to take her apart, layer by layer, until he found the essence of her.

She stiffened as a man appeared in the doorway. Crossing his arms over his chest, he stood and surveyed the room. He was tall and thin, with a powerful presence that immediately gained everyone's attention. Everything about him seemed sharp: his piercing blue eyes, proud beak of a nose, and jutting chin, the smooth platinum hair that rose in an angular crest above his head.

"I'm Stanton. Welcome to Oakhurst," he said. His voice was harsh, even his words clipped and sharp-edged.

Stephen rose to his feet and came forward to shake hands. "Thank you for offering us the use of your home, Mr. Stanton. I'm Stephen Hawkes."

Stanton's penetrating gaze swept over the younger man's face. In that moment, Stephen felt himself inspected, weighed, and judged. And accepted, if he could count that brief stretching of the old man's lips as a smile.

Edward Eldridge came forward, his hand extended. "Mr. Stanton, it is indeed a pleasure to meet you. I want to compliment you on your home — French Renaissance, is it not? — and the efficiency of your staff. A residence worthy of its owner, I must say. And I want to add my gratitude for your kindness in having us here. Although *I* would be quite willing to take any sort of accommodation offered in town, of course, there are ladies in our group who are unused to rough conditions of any kind."

As Eldridge pumped Stanton's hand enthusiastically, the old man looked him over without approval.

But the spiritualist, undaunted by that boreal stare, continued blithely. "I've heard so much about you, even in England. Your exploits — "

"Slander!" Stanton barked. "Every word patently untrue!"

Completely dumfounded, Eldridge could do nothing but gape openmouthed at his host.

Stanton removed his hand from Eldridge's grasp, then turned away and began greeting the rest of his guests.

Stephen repressed a chuckle. It was the first time he'd ever seen Eldridge at a loss for words. And Stanton hadn't even cracked a smile. The old man seemed to be everything he was rumored to be — tenacious, cunning, and ruthless, a wily old badger with plenty of scars to show the fights he'd been in — but he had one hell of a sense of humor.

Lauren was only dimly aware of the conversation as she struggled to retain her composure. Stanton was slowly making his way towards her, and she wasn't sure she could trust herself to act normally when her turn came. Softly, she told herself, take a deep breath. Pretend he's a complete stranger. That shouldn't be hard; to all intents and purposes, he was, for he had removed himself from her mother's life before she was born. And probably hadn't spared them a moment's thought since.

Stanton reached Portia's chair. "Don't I know you, madam?"

"You have an excellent memory, Mr. Stanton. We met a great many years ago," she said. "You had some business dealings with my husband, Thaddeus Danforth."

"I remember Danforth." He nodded, a single, curt jerk of his head. "One of the few men whose word was as good as mine."

"Why, thank you, sir," Portia said with a smile. "He said the same about you."

He bowed, a courtly gesture at odds with his countenance and clipped words. "That's a compliment, coming from him."

Pride brought Lauren's head up as Stanton came to stand in front of her, and she met his piercing gaze with cool dignity. No one was going to make her cringe like a coward, no one! "My name is Lauren Wakefield," she said, pleased to find that her voice was as composed as she wished. "I, too, would like to thank you for your hospitality."

"My pleasure, Miss Wakefield," he said.

He turned away almost immediately, and Lauren let her breath out in a sigh that was part relief, part disappointment. Did you think he was going to recognize you? she asked herself in self-disgust. Did you think he was going to point at you and announce "This is my granddaughter?" Fool! If he knew who she really was, he'd probably throw her out of the house. And yet, even as that thought echoed through her head, unshed tears made her eyes ache.

Stanton reached the doorway and turned to inspect his guests again. "When you've finished eating, the servants will take you to your rooms to bathe and rest," he said, pausing in the doorway. "We'll see what we can do about fresh garments for all of you. Dinner is at seven."

He left as abruptly as he'd come.

Lauren slipped away while the others were lingering over dessert. The air in the corridor felt damp and chill; the weather had turned sharply colder this afternoon, and her body hadn't yet adjusted to the sudden change in temperature.

As she passed the library, she caught sight of a portrait that irresistibly pulled her into the room. It was a painting of her mother as a young girl of sixteen or seventeen. Alanna was as beautiful as a woman could possibly be, and her eyes held none of the broken dreams that had shadowed them in later years. With shaking hands, Lauren smoothed the skirt of the sapphire velvet dress she'd been given.

"Lovely, wasn't she?" Caldwell Stanton asked from behind her.

Lauren whirled to see the old man standing in the doorway. *"Was?"* she asked.

"That was my daughter." He came farther into the room, his attention on the portrait.

"She isn't any longer?"

His flinty gaze swung to her. "No. Not for a long time."

Anger rose in her, making her chest heave. What

accident of fate had given Alanna—beautiful, tender Alanna—to such a cold, grim father? He had money, position, power. He could have defied society and supported his daughter's decision to keep her child. Instead, he had turned away from her, leaving her to the questionable mercies of a cruel, faithless world, and even more faithless men.

"What's the matter with you?" he asked, his eyes narrowing as he saw her anger.

"Not a thing, Mr. Stanton." Lauren turned back to the portrait, disturbed that he had read her so easily. She was off balance with him, her normal composure and reticence shattered by his total lack of conventional manners. Well, she thought, if you can use rudeness to get beneath people's skins, so can I. "What happened to your daughter?" she asked with deliberately harsh bluntness. "Did she die?"

"I don't talk to people's backs," he growled.

Her rage went up another notch. Raising her chin defiantly, she swung around to face him. "Well, did she die?" she repeated.

"I didn't say that."

His grizzled eyebrows contracted in a scowl, and Lauren was pleased to see that he was becoming thoroughly annoyed with her. Perhaps I'll get some answers now, she thought triumphantly. Looking down her nose at him, she asked, "Then what did you mean when you said that she wasn't your daughter any longer?"

"I *meant* that she's gone. She wouldn't listen to me. She never listened to me, and she came to grief because of it. So I threw her out." He came to stand directly in front of her, his jaw thrust forward pugnaciously. "What do you think of that, eh?"

Lauren lost her temper completely, and a reckless

part of her reveled in the surge of emotion that went through her. She felt wonderfully free and bold, as though a heavy chain had been lifted from her soul. He might throw her out afterward, but she was going to have her say! "I think it's horrible. I think *you're* horrible!"

"So? What the hell business is it of yours?" he growled, completely forgetting that he'd asked her opinion. *"She,"* he jabbed his thumb towards the portrait, "is my concern."

"Indeed?" Lauren met his enraged stare levelly. "If you'd had a bit more *concern* for her, Mr. Stanton, she might be here today."

"By God, I ought to—"

"Ought to what?" she challenged. "Knock me down for speaking the truth? Call me out, perhaps? Pistols at twenty paces?"

"Goddamn!" His voice rose to a roar. "Insulted in my own house! By a woman I invited out of the goodness of my heart—"

"Heart!" she shouted back. "What heart?"

He drew in his breath, prepared for another bellow. Then, suddenly, he began to laugh. She stared at him, outraged, and that only made him laugh harder. Finally he regained control. Pulling his handkerchief out to wipe his streaming eyes, he wheezed, "Thank you, Miss Wakefield. That was the best damn fight I've had in years. Not many people have the balls for a good fight."

Lauren was too shocked to speak for a moment. "How dare you use that language—"

"Are we having fun?" Stephen asked from the doorway.

"Yes, as a matter of fact," the old man said.

Lauren turned to see Stephen lounging against the

door frame, his big, broad-shouldered body encased in a shirt that was too large and a pair of pants that were too tight for comfort. *Her* comfort, that is. He didn't seem to mind at all that everything he had was clearly outlined by the fabric. Her breath came shallowly, and even her anger paled in comparison to the desire she felt at the sight of him. This was the man she loved. Loved, wanted, and feared. Oh, she didn't fear *him,* precisely — she feared the power he had over her.

Stephen's eyes narrowed as he felt her scrutiny. If she had any idea how sultry she looked just now, she'd blush to her toes. And if she continued to stare at his crotch like that, his reaction was going to embarrass her even more.

"Well, what do you want?" Stanton asked, distracting him.

Stephen grinned at him. "I could hear you yelling all the way down the hall." His gaze swung to Lauren, and his eyes darkened. "Both of you."

"Nothing like a good argument to clear the head," Stanton said cheerfully.

"You know," Stephen mused, "that's the first time I've ever heard Miss Wakefield raise her voice."

"A charming young woman, our Miss Wakefield," the old man replied, showing the edges of his teeth in a dagger-sharp smile. "Already she has seen fit to pry into my personal life, and when I objected, insulted me most foully." He took Lauren's hand and tried to raise it to his lips, but she resisted him, scowling. He laughed. "I like her. Not many people have the guts to insult Caldwell Stanton to his face."

Stephen ran his thumb over his jaw thoughtfully. Lauren was doing it again, throwing her sly, charming net over everyone around her — everyone, that is, who

198

might be of use to her. By god, she had brass aplenty to try it on a man like Stanton. But she'd done it. She'd managed to find exactly the right way to endear herself to the old man. Chameleon, changing herself to suit the situation. Oh, it's going to be a pleasure to take her down, Stephen told himself.

Stanton's rough voice cut through his grim thoughts, however. "Come with me," the old man said. "I'm supposed to meet Mrs. Danforth in the drawing room to talk about old times."

"What about the rest of your guests?" Lauren asked.

The old man snorted. "Cattle. Nice enough, but cattle nonetheless. Your lot are the only ones with anything interesting to say."

With a sardonic grin, Stephen offered Lauren his arm. She took it, and her body instantly responded to his nearness. And he knew it as well as she, for he made sure that his arm brushed the side of her breast with disturbing frequency as they accompanied Stanton towards the drawing room. Somehow Stephen managed for them to fall a few paces behind, giving him the opportunity to caress her more fully.

"Stop it!" she hissed under her breath.

"Stop what?" he whispered with mock innocence, moving his arm against her softness again. "This?"

"Yes. Stop it."

"No. I like it." His gaze, smoky with arousal, traveled leisurely over the smooth swell of her breasts, then rose to her face, noting the way her lips had parted unconsciously, and the sensual heat that flared in her dark eyes. "And so do you."

She disengaged her arm, glaring at him with what she hoped was haughty disdain. Somehow she had to gain control over herself, or she was going to give him

199

free rein to hurt her. But how? How was she going to stay away from him, when her very bones seemed to melt at his touch?

Stanton reached the drawing room. Before opening the door, however, he glanced over his shoulder at the two younger people behind him. "Are you coming in, or are you going to stand there and gawk at each other for the rest of the evening?" He laughed as Lauren blushed scarlet.

"I wasn't gawking," she snapped. Her head held high, she opened the door and swept past him.

Chuckling, the two men followed her in. All three stopped short in surprise, however, when they saw Portia and Eldridge sitting on either side of a small table, their hands tightly clasped, their eyes closed.

"What the hell is going on here?" Stanton demanded.

Eldridge jumped to his feet and came forward, his hand extended. "Mr. Stanton, dinner was wonderful. Your cook—"

"I asked you a question!" the old man snapped.

"They were communing with the spirits," Lauren said, her voice fairly dripping with contempt. "Mr. Eldridge is a medium."

Stanton blinked. "What?"

Lauren smiled challengingly at Stephen. "And so is Mr. Hawkes."

"WHAT?" Stanton bellowed.

Clever, clever girl, Stephen thought in rueful admiration. Get the old rogue to like you, then use him to pry the competition away from Mrs. Danforth.

Stanton drew himself stiffly upright, even his crest of silver-white hair seemed to swell with anger. His outraged gaze snapped to Stephen. "What twaddle is this?"

Stephen crossed his arms over his chest and grinned at him. "Do you have any ancestors you'd like us to contact? That is, once we've put Mrs. Danforth in touch with her husband."

Seeing her host's face turn red, Portia half rose from her chair. "Stephen, perhaps you shouldn't have—"

"Haw, haw, haw!" Stanton slapped his knee in mirth, startling them all. "Now, if that isn't a novel idea! Haw! Madam, do you have any idea what old Thaddeus would have to say if you *did* manage to contact him?"

"Well—"

"You haven't given them any money, have you?" he barked.

Portia jumped. "No, I—"

"Well, don't." Stanton pinned first Eldridge, then Stephen with a withering glare. Eldridge flushed; Stephen grinned. The old man shouted, "And if you try any of your bullshit here—"

"Mr. Stanton!" Portia cried in horror.

". . . I'll shoot the goddamn ghost first, and then the man who brought it into my house," Stanton continued. "Is that clear?"

Stephen looked at the old man from under lowered lids. "Some might take that as a challenge, Mr. Stanton."

"Take it any way you like." The old man grinned, taking them aback with another of his mercurial mood changes. "*You* might even manage to get away with something. Liven up the place a bit. Is that why you've got them, Mrs. Danforth? Bored, eh?"

Although Portia tried to look severe, her blue eyes gleamed with laughter. "I'm sure I don't know what you're talking about," she said.

"Sure, you don't." Stanton gave a short bark of laughter. "Where were you going before that train crashed on my doorstep?"

"We planned to spend a week or two at my house in Peekskill," Portia said.

Stanton went to the sideboard and poured himself a whiskey. "Why don't you spend the time here instead?"

"Oh, we couldn't do that!" Portia protested.

"Why not?" Stanton asked.

The widow spread her hands. "Well, I just—"

"Tomorrow or the next day, the rest of my guests will leave here to go on with their mundane lives. An hour after they're gone, I won't even remember their names. But you four," Stanton reluctantly included Eldridge in the group, "are different. I could use a little entertainment. How about it, Mrs. Danforth?"

"Well . . ." Portia nodded in sudden decision. "All right."

Oh, no! Lauren thought. Oh, no! She was trapped. Trapped with Hawkes and her grandfather. The man she loved, and the man she hated—and both equally dangerous.

Chapter Fourteen

Lauren was just drifting off to sleep when she heard a soft noise in the corridor outside her door. It was not repeated, and she closed her eyes again.

Suddenly she became aware of movement nearby, of quiet breathing that was not her own. She sat bolt upright with a gasp. There was a shadowy form standing beside the bed, a deeper, more solid blackness against the darkness of the room. A hint of musky cologne came to her, and her nostrils flared. Stephen. Like his scent, the awareness of his desire drifted to her on the still air. She knew what he'd come for, what he wanted. And if she wanted to keep her heart intact, she couldn't give it to him.

The mattress shifted as his weight came down on it. With a sudden flurry of movement, she hurled the covers aside and leaped out of bed. She heard a muffled curse behind her, as he grappled with the thick comforter for a moment. Then his feet hit the floor, and he began to stalk her through the dark room. Lauren backed away hastily, trying frantically to think of a way out of this mess.

"If you run, I'll come after you," he growled. "Right into the hallway, if necessary."

Anger rose in her, and she welcomed it, using it to

hold her fear at bay. "Why should I run? I'm not afraid of you," she said. But it was a lie; her heart was pounding, her body trembling. Her time had come. Her lover had come to claim her, and she didn't think she had the strength to resist him.

Stephen lit the gaslight, flooding the sumptuous room with golden radiance. He was going to make love to her. After tonight, there would be no doubt as to who was the master in this game. He leaned against the massive, twisted bedpost and watched her, a sardonic smile on his mouth. Truly, she was a consummate actress; her heightened breathing, her trembling lips and apprehensive eyes all belonged to an innocent maiden and not a conniving little schemer.

"What do you want?" she asked breathlessly.

"You."

She took a step backward, shaking her head. Her gaze, unable to meet his, moved lower. He was wearing a white shirt that was partially unbuttoned, revealing a wedge of dark chest hair, and those too-tight trousers, which revealed a great deal more. The long, thick line of his erection was clearly outlined by the fabric, and the sight of it made her breath catch in her throat. Liquid warmth flooded into her lower body, tempting her, weakening her.

"How did you get in here?" she asked, as though words would dispel the sultry atmosphere of desire that permeated the room.

"Did you think a lock would stop me?" He crossed his arms over his chest, his smile widening. "I tasted your passion once, and the memory of it has haunted me ever since. I want to taste it again. Completely. And so do you."

She shook her head, but he knew she was lying, for her eyes—those dark, fathomless eyes in which a man might drown—were slumberous with remembered passion. At this moment he didn't give a damn about her lies, his duty, or the case. He just wanted her.

"I'm going to make love to you," he said. His voice was intimate, throaty with desire.

Those velvet tones went over Lauren like a caress, sending a shiver of mingled desire and dread up her spine. She closed her eyes, seeking the strength to fight him, to fight the treacherous weakness of her own body. "What we did was wrong. Terribly wrong, and it must never happen again. I beg of you, leave me alone!"

"Leave you alone? Ahhh, Lauren, you don't believe I'd ever agree to that." Sly little enchantress, he had to have her. Reality be damned. Tonight, he was going to believe the illusion. Drown in it, in her. Whatever she was yesterday and would be tomorrow, tonight she was his.

He pushed away from the bedpost and walked towards her. Lauren stared at him, mesmerized by the feral grace of his wide-shouldered, slim-hipped body. He was all man, and she wanted him so badly her knees shook. *Let him come,* a sly voice whispered in her mind. *You love him. He's taken your heart already; there's nothing left to lose. But you do!* the rational part of her mind screamed back. *You still have the things that matter the most: your pride and your self-respect! He'll take those, too, if you let him!*

"No!" she cried. "I won't let you do this to me!"

Whirling, she ran from him. He flung himself after her, catching her around the waist with one arm and drawing her back against him with a jerk.

"You don't want to get away from me," he rasped in her ear. He turned so that they were facing the mirror of her dressing table. "And I intend to prove it."

Lauren stood stiffly, refusing to look at her reflection. "Take your hands off me," she said. But her voice lacked conviction, even to her. She was supremely aware of his muscular thighs pressing against her buttocks, his hard arm encircling her waist.

"You don't mean that." The feel of her soft curves rocked him to his toes, and he took a deep breath in an effort to restrain his raging desire. He intended this to be a slow, deliberate seduction, where he was in complete control. After tonight, she would be under no illusions as to their relationship; he wanted her to admit that she needed him, female to male, flesh to flesh. He wanted her to admit it to him, and to herself.

With his free hand, he unbraided her hair, draping it around her shoulders. His fingers delved through the bright, silken mass, combing it, reveling in its fragrant softness. He pressed tiny, nibbling kisses along her temple and the curve of her jaw.

"We stood like this once before," he murmured, his breath teasing her ear. "Remember?"

Yes, she remembered. The night of the party, when he had touched her so possessively, so incredibly gently, that she had wanted more. Just as now she wanted more. She closed her eyes.

"You have a lovely neck," he bent forward to graze the side of her throat with his lips, "and shoulders, cheeks, eyebrows." He kissed each feature as he named it, his long fingers turning her head from side to side so he could reach. "Mmmm, and ears. I especially love your ears." He sucked her earlobe into his mouth, his tongue rasping over it in an incredibly arousing caress.

Lauren gasped, dazed with the feel of him, his scent, his passion. Her whole body was throbbing. If

206

he hadn't been holding her, she would have fallen to the floor at his feet.

His free hand went to the row of tiny buttons at the front of her nightgown. Unfastening them deftly, he slipped his fingers beneath the fabric. He began to trace a light, teasing path in the cleft between her breasts, coming close, but not actually touching the curving flesh. When she shifted, unconsciously seeking greater contact, he grinned. "Do you want me to touch your breasts?" he murmured. "All you have to do is ask."

"I can't. I can't," she said in automatic denial. But her head dropped back against his chest.

"Of course, you can." He opened her nightgown fully, exposing her breasts. "I wanted to do this that other time, before that other mirror," he said hoarsely.

Again he had to exert stern control over himself, lest he take her right now. God, she was beautiful! Her breasts were swollen, her nipples taut, rosy peaks that beckoned him, begging him to touch them, taste them. He managed to resist that sweet lure, although it took every ounce of will he possessed. He reached up to clasp her throat with one hand, pleased beyond measure to find that her pulse was racing as fast as his. "Look at yourself," he said.

She shook her head, keeping her eyes tightly closed.

"Look!" he commanded. His voice was like a lash, forcing her head up and her eyes open.

She saw her own skin, pale against the darker skin of his hand. Her breasts rose and fell with her breathing, the erect and reddened nipples betraying her arousal. She looked at his reflection in the mirror, and the sight of his passion-flushed skin and taut jaw was incredibly stirring. He was controlling himself, but just barely, she realized. The thought that he wanted her so very much sent a powerful surge of heat through her lower body. She ached for him, for his hands, his mouth.

"Do you want me to touch you now?" he asked, his fingertips tracing a teasing path around her breasts. Then he took a lock of her hair and used the end of it to lightly brush her nipples.

Lauren gasped, arching upward. If she didn't feel his hands soon, she was going to go crazy. She had lost control of her own body to him, and it was a sweet torment that only he could ease. Meeting his gaze in the mirror, she said, "Touch me, Stephen."

"Ahhh, love!"

His hands cupped the full weight of her breasts at last, lifting them, caressing them while she watched, spellbound. His thumbs circled her nipples once, twice, and she moaned.

Stephen drew in his breath in a sharp sigh of pleasure. "You're a woman, Lauren. A beautiful, sensual woman. Never, never be afraid to ask me to touch you again."

She trembled. Beautiful, he'd called her. At another time she would have dismissed it as a facile compliment, empty of meaning. But now, watching the way his hands moved over her skin—possessively, lingeringly, almost reverently—she believed him.

He slid the nightgown over her shoulders and down, letting it fall to the floor around her feet. Lauren gazed at her naked self in the mirror and, oddly, felt not the slightest shred of embarrassment. Stephen was pressed tightly against her back now, his hands moving over her breasts, waist, hips, thighs . . . everywhere. He nuzzled his way through the tumbled mass of her hair, to trace the smooth curve of her shoulder with his tongue. As he bit gently at her flushed and sensitive skin, her hands moved restlessly over his narrow hips and the hard-flexed muscles of his thighs.

"God, Lauren!" He spun her around and claimed her mouth with bold aggression. His tongue sought hers, stabbing deeply into her mouth, groaning when she sucked it even deeper.

His hands slid over her shoulders, her ribs, the long, lovely line of her back, then dropped to her buttocks, his fingers closing over the curving flesh with urgent possessiveness. Then, so suddenly that she gasped, he swept her into his arms.

"What are you doing?" she murmured dazedly.

"I'm taking you to bed." He laid her on the coverlet and came down beside her, one hard thigh possessively across her legs.

She stared up at him, trying to gather her scattered wits. But he was so close, his chest heaving with deep, ragged breaths, that all thought fled. There was only him. Almost of its own volition, her hand went out to stroke over the hard muscles of his shoulders and chest. A shudder followed her hand, and she reveled in the knowledge that she affected him as deeply as he did her. She explored him, fascinated by his smooth skin and prickling hair, the ridged tautness of his narrow waist. But she didn't have the courage to move beyond his waistband, where that interesting arrow of hair disappeared.

"Shy?" he asked. Swiftly, he stripped off his shirt and discarded it.

"Afraid," she whispered.

"Of me? I'm just a man, Lauren." He took her hand and placed it on the throbbing shaft of his manhood. "One who wants you very much." That was an understatement! He wanted her more than he'd ever wanted a woman before, more than he'd believed he could ever want a woman.

Lauren caressed him, marveling at the hard, springing strength of him. Boldly now, she unbuttoned his trousers to touch him without the interfering fabric. Her fingers closed over him, stroking, teasing, and as he arched beneath her, gasping as he struggled to maintain control, she reveled in her power over him.

Almost beyond the edge of restraint, Stephen surged up to his knees, taking her by surprise as he snaked his arm about her waist and pulled her against him.

She gazed up at him, passion smoldering in her dark eyes. "I want to touch you," she murmured.

"Later, you can touch me all you like, my fire-haired beauty, but right now I can't take it."

"But—"

He tipped her backward onto the bed, pinning her hands above her head and silencing her with a burning kiss. When she moaned, he slid downward, his tongue making a moist path down her throat and between her breasts. He paused for several pleasurable moments to suckle her nipples, then moved lower to taste her navel and trace the graceful line of her hipbones with his open mouth.

Lauren writhed, tormented by the spiraling tension in her body. She ached. She wanted, she needed . . . When his hands urged her legs apart, she obeyed without thought. Eagerly. Whimpering. Ready.

"Ahh, honey, you're driving me crazy," he muttered thickly. "I'm going to know every inch of you tonight. Over and over and over." He slid farther down her body, his tongue delving through her nest of auburn curls to taste the sweet, tender flesh below.

Lauren's hands clenched in the thick darkness of his hair. Oh, it was too much! Surely she was about to die from the sheer pleasure of his stroking tongue! She arched upward with a gasp, trying to escape, but he merely pressed her back down and continued to torment her.

"Please, oh, please!" she moaned.

Her words were nearly his undoing. He pressed himself into the bed, willing restraint. When he had regained a measure of control, he pushed up on his elbows to look at her. Her lips were parted, her breasts swollen with passion, her hips moving in love's unconscious rhythm. As much as he'd wanted to bring her to the edge—no, over the edge—before allowing himself his own fulfillment, her white-hot need was an irresistible lure.

"Do you want me?" he demanded hoarsely.

"Yes," she gasped. "Yes!"

He slid his trousers off, tossing them carelessly to the floor. Then he knelt between her legs, using his hands to spread her knees even farther apart, exposing her completely to his gaze.

"Tell me you want me," he rasped, caressing her wet, swollen flesh with sure, skilled fingers. "I want to hear the words."

Lauren whimpered, arching against his hand in wild abandon. "I want you, Stephen. Please!"

"God, Lauren!" He slid up her body to claim her mouth once again.

Lauren stiffened as the tip of his manhood touched her untried entrance. He felt huge. How was she ever going to accommodate him? She couldn't possibly, oh, she couldn't . . . Pulling her mouth from his, she panted, "Stephen, I just . . . I can't . . . !"

"It's far too late to stop now, little wanton," he murmured. He claimed her mouth again, silencing her. Trembling with long-restrained need, he poised himself, then plunged into her with a smooth, hard thrust. He heard her cry of pain, felt her virgin's membrane split beneath his assault, and froze in astonishment. He'd thought her innocence an act! And she'd been so bold with her caresses, so seemingly experienced in her responses! God, if he'd known she really *was* a virgin, he'd have been much more gentle.

"I'm sorry," he said, kissing the tears that had gathered at the corners of her eyes. "It will never hurt again after this. Trust me, love." With almost superhuman control, he held himself motionless to give her time to adjust to him.

Lauren slowly relaxed as the burning pain eased. Still he gave her time, kissing her, his hands leaving her hips to caress her breasts, her throat, her waist. Soon the pain disappeared entirely, leaving her instead with a delicious awareness of the hard shaft that was imbedded deep within her flesh.

Feeling her velvet flesh contract around him, Stephen released her mouth to tenderly kiss her closed eyelids. Then, slowly, carefully, he began to move, withdrawing almost completely before plunging into her wet, hot depths again. So tight, so sweet, he thought, my little wanton virgin. Triumph—pure, primitive male possession—coursed through him. No man but him had ever claimed her. And no man ever would.

"You belong to me," he growled.

"Yes," she gasped.

He lifted her hips to slide even deeper into her throbbing flesh. "Say it!"

Her eyes flew open at the spiraling pleasure that caught her body. Even the memory of pain vanished in that wild coiling of desire. "I belong to you," she said.

He laughed, a triumphant, excited sound, and increased the depth and the pace of his strokes. She met him eagerly, thrust for thrust, gasp for gasp, and he groaned with the sheer delight of it. What passion! he thought. What a sensual, beautiful woman she was!

"Wrap your legs around me, honey. Ahh, that's it," he muttered hoarsely when she obeyed. "That's perfect."

The tension in her lower body increased until it was almost unbearable. Lauren moaned and clung, her fingers digging into the long, flexing muscles of his back. He took her higher, and higher yet, until she found herself begging for release.

"Help me!" she gasped. "Please, Stephen. Help me!" The first tiny tremors began, deep in her body, and then a tremendous wave of shuddering, clenching sensation washed over her.

Stephen groaned, burying his face against the fragrant skin of her neck as he drove into her with flashing power. He felt her contract around him in the throes of her climax, pulling him over the edge with her.

Lauren clasped him to herself, feeling his strong body shudder, loving the way he moaned her name as he reached his fulfillment. Then he collapsed upon her, spent, and she welcomed his weight. After a moment, he rolled onto his side, bringing her with him. Pillowing her head on his shoulder, he absently combed the tangles out of her hair with his fingers.

Lauren raised her head to look at him. "Stephen, I—"

"Shhh. Don't say anything," he murmured, pulling

her back down. "After *that,* there isn't anything either of us need to say."

Lauren sighed. If it had been as wonderful for him as it had been for her, perhaps there *wasn't* anything that needed to be said. Surely only two people who loved each other could experience such fulfillment. Perhaps this was what her mother had searched for all this time and never found. With another sigh, Lauren kissed the firm flesh of his shoulder, then closed her eyes.

Stephen felt her relax against him and realized that she'd fallen asleep. He was satiated, totally drained — at least for the moment. She'd been a virgin. A virgin, and she had given herself with such passion! Never before had he experienced anything or anyone to compare with her.

But, he reminded himself regretfully, this is the woman who has spent two years ingratiating herself into a gullible old woman's house and heart. It wasn't Lauren's grasping for money that galled him the most. It was the fact that she was willing to break Portia's gentle heart to get it.

"Damn!" he hissed between clenched teeth. He laid Lauren down beside him, propping himself on one elbow so he could study her. Beautiful, responsive, everything he'd ever hoped to find in a woman — and it was all a lie! He scowled, a slow-burning anger rising like a scourge in his soul, for even now he wasn't able to purge himself of his love for her.

Despite his anger, he felt a renewed stirring of desire for her. His hand stroked slowly over her slim, straight back, her curving hips, then moved up to cover one pink-tipped breast. He drew his breath in sharply as he felt her nipple harden against his palm. Even asleep, she responded to him. She looked vulnerable and completely desirable, with her lashes lying in sweeping curves against her cheek, and her hair spread out around her in a froth of tumbled curls. He traced the delicate curve of her cheekbone with his fingertip, and she murmured his name sleepily.

With a muttered curse, he got up. In another minute he'd be making love to her again. He had to get out of here now, before he lost what little sense he had left. Damn it, he'd known better than to get involved with her! But she had wrapped him up with her beauty, her intriguing, hidden fire, and air of innocence, and every time he touched her it only tightened the bonds around his heart.

Well, my clever little Siren, he thought, two can play that game. Now we'll play by *my* rules for a while. I'm going to wrap you up as thoroughly as you've wrapped me. Let's see if you can take it as well as you can give it to others. Pulling on his clothes hastily, he turned off the light and tiptoed out of the room.

Chapter Fifteen

Lauren paused before the closed door of the dining room, listening to the drone of conversation within. What was she going to do if Stephen was there? After last night, what was she supposed to say to him? How was she supposed to act?

"Well, go on in," a low, gruff voice said from behind her. "Or are you trying to avoid someone? Stephen Hawkes, perhaps?"

Caldwell Stanton's voice. She stiffened, her chin going up in automatic defiance, then turned to face him. "I am not trying to avoid Stephen Hawkes — or anyone else, Mr. Stanton."

He grinned evilly. "Of course not." His smile faded suddenly, and he rubbed his chin with one hand. "He bothers me, too."

"Why?" she asked in surprise.

"This spiritualist nonsense of his. I had him pegged as a different kind of man entirely."

"Oh?" She cocked her head to one side and regarded him curiously. "What kind?"

"The kind who has better things to do than spend his time snookering old women. He's got a bigger game going, in my judgement."

"Oh, really?" No matter what she might think

about Stephen's actions, her every instinct rose up in his defense. How dare this old . . . devil accuse him? "Did it occur to you that your judgment might just be wrong?"

He grunted. "Never been wrong before."

"Never?" she asked, her voice seething with sarcasm. What about Alanna? she added silently.

His sharp gaze pinned her. "I said I'd never been wrong. I didn't say I never had regrets."

Lauren was startled by his admission. Could it be possible that he was actually sorry for what he'd done to his daughter? For a moment, she almost relented. But the memory of what this man's cold self-righteousness had cost her mother soon hardened her heart again, and she frowned at him.

He chuckled. Taking her arm, he opened the door and escorted her into the dining room. Lauren smiled at Portia and nodded coldly to Eldridge, who was seated beside the widow. Then she saw Stephen, and the rest of the occupants of the long, gleaming table faded into a blur as her gaze fastened upon the man to whom she had given herself the night before.

His smile was welcoming, his gaze as caressing as his hands had been. Her pulse hammered in her ears as she read the promise in the smoky depths of his eyes. Dear God, she wanted him—wanted him more than ever. Was it as obvious to him as his desire was to her?

Stanton drew her forward, seating her in the vacant chair next to Stephen's, then moved to his own place at the head of the table. A servant rushed to offer her a selection of hot, fragrant food. Overly conscious of Stephen's gaze upon her, she chose randomly among the proffered dishes.

Stephen studied her, shaken by the effect her sudden appearance had had on him. Lovely, lovely, as pure-seeming and as serene as always. His mind brought up the memory of how she had looked last night, her hair tumbled around her in a bright cascade as she wantonly returned his passion. He'd hoped that bedding her would have cooled his desire for her, but it had only sharpened his need to a fever pitch. Waking up alone in his own room this morning, he'd sorely regretted his hasty action in leaving her.

"Good morning, Miss Wakefield," he said. "Did you sleep well?"

She glanced at him, then away. "Yes."

He dropped his napkin on the floor between them. As he bent to retrieve it, he whispered, "Lauren, my love."

She trembled. Love, he'd said. His love. Almost, she leaned towards him. But, recalling where she was, she controlled herself. Afraid that her feelings were written on her face for all to see, she dropped her gaze to her plate.

The butler came into the room and whispered something in Stanton's ear. The old man nodded, then turned to his guests. "The telegraph line has been repaired. A message was sent to the railroad, which is dispatching a train to take all of you back to New York."

A babble arose, to be instantly squelched by Stanton's up-raised hand. He continued, "Centerville has no station, you understand, so the train

218

will wait for you at the point where the tracks are nearest the town. I'll have my servants drive you there."

"What about our luggage?" a woman cried. "I fully expect to be reimbursed—"

"Take it up with the railroad, madam. Do I look like a goddamned ticket-puncher?" Stanton growled, his crest of hair nodding aggressively.

There was a moment of shocked silence, then Portia cleared her throat. "Well, ah, this certainly is a wonderful breakfast, isn't it?"

"Yes," the woman who had complained about her luggage said. Her face was set in stony disapproval as she rose from her seat. Without another word, she stalked from the room. The rest of the guests followed, all but Lauren, Stephen, Portia, and Eldridge.

"What did I tell you?" Stanton said when they were gone. "Cattle! One moos, and the rest fall into line."

Lauren looked down her nose at him. "Some of us moo, and some bray," she said, her voice as sweet as honey. "Who is to say which is better?"

Stephen nearly fell into his plate in astonishment. Then he threw back his head and laughed. God, she was something! Calling the old bastard a jackass to his face, and with that dulcet tone of voice that made her words seem even more sarcastic by comparison. No wonder Stanton enjoyed her company! Two of a kind, she and the old man. Both possessed the same quick, ruthless humor, and although Lauren's was the rapier to Stanton's broadsword, both were equally lethal.

Outraged, Stanton glared at Stephen. "You think that's funny, Hawkes?" he barked.

"Yes," Stephen gasped.

Before another word could be spoken, Portia said, "I think we should send cables to our friends in New York as soon as possible. Jane will be terribly worried."

"I'll go," Lauren offered.

"Do you want a carriage or a horse?" Stanton asked. He smiled at her in another of his abrupt changes of mood.

"A horse, please!" Lauren said eagerly. How wonderful it would be to ride again! Since Portia didn't keep a stable, she hadn't ridden since she'd left England.

Stanton nodded, stabbing a forkful of ham into his mouth. "I'll get one of my grooms to escort you."

"I'd like to borrow a horse, too, if you don't mind," Stephen said. "I've got a few telegrams of my own to send."

Stanton gave a short bark of laughter. "To whom? Your pet ghosts?"

"Perhaps." Stephen grinned, completely unfazed by the comment. "What about you, Mr. Eldridge? Do you have anyone you'd like to contact?"

"Besides Thaddeus Danforth, that is?" Stanton asked. He slapped his hand down on the table and roared with laughter.

Portia patted her lips daintily with her napkin. "Really, Mr. Stanton! I do wish you'd treat the matter with more respect. Mr. Eldridge and Mr. Hawkes are trying their very best to help me."

Stanton snorted. After shooting a glare at the two younger men from under his brows, he pushed his chair back and rose to his feet. "Come, Miss Wakefield. I'll escort you upstairs. We'll see if we can find a riding habit for you to wear."

"Why, thank you, sir," she said, rising to her feet.

He tucked her hand into the crook of his arm and turned her towards the door. When they were gone, Portia sighed and said, "Poor Mr. Stanton. I do believe he's as lonely as I ever was."

And just as vulnerable to Miss Wakefield's gentle manipulations, Stephen reflected.

Lauren glared over her shoulder at Stephen, who was in the process of reading the message she was writing to Jane Talmadge. He had read the one she had sent to Richard, too. "Do you mind?" she asked. Conscious of the nearby telegraph operator, she lowered her voice to a whisper. "I gave *you* privacy for your messages, and I'm certain you have a great deal more to hide than I do."

"One can never be certain when it comes to secrets," he replied. Reaching around her, he picked up the papers and handed them to the operator. He grasped her elbow and urged her outside to the boardwalk that bordered Centerville's cobblestone main street.

"What has got you so upset?" she asked.

"You didn't break with Farleigh." he growled. "Why not?"

She averted her face. Despite his demand, he

hadn't offered to take Richard's place. But then, she hadn't expected it. She loved Stephen Hawkes—charlatan, thief, rake, whatever. Once she had admitted that to herself, she had committed herself to taking what he was willing to give. Her head lifted proudly. So, she had given herself to the man she loved. That didn't mean that she had to throw aside her dignity as well.

"I asked you a question." His grip on her elbow tightened. "You'd better not even think about playing games with me. I'm not about to share you with another man."

"I am not playing games." Lauren met his anger-darkened gaze levelly. "I fully intend to break with Richard; how could I not, considering the circumstances? But I intend to tell him to his face, not in a telegram. *Anyone* deserves better than that."

Stephen raked his free hand through his hair. That answer was completely consistent with the woman she professed to be. Damn, but he was confused! She seemed so plausible, so brave, so honorable. Could anyone be that good an actress? But her innocence hadn't been an act; he'd had incontrovertible proof of that. But, his cynical policeman's mind whispered, she wouldn't be the first woman to trade her virginity for something even more valuable. In this case, confounding a competitor who was coming much too close. And it had worked, he thought bitterly. Oh, yes, it had worked.

They reached the spot where the groom was waiting with their horses. After lifting her into her sidesaddle, Stephen mounted his own animal. In a

222

few minutes, the three of them had passed out of town and into the forest beyond, sere and brown in its winter dormancy.

Lauren rode a little ahead of the two men, reveling in the beauty and serenity of her surroundings. She loved the dry leaves crunching beneath her horse's hooves, loved the crisply biting air and the brooding trees, bare now, that would magically bring forth new life in a few short months.

"It's lovely here, isn't it?" she asked, glancing over her shoulder at Stephen.

"Yes, it is." He wasn't looking at his surroundings, however, but at her. Her dark eyes were shining with excited wonder, and her bright, curling hair was beginning to escape the confines of her chignon. Her deep green velvet habit and plaid woolen cloak lent an air of verdancy to the winter landscape. Sprite, he mused. A graceful tree nymph, come home to the woods at last. Or was she some fell Siren, who would lure him to his doom in the secret heart of the forest? Perhaps, he thought. Perhaps. But even knowing so, he would follow her. It would be worth any risk just to taste her lips again.

"Sir," the groom called from behind him, breaking into his reverie.

Stephen glanced over his shoulder. Seeing that the groom had dismounted and was examining his horse's right front hoof, he turned his own mount back. "What's the matter, Yancy?"

"She's picked up a stone, sir. I'll have to lead her."

Stephen pulled his left foot out of the stirrup

223

and held out his hand. "Here. We'll ride double."

"Very kind of you, sir, but Curran," the man thrust his thumb at the handsome chestnut stallion Stephen rode, "won't allow it. You go on ahead."

"Very well. We'll send someone back for you." Stephen wheeled his mount and went to join Lauren, guiltily pleased that things had worked out so well for him.

"What happened?" she asked.

"His horse picked up a stone. He'll be coming along on foot."

She looked at the groom, her brow furrowing in concern. "But couldn't we try to take him on one of our mounts?"

"He says not." Stephen urged his horse forward. "Come on, Lauren. He'll be perfectly fine, and we'll send someone back for him as soon as we return to the house."

She followed him, looking over her shoulder from time to time. "Are you sure he'll be all right?"

"Completely." He ducked under a low-hanging branch. "Watch your head."

They passed single file around a long, sweeping curve of the trail and came to the edge of the woods. Stephen's stallion tossed his proud head and pranced out into the grassy meadow beyond. Firmly, Stephen reined him in, half turning him to watch Lauren emerge from the woods. She took his breath away. Her skin looked like cool alabaster, white and perfect, and her hair caught the sunlight like a new-minted coin, reflecting a warm molten glow.

Drawn to his smouldering gaze like a moth to a flame, Lauren urged her mare beside the stallion. Would she always come to Stephen, beckoned irresistibly by his desire? she wondered. Was love like this for others—this sometimes wonderful, sometimes terrible force that had the power to sweep all reservations, all logic aside?

"Alone at last," he murmured.

"Did you have anything to do with that horse picking up a stone?" she asked, half in jest, half in exasperation. She wouldn't put it past the rogue.

"My sweet, if I could have arranged such a thing, believe me, I would have done it long before now." He moved his horse closer. "I can't stop thinking about last night."

Lauren felt the heat rise into her face. She couldn't stop thinking about it, either. Their lovemaking had been so beautiful, such a deep sharing of everything she felt for him, that she had not the slightest shred of remorse for giving herself to him. But she couldn't quite bring herself to adopt his openness about it.

"You're not embarrassed, are you?" he teased. "Not with *me!*"

Lauren only blushed hotter, turning her face from him to hide it. "Please, Stephen!"

"I can't help it," he said. "You act so prim and ladylike in the daylight, and I'm just trying to reconcile this Lauren with the wanton from last night." He put one finger beneath her chin and forced her to look at him. "You should learn to play a bit, love. Life doesn't have to be serious all the time."

"I'm a serious sort of person," she said. Besides, she thought, love *should* be a serious thing.

"Then I'll have to teach you how to relax." He let his fingertips brush her knee. "Wouldn't you like to get down for a while?"

"Here?" She glanced around in confusion. "Why?"

He moved his hand upward along her thigh, thoroughly enjoying the delicious tactile combination of velvet and the firm flesh beneath. "It's been a long, tiring ride. We could rest."

"Don't be ridiculous," she protested. But a shiver went through her, for even through her clothing she felt the simmering desire in his touch. It kindled her own desire, bringing a sweet, heated rush through her body. Such power he had over her!

Stephen saw her response in the unconscious parting of her lips, and rejoiced in it. "Let's get down."

She closed her eyes, trying to ignore the urgings of her body. "We can't, Stephen. The groom —"

Stephen nearly groaned in frustration. He'd been so wrapped up in Lauren he'd forgotten the man who was only a few minutes behind them. Damn it to hell! "If he weren't coming," he asked, his voice low and hoarse with desire, "would you do it?"

Lauren looked down at the mare's coarse black mane, not wanting him to see how very close she was to climbing down from her saddle even now. Yes, she would! When he looked at her with those smoky eyes that fairly blazed with desire, she could deny him nothing. Here in the woods, in a bed, anywhere! Cool, composed Lauren Wakefield, who never let anyone stir her emotions, would make love with him in the mud if he wanted. But I can't say it. I just can't!

"Would you?" he asked again. He didn't know why he was insisting on an answer, but he wanted one nearly as badly as he wanted her.

She intended to say no. She opened her mouth to say no. But what she did say was, "Yes." It was a whisper, almost inaudible, but it was her admission of his power over her. "Yes," she said again, louder. "I would."

He drew in a ragged breath, trembling from the force of the emotions she roused in him. Not only physical desire—if only it were that simple! But he was filled with a wild mixture of anger and raging need and a man's will to possess his woman utterly, mingled inextricably with the sinking feeling that he was riding another runaway train to disaster—with no way to stop. For a man who had always held iron control over his emotions, it was a damned uncomfortable revelation. It hurt, and made him angry, and anger made him want to hurt her in return.

"You're a hot little piece, aren't you?" he growled. "I don't think you'd give a damn if the whole world were watching."

Lauren gasped in shock and outrage. How dare he say such a thing to her! How dare he treat her like some . . . whore! Without thinking, she slashed her riding crop across his arm as hard as she could. Cursing, he let go of her, and she urged her mount into a gallop. The mare tore across the

227

meadow, her churning hooves throwing up clods of dirt in her wake.

Lauren leaned forward, hoping the wind would scour the hurt from her. Faintly, she heard the drumming of the stallion's hoofbeats, and knew Stephen was coming after her. She had to get away! If he touched her again — if she let him — she'd lose the little self-respect she had left. Is this what he wanted, to strip her of everything she held precious?

"Come on, girl!" she cried to the mare. "Fly! Fly!"

They plunged up the slope of the next hill. Reaching the crest, they hurtled towards the light-flecked blue ribbon of the stream below.

"Lauren, stop!" Stephen shouted from behind her. "You'll never make it!"

Hearing the stallion's hoofbeats, closer now, she urged her mare to greater speed, straight towards the water.

Chapter Sixteen

Stephen reached the top of the hill a few lengths behind Lauren, and terror clutched his throat when he saw her head the mare towards the stream. She was going to break her neck trying a jump like that! He was going to lose her now, this instant, and he couldn't bear it.

"Lauren, don't!" he roared. He kicked his heels into the stallion's flanks, but he knew with gut-wrenching certainty that he'd never catch her in time.

Time seemed to stand still as he watched the mare reach the bank of the stream. He saw the horse's hindquarters bunch, then relax as she sprang forward. Lauren's plaid cloak fluttered straight out behind her, as the mare soared in a graceful arc over the water. And then, to his astonishment and utter relief, the pair landed safely on the other side. Without a backward glance, Lauren urged her mount back into a gallop and hurtled up the slope of the hill beyond.

Stephen felt the stallion's muscles flex as they neared the stream. Then, with a smooth, powerful surge, they were over, and the big horse's long-reaching stride made steady gains on the mare's lead. Watching Lauren expertly squeeze the most out of her horse's abilities, Stephen knew he wouldn't have a prayer of a chance of catching her, if he weren't riding the stronger animal.

He couldn't wait to get his hands on her, although he wasn't sure if he was going to kiss her, or turn her over his knee for scaring him half out of his wits! Slowly, he regained control of his churning emotions.

Soon the mare and her rider were only a length ahead of him, then half a length, then so close that he could touch the animal's heaving flanks. "Lauren, stop!" he shouted.

She ignored him. He urged the stallion to a further burst of speed and came up beside her. Leaning precariously over to the side, he grabbed the mare's bridle and held on as the two horses slowed to a canter, then a walk. When they had stopped completely, he plucked Lauren out of her saddle and placed her sideways across his thighs.

"Don't hit me again," he warned, wrenching the riding crop from her hand and tossing it away.

"Just leave me alone!" She turned her face from him, unwilling to let him see her cry.

He grasped her chin and forced her to look at him. "Are you mad, to take such a chance? You might've killed yourself!"

"What do you care?" she cried passionately, all her pent-up emotion coming out in a flood. "I gave you the only things I could truly call my own—my innocence and my heart. I came to you in love. How dare you treat it as a lewd joke!"

He grew very still, his blood pounding in his veins. The last thing he'd expected to hear from her was a declaration of love. It was surprising and disturbing, and incredibly welcome. Had he pierced her armor at last? Had he finally reached the real Lauren, or was it merely a new move in her game? God, he wanted to believe her!

"What do you mean?" he asked softly.

" 'You're a hot little piece, aren't you?' " she hissed, mimicking his tone perfectly. Her fist beat at his chest. "If you think you're going to treat me like some common—"

He put his hand over her mouth, silencing her. "Not that. What you said before. About coming to me in love."

She tried to turn her face away, but he wouldn't let her. His gaze held hers, and the need in his eyes was so compelling that she trembled. She hadn't meant to tell him she loved him. It had been a slip, wrung from her by the hurt she had suffered at his hands.

"Tell me," he whispered, lowering his hand from her mouth.

She couldn't help herself. "I love you," she said. More than pride, more than shame, more than anything.

He kissed her then, his mouth slanting over hers with a gentleness that brought fresh tears to her eyes. He kissed the crystal drops from her cheeks, the pulse in her throat, and the windblown hair just above her ears. "Say it again," he murmured against her temple.

"I love you, Stephen." It was easier to say the

second time. And still easier the third. "I love you."

The words were sweet triumph to him. "You love me," he repeated, kissing the curve of her jaw. "How could I know?"

She put her hands against his chest and held him away. "How could you not?"

"You've never come to *me*. I've had to tease and tempt and cajole, just to get near you. Even last night, when you 'came to me in love,' I had to chase you down and convince you to let me touch you."

She looked searchingly into his eyes, as though to plumb the gray depths for some clue to the thoughts below. "What are you saying?"

"If you love me," his thumb caressed the delicious curve of her full bottom lip, "you won't be afraid to show me that you want me as much as I want you."

"I don't understand," she said. But she did, and it made her tremble. He *did* want everything from her. Everything. And she would give it.

"I don't intend to chase you any longer, Lauren. Either we're equal partners in this relationship, or you need to rethink what you expect from love." With an easy motion, he lifted her and set her back in her own saddle. "Do you want me to come to your room tonight?"

"Yes," she whispered. "I want you to come to my room tonight."

"And will you make love to me when I do?"

Lauren closed her eyes for a moment, then opened them and met his gaze steadily. There was

232

no shame in her, just a need to hold him again. A need to have him again. "Yes, I'll make love to you."

"Then, lover, I'll come to you." He took her hand and drew it to his lips, then pressed his open mouth against the wildly throbbing pulse in her wrist. "I'll always come to you."

Lauren took a deep, shuddering breath. God help her, her body was even now reacting to the promise in his deep voice. Yes, he wanted everything from her. Yes, she ran the risk of becoming pregnant, just as her mother had. But Stephen had just given himself to her in a way she'd never expected. He was hers. He would always be hers, and in the deepest recesses of her heart there was the absolute certainty that he would always take care of her. Tonight she would show him just how much she loved him. The thought was incredibly moving, and a liquid rush of warm desire settled between her legs. She pressed her thighs together—not to deny it, but to savor it.

Reluctantly, Stephen released her hand. The sultry passion on her face was oh, so tempting! He burned to make love to her now, this instant. But he wanted even more to see if she truly intended to keep her promise. She was so hot, so incredibly sensuous, even when she was trying to resist him, that he was powerfully stirred by the prospect of what she'd be like when she took the initiative.

"Let's go," he said. "We've got to send someone back for the groom." Before she could urge her horse forward, however, he grasped her reins once again. "It's going to be a long, long day, love. I can't wait to touch you again."

Lauren lowered her gaze, unable to face his directness. He was allowing her no coyness, no hiding beneath conventional speech, and she wasn't sure how to respond. Did all lovers speak so bluntly to one another? Certainly her mother had never spoken so in her daughter's presence. "I . . . ah . . . I suppose we ought to go," she said, flustered.

Stephen grinned at the scarlet blush that spread over her face and throat. Did it indicate a few second thoughts in that pretty little head of hers? He couldn't wait to find out.

Lauren paced back and forth in her room, her nervousness increasing as the house slowly became quiet. Over and over, she had planned how she'd greet Stephen, but now, when the moment was nearly upon her, she was losing her courage. Hearing footsteps in the hall outside, she froze, clutching the collar of her dressing gown tightly around her throat. But the steps moved away, and she began pacing again.

"Oh, I'm no good at this," she muttered. "Perhaps I could just smile in a *very* friendly manner?"

No, that wouldn't do. Not for him and not for her. More than anything, she wanted to move Stephen irresistibly. She wanted to make him lose control, to want her so badly he couldn't think of anything but loving her. Her back straightened in determination. She would be the bold seductress, something that would have been unthinkable for her even two days ago.

There was a soft noise at the door. With a gasp, she threw her robe aside and, naked but for stockings and garters, rushed to lie down on the chaise. Sternly, she restrained the urge to cover herself. She had played this scene over and over in her mind, but she hadn't envisioned this horrible moment of embarrassment. What if he didn't find her alluring? Oh, God, what if he *laughed?*

She heard the door open at last, heard his soft footsteps as he came into the room. She couldn't look at him, she just couldn't! And it was far too late to change her mind. With a silent prayer, she closed her eyes and waited for him to find her.

"Lauren?" Stephen whispered, closing the door behind him and locking it again. The bed was empty, the room dark but for the coals of a dying fire that smouldered redly in the fireplace. Disappointment stabbed through him.

He moved farther into the room, then stopped in astonishment as he spied Lauren at last. She reclined against a nest of pillows on the chaise near the fire, naked but for garters and sheer white stockings, her hair spread out over the pillows in a glorious riot of auburn curls. In the ruddy firelight, her skin gleamed like mother-of-pearl against the dark burgundy velvet upholstery beneath her. The simple, astonishing fact of her audacity rocked him to his toes.

Then he saw her hands twitch slightly, and Stephen realized that she was trying very hard to keep from covering herself. He realized, too, the extent of the sacrifice she was making. Beautiful, daring woman, he thought, going so far out of

235

character to prove how much she cared for him. No woman had ever offered him so much, given herself so generously or with such innocent sensuality. Drawn like a moth to a flame, he walked towards her.

Helpless to stop herself, Lauren raised her head and looked at him. Suddenly, all her shyness fell away, burned away by the leaping flare of desire in his eyes. He was on fire for her, powerfully and immediately, and yet there was such tenderness on his face that she caught her breath in a little sob of happiness. *This* was what she had imagined. *This* was what she had put a lifetime of reserve aside to see.

Her breathing quickened. He was shirtless, barefoot, his broad, furred chest and wide shoulders, muscled arms and lean, flat belly making him look primitive, as untamed as any fierce jungle predator. He stopped beside the chaise, looking down at her, and she met his smouldering gaze boldly. This was her love, her lover, the man she had chosen.

"Is this what you wanted?" she asked softly.

"Yes," he growled. Bracing his hands on either side of her, he leaned down and kissed her with savage intensity. "Yes, and yes, and yes!"

She wound her arms behind his neck and tried to pull him down, but he gently disengaged himself. "No, I want to look at you," he said hoarsely.

She smiled, pleased at the note of tightly leashed passion in his voice, and folded her hands behind her head. She felt reckless, utterly abandoned. "Is that all?"

"Oh, no," he murmured. "But it's a start." His

gaze moved over her leisurely, taking in her upstanding breasts, lifted even higher by her position, and the hard-peaked nipples that crowned them. In a moment I'll taste them, he promised himself. Soon. But for now he held back, wanting to feast his eyes upon the bounty spread out before him before allowing himself to touch her.

"This is a most unexpected treat," he said, running his fingers lightly down the length of her silk-clad legs.

"Why unexpected?" She repressed a gasp as he began to play with her toes.

"I never thought you'd be so bold." He caressed the slim curve of her ankle, then moved to stroke her calves.

"Neither did I," she confessed.

"You locked the door."

"Considering my dishabille, wouldn't it have been a bit embarrassing if Portia had decided to pay a call before retiring?" She smiled. "Besides, when did a lock ever stop you?"

"Lover, iron bars wouldn't keep me from you." His hands moved upward to stroke her hips and waist. Then he ran his palms along her ribs, brushing the curving sides of her breasts. Although he ached to caress her more fully, he held back.

How long is he going to tease me like this? she wondered, wishing he would touch her more intimately. And then she knew. He was waiting for her to take the lead. Very well, if that was what she had to do . . . With a smooth, supple movement, she rose to her knees and pressed herself against his chest. "I see that I'm forgetting my agreement to initiate our lovemaking tonight."

He drew in a sharp breath. "Did you have more in mind than this delightfully bold greeting?"

"Is it enough to satisfy the terms of our agreement?" she asked coyly.

"Perhaps." He laughed softly, delighted by her playfulness. This, too, was her gift to him.

"Let me know when you decide." She started to pull away, but he grasped her waist, pinning her against him.

"If you have a plan," he murmured, his lips poised a scant inch above hers, "I'd be willing to listen."

"I'd rather show you than tell you," she whispered.

"Show me, then."

Feeling incredibly bold and free, recklessly uninhibited, Lauren moved upward to close the small distance that separated their lips. His mouth opened in invitation, and her tongue made darting little passes inside, reveling in his heat, teasing him, tempting him to take control.

With a groan, he crushed her against him and kissed her hard, his tongue stabbing deep into the honeyed sweetness of her mouth. Restlessly, his hands stroked down her back and over the curve of her buttocks, then back up again. She arched like a cat into his caress, eliciting another groan from deep in his chest.

"You're the most tempting, sensuous woman I've ever known," he muttered, his hands tangling in her hair to pull her head back. He took her mouth, fiercely, drowning himself in her taste, her scent, the feel of her skin.

Lauren ran her hands over the flexing strength of his arms and back, the hard swell of muscles in his chest. Frantic to get to his skin, she unbuttoned his trousers and pushed them down over his hips. Tearing her mouth from his, she leaned back to admire the magnificent male strength of him. "You're as perfect as a man could be," she said breathlessly.

He stepped out of his trousers. Kicking them aside carelessly, he pulled her close again, rubbing her taut nipples against the crisp hair of his chest.

"Oh!" she gasped, a shaft of heat stabbing through her body. She was exquisitely aroused by his action, her nipples throbbing, the flesh between her legs swollen and wet. In sweet retaliation, she rubbed her silk-clad leg against his erect manhood, then straddled him, capturing him between her thighs.

He grasped her upper arms and held her away from him, fighting for control. "If you do that, I won't be able to hold back," he rasped.

"I don't care," she said, yearning towards him.

He shook his head. "Tonight I'm going to make slow, easy love to you, and when it's over, I'm going to do it all over again." Gently, possessively, he stroked the silken tumble of her hair. "Lie down, honey. Let me look at you again."

She obeyed, stretching out against the pillows, but she was afire for him. God, if he didn't touch her soon, she was going to go crazy. Hoping to push him over the edge, she put her hands behind her head. She knew what the position did for her breasts, and knew he liked it.

He liked it. She was more luscious than anything he could ever have imagined in his wildest dreams, every creamy, silken inch of her. Sumptuous, hot, beautiful. He was firmly in control now; all his attention was focused on her.

His lips curved upward in a smile as he sat beside her. "No, don't," he admonished when she reached for him. "Put your hands back where they were."

Reluctantly, she put her hands behind her head again, looking up at him as though the very intentness of her gaze would bring him to her. When he leaned down to kiss her at last, she moaned against his lips in relief. His slightly calloused palms closed over her breasts, welcome, exciting warmth, and she arched into his hands. Nothing had ever felt so good, so welcome! And greedy as she was, she wanted more. She moaned a plea into the hot depths of his mouth.

"God, Lauren," he muttered hoarsely, moving down to nibble her chin, then her throat, then the graceful line of her collarbone.

She held her breath in anticipation as he moved downward again. But he wasn't through tormenting her, she soon discovered, for he bypassed her aching nipples to taste the sensitive skin of her ribs. She gave up obedience and wound her fingers into his thick, silver-shot hair, directing him to her breasts. Still he resisted. As he teased the curving underside of her breasts with his teeth and tongue, Lauren thought she'd go mad with frustration. Her fingers clenched tightly in his hair, moving his mouth towards her nipple. "There," she murmured.

"I need you there."

His mouth closed over her, sucking, tugging gently, his tongue coming forward to rasp over the rosy peak again and again. Heat, wonderful, searing heat went through her, beginning at her breasts, coiling through her body until it settled at last in the core of her. He moved to the other breast, and her legs moved restlessly on the chaise.

When she whimpered, he raised his head and looked down at her. "Is that what you wanted?"

"Yes," she breathed. She was floating, dazed with passion.

"There's more. Much more." He slid her garters down and off, then tossed them over his shoulder.

Lauren gasped as he rolled her stockings down her legs, kissing each every inch of skin as he exposed it. He leaned one knee on the edge of the chaise and looked down at her, raging, naked need in his eyes, then bent to her again. Beginning at her toes, his tongue and hands caressed their way up her legs. When his fingertips touched the tender places behind her knees, Lauren writhed in pleasure, a soft moan escaping her.

He paused in his exploration to look up at her. "Is that sensitive?" he asked.

"Yes," she breathed, her eyes half-closed.

"There are other spots even more so," he said. "Tonight, I'm going to find every one of them."

His caresses continued, always moving upward. Lauren trembled as he reached her thighs. Her whole body was afire with sensation, with need. When his palms urged her legs apart, she obeyed mindlessly. And then he reached the core of her.

241

As his tongue flicked out to taste her woman's flesh, she arched her hips to meet him. Slowly, surely, with devastating finesse, he drove her to the edge of ecstasy.

"Please, Stephen, I want you," she moaned. "Come to me!"

"Soon, soon," he soothed, smiling tenderly at her.

And then he slid two long fingers into her quivering depths, pushing her over the edge in one beautiful, frantic moment. Wave after wave of rippling pleasure caught her, and she cried his name as she gave herself up to it.

When she could breathe again, she opened her eyes to see him leaning over her, smiling. There was sheer male triumph in his eyes, as well as a raging bonfire of long-restrained passion. Oh, she loved him! Always, he thought of *her* fulfillment before his own. Always, he put her first. She said a silent prayer of gratitude for his tenderness and his strength.

"I want to touch you," she said, daring him to tell her no.

His eyebrows went up. "Where?"

"Everywhere." She sat up, then pulled at his arm. "Lie down, Stephen."

He gauged the width of the chaise, then shook his head. The thick Persian rug would cushion them as well as any furniture, he thought, and provided much more room for them to play.

"I'm at your disposal, my love," he said, sitting on the rug before the fire and patting the spot beside him.

"I know." She rose from the chaise and came towards him, stopping to stand over him, her arms akimbo.

Stephen took a long, leisurely look at her, beginning at her toes and moving upward. Her legs were slightly parted, giving him a most enticing view of the paradise between, and her breasts were swollen, her nipples still hard. Her skin was flushed, and not from the firelight. *He* had put that rosy glow on her body. And with that marvelous auburn hair falling in wild curls around her shoulders, she seemed to be a creature of flame. Flame and passion.

She knelt beside him, then put her hands to his chest and pushed him backward. "It's my turn now," she said.

"Your turn," he agreed hoarsely. When she bent to lick his flat, male nipples, he arched upward with a groan. Easy, he told himself. Think of your job, think of the weather, think of anything but the pleasure this beautiful woman is giving you. Great drops of sweat broke out on his forehead.

Lauren smiled, feeling gloriously in control. Her hands moved over him, reveling in the contrasts of silky hair and hard-ridged muscle. She put both her palms flat on his taut belly, just above his erection, and felt him draw in a long breath of anticipation. "Do you want me to?" she asked.

His eyes were slitted nearly closed. "Please."

She grasped his throbbing manhood. Gently but firmly she stroked it, bringing a groan to his lips. This is true power, she thought, a woman's power over a man. Then his hand came to caress the swollen flesh between her legs, instantly bringing her to a state of eager readiness, and she knew he had equal power over her.

"God, Lauren!" Stephen gasped, arching in almost unbearable pleasure. "I've got to have you now, this instant, or I'm going to die!"

"Take me, then," she said, falling forward to kiss his chest, his neck, his lips.

His big hands closed on her waist, lifting her so that she straddled him. He held her there for a long, breathless moment, then lowered her onto his manhood. He filled her totally, wonderfully, and she sighed with delight. Lost in the wonder of it, she spread her hands out over his chest and began to move. She watched the play of emotions upon his lean, handsome face, and reveled in her effect on him. If she belonged to him, so did he belong to her!

Stephen groaned. God, the utter delight of being in her! He lifted his hips to meet her, easing himself even further into her tight, hot depths. She was perfect, perfect, riding him with an instinctive sense of what rhythm he liked best. But he had to take control now, or this was going to be over much too soon. He wanted it to be good for her. Tonight was hers.

With a surge of coiled muscles, he heaved upward to a sitting position, lifting her off him as he did. She cried out in surprised protest. "Shhh," he murmured, turning and placing her on her back, then coming down on top of her, his lean hips nestled between her widespread legs. Before she could react to this new position, he slid into her. Fully, aggressively, staking his claim irrevocably. His toes digging into the rug for purchase, he began to thrust into her, driving deep.

Lauren gasped, both surprised and excited by his loving invasion. She wrapped her legs around his hips, moaning when that allowed her to take even more of him. And then the ripples of another climax began, then swelled into a tremendous, shuddering tide of sensation. She surged up against him, crying out, her nails digging into the hard, thrusting muscles of his back.

Stephen lost the few, ragged remnants of control that still remained. Lunging against her again and again, he poured himself into her depths. "Lauren," he groaned. "Lauren."

As he collapsed upon her, spent, he realized that the game had turned against him. She'd wound him up even more tightly than before—not with lies, not with clever distractions, but with this generous giving of her love. No matter what happened, he'd carry her in his heart forever.

Chapter Seventeen

"Lauren," a deep, beguiling voice whispered. "Wake up, love."

Lauren rolled over onto her side and snuggled deeper into her pillow. She opened her eyes partially, saw the faint glimmerings of light behind the curtains, then closed them again. "Stephen?" she asked sleepily.

He chuckled. "Were you expecting to wake up beside someone else?"

"I don't want to wake up at all."

"No?" He moved so that he was pressed up against her back, his body curved possessively around hers. "Perhaps I can convince you to change your mind."

"Mmmmm." Lauren snuggled against him as he kissed the tender skin beneath her ear. She was not surprised to find him well-warmed and ready, his aroused manhood a searing brand against her buttocks. He had awakened her thus at intervals throughout the night. Insatiable, but then so was she; already her body was responding to him, springing to sensual life at his behest.

"You're beautiful," he murmured against her hair, his hands gliding over the smooth, satin curve of her thigh and hip. He couldn't seem to stop touching her. He felt greedy, almost desperate, as if he had to cram a lifetime of loving her into this single night.

"Aren't you tired?" she teased.

"No. Are you? Do you want me to stop?" He buried his face in the thick hair at the nape of her neck, breathing in her faint violet scent. "The last thing I want to do is hurt you."

Feeling the swollen presence of his manhood hard against her buttocks, Lauren reveled in his care of her, in his restraint. Hurt her! He'd done nothing but pleasure her, over and over. And she wanted nothing more than to feel him loving her yet again. Instead of reassuring him with speech, she rubbed her behind against him in eager acquiescence.

"Ahhh, love!" he muttered hoarsely. His hands slid over her chest and downward to cup the gentle weight of her breasts. He lifted them, his fingers rolling her nipples into tight peaks.

His hand glided downward over her taut belly and quested through the auburn curls below. Her legs parted to accommodate his search. Holding his breath in anticipation, Stephen found the core of her. She was wet and hot and completely welcoming, and he had to restrain the sudden, violent upsurge of need she roused in him. Every time was like the first—impatient, trembling, white-hot. Would he ever have his fill of her? he wondered. Hearing her moan softly, he realized that he would never have enough. No matter what the future brought, no matter what he had to do, he would always want her.

Lauren arched her back, as his fingertips found the tiny nub that was the center of her desire and began to stroke her expertly. She murmured a wordless plea of passion. She needed him—she needed him *now*. Although she tried to roll onto her back, he held her pinned against him, trapping her against the hard, throbbing shaft she wanted so badly.

"Do you love me?" he asked, uncaring at this moment whether she lied or not. He had demanded those words from her over and over throughout the night, and no matter how many times he heard them, it was never enough.

"Yes." Her hands crept back to clasp his hard, muscular thighs, trying to urge him to her. "Stephen, please!"

"Say it!" His voice was ragged; his breathing even more so.

"I love you." She gasped as he slid up into her aching warmth. He filled her—filled her body even as her heart overflowed with tenderness for him. "I love you, I love you!" she moaned, helpless in the demanding grasp of her passion.

Stephen held himself motionless within her, reveling in her taut warmth. Then he began to move, slowly and leisurely, stroking her with his body as his hands caressed her waist, her breasts and the smooth curve of her throat. One hand slipped up to her face, his fingers lightly tracing the moist beauty of her lips.

She moaned as sweet, coiling pleasure settled deep in her body, inflamed by his lingering caresses. She wanted more. After last night, she knew the extent of his restraint. But she also knew that she had the power to break his iron control. When his hands moved over her lips again, her tongue darted out to rasp over his fingertips.

"God, Lauren!" he muttered raggedly, unbelievably stimulated by that seemingly simple caress. He groaned in delight. Control was a thing of the past. It had no place in this bed, with this woman. There was only sensation, the incredibly seductive feel of her velvet heat around him, holding him, urging him on. She was so tight, so hot, and at this moment, so utterly his, that he couldn't resist telling her how he felt. Just once. "I love you, my fire-haired wanton," he whispered.

Lauren gasped, the unconscious writhing motion of her hips stilling. "What did you say?" she asked. "Please, Stephen, I have to hear it again."

"I love you," he whispered again. His hands, shaking with the force of his emotions and his passion, roved from her breasts to her hips and back again. "I love you."

Lauren closed her eyes against tears of happiness. He'd admitted it at last! He was hers, totally and irrevocably, just as she belonged to him. "Oh, Stephen, I—" She broke off as he grasped her hips and began to thrust into her strongly, and soon she was incapable of speech, incapable of anything but surrendering to the incredible sensations he was creating in her.

She met every deep, surging stroke with equal violence, her nails digging into the heavy, hard-flexed muscles of his thighs. Higher they went, and higher still. Gasping, trembling, their moisture-sheened bodies strained together toward the beckoning ecstasy. They reached it together, eagerly drowning themselves in a rippling maelstrom of sensation-shattering, total fulfillment. His deeper voice echoed her cry of release, a primitive, mutual paean of triumphant passion.

They clung to one another afterward, drifting lazily through layers of returning awareness. Then Stephen turned her to face him, wanting to taste her honey-sweet lips. He stiffened in shock when he saw tears running down her cheeks. "Did I hurt you? Lauren, darling, what's wrong?"

"Nothing! Oh, nothing!" Smiling through her tears, she wound her hands in his thick hair and kissed him, a hot, openmouthed caress that had her whole heart in it. "You said it. You actually said that you loved me!"

"I *do* love you," he said. Fool that he was. But he'd be an even greater fool if he failed to take advantage of that kiss. He held himself over her with braced arms and claimed her lips in a reawakening of desire that surprised even him.

Someone knocked softly on the door. "Lauren?" Portia called. "It's nearly nine o'clock, dear. Aren't you coming down to breakfast?"

"Oh!" Lauren tried to bolt from Stephen's embrace, but he pulled her back into his arms and held her tightly.

"Don't panic, love," he whispered into her ear. "She can't see through the door." God, she was adorable with her chest heaving and her eyes wide with consternation! Truly, she was unique—so wan-

250

ton at some moments, so virginally innocent at others.

Lauren took a deep, calming breath. "I . . . just woke up, Portia," she called. "I'll be down shortly."

"Very well," the widow said. "I wonder where Stephen is? I can't find him anywhere."

"Perhaps he went . . ." Lauren looked into Stephen's eyes, saw the sparkle of laughter there, and had to take another breath before continuing. "Have you tried the garden?"

"Not yet, but I will. I want him to go into town for me, to see if Jane has replied to our telegram. Surely she'll want us to return . . ." Portia's voice trailed off as she moved away.

Lauren sighed in relief. Stephen collapsed upon her, his body shaking with silent laughter.

"You were going to suggest that I'd gone for a ride," he wheezed. "God, that's rich! And what a ride it's been!"

She glared at him in outrage, then wriggled out from beneath him. Grabbing a pillow, she raised it high overhead. "Such a statement never occurred to me," she hissed, punctuating each word with a blow to his broad, heaving back. "Stop laughing at me!"

"I can't." He rolled over, raising one hand to defend himself from the flailing pillow. "You should have seen the look on your face."

"How do you expect me to look?" she demanded. "*I'm* not accustomed to being interrupted while abed with a lover."

"Now that's a jealous statement if I ever heard one." He put his hands behind his head, com-

251

pletely unconcerned by his nakedness.

Lauren stared at him with narrowed eyes. The sight of his broad, furred chest and hard-ridged belly, and most especially the magnificent maleness that was even now responding to her gaze, did strange things to her insides. Yes, she was jealous! Jealous of every woman he'd ever looked at, let alone touched. But pride made her say, "Don't flatter yourself."

"You know, you're especially beautiful when you're jealous," he murmured. It was true; her chest was heaving in a most intriguing manner, and even more interesting, her nipples had risen up into taut points, betraying the true direction of her thoughts. Ah, the wanton had surfaced again! He propped himself on one elbow and tweaked one of those rosy, inviting peaks. "And eager. If this is the result, I think I'll keep you in a veritable frenzy of jealousy."

"You're insufferable!" But her exasperation was rapidly dissipating. How could she be irritated at him when all she wanted to do was fall into his arms and be loved again? But really, he was just too arrogant to be left unpunished, she chided herself. Half in earnest, half in play, she raised the pillow overhead again.

He surged to his knees, his right arm snaking around her waist and pulling her against him. With his other hand, he removed the pillow from her grasp. "Are you looking for reassurance, Miss Wakefield?"

"Certainly not!" She held herself away from him with stiffened arms.

"Are you looking for compliments, then?" he asked, pulling her closer. Her arms bent, and he was gratified to feel her soft breasts against his chest at last. "Do you want me to say that you're the most beautiful woman I've ever known, and that I've fallen so completely under your spell that no other woman will ever do?"

"Yes!" she said, capitulating, demanding.

He toppled her backward, his weight pressing her into the mattress. "I'd rather show you than tell you."

"Please, Stephen, don't," she whispered, wishing she had her mother's courage. Alanna would have smiled up into her lover's eyes, damned the consequences, and drawn him back down. But Lauren couldn't. Coward that she was, she just couldn't. "I'm expected downstairs."

"So you'll be late." He thrust one hard thigh between hers.

Heat, instant, volcanic heat, coursed through her, chasing away the remnants of her caution. When he reached between them to stroke her wet, swollen woman's flesh, she slid her legs farther apart in instinctive welcome.

There was another knock at the door, and they both stiffened. "Miss Wakefield, it's Nora," her maid called. "Will you want a bath now?"

Lauren took a deep breath, trying to control her frantic heartbeat. "No, Nora. I . . . I think I'll wait until after breakfast. Tell Mrs. Danforth that I'll be down in a few minutes."

"Yes, Miss." The maid's footsteps soon faded away.

Stephen sighed. Reluctantly, he rolled to one side. "Fate is against me, not to mention the whole damned household," he growled.

Lauren sat up, smiling at his discomfiture. "Really, Stephen. It isn't as though you haven't had adequate—"

"Adequate! " He pulled her down and kissed her thoroughly. "I don't think I'll ever have enough of you. I ought to keep you here openly, and damn the rest of the world!"

"We can't do that. *I* can't do that." Lauren knew the consequences of such recklessness all too well. Held up to public regard, the lovemaking that had been so beautiful, so completely generous, would be branded ugly and sinful. Even Portia, who cared for her, would not be able to condone what they had done.

"Let me go, Stephen," she said. "I have to get dressed."

"Are you ashamed?"

"Not with you. But others would shame me for it."

He sat up, pulling her up with him. "Does it matter? Do you care that much about what the rest of the world thinks?"

"There's a very high price to be paid for flouting the world, Stephen."

He snorted. "Only if you care for their opinion."

Mother didn't care—at first, Lauren thought. But she paid and paid and paid. And if I become pregnant from my joining with Stephen, I'll pay, too. "But I do care," she said slowly, choosing her words carefully. "In particular, I wouldn't want to lose Portia's good opinion of me."

Or her patronage, he thought. "She loves you. She'd understand."

"No." Lauren shook her head. "To Portia, and to the rest of society, what we did would be considered very wrong."

His eyebrows went up. "Why should it be wrong for two people who love each other to express that love in the most natural of ways?"

"Because we're not married," she said, looking down at her hands. Her heart swelled with hope. If he had any intention of proposing, this would be the time. Please, she begged silently. Please love me enough!

Stephen knew from the look in her eyes what she wanted him to say. But a policeman's long-ingrained caution stilled the words in his throat. He *thought* he knew the woman she was. No actress, no matter how skilled, could fake such caring, such generosity, and passion. But, that cool, professional part of his mind told him, she still hasn't told you her real name! It was damned hard for him to turn away from the hope in her eyes, but until she trusted him enough to reveal her secret, he couldn't bring himself to ask her to be his wife.

"I suppose I'd better get to the garden and let myself be found," he said, releasing her.

He wasn't going to ask! Lauren felt as though she'd been stabbed through the heart. Don't let him see! she told herself harshly. Remember, you went to him freely, without promises from him. He'll not welcome regrets or recriminations. Just love him, and hope that if you love him enough, for long enough, you'll change his mind. "Yes, you should go," she agreed quietly.

"For now," he growled, abruptly jerking her against him again.

She reached up, tracing his firm mouth with trembling fingertips. "Yes. For now, my love."

Stephen strode out of the telegraph office empty-handed, mentally cursing his luck for being sent on a useless errand, when all he wanted was to be with Lauren. This time with her was a precious interlude in the midst of reality, and he was jealous of every lost moment of it. Tonight, though . . .

"Mr. Hawkes?"

Stephen whirled, and was startled to see a man from his own department. "Mayes? What the hell are you doing here?"

"The Commissioner sent me." Mayes was a blond, blunt-faced young man in his early twenties, recently promoted to detective.

Stephen's chest contracted with dread. "Come on. I'll buy you a drink."

A few minutes later, seated at a table in a nearby drinking establishment, Stephen sipped his whiskey and studied the younger man. Something was up, something important, and he knew he wasn't going to like it.

"Well?" he asked.

"We're to go to Boston," Mayes said.

"Boston! *Now?*" Stephen muttered a curse under his breath. "Has Padgett forgotten that I'm on a case?"

"This *is* your case. Seems that Eldridge came into the country a bit earlier than we supposed. He took up with a rich widow in Boston."

Stephen nodded. "She lost some money and decided to complain?"

"Her family decided to complain. She died suddenly four months ago—the day before Eldridge left Boston in a big rush." Mayes grinned. "We're to oversee the exhumation and autopsy."

Stephen rolled his eyes at the younger man's obvious eagerness. Well, the examination of a four-month-old corpse ought to cure him of that. "I've got to stop in New York and pick up some clothes."

"No, you don't," Mayes said cheerfully. "The Commissioner had me pick up some things for you. We're to head for Boston immediately, he said."

"All right. I'll have to send a message to the others," Stephen growled peevishly. He wasn't worried about Eldridge; he could trust Stanton to keep him in line. But damn it to hell, he didn't want to go! He had plans—detailed, incredibly pleasant plans—for the next several nights. And none of them included sitting in a clattering railcar with another policeman. "Barkeep! Bring me some paper and something to write with, will you?"

When the paper and pen were brought to him, he scrawled Lauren's name across the top sheet. Then he hesitated, trying to decide what to say. He wanted to tell her he loved her all over again. Damn it, he wanted her to miss him while he was gone, to crave him, body and soul, the way he would her. He wanted . . .

"Oh, yes, there's something else," Mayes said, interrupting his thoughts. "About the Danforth woman's will."

"Well? What the hell is it?" Stephen demanded impatiently.

"Other than a few minor bequests to servants and charities, the bulk of her estate is to go to Lauren Wakefield. About a quarter of a million dollars, all told."

Stephen's breath went out in a long sigh. He sat back in his chair, trying to assess the extent of the blow those words had dealt him. A week ago, he would have expected this. But he'd become so wrapped up in Lauren, that he'd almost managed to convince himself that she was exactly what he wanted her to be. His guts twisted with the pain of it. Pain that she'd fooled him, but even more so, that he'd fooled himself. Damn her. Damn her beautiful, lying eyes!

He crumpled the unfinished note in his fist, then hurled it into the far corner of the room. After scribbling a quick note to Portia, he rose to his feet.

"Let's go to Boston, Mayes," he growled. "We've got work to do."

Chapter Eighteen

"Lauren, dear, you really ought to wear that color more often," Portia said, looking admiringly across the bridge table at the younger woman. "You look quite lovely."

"Thank you." Lauren paused in the midst of dealing to glance down at the emerald green gown the maid had brought to her this morning. It was comfortable and flattering, its slim bodice and bell-shaped gown harkening back to an earlier era. She wished Stephen could see her now. That leaping flame of desire would flicker in his eyes, and she would smile in the secret knowledge that he would come to her again tonight. And as for marriage, well, he certainly wasn't the first man who needed a little time to get used to the idea. But sooner or later . . . Absently, she finished dealing out the rest of the deck.

Portia glanced over her cards at Stanton. "Lauren seems to have blossomed during the last few days. I've never seen her so beautiful—or so happy."

"Evidently train wrecks agree with her," the old man growled.

No, not train wrecks, Lauren mused dreamily, in

too good a mood to be offended by his baiting. It was love that agreed with her. Love and passion and the touch of a man who made her very blood sing. If she was beautiful, it was because Stephen believed her so, and had made her believe it, too.

"Wake up, Miss Wakefield," Stanton said. "It's your bid."

Lauren came down to earth with a jolt. "Sorry." She looked at her cards, quickly adding up her points. "I'll open with one no trump."

"Pass," Eldridge said.

Portia fanned herself with her handkerchief. "Three spades."

"Three?" Stanton demanded. "Are you sure?"

The widow smiled. "Quite sure."

"Hell!" Stanton shuffled his cards despondently. "Pass."

"Six no trump," Lauren said.

Portia beamed. "I'm dummy again. May I get you a drink, Mr. Stanton? You look as though you could use one."

"I could use several." He gave a growl of irritation. "I think I've been well and truly snookered. How much do I owe you two ladies, anyway?"

Lauren quickly scanned the score sheet. "If . . ." With a smile, she corrected herself. *"When* we make this small slam, you'll owe us thirty-six dollars and seventy-five cents."

"You're enjoying this, aren't you?" he growled.

"Indeed I am, Mr. Stanton." Lauren studied the old man from beneath half-closed lids. Perhaps her unholy delight at beating him at something, even at bridge, showed a serious flaw in her character, but

260

she couldn't help herself. She was going to take her share of his thirty-six dollars and seventy-five cents and give it to her mother. A pittance, but rich in satisfaction.

The butler came into the room, holding out a folded piece of notepaper. "Mrs. Danforth, this came for you a moment ago."

"Thank you." Her forehead creased in a frown, the widow took it from him. "I wonder . . . Oh! Oh, my goodness!"

"What's the matter?" Lauren asked.

"Stephen had to leave," Portia said.

"Leave?" Lauren's chest felt constricted, as though an iron band had closed around it. "Did he say where he was going?"

Portia shook her head. "He just said he had some business to take care of, and that he doesn't know when he'll be back." She turned the paper over and over, as though another message would magically appear. "I don't understand what could have made him leave so precipitously."

"Perhaps Mr. Hawkes has already obtained sufficient entertainment from us, and has moved on," Eldridge murmured.

Lauren felt her newfound happiness collapsing, breaking into icy splinters around her heart. There was room for only one thought in her numbed mind: Stephen is gone. Without a kiss, a word, without so much as a hasty postscript on Portia's note. He had taken everything she had to give, and it hadn't mattered. She hadn't mattered.

"Miss Wakefield!" Stanton barked. "Are you going to play that hand or not?"

His grating tone stiffened her spine. She fanned her cards open, forcing herself to concentrate on them. You will not cry in front of him, she told herself savagely. You will not let him see your weakness. Biting down on her inner cheek so hard that the blood came, she began to play.

She felt as though she'd been trapped in some horrible nightmare, her mind tallying cards and her hands moving in precise, accurate motions, while her heart tore itself into pieces. Finally the last card was played, and she looked down in some surprise to see that she had made her bid.

"Well played," Stanton said. His gaze sharpened as he noted her pallor. "Are you ill, Miss Wakefield?"

"A headache," she replied faintly. "I think I'll go lie down for a while."

Stanton rose and helped her to her feet. "Shall I send for the doctor?"

"Of course not. I'll be fine." She smiled reassuringly at Portia, feeling as though her face would crack with the effort of it. Before the widow could say anything, Lauren turned and left the room.

"Rather a sudden illness, don't you think?" Eldridge murmured, waving his hand languidly. "Perhaps it was the news of Mr. Hawkes' sudden departure that caused it."

Stanton's brows lowered as he turned a frigid glare on the spiritualist. "Disappear," he growled. He waited until Eldridge slid out of his seat and hurried out of the room, then turned to Portia. "It's hell to be young and in love."

She sniffed. "Men can be such fools!"

"So can women."

"Sometimes," the widow agreed sadly. "Sometimes."

Lauren lay on her bed, drained of tears for the moment. She had cried and cried, hours of wracking sobs, but there had been no release, no lessening of the pain in her heart. Stephen had left her. Two nights were all she'd had. Two short, shatteringly beautiful nights, and then he had walked away. Oh, she'd told herself this might happen. But not now, not like this!

"Oh, Stephen! I thought I'd have more time," she sobbed into her pillow. "I thought I'd be able to see some sign of it and prepare myself!"

Her fists beat the mattress. Why did you say you loved me? she railed in silent agony. I had already given myself to you, asking nothing but what you were willing to give! Why did you say those three words? Slowly, she rolled onto her side, curling around her pillow in an attempt to ease the stricture in her chest.

She was bewildered, hurt, humiliated beyond her wildest imaginings. This went beyond the pain of her childhood, when she'd had to endure being called a bastard, even when she'd had to answer the taunts of those who called her mother a whore. Then, she'd been able to tell herself that her tormentors were unimportant. But she'd loved Stephen. She had given him everything that had been in her power to give another human being. More, she had put her very nature aside last night to lie naked on that chaise, like some Middle Eastern houri, waiting for her man's pleasure. It hadn't meant a thing to him. Except, perhaps, a few hours of carnality.

How could he have left without a word of farewell? She couldn't believe he'd been afraid to face her; no matter what else he might be, Stephen was no coward. He just hadn't cared. Empty words of love, meaningless acts of passion. And she, who certainly should have known better, had fallen for it.

"Miss Wakefield?" A maid tapped softly on the door. "Are you awake?"

"Yes," Lauren called, schooling her voice to normalcy. "Is it time for dinner already?"

"Oh, not for an hour or so," the girl said. "But there's a gentleman here to see you."

Lauren sat bolt upright. Could it be . . . "Who is it?" she asked breathlessly. Could it all have been a misunderstanding? Could Stephen have come back for her? "Is it Mr. Hawkes?"

"No, Miss."

I should have known better, Lauren thought, damning herself for the stupid hope that had brought her upright so abruptly. Still the fool! Even after what he did to you!

The maid continued, "It's a Mr. Richard Farleigh, Miss. He's waiting in the drawing room."

Richard? Lauren's eyes widened in shock. What was Richard doing *here?* How was she going to deal with him now? She was a mess, physically and emotionally, and Richard was the last person she wanted to see just now.

"Miss?" the maid called. "Are you awake?"

Lauren sighed. "Please tell Mr. Farleigh that I'll be down shortly."

"Yes, Miss." The maid's footsteps retreated.

Lauren scrubbed at her wet cheeks with the back of her hand. Oh, God, why had Richard come now? Because he loves you, she scolded herself, hating herself for her lack of consideration for him. He loves you, and he's worried about you. And now you're going to have to send him away.

Squaring her shoulders, she rose from the bed and splashed water on her reddened eyes. Richard would have to be faced. *She* was not about to cast someone aside without an explanation. Swiftly, she straightened her dress and bound her tumbled hair into a neat knot at the back of her head, then went downstairs.

Richard, Portia, and Stanton were waiting for her in the drawing room. As she entered, Richard jumped up from his chair and rushed to her.

"Darling!" he cried, catching her up in his arms. "I've been frantic with worry since I got your cable! I got here as soon as I could, knowing you'd need me."

Lauren turned her head so that his kiss landed on her cheek instead of her lips. "Richard, we must talk." Over his shoulder, she looked pointedly at Stanton. "Alone," she said.

The old man grimaced at her, but obligingly rose from his seat. Extending his arm to Portia, he said, "Come, Mrs. Danforth. Let's leave them to their billing and cooing."

"Caldwell," the widow said as she was led out of

the room, "this is not the time for levity, believe me."

Lauren extricated herself from Richard's grasp and went to close the door. He approached her again, his arms outstretched, and she shook her head. "Please, don't. Sit down, Richard."

Frowning, he took a seat on the sofa. "What's the matter, darling?"

"I . . ." She took a deep breath, willing herself to continue. "I can't marry you."

"What?" he asked blankly.

"I can't marry you. I'm sorry, Richard."

He looked away, knowing he had to hide the murderous rage in his eyes. How dare she! He needed her—needed her grandfather's money! "Why can't you marry me?" he asked, gritting his teeth to keep from screaming it at her.

"I had the best of intentions when I accepted your proposal. I thought—" Her hands twisted together in agitation. "There is no excuse for the way I deceived you. I'm sorry, truly sorry."

For a moment he stared at her uncomprehendingly. Then he knew. Knew as though it had been painted in fire upon his brain. "Another man?"

She nodded. Her arms crossed, hugging her chest in misery.

"Are you going to marry him?"

"No," she said softly. "I doubt I'll ever see him again."

Ah, hope! He bounced up from the sofa so suddenly that she took a step backward. "Then what's the problem?"

She closed her eyes. There was no way to avoid

266

plumbing the depths of her shame, then. But she had wronged Richard terribly, and she must face the consequences. She must tell him the truth.

Opening her eyes, she met his gaze. "We can't marry because I . . ." The words stuck in her throat. Say it! her conscience screamed at her. Say it! "I can't marry you because . . . well . . ." Say it! "Because I am no longer chaste."

He flung himself away from her. Turning his back on her, he struggled for control. *He* had wanted to be the one to take her innocence! He had dreamed about it, planned every delicious moment of it. He'd been cheated, cheated!

He whirled to face her, wanting to strike out somehow, to punish her for what she had taken from him. But a small, calm corner of his mind whispered, "Think of the money! You've killed a man for it—you can't give it up now." Yes, he thought. The money. She can be punished *after* I have the money.

"Lauren." He went back to her, going down on both knees before her. "Darling, it doesn't matter. Marry me. I'll make you forget him."

Lauren cringed inwardly. Marry him, go to his bed, have his children? Oh, no. Even though Stephen had cast her aside, she couldn't bear the thought of another man touching her. "No. No, it's impossible."

"Anything is possible when a man loves a woman as much as I love you." He buried his face against her thighs, clutching the fabric of her skirt in both hands.

Lauren's skin crawled at his nearness, and she

had to fight to keep from pushing him away. But then she heard a sob escape him, and tears of distress began to flow down her cheeks. "Please, don't. Richard, don't do this to yourself!"

"Tell me you'll think about it," he begged.

Stephen's lean, vital features rose compellingly in her memory. Her love, her lover—the man who had taken her with such strength and gentleness, that even now she couldn't endure the thought of another. "I'm sorry, Richard, but no. It will never work. Go back to New York and your gay life. Tell your friends that you threw me over. Tell them anything."

He rose to his feet. "I'll change your mind. I'm going to ask you to marry me—every day, if necessary—until you do."

She shook her head. "There are plenty of other women for you to marry. Better women than I."

"No, there aren't. We belong together. Someday you'll realize that." He'd convince her. He hadn't met a woman yet who could resist him. Reaching out, he slid his hands over her shoulders. His anger diffused, to be replaced by desire. She *did* have marvelous skin, and that hair . . .

Unable to bear his touch again, Lauren stepped back, away from his hands. "I think you'd better go, Richard."

"For now," he said. Raising her limp hand to his lips, he kissed it lingeringly. "I'll be waiting for you in New York, my love."

Numb with despair, she watched him walk out of the room. For now, he'd said. Those had been Stephen's last words to her this morning. An empty promise, as empty as his words of love . . . given in the heat of passion, and quickly retracted when the moment had passed.

She left the drawing room, but instead of going upstairs to her own chamber, she headed towards the library. Slipping inside, she lit the gaslights against the growing darkness and stood before the portrait of Alanna Stanton.

"I never really understood before," Lauren whispered, tears flowing unheeded down her cheeks. "But now I do. It hurts, Mother, it hurts."

There was no answer, of course.

Lauren sighed. Was there some quirk in Stanton women that made them choose men who didn't value them? How brave her mother was, to trust in love again and again! Lauren didn't think she had that sort of courage herself; she'd settle into her spinster's life, hoping this terrible pain would someday fade.

Alanna smiled down at her. Beautiful, happy, silent. But somehow, Lauren felt comforted. She sat at the rosewood desk and put her head down on the cool, polished wood, letting the welcome serenity wash over her. Without even knowing it, she slipped into a doze.

A few minutes later she awoke with a start, realizing that someone had come into the room. Turning, she saw Caldwell Stanton standing before his daughter's portrait, his hands clasped behind his back. She rose to her feet, intending to leave, but he said, "Don't go."

Lauren sank back into her chair.

"You cut the young pup loose," he said.

"Did he tell you that?"

"No. I knew you would. He's weak. You'd never stay with a weak man."

"Oh, really? What makes you think you know what I would or would not do?"

His attention didn't waver from the portrait. "You're strong, and you admire strength in others. The moment you clapped eyes on Hawkes, that fancy boy didn't have a chance."

Neither did I, she thought. Neither did I.

There was a long stretch of silence, then Stanton said, "Alanna will be forty years old next month. Her child, twenty-two. I never knew its name."

"You never tried to know." Lauren searched for her anger, but it was gone, burned to ash by the agony Stephen had burned into her heart.

"No, I didn't." He turned to face her, jamming his hands deeply into his pockets. "Do you think my daughter would ever forgive me?"

There wasn't the slightest softening of the harsh lines of his face, the slightest sag to his bony shoulders. But Lauren, who had learned to stand erect and unflinching through hurt and humiliation and despair, knew his pain. She could not turn away from it. A week ago — yesterday — she might have.

"Do I think she would forgive you?" she repeated, rolling the words around her mouth as though tasting them. Truly, she couldn't know what Alanna would do. "Why do you ask *me?*"

"Because you're the only person whose opinion I give a goddamn about." He met her gaze unflinchingly. "Well, maybe not the only one.

Not that I'd ask her, mind you, but Mrs. Danforth is too damned nice to be objective about such a thing."

Lauren clasped her hands in her lap and stared down at them. If she wanted revenge, here it was. She could tell him no, crush his hopes and send him to his grave without a chance of being forgiven. But there was no room in her any longer for bitterness or recriminations. She had lost her will to judge this man. If Alanna wanted to forgive him, it was her right. If she didn't want anything to do with him, that, too, was her right.

"I think anything is possible," Lauren said at last. "I think the woman in that portrait has great capacity for love—and forgiveness."

"I don't even know where she is." For the first time, his shoulders sagged.

Lauren closed her eyes, praying that she was doing the right thing. It was a leap of faith, of trust in her mother's gentleness. "If she were ready to come home, Mr. Stanton, she would go back to the place where it all began."

"You're suggesting that I reopen the house in New York?" he asked. "Sit there like a damned spider, in case she sees fit to come to me?"

Lauren nodded, amusement bubbling up at the picture his words evoked. "A certain amount of humility is called for when one wants forgiveness, you know."

"What if she doesn't?" he growled.

She met his gaze levelly. "Then you lose."

"Fair enough." He extended his arm. "Come, Miss Wakefield. I've got plans to make. Do you think Mrs. Danforth would object to returning to New York early?"

"I think the attraction of a country idyll has paled for all of us." All she wanted to do was to try to forget Stephen. Once out of this house — and away from the bed they had shared for such a few, fevered hours — she would. Somehow.

Chapter Nineteen

"Ahhh, New York," Stanton said, as the train entered Grand Central Station. "Too damned big, and getting bigger and more damned every day. What do you say, Miss Wakefield? Maybe you've come to like the damned, what with all the ghoulies and ghosties floating about the house."

Lauren clamped her lips together to still her retort. He had been at her the entire trip, goading her, insulting her, doing everything in his power to get her into an argument. Well, she wasn't some dancing bear to hop to his whims. Dear heaven, what had ever prompted her to feel sorry for the old devil?

The train squealed to a stop in a cloud of steam. Lauren stared out the window at the crowd that thronged the platform. Grand Central was a true melting pot of humanity; poor and rich, men, women, and children of all classes and nationalities mingled freely here. She couldn't help but scan the faces that were staring curiously at Caldwell Stanton's luxurious private car, half-hoping and half-dreading to find Stephen's among them. And what if you do? she asked herself with brutal honesty. What if you come face to face with the man who discarded you? Her chin lifted. She would do what her mother had always done: walk away with dignity and pride, and never show the shameful hurt inside. Loving and losing had been a hard lesson, but she had learned it. Never again, she vowed. Never, never again. Once she managed to pry Portia out of Eldridge's grasp, she'd take her savings and find a little house out in the country somewhere. She'd live her spinster's life there, alone, and if not happy, at least content. And safe. When Alanna needed a place to go and heal herself, she would be welcome to share that life for however long she needed.

Edward Eldridge leaned his elbows on the back of her chair, his face a leering caricature in the glass. "Don't bother looking for your lover," he whispered. "You'll never see him again."

Lauren stood up abruptly. She'd told herself the same thing a hundred times, lashing herself with it, but his gloating whisper was unbearable. Unfortunately, there was no way to respond to his jibe without leaving herself open to even more pointed remarks. Then she noticed the pallor of Portia's normally pink cheeks, and forgot all about the spiritualist.

"Portia, are you ill?" Lauren asked, moving to put a cloak around the widow's shoulders and help her rise.

"Just a headache," Portia said, patting Lauren's hand before pulling away. "A breath of fresh air, and I'll be as good as new." She turned to Stanton. "Are you sure you'd rather stay in a hotel? Truly, we've plenty of room."

274

He gave her one of his sharp-edged grins, then shot a sardonic, sideways glance at Lauren. "Absolutely. The St. Nicholas may be boring, but I'm damned if I'm going to sleep with Mr. Eldridge's ghosts."

"You'll visit, then?" Portia asked.

"Wouldn't miss it," he said, raising her hand to his lips in an uncharacteristically gallant gesture. Then he turned to Lauren, his grizzled brows going up. "And what do I say to you, Miss Wakefield?"

"Goodbye seems appropriate," Lauren replied, falling back on the facade of composure that had stood her in such good stead all her life. She wasn't going to allow him to tweak her emotions any longer; she'd allowed Stephen to delve beneath her armor, and it had resulted in nothing but pain.

Stanton grunted, disappointed. He plopped his derby on his head, nodded coldly to Eldridge, then stomped towards the door. "I've ordered a carriage for you," he growled over his shoulder. A moment later he was gone.

"Such a nice man," Portia said. Both Lauren and Eldridge stared at the widow in astonishment, and she added, "A bit gruff at times, but one must look past that."

"Not I," Eldridge said, offering the old woman his arm. "Come, my dear. Let us go home."

"It doesn't seem like only a week has passed since we left," Portia said, as the spiritualist helped her down to the platform.

No, it didn't seem like only a week, Lauren agreed silently, accepting the arm of the porter who rushed to assist her. She had left New York a proper young woman, engaged to a proper young man. She returned without a fiance, her innocence, or her heart—and without the man who had taken them all.

The porter led them to the closed carriage that was waiting outside the station. Eldridge took the seat facing the rear of the carriage, Portia and Lauren the one across from him.

"Are you feeling better now?" Lauren asked, tucking the rug around the widow's legs.

Portia nodded. "I'll just close my eyes for a few moments."

As the carriage pulled out into the crowded street, Lauren was aware of Eldridge watching her, a smug, all-too-knowing smile on his face. Anxious to avoid his glance, she kept her gaze fixed on the window. The sounds of the city surrounded her: the general underlying clatter of traffic, pierced frequently by the imperative shrillness of a policeman's whistle, and more sweetly, by the lilting music of the organ grinders and other musicians who plied their trade on the streets. But she saw none of it, for Stephen's lean-jawed visage swam into her memory. Laughing, his eyes half-closed in passion, his face haunted her. She tried to push the image away, but it came back even more strongly. Illusion—just as his professed love had been—but at this moment, more real to her than the scene outside. She'd known the kind of man he was. She'd known he would leave her someday. And even knowing that, she had fallen in love with him. Because she had known what loving him would cost, her actions were more foolish, more reckless,

276

than her mother's had ever been.

Deep in her somber thoughts, she was startled when the carriage drew to a stop in front of Portia's house. She turned to the widow, who was asleep, and shook her gently.

"We're home, Portia," she murmured.

Portia's eyes opened. Putting a shaking hand to her brow, she moaned, "Ohhh, Lauren, I feel so bad! Dizzy, and it's hard to breathe. I don't . . . I don't think I can walk just now!"

"You don't have to, dear," Lauren soothed. She turned to the spiritualist. "Help me get her inside, Mr. Eldridge."

With his help, she half lifted, half dragged the widow from her seat. The driver came around to help, and Lauren rushed up the steps to the door, while the two men lifted Portia from the carriage.

"Please, be careful with her!" Lauren reached above the lintel for the spare key, then unlocked the door, and flung it wide. Glancing over her shoulder frequently to make sure they obeyed, she led the way upstairs to the widow's bedroom.

They placed Portia on the bed, then stood back helplessly while Lauren felt the old woman's forehead. "She's burning up with fever," she said. "Driver, please go to Dr. Lindsay's office on Third Avenue. Bring him here immediately."

As the man hurried out, Eldridge tried to follow.

"Mr. Eldridge." Lauren spoke sharply, stopping him in his tracks. "Would you please light the stove and set a pot of water to heat? Just to lukewarm, now."

"I don't know how to light the stove."

Lauren looked at him over her shoulder, hoping her eyes were as fierce as her thoughts. "Then learn."

He turned on his heel and left the room. As soon as the door closed behind him, she began undressing Portia. The old woman was barely able to lift her head, and getting her out of the corset and the layers of petticoats was a long and frustrating process. But Lauren managed finally, breathing a sigh of relief when she finished tying the last ribbon on the widow's nightgown.

"Just lift your legs a bit, dear, and we'll have you under the covers," Lauren said. A moment later the widow was tucked into bed, the counterpane pulled up to her chin.

"Thank you," Portia murmured weakly. "I'm sorry to be such a bother."

"Oh, Portia! You're no bother at all." Lauren laid the back of her hand against the old woman's hot cheek. The fever seemed even higher than before. I've got to try to get it down, she told herself worriedly. I need that water! Someone knocked urgently at the front door, and Lauren nearly gasped with relief. "That must be Dr. Lindsay. Will you be all right for a few moments, while I let him in?"

Portia nodded, and her eyes drifted closed. Lauren stood looking down at her for a moment, noting the dry, papery thinness of the skin around her eyes and her shallow, rapid breathing.

Fear churned Lauren's stomach. Dashing a tear from the corner of her eye, she turned and hurried downstairs and opened the door. "Dr. Lindsay, thank you for coming! She's upstairs."

278

The doctor, a short, white-haired man with ruddy skin, gentle brown eyes, and an even gentler manner, tossed his coat carelessly over the bannister and hurried upstairs.

Lauren rushed ahead of him to lead the way into the bedroom. "She seemed fine when we began the trip here," she said. "But then she collapsed, and her fever keeps going up."

Quickly, the doctor examined Portia. To Lauren's concern, the old woman didn't wake even when he rolled her onto her side. His face creased with worry, the doctor said, "It's pneumonia, Miss Wakefield. She'll need constant care, I'm afraid."

"Just tell me what to do, doctor."

He studied her closely, then nodded. Pulling a paper and pencil from his bag, he scribbled a list of instructions. "Send someone for these medicines. Bathe her to get the fever down, and make sure she drinks plenty of liquids. I'll be back tomorrow to check on her."

"Thank you." Lauren brushed a stray lock of hair back from the widow's cheek, as the doctor repacked his bag and left the room. "You'll be all right," she said softly. "I won't let anything happen to you."

Lauren sat in the chair beside Portia's bed, mending one of the old woman's nightgowns. Three weeks had passed since the widow had fallen ill, three weeks that had passed in a blur of work and worry. With a sigh, Lauren laid her sewing aside and rubbed her eyes. She was tired, bone-

279

tired. She had hired five maids during that time, but each one had quit after just a few days, because of Edward Eldridge's ghostly pranks. So, whenever her nursing duties permitted, she also did the cooking, laundry, and most of the heavier work. But by the grace of God, Portia was on the mend at last.

Although her eyes burned from lack of sleep, Lauren refused to give in to her fatigue. If she slept, Stephen would come into her dreams. It was then, relieved of her mind's restraints, that her heart revealed the depth of the blow it had taken. It was as though a great, aching void inhabited the center of her chest, a yearning that could never be assuaged. Her body craved his touch with a burning intensity that woke her, trembling with need. No matter how she damned herself for her weakness or vowed not to let herself dream about him, his memory refused to be banished. It was as though he had imprinted himself on her very soul.

She sighed, shifting into a more comfortable position. If she was ever to find serenity again, she must purge herself of this obsession. During the past three weeks, she hadn't been able to abandon the hope—the blind, foolish, irrational hope—that he would try to contact her to explain his actions. But there had been nothing. Stephen was gone. She must go on, wiser now, and not let his rejection of her love taint the rest of her life. And as Portia was well enough to be left alone for a few hours, Lauren was going to visit her mother. To apologize. She'd thought Alanna to be a weak woman, someone who needed protection from harsh reality. Only now did she realize how strong her mother truly was, how much courage it had taken for her to face life with grace and joy, despite the betrayal of her love. Lauren's chin lifted. She would never be able to forget Stephen Hawkes, but she *would* find happiness again. Alone, most likely. But she would.

"Miss Wakefield?" the maid called through the closed door, shattering Lauren's reverie.

Lauren rose from the chaise and tiptoed to the door. "Yes, Jeanne?"

"I won't be back after today, Miss. I'm sorry." The woman's hands twisted her apron nervously, crumpling the starched linen into a wrinkled mess. "There's funny things going on in this house. I tried, Miss. But I'm frightened, and I'm leaving."

Not again! Lauren thought disgustedly. Couldn't Eldridge stop his tricks for a moment? "Are you sure I can't change your mind?" she asked.

"I'm sure. Now, you've already paid me for today and yesterday, Miss, so we're settled." The maid bobbed a frantic little curtsey, then hurried towards the stairs. A moment later the front door slammed closed behind her.

"That's the third one this week," Portia said.

Lauren whirled. "You were supposed to be asleep."

"Help me sit up, dear." When she had been propped up against her pillows, the old woman folded her hands on the counterpane. "You've been doing far too much. Laundry, cooking, waiting on me hand and foot—"

"You know I don't mind," Lauren protested.

"Truly, Portia, it's going to be very hard to hire anyone right now. Word of what is going on in this house has spread. People are afraid. Jeanne only agreed to try because Mrs. Talmadge begged her."

Portia shook her head. "I won't have you working yourself into exhaustion. You simply must find someone."

With a sigh, Lauren sat down in the chair. "Richard told me he knew a girl who might do, even with the goings-on here. But I hadn't wanted to ask him for anything. Under the circumstances . . ."

"Send a message to him this evening."

"But —"

"This evening, Lauren."

Lauren didn't dare disobey the note of command in the widow's voice. So she merely ducked her head and said, "Yes, ma'am."

"Very good." Portia smiled. "Now, tell me what has you so reluctant to ask a favor of Mr. Farleigh. Has he been calling?"

"Every day," Lauren murmured.

"And has he tried to convince you to change your mind about marrying him?"

Lauren sighed. "Every day." Frustrated, she rubbed her forehead with the back of her hand. Richard's visits and repeated proposals had been more of a burden than the housework, for they only kept the raw edge on her guilt. Oh, why couldn't she have fallen in love with him instead of Stephen? "But my relationship with Richard isn't the issue here, Portia. Eldridge is. We have to do something about him. Why don't I go to the po-lice—"

"And what will you tell them?" Portia asked. "Mr. Eldridge has done nothing illegal, you know. And after inviting him into my home to contact Thaddeus' spirit, who am I to complain if a few extra ghosts get out?" With her palm, she smoothed a wrinkle in the counterpane. "I know what people have been saying about me the past few months. 'Poor Mrs. Danforth! She's really gone soft in the head. Someone ought to do some-thing about that crazy old woman for her own good.'"

Lauren bit her lip. "Nonsense. No one thinks—"

"Please, Lauren. Don't." The widow patted the bed beside her, and Lauren obediently perched on the edge. "You've always defended me. But no matter how much you resist it, the fact is that the rest of the world thinks I'm a dotty old woman. Bring the authorities into this, and I'll probably end up in Bloomingdale Asylum."

"Oh, no!" Lauren took Portia's hands in hers. "But what are we going to do? This can't go on in-definitely!"

A spell of coughing caught the old woman sud-denly, and Lauren jumped up to support her shoul-ders. When it was over, the widow lay back against her pillows, her eyes closed. Lauren covered her, then tiptoed towards the door, reviling herself for being so selfish as to worry the poor woman when she was still so weak.

"I wish Stephen would come back," Portia said softly.

Lauren stopped. It was the first time she'd heard his name spoken in many days, and the sound of it made her heart contract with pain. Slowly, she turned to look at the widow. "Why?" she asked.

"Because I like him." Portia opened her eyes and regarded the younger woman levelly. "And because Mr. Eldridge is afraid of him."

"Stephen would only add to our problems," Lauren said, a bit more forcefully than she intended. "Besides, he's gone. We'll never see or hear from him again, so we'd better learn to solve our problems without him."

Portia cocked her head to one side. "Of course, we'll hear from him, if only to tell us where to send his things. He left a number of his belongings here, you know. I noticed that before we left for Peekskill."

"I haven't been in his room." Lauren drew in a deep breath, incensed at the possibility of receiving an impersonal little note instructing her to pack his belongings and send them on so he could strut for the next woman in his life. Her eyes narrowed. Well, I'll take care of *that* the first chance I get, she promised herself. A symbolic ridding of her memory of him. She'd clear out her life as she cleared his possessions out of the room he had used. Rather as he'd used her.

Richard took Lauren's note from his manservant and opened it. "Well, well, well!" he murmured, reading it as he went upstairs to his room. "So you've decided to take my offer, my sweet Lauren?

284

Excellent!"

Bianca lay upon his bed, naked, her abundant femininity an opulent visual feast against the red velvet coverlet. "Back for more?" she asked, propping herself on one elbow to smile at him.

"Yes, indeed." He joined her, running his hand along the plump curve of her hip. "Afterward, I've another job for you."

"More fun than this?" She unbuttoned his trousers to take his already swollen manhood in her hand.

He pushed her down onto her back and buried his face against her throat. She smelled of sweat and lust and cheap perfume, and he reveled in her coarseness, even as he quivered for Lauren's lilac-scented coolness. He pushed Bianca's legs apart and thrust abruptly into her, riding her to his quick and utterly selfish release.

He withdrew from her to straddle her hips. Reaching down, he grabbed a double handful of her fiery hair.

"Ow! That hurt!" she gasped.

"Dye this," he said. "Black, I think."

"Ow! All right!" She pried his fingers open, releasing her hair. "Is this for the new job? What is it? One of your fancy friends likes brunettes?"

He laughed. "Bianca, darling, I'm teaching you a whole new profession. Starting tomorrow, you're going to be a maid!"

Chapter Twenty

Stephen stalked down the steps of Police Headquarters and hailed a carriage with a curtly imperious gesture. Climbing into the vehicle, he said,
"Twelve Gramercy Park. And make it quick."

He settled back against the cushions, his arms
crossed over his chest, his brows lowered in a black
scowl of irritation. He'd spent most of a month
dealing with a family reluctant to allow their
loved one's exhumation — something Commissioner
Padgett hadn't bothered to mention — only to have
the autopsy reveal nothing of use in his case. Then,
tired to the bone, he returned to New York to find
that Lauren and Portia had returned weeks earlier
and were alone with Edward Eldridge and his
tricks. When he'd learned that Portia had been extremely ill, he'd actually shouted at the Commissioner. To no purpose, of course. Padgett had
merely grinned and sent him to resume his place in
Portia's home.

"Damn your evil hide, Padgett!" Stephen muttered under his breath. "I'll shoot myself before I
let you give me a case like this again!"

As the carriage wove through the traffic, he tried

to get control of his seething emotions. He'd left Lauren without a word, intending to sever their relationship. Fool that he was, he'd been sure that his love for her would fade with time and distance. But it hadn't, anymore than the knowledge of her lies had lessened his desire. He had burned for her, dreamed about her — vivid, scorching dreams — feeling her silken skin, hearing her laughter, smelling the lilac fragrance of her hair. All during the journey here, the train wheels had seemed to whisper, *Lauren, Lauren!,* feeding the fires of his need and his anger, until he was in a worse state than when he'd left. Even if his job hadn't required it, he would have been drawn back to her.

The vehicle turned the corner onto Gramercy Park South, and Stephen looked down the line of graceful brownstone buildings that stood shoulder to shoulder along the street. From here, he could see Portia's house. He drew in his breath sharply when the front door opened and Lauren, her arms laden with a bulky bundle, came out onto the stoop. The sun caught her hair, turning it to a fiery nimbus around her head. The sight of her was like a blow to his chest, making his pulse race and his fists clench with desire. *Damn her!* he thought savagely. *Damn her for wrapping my heart up in her sticky little web!*

Lauren shifted the bundle of Stephen's clothing, peering over it for the elderly ragpicker who came most mornings to sift through the neighborhood's discards. For a moment she was afraid she'd missed him, but then she saw him shuffle out of the nearby carriageway, a high-piled sack upon his stooped shoulders. "Mr. Galt!" she called.

The old man made his way to her and raised his battered hat respectfully. The young lady at Number 12 always had a kind word, even for the likes of him, and saw that the household's discards were set aside for him so that he didn't have to paw through stinking garbage for them. "Got somethin' for me, Miss?" he asked.

"Yes," she said, holding out the bundle. "We won't be needing these any longer, and I thought . . . Oh!" A gasp was wrung from her as she saw Stephen's carriage approaching. Stephen. Her lover, her seducer, the man who had thrown her love aside as though it had been nothing.

She stood frozen, the bundle held at arm's length, as the vehicle came to a halt before her. Stephen paid the driver, then jumped nimbly down to the ground.

"Why the hell didn't you stay at Stanton's?" he growled.

Lauren tightened her grip on the bundle of clothes, anger instantly dispelling her shock at his unexpected appearance. The nerve of the man! How dare he show up, after tossing her love aside so carelessly! How dare he address her in that accusatory tone of voice, when any other man would at least have the decency to be embarrassed! Arrogant, selfish . . . He was *not* going to do this to her! Charlatan, thief, rake—everything she'd ever thought about him was true. She met his challenging charcoal-gray gaze levelly for a moment, then turned back to the ragpicker.

"Please take these, Mr. Galt," she said. Without

another word, she went into the house and closed the door.

"Hey! Those are my clothes!" Stephen shouted, catching sight of the contents of the bundle. He took a step towards the ragpicker, intending to retrieve his belongings. Galt backed up warily. Stephen sighed, then reached into his pocket. "All right, how much do you want?"

Inside the house, Lauren stood with her back to the door, her chest heaving with reaction. Desperately, she looked around the foyer, like a rabbit searching for a bolthole. Stephen obviously intended to walk back into this house as though nothing had happened. She wanted to run and run and never look back. But now, more than ever, Portia needed protection from the two spiritualists who would surely drain her dry. For her sake, this dreadful situation must be endured. But oh, how hard it was going to be!

Lauren straightened her spine, stubborn determination replacing her panic. This was the price she must pay for allowing herself to indulge in an illusion, no matter how compelling. Well, Stephen's love had been a dream; this was cold, hard reality, and must be faced. She'd had a great deal of practice in hiding her emotions, and it would serve her well now. It must.

"Lauren, I know you're there," Stephen called. "Let me in."

His voice propelled her away from the door. Tossing her head in disdain, she walked upstairs. The new maid could let him in, she thought. And if the girl moved at the same rate as she did housework, it would be a while.

By the time Stephen came in, Lauren was ensconced in the chair beside Portia's bed, sewing with intense concentration. She had to have some occupation, so she'd have an excuse not to look at him. Hearing his footsteps on the stairs, she missed a stitch.

"Mrs. Danforth?" he called, tapping upon the widow's door.

Portia sat up straighter and gave a squeal of delight, startling her cat Nero from his warm nest in the pillow beside her. "Why, Stephen! Come in, come in!"

Stephen walked into the room and bent over the bed to kiss the old woman's cheek, noting how much weight she'd lost, and the deep creases that now bracketed her mouth. "You've been ill?"

"Pneumonia, I'm afraid," she replied. "A horrible illness. There were times when I was sure I wouldn't make it."

He sat down on the edge of the bed, lifting the purring cat into his lap. "You're better now, I trust?" he asked.

"Oh, yes. Lauren nursed me day and night. I don't know what I would have done without her."

Stephen glanced at Lauren. She was wearing one of those ugly mouse-gray gowns again, her body stiffly corseted, her beauty and fire hidden behind layers of wool and that damned frigid air of serenity.

"Did you miss me?" he asked. Although he was looking at Portia, his attention was on Lauren.

"Terribly," the old woman teased. "Lauren was sure we'd never see you again."

"Evidently. I caught her giving my best suit to a ragpicker."

Portia giggled. "I'm sorry, Stephen. But it *is* funny."

"Funny!" He crossed his arms over his chest. "It cost me twenty dollars to ransom my clothing from that old blackguard."

Steeling herself to speak with cool dignity, Lauren met his gaze calmly. "Since it was my mistake, I'll reimburse you for your loss, Mr. Hawkes."

So we're back to Mr. Hawkes, are we? he thought. Well, my girl, it isn't going to work. "Don't be ridiculous."

"I insist," she said. To her surprise and pleasure, she found that her voice remained politely unemotional, revealing nothing of the turmoil that wrenched her insides.

He studied her with narrowed eyes, stung by her continued coolness. "I won't take it."

Lauren's hands jerked inadvertently, and the needle sank into the tip of her index finger. With a hiss of pain, she put the injured finger in her mouth. For a moment the sharp, metallic taste of blood stung her tongue, then her awareness of it faded as she saw the look on Stephen's face. His gaze was riveted on her mouth, his eyes aflame with desire. He wanted her. To her shame, her own body reacted to that knowledge, a deep, flooding warmth settling deep within her. Hastily, she lowered her hand.

Stephen tried to grin, but couldn't, for her seemingly innocent gesture had hit him like a physical blow. The sight of her full, red mouth sucking her finger was incredibly erotic, arousing in him an almost uncontrollable urge to take her hand and raise it to his own mouth, to slide his tongue over the spot hers had touched, then to taste her lips and the sweet depths beyond. Easy, son, he cautioned himself. You can't run panting after her like some callow boy. Make her come to you.

"Well, Stephen," Portia said, breaking into the uncomfortable silence, "Have you come back to stay?"

"How could I not?" he said gallantly. His gaze drifted back to Lauren's mouth. "Besides not being fool enough to abandon two such lovely ladies, I haven't accomplished what I came here to do. I must still contact Thaddeus for you."

"Do you think you can?" the widow asked.

"Yes." He smiled. "I have some very interesting ideas I'd like to put into practice as soon as possible."

The widow straightened the sleeve of her silk bed jacket. "Another séance, Stephen?"

"Indeed, madam."

Lauren put her sewing aside and stood up, unable to bear another word. Did the man have no mercy at all? Must she not only face him after being cast aside most brutally, but also be forced to watch him hurt Portia, too? "Mr. Hawkes, surely you must realize that Mrs. Danforth is far too weak to be bothered with such things," she snapped.

He was pleased to hear some heat in her voice at

last. "That is for Mrs. Danforth to decide, surely."

Lauren stiffened. "How dare you come around with your wheedling and false promises, upsetting her—"

"I'm not upset—" Portia began.

"Why do you insist on burying her in this room with no company but yours?" Stephen asked, ignoring the old woman's protest. "It might do her good to return to normal activities—"

"Normal!" Lauren laughed derisively. "Spooks and hauntings and voices in the night? Really, Mr. Hawkes!"

"Stop!" Portia cried before Stephen could reply. "This bickering is far more distressing . . ." She began to cough, and Lauren ran to support her shoulders until the spasm passed.

Stephen took the widow's hands in his, his forehead creased with concern and guilt for his part in bringing on her attack of coughing. Perhaps Lauren had been right about the old woman's fragility, after all. "I'm sorry for upsetting you, Mrs. Danforth. Shall I go for the doctor?"

"Oh, no," Portia said. "This happens from time to time. Perfectly normal, the doctor says."

Stephen released her hands and leaned against the bedpost to watch Lauren. Interesting, the way she reacted far more to the idea of competition for the widow's favor than to his sudden reappearance. Interesting, and damned irritating.

Portia reached up to pat Lauren's cheek. "It's over, dear. You can stop clutching me now."

"Are you sure you're all right?" Lauren asked.

Portia nodded. "I'll just take a short nap, and

perhaps I'll be able to come down for tea. And I would appreciate it if you would get Stephen settled in his old room."

"I wish you would reconsider," Lauren said.

"Truly, dear, it's for the best." The old woman wriggled deeper into her pillows, patting the mattress beside her to beckon Nero back to his accustomed sleeping place.

After making sure the widow was tucked in securely, Lauren turned towards the door. Hearing Stephen's footsteps behind her, she stiffened, her skin tingling with awareness of him. If only one of Eldridge's spirits would materialize now and carry her away! She wanted to run, but pride made her walk at her normal pace.

Stephen closed Portia's door behind him, then moved quickly to block Lauren's path. "Lauren, we've got to talk."

"Words are not necessary, Mr. Hawkes. Your actions speak for you," she said. Don't drop your guard for an instant, she told herself firmly. Show him one instant of weakness, and he'll use you and discard you all over again.

The utter coldness of her voice and eyes took Stephen by surprise. Any normal woman would cry, ask questions, or perhaps scream recriminations—*something*. He could soothe tears, come up with facile answers, or kiss away the recriminations, but this total absence of emotion gave him no opening at all. Damn her eyes! he growled inwardly. I'll *make* an opening.

"You're not angry?" he asked.

"Should I be?" Her gaze didn't waver.

"Any other woman would be."

"I am not any woman." At least to *me,* she added silently and bitterly.

He smiled, remembered passion warming his eyes. "Now *that* is definitely the truth."

Lauren clasped her hands in front of her with feigned composure, and forced herself to look at him with the same polite expectation she'd show a stranger. "Is there anything else, Mr. Hawkes?"

"Plenty. But I doubt you'd be interested in hearing it in your present mood."

"Now that is *definitely* the truth," she said. "I'm glad you recognize it."

He let his breath out in exasperation. "And when will you be in a mood to discuss it?"

"Never." Lauren started to walk past him, but his arm shot out, blocking her path.

"It's not over between us." he said softly.

Lauren schooled her rising temper to obedience. If he were seeking some perverse sort of satisfaction by delving into the depths of her hurt and shame, he wasn't going to find it. Looking down her nose at him, she said, "I do not intend to allow your importunities to bother me, sir. Mrs. Danforth is my main concern—my only concern—and I warn you, I will protect her any way I can."

"Is that a threat?" he asked softly.

"Absolutely."

He took her by the shoulders, stopping her from turning away. "Exactly what did you have in mind?"

"I prefer to retain the element of surprise, Mr. Hawkes." Actually, she had no idea what to do if he called her bluff. But if a vague threat would keep him from bedeviling her, she'd use it.

"Hasn't our relationship gone a little too far for this Mr. Hawkes nonsense?"

"Our relationship did indeed go too far," she replied, trying unsuccessfully to step back, away from his hands.

"That isn't what I meant."

"No? But then your perspective is different, isn't it? You didn't take the same risks I did."

"What the devil—? Are you with child?" he demanded, his pulse roaring in his ears.

"No! Thank God, no!" she gasped, momentarily shaken out of her composure. "At least I was spared *that!*"

"You're mighty damned pleased about it," he growled, unaccountably stung by her obvious relief. *He* was supposed to be the one most pleased by the news. He lowered her until her heels were touching the floor once again, but retained his hold on her shoulders.

"Shouldn't I be?" she asked. But the image of a child with Stephen's fathomless gray eyes rose in her mind, and her heart contracted with pain at the thought that it was never to be. She lifted her chin, burying her churning emotions beneath a tightly held shield of icy composure. "Are you saying, Mr. Hawkes, that I should be disappointed that I won't be branded a whore and cast out of polite society?"

Stephen was infuriated by his inability to get the response he wanted from her. Even her hatred would be better than this total absence of emotion.

296

"Whores sell their favors," he said. "What did you purchase with yours?"

She tilted her head back to meet his gaze squarely, but she was sick inside. "I expected nothing, and I received nothing."

"Not even pleasure?" he asked, letting his hands slide down her arms.

Lauren wanted to scream. She wanted to cry, slap his face, beat her fists upon his chest, anything to loosen the tight band of pain around her heart. Fury and shame, hurt pride, and the desire for revenge warred within her, until she thought she was going to burst. But if she revealed her feelings to him, he would surely use them against her. Well, she wouldn't give him the satisfaction! With all the self-discipline at her command, she forced herself to shrug carelessly.

"Stubborn, aren't you?" he murmured, running his hands back up to her shoulders, then sliding them slowly down her sides to her waist, as he watched her reactions intently. Her chin went up another notch, but other than that, he might have been caressing a statue. Frustration knotted his guts. Damn you, Lauren! he raged silently. Let me in!

"Are you finished, Mr. Hawkes?" she asked calmly. "Or do you intend to rape me here in the hallway, to prove just how ignoble you can be?"

Her words drove him back a step, and he shook his head as though to clear it. This was crazy! He'd intended to use the same tactics that had been so successful in battering down her defenses before, but they weren't working. Her continued indifference stung badly, and it wasn't just his ego that was hurting. No matter what she was, he still wanted her. He wanted her so badly, his hands shook with it. Frustration, anger, and the drive to possess her clenched his heart. Damn her to hell, he didn't dare touch her lest he lose control completely. Yes, at this moment he was capable of taking her right here on the floor, pleasuring her until she cried out in need and capitulation.

"Deny it all you like, but I *know* how hot your passion burns," he said huskily, remembering how he'd basked in her heat, and how she had raised his own desire to a fever pitch he'd never experienced with another woman.

Seeing the smoky look of awakening desire in his eyes, Lauren trembled. Yes, her desire for him had burned hotly. And yes, she admitted to herself, it burned still, for she felt the sultry coiling of passion rising within her. Fire called to fire, flesh to flesh, responding to the sensual call of the man she had once chosen as her mate. Treacherous, liquid warmth settled in her lower body, weakening her legs, sapping her will. Almost she took a step towards him, so great was his power over her.

"Miss?" The new maid's rather flat, nasal voice came from behind Lauren, shattering the dangerous, sensual spell that had held her in thrall.

Lauren turned to look inquiringly at the young woman Richard had brought this morning. Although he'd said that Bianca Marelli had served him satisfactorily, in Lauren's opinion, she was slow and unsure at even the simplest of household tasks. "Yes, Bianca?"

"I can't find the broom," the maid said. Her dark gaze traveled Stephen's lean, muscular body appreciatively.

"Did you look in the closet downstairs, where the dust cloths are kept?" Lauren asked, frowning. She'd put the broom there herself this morning!

"Uh-huh. But, you know," Bianca took a deep breath, severely straining the buttons of her bodice, "things tend t'move around a bit in this here house."

"Ah, yes, Mr. Eldridge's spirits." Stephen's brows went up. "They don't bother you?"

"Nothin' bothers me," Bianca said. "I ain't the fanciful type. Now, what about that broom, Miss Wakefield?"

"I'm sure it will turn up eventually. Why don't you just go on to your other duties until it does?"

"Cleanin' the silver? Eck." Bianca flounced off down the hall.

Lauren shot a glance at Stephen. Bianca was an extravagantly curved young woman, lush and ripe and, with her wide mouth and insolent dark eyes, quite pretty. Eldridge was quite taken with her. Would Stephen, too, be drawn to the maid's abundant charms? The thought hurt, a cruel knife-twist in Lauren's already battered feelings. Ridiculous, she told herself. I'm finished with him, totally and irrevocably. But she was unaccountably reassured to note that he was looking at her, not at Bianca's retreating figure.

Realizing that she was about to lose her chance to get away from him, Lauren began to walk towards the stairs. "I have a great many things to do.

If you'll excuse me"

"Running away?" Stephen asked.

That statement stopped her in her tracks. "Certainly not," she replied with cool dignity. "But you and Mr. Eldridge are our guests, and I must see that you're served a proper meal tonight."

"Should I bring a food taster with me?"

"Oh, no!" She turned to face him, allowing a slight, malicious smile to curve her mouth. "Why don't you and Eldridge taste each others'?"

"I'd rather taste yours," he murmured.

She gave him a frigid look of disgust, then turned and stalked away. But her disgust was really directed at herself, for the sweeping shiver of heat his words had sent through her.

Chapter Twenty-one

It began to snow that afternoon, a soundless drifting of big, wet flakes that soon covered everything with a fairyland glaze of white. Lauren donned her warm woolen cloak and went to sweep the back stoop. It was a futile, unnecessary chore, but she was desperate to escape the house . . . and Stephen.

But deep in her heart, she knew she was really trying to get away from the one thing she couldn't escape: herself. In the past few weeks, she had come to terms with the pain caused by Stephen's rejection of her love. She had found strength she never knew she possessed, and she was prepared to go on with a measure of contentment, if not happiness. But Stephen had torn it all away.

"You thought you had all the answers again," she muttered, her breath rising in a steam cloud upon the cold air. "And again you were wrong, wrong, wrong!"

Cool, composed Lauren Wakefield, thinking she had regained control of her life. After one look at Stephen, she was a muddled mess of emotions, teetering wildly among anger, hurt, hatred, and yes, God help her, love. Still love, after everything he had done to her. His smile, the vitality of his handsome face, caused the same treacherous warmth to flow through her as it always had. His every gesture reminded her of those two fevered nights they had spent together, the passion and unforgettable pleasure they had shared. But pain had followed that pleasure. The humiliation of being cast aside must temper her memories and harden her resolve, or she'd have no dignity left at all. Even as she made that vow, however, she burned to know why he had left her, where he had gone, and most important of all, who he'd been with.

There was an imperative scratch at the door behind her, and she opened it to let Nero out. "So you needed some fresh air, too?" she asked, sweeping a clear spot for the cat.

He planted his broad, furry behind on the place she had prepared, and stared at her with unblinking golden eyes.

"Don't you dare look at me like that," she scolded, moving to sweep the top step. "I know you like Stephen Hawkes. You always have. But really, you ought to have better taste." Snow flew in all directions as her motions grew more vigorous.

The Persian sniffed at a clump of snow that landed beside him, then shook the clinging stuff from his whiskers. *"Miaoooow!"*

"And don't bother defending him." Lauren moved down another step. "You're as bad as Portia. If you knew what he was really like, you'd claw him to shreds. *I'd* certainly like to."

She finished the last step and moved out into the brick walkway. She'd like to sweep her way right out into the street and away, never to set eyes on

Stephen Hawkes again. How many cast-off mistresses were forced to live in the same house with their former lovers? Yes, she had gained strength. Yes, she had gained confidence in her ability to survive the destruction of her girlish illusions. But were strength and confidence enough to see her through day after day of facing the man who had betrayed her trust?

"This is all your own fault, for being stupid," she muttered under her breath. "Portia needs you more than ever. Stop feeling sorry for yourself and try to find a way to help her."

She let out her breath sharply. So, she hadn't yet managed to purge her love for Stephen from her heart! That didn't mean she had to let him see it, and it certainly didn't mean she hadn't the sense to keep him from using her ever again. Eventually, she would learn not to care at all. And the sooner, the better!

"I see the broom turned up at last," Stephen drawled from behind her.

Lauren froze; she'd been so wrapped up in her thoughts that she hadn't heard the door open. And despite the resolution she had made a scant moment ago, her heart began to pound in response to his deep voice. Without turning, she said, "Things always turn up eventually. Our ghosts are playful, not destructive." She resumed sweeping, attacking the snow on the walkway with renewed vigor.

"You're going to wear that broom out," Stephen said with considerable amusement.

She turned slowly towards him, her hands tight on the broom handle. "Did you come out here for a reason, Mr. Hawkes?"

"Mrs. Danforth sent me to tell you that she'll be down for tea." How lovely she was with a dusting of snowflakes in her hair! he thought, bending to scoop Nero into his arms. "And to fetch this lazy cat."

As he straightened again, his gaze locked with Lauren's. She knew she should turn away. But there was admiration in his eyes, as well as a challenge that made her heart come up into her throat with dread. He was going to play his games all over again, just like a cat with its tormented prey. If he would only give her a chance to get a hold on her emotions . . .

The door opened, and Bianca peered out. "Miss Wakefield?"

Saved again! Lauren thought. Whether she could dust or not, Bianca was worth her weight in gold! "Yes?"

"Mr. Farleigh is waitin' in the parlor," the maid said, then ducked back inside, banging the door closed behind her.

Lauren leaned the broom against the side of the house and hurried up the steps, hoping to get past Stephen without further confrontation. But he caught her arm as she went past, immobilizing her.

"Still trailing Farleigh along?" he asked.

"My plans for the future are no concern of yours," she said, keeping her face resolutely turned away from him.

Stephen's ascot suddenly felt too tight. Although he'd never expected her to let as rich a plum as Richard Farleigh get away unplucked, the thought of that giggling fop prancing around her made him furious. "I ought to break his neck," he growled.

Lauren's chin came up, and she met his angry gaze calmly. With the same tone with which she might discuss the weather, she said, "Such an uncharitable attitude, Mr. Hawkes. *You* didn't want to marry me. In fact, you went to great pains to disassociate yourself from our relationship. Why do you object now, if another man wishes to share my life honorably?"

"Because you belong to me," he said.

"I don't belong to anyone," she said, keeping her voice calm with difficulty. She couldn't stop herself from adding, "And most especially, I do not belong to *you*."

A muscle jumped spasmodically in his jaw. "Don't push me too far, Lauren. It wouldn't take much for me to throw your goddamned fiancé out on his ear."

Why, he's jealous! she realized with a sudden rush of surprise. Then her eyes narrowed. She'd been fooled once into misinterpreting his actions as love. He didn't want her, not really. He just didn't like the thought of losing possession to another, an emotion that might as easily have been caused by ownership of a piece of furniture. Bitter, bitter knowledge, she thought.

"Go away, Mr. Hawkes," she said quietly. "You're not wanted here."

"I don't give a damn what you want." He flung the door open and urged her into the house, pausing long enough to divest her of her cloak and sling it carelessly over a chair before grasping her arm again. "Put a nice smile on for your sweetheart, love," he growled.

Lauren allowed him to tow her into the parlor—

docilely, if not willingly. If his scowl and belligerently outthrust jaw were any indication of his mood, he'd probably drag her in by the hair if she tried to resist.

"Lauren, darling!" Richard said, jumping up from his chair and coming forward. His gaze swept over Stephen assessingly, then returned to her. "I've brought my lovely sister with me today."

Surprised, she looked past him to see Clarissa seated on the sofa, one languid white arm stretched across the upholstered back. What on earth brought her here today? Lauren wondered. Clarissa had hardly been civil to her, even when she had been betrothed to Richard. "Hello, Clarissa," she said. "I hope you've been well."

"Well enough," Clarissa said.

Lauren tried to pull away from Stephen. Failing in that, she held her arm stiffly and pretended that he wasn't touching her at all. But his hand was hotly possessive, even through the fabric of her sleeve, and she knew he was treading a fine line between restraint and open anger, and it wouldn't take much to push him over. The last thing she wanted was to have him create a scene here, in front of gossip-loving Clarissa Farleigh.

"You look especially lovely today, darling," Richard said, taking Lauren's free hand and raising it to his lips.

Stephen wrestled his temper into abeyance. He told himself that Farleigh was an innocent dupe, inveigled into a betrothal by a cunning, greedy woman. But the sight of the fellow's pale, manicured hand clutching Lauren's slim fingers sent daggers of jealousy through his brain.

Lauren's peripheral vision caught the angry swell of his chest. Her own temper flared, although she didn't let it show. How arrogant! And how unfair! He had walked away from her without so much as saying farewell. And now he had the gall to waltz back into her life as though nothing had happened, expecting her to accommodate his every desire.

Clarissa rose, flicking her cerese watered-silk train behind her with a practiced gesture. "Stephen, dear, how marvelous to have you back again! Are you planning to stay this time?"

"It depends," Stephen said, his gaze darting to Lauren's profile. She seemed to be completely oblivious to him, despite his hold on her arm. What incredible self-control she had to stand here beside him, surely as aware of him as he was of her, and not let the slightest trace of it show.

"I was terribly worried about you, Stephen." Clarissa swayed forward, offering her hand for him to kiss. "I happened to be driving down Mulberry Street today, and noticed you coming out of Police Headquarters with *such* a black look on your face."

Well, Lauren thought, that explains her visit. Good heavens, she must have run to Richard straightaway and begged him to bring her here! Jealousy, sharp and ugly and very unwelcome, added its sour tang to Lauren's already confused emotions. Don't care. she told herself. Don't care.

"Police Headquarters, you say?" Richard drawled. He turned to Stephen, his eyebrows raised in surprise. "Are you in some sort of trouble, Mr. Hawkes?"

"Not yet," Stephen said, showing the edges of his

teeth in a rueful smile. Damn his luck for being seen there! "I have the warmest of relations with the police, actually; they most kindly retrieved some property that had been stolen from me a few months ago."

"In your profession, I'm sure you have a very *long* history of dealings with the police," Lauren murmured.

His smile became one of genuine amusement. "Truer words were never spoken, my dear Miss Wakefield."

Richard put his hand at the small of Clarissa's back and pushed her closer to Stephen. "Clarissa, why don't you and Mr. Hawkes get reacquainted over on the sofa. Darling," Richard linked his arm with Lauren's, "I have something to show you."

For a moment Lauren was afraid that Stephen wasn't going to let go. How humiliating to be caught between them, tugged first one way and then the other, like a bone claimed by two snarling dogs! But after a warning squeeze on her elbow, Stephen released her. Seething with resentment, Lauren glanced back over her shoulder at him as Richard led her towards the settee. That squeeze, no matter how gentle, had spoken volumes. Pure male possession had been conveyed in it, as well as a promise that he wasn't finished with her.

Richard helped her to her seat, then took the place beside her. "Look what I brought you, my love," he said, pulling a long jeweler's box from his pocket and handing it to her.

Lauren opened it to see an exquisite pearl necklace nestled against a black velvet lining. Exquisite, and totally inappropriate for a lady who was not

308

his betrothed. She could feel the heat rush into her face. Was Richard merely overeager, or was he flouting the conventions because he knew she was no longer chaste?

"It's lovely, Richard," she murmured. "But you know I can't accept it."

"I know it isn't the proper gift to offer you now," he said. "But we can rectify that if you'll just say 'yes, Richard, I'll marry you.'"

"I can't," she whispered.

"Damn it, Lauren, if we didn't have an audience, I'd go down on my knee and ask you properly."

"My answer would still be the same," she said. Helplessly, her gaze drifted to Stephen, to find him staring at her with storm-dark eyes, and the box shook slightly in her hands. "I'm sorry, Richard."

"So am I," he said, taking the box and putting it back in his pocket. "But I'm planning to ask you again tomorrow and the next day and the day after that, until you finally say yes."

"I wish you wouldn't." Lauren leaned forward and touched his wrist. "You know it's impossible, and you know why. It would be better for us both if you wouldn't come—"

"Please, darling, don't send me away!" Richard put his hand over hers and gazed earnestly into her eyes. "I'll make you a promise: no more proposals, at least for a few days. I'll be your friend, your confidant, your undemanding companion. Will that do?"

She relented, unable to deny his imploring eyes. "Yes, Richard, that will do."

He took her hand from his arm and raised it to his lips to kiss it lingeringly. Lauren stole another glance at Stephen. He was sitting with his arms crossed over his chest, glaring at her with eyes that had turned silver with rage. She had never seen such a look of barely restrained violence on his face before, and it frightened her. Hastily, she removed her hand from Richard's grasp.

Clarissa tapped Stephen on the arm. "Stephen, would you like to accompany me to a party next Saturday night?"

"No, thank you," he said, without looking away from Lauren.

Clarissa's eyes narrowed as she realized who he was watching so intently. Then a malicious smile curved her lips, and she said, "Dickie will be there."

Stephen turned to look at Clarissa at last. If Farleigh was going, Lauren would probably be there, too. "All right, Clarissa, I'll go," he said, determined to make an uncomfortable evening for the happy couple. He was going to haunt Lauren like one of Eldridge's spirits. He was going to pursue her, tempt her, and provoke her out of that damned unnatural calmness. And he wasn't about to let Richard Farleigh interfere.

"Good afternoon, everyone," Portia said from the doorway. She looked very shaky, and was leaning heavily on the spiritualist's arm. Extending her free hand, she murmured, "Stephen, may I borrow your strength for a moment?"

He strode to her side, offering his arm in a courtly gesture. "Always, dear lady."

Lauren pulled a comfortable armchair closer to the fire and shook out a knitted throw. "Bring her here, please."

"Thank you," the old woman murmured, as the three of them settled her in the chair. "I find I'm not nearly as strong as I'd hoped."

"You'll get stronger every day," Lauren assured her, tucking the throw securely around her legs.

"Please sit down, gentlemen. Don't make me strain my neck by looking up at you," Portia said.

Clarissa beckoned Stephen back to his seat beside her, while Richard sank back onto the settee, and Eldridge claimed the chair nearest the widow's. Lauren stood behind Portia, deeming it the safest spot in the room. Coward! she railed at herself. If you had any backbone at all, you wouldn't care what Stephen thought or did. You wouldn't worry about his intentions or his motives, and most of all, you wouldn't worry that you might succumb to his enchantment again.

"Well, Clarissa, this is a pleasant surprise," Portia said, folding her hands in her lap. "What brings you here today?"

"Just a friendly visit, Mrs. Danforth," Clarissa replied, smiling coquettishly at Stephen. "Isn't it nice to have Stephen back?"

"Indeed it is," the widow agreed. "I can't wait for him to conduct another séance."

"A séance!" Clarissa clapped her hands in delight. "Oh, may I come?"

Lauren gripped the back of Portia's chair with white-knuckled hands. "I don't think Mrs. Danforth will be well enough to plan on having one any time soon."

"Oh, don't be silly, dear," the old woman protested. "I've already decided that next Friday will be an excellent day for it. We'll invite the Talmadges—Jane had *such* a good time at the last one—and Mr. Stanton. He's been so kind, sending flowers and fruit and charming little notes. It would be so nice to see him again."

Lauren drew in a deep breath, almost as disturbed by the thought of seeing her grandfather again as by the talk of another séance. Caldwell Stanton wasn't someone she wanted to deal with just now, especially as she hadn't had a chance yet to visit her mother, to tell her that her cold, hard, imperious father wanted to see her again.

"What about *my* séance?" Eldridge demanded, his resonant voice quivering with indignation. "I've been patient for weeks, and now you let Hawkes have the first chance!"

The widow turned to him, her blue eyes wide with surprise. "But Edward! You always preferred private séances, just the two of us. But if you'd like Mr. Stanton to attend—"

"Not Stanton!" Eldridge waved his hands in a dramatic gesture of negation. "No spirit would come within a mile of this house with him in it!"

"Oh." Portia turned to look inquiringly at Stephen. "Do you want to exclude dear Mr. Stanton from your séance as well?"

"Not at all." Stephen grinned, thinking what a marvelous magician's assistant the old devil would make—if he could be trusted not to take over the show. "I'll even let Mr. Eldridge come. Perhaps he'll learn how to conduct a *real* séance."

Eldridge's eyes were as flat and cold as a snake's. "I wouldn't want my presence to give false validity to your amateur's tricks."

"Oh?" Stephen's eyebrows went up. "Yours are

312

professional tricks, then?"

"Here's our tea!" Portia said, hearing the rattle of the tea caddy in the hall outside.

Bianca pushed the laden caddy into the room. Lauren moved to help her, unobtrusively reaching under the cozy to feel the side of the teapot. It was barely lukewarm. With a sigh of resignation, Lauren then lifted the embroidered linen towel from the tray of food, to find that many of the tea cakes she had made this morning were gone. Evidently Bianca liked tea cakes.

"You gentlemen look hungry," Lauren said, picking up the teapot. "I'll just go make some sandwiches." She lowered her voice to a whisper. "Bianca, please fold the napkins before giving them to the ladies and gentlemen."

"Yes, Miss."

Stephen watched the exchange curiously, catching the insolent expression that crossed the maid's face as she watched Lauren leave the room.

"I'm very grateful that Richard was able to find Bianca for us on such short notice," Portia said, noticing the direction of Stephen's gaze. "It's been terribly hard keeping servants, what with the, well, strange reputation we seem to have acquired, but Bianca doesn't seem to mind a bit. I was terribly concerned about Lauren pushing herself so hard trying to do everything. Good heavens, the child was even scrubbing the floors!"

Stephen ran his thumb along his jaw thoughtfully. If Lauren was only after Portia's money, all she had to do was sit idle and let the old woman die. But she hadn't. She'd nursed Portia loyally, and had taken on the most menial tasks without complaint. Oh, yes, there was still the matter of her lying about her identity, but even the most hardened part of his policeman's mind wasn't cynical enough to believe that she would do anything to harm Portia.

He glanced at Bianca again. She was staring at Richard, her tongue stroking her upper lip in a very lascivious manner. Oho! Stephen thought in surprise, when he saw Richard's right eye close in an answering wink. Bianca might be serving Portia as a maid, but I'll bet she serves Richard in a very different way.

As the conversation went on around him, Stephen studied the young man he had earlier dismissed as a gullible puppy. There were hidden depths to Farleigh, if he had the gall to send his mistress to dust his fiancée's furniture. And not nice depths, either. It was bad enough to watch the fellow fawn over Lauren, but to watch it knowing that Farleigh was betraying her under her own roof was intolerable. Every instinct Stephen possessed urged him to protect her. He didn't know what game she was playing with Farleigh, or why, but the seemingly mild-natured, earnest suitor was really a snake in disguise, and snakes could be dangerous.

Lauren came back into the room, carrying a cloth-covered tray in one hand, the steaming teapot in the other, and every fiber in Stephen's body responded instantly to her presence. Although she looked as prim and proper as any spinster governess, his memory put her in another guise entirely. The seductress, her unbound hair framing her nakedness in a froth of silken fire, as she kindled him

314

to heights of passion he'd never known with any other woman.

"I'm going to claim you again, my flame-haired wanton," he muttered under his breath. "For your own good. And mine."

Almost as though she'd heard him, Lauren looked up. Her gaze was as cold and impersonal as if he were part of the sofa. Stephen nodded in determination. Whatever obstacle she put before him, he'd overcome. Whatever challenge she offered, he'd meet. And whatever mystery had prompted her to begin this devious game, he would solve.

"Stephen, why don't you come for me at nine next Saturday?" Clarissa said, interrupting his thoughts. She leaned closer, pressing the side of her breast against his arm. "That should give us plenty of time to get into the proper mood."

Stephen could think of nothing he'd like less than squiring this chattering, overbold woman to an idiotic society party. Only the thought of sitting here while Farleigh danced with Lauren kept him from refusing the invitation. Well, he thought grimly, there's no help for it. "All right, Clarissa. I'll be there at nine."

Lauren nearly dropped the teapot, shocked at such inconsiderate behavior, even from him. She'd given up her virginity, her pride, even her one chance at a respectable marriage to love him, and he'd tossed it all away. It was bad enough that he'd come back expecting her to fall into his arms, as though nothing had happened. But now, only minutes after claiming her in no uncertain terms, he was deliberately flaunting his pursuit of Clarissa. Was it just meanness, or did he actually think she would share him with another woman?

It took every ounce of her control to set the teapot gently on the table, when she really wanted to fling it against the wall. So, this was the real Stephen—cruel, calculating, empty of compassion. How could she have been so stupid as to fall in love with such a man? What a fool she'd been! And still was, for letting him continue to hurt her. She began sorting the sterling flatware that Bianca had put down in a jumbled mess, but her hand shook uncontrollably for a moment. With an effort, she forced herself to steadiness.

Although she faltered only briefly, Stephen saw it. She still cares! he exulted. No matter how deeply she tries to hide it, she cares. It was the chink in her armor, the Achilles' heel that would put her in his arms again.

Lauren felt the sudden stinging of tears against her eyelids and sternly willed them away. "Bianca, will you distribute the plates, please?" she asked. Noticing suddenly that the maid's hands were none too clean, she amended hastily, "Never mind, I'll do it. Would you put one of those small tables in front of Mrs. Danforth's chair?"

"There's nothing like a real English tea," Eldridge said, eying the tray of cakes greedily. "But I thought you planned to make scones today, Miss Wakefield? I'm particularly fond of scones."

"Yes, I know. But I'm afraid I ran out of time, Mr. Eldridge." Lauren whisked the towel from the gleaming Lusterware teapot. "Will you be mother, Mrs. Danforth?"

"I'd love to, dear," Portia agreed, beaming with pleasure.

316

Lauren picked up the teapot and turned around. "Oh!" she gasped as Bianca bumped into her with some force, causing the pot to fly out of her hands.

A stream of hot tea made an arc through the center of the room, spattering the rug, one arm of the sofa and the hem of Clarissa's elegant day gown. With a shriek that rattled the windows, Clarissa leaped to her feet.

"Are you burned?" Lauren cried, rushing forward.

"My dress is ruined!" Clarissa screamed, whirling to point an accusing finger at Bianca. "You stupid cow!"

"Are you speaking to me, Miss Farleigh?" Lauren asked with frigid dignity. "*I* dropped the teapot." No matter what Bianca's failings as a maid might be, she was not going to be abused in this house.

Bianca looked at Lauren, her mouth open in surprise, then grabbed a towel and began mopping the mess on the floor.

Clarissa sniffed with haughty disdain. "Stephen, take me home."

"Didn't you come with your brother?" Stephen asked, his dark brows raised in Satanic-looking arcs.

"She did." Richard reluctantly rose from his comfortable place on the settee. "Oh, very well. Come along, Clarissa."

"I'll see you out," Lauren said, leading the way to the front door. Pain throbbed in her temples. What a horrible day! Horrible! And with Stephen here in the house, tomorrow would be the same, and every day thereafter.

317

Clarissa sailed out without a word, but Richard lingered a moment, taking Lauren's hand in both of his. "Until tomorrow, darling," he murmured.

"I'm sorry, Richard, but tomorrow will be impossible. I have a great many things to do."

Richard's gaze went to the parlor door, where Stephen Hawkes lounged in the opening. Bastard! he thought. Somehow I've got to get myself married to Miss Wakefield/Stanton before that man queers things for me. "Will you miss me, darling?" he asked, loud enough for Hawkes to hear.

Lauren pulled her hand away. "Please, don't."

"I'll be back soon, my love," Richard said, hiding his anger beneath a pleasant smile. Revenge is sweet, he vowed silently, and mine will be especially so, since it will be visited on your lovely self. He put his derby on, adjusted it to a rakish angle, then strode away.

Lauren shut the door, leaning her forehead against it for a moment, then turned back to the parlor. The sight of Stephen standing in the doorway stopped her in mid-stride. He was smiling at her, his gray eyes as warm and caressing as his hands had been during those sultry nights of lovemaking. Her chest tightened, and her legs grew weak at the memory of the passion they had shared. Why does this man affect me so? she wondered. What does he have to do to me before I no longer care?

"Eavesdropping again, Mr. Hawkes?" she asked, gathering her courage around her like a cloak. She moved forward again, but Stephen remained where he was, leaving her to falter to a stop or walk right into his chest.

318

"I like to eavesdrop," he said. "I learn the most interesting things that way."

Lauren clasped her hands in front of her, trying to decide what to do. Did she order him to move — which probably wouldn't work — or stand here and let him intimidate her? Either way, she'd lose ground in this battle of wills. Finally deciding that anything was better than to back down, she said in her calmest voice, "You may not have noticed, but you're blocking the doorway."

"I noticed."

Eldridge's irritated voice came from behind him. "Well, you're blocking me, too. Why don't you continue this touching little scene somewhere else?"

Stephen grinned at Lauren. "Yes, why not?"

"Because I have better things to do," she said, peevishness creeping into her voice at last. "Get out of my way."

"How can I resist such a gracious request?" Still grinning, Stephen stepped back into the parlor. Ah, the ice is beginning to crack, he thought in triumph.

Chapter Twenty-two

Lauren busied herself preparing the dough for the day's bread. She always enjoyed this homely chore, savoring the yeasty odor and satiny feel of the dough. Behind her, the big cast-iron stove radiated heat and the delicious smell of baking biscuits. She took a deep, appreciative sniff, imagining the aroma wafting upstairs, sliding under Portia's door and luring her out of bed. Portia loved hot biscuits in the morning. So did Stephen, although he was seldom up early enough to find them still hot.

Lauren sprinkled a handful of flour on the board, flipped the ball of dough over, and began to knead vigorously. No, Mr. Hawkes was never about early these days; he spent nearly every night out, leaving right after dinner and not returning until long after midnight.

"And how do you know that?" she murmured. "Why, because you can't seem to get to sleep until you hear his footsteps coming down the hall. Twit." She dug the heels of her hands deeply into the ball of dough. "Fool, nitwit, imbecile!" She'd thought he was going to make her life miserable by pursuing her. Instead, he'd all but ignored her. Out gallivanting, she reflected sourly, and probably with Clarissa. "And why do you care?" she muttered under her breath, giving the dough a thorough mangling. "Because you're stupid, that's why."

There was a faint noise from the stairs behind her, and Lauren's ill humor evaporated. She smiled as she placed the ball of dough in the trough of the doughtray to rise. The biscuits must smell especially good this morning; Portia hadn't wasted a moment in coming down.

"They're not even cooked yet, you greedy thing," she teased without turning around. "Sit down, dear, and let me get you a cup of tea while . . . Eeek!" The cry was torn from her as she felt a pair of warm lips caress the nape of her neck.

She whirled to see Stephen standing behind her, close enough to touch and grinning like a jackanape. He was already dressed in a fresh white shirt and brown trousers, but he hadn't yet put a collar on, and she could see the corded muscles of his neck and the beginnings of dark chest hair. Unbidden, the memory of his naked body rose up in her mind like a flaming brand. She wanted to step back, away from the man and the memory, but it felt as though her shoes had been nailed to the floor.

"So I'm 'dear' again," he said, smiling down at her. "I must admit, it's an improvement from Mr. Hawkes."

His comment released her voice—and her irritation. "I thought I was speaking to Portia," she said. "Actually, I can't think of anyone less a 'dear' than you."

He chuckled. "Even Caldwell Stanton?"

Lauren took a wet washrag and scrubbed the flour from the oak table. "Caldwell Stanton might be the

321

rudest man on the face of the earth, but at least he's honest."

"Am I to consider that a personal attack?" Stephen asked, his brows going up in sardonic arcs.

"Mr. Hawkes." Lauren put her hands flat on the table, praying for the strength to maintain her composure. "Did you come down here for a reason?"

"I don't think I've ever smelled anything as good as those biscuits." Except for you, he added silently. Lilac and Lauren, the headiest scent he'd ever experienced. Putting his hand over his heart, he asked plaintively, "Please, Miss Wakefield, may I have some?"

He smiled, and his grin was so much like a mischievous small boy's that Lauren couldn't help but smile in return. "They'll be ready in a few minutes. Why don't you get yourself a cup of coffee and wait in the dining room?"

"Why don't I just eat in here?" he asked, eyeing the neat grouping of porcelain bowls holding butter, apple preserves, and strawberry jam that occupied the center of the glistening tabletop. "Evidently you were planning to entertain *someone* this morning. I'll just join you."

"But Portia might not be down for—"

"Quite a while," he finished for her, elated that she had unwittingly answered his implied question. "Are you afraid to be alone with me? What if I promise to be very good?"

She studied him suspiciously. "What do you mean by that?"

"You wound me, beautiful lady." He went to the cupboard and took out a cup and saucer. "I just don't want to sit in that big, drafty dining room all alone, when I can enjoy the cozy comforts of this wonderful room, as well as a bit of conversation."

"Well . . ." Lauren hesitated, both dismayed and drawn by the idea of spending some time alone with him. "All right. But I haven't got time to talk; I have to fix breakfast and—"

"Oh, don't mind me. I'll just watch you cook." He winked. "There's nothing more soothing to a man than seeing a woman work around the kitchen."

A faint blush stained her cheeks. She hid her nervousness by busying herself slicing ham. Why couldn't she hate him? He surely deserved it after what he had done to her. But somehow he seemed always able to make her laugh, even when she knew better than to respond to him in any way.

Stephen poured himself a cup of coffee and sat down at the table. Evidently she and Portia had gotten in the habit of having a cozy little breakfast here, while the rest of the household was asleep. A twinge of jealousy went through him. He really had it bad, he reflected cynically, when he even begrudged the attention she gave the old woman.

"Why don't you sit down and have a cup of coffee with me?" he asked.

"Because I'm busy," she said shortly. "And you seem to have forgotten the promise you made only a few minutes ago."

"All right, all right," he said good-naturedly. "You can't fault me for trying."

She returned to her chore of slicing ham, overly conscious of his bold regard. She felt as though his gaze was peeling her clothing off layer by layer and, instead of being repelled by that thought, a treacherous warmth was creeping into her limbs. To hide her flushed face, she hurried over to the oven to check the biscuits.

Stephen swiveled in his chair to watch her, admiring her quick efficiency and the graceful sway of her bustle as she moved. There was a dusting of flour on her forearms and bright tendrils of hair sticking to her work-dampened face. Seeing her like this, tending to these simple domestic tasks as though she'd spent her life doing them, only made him desire her more. Easy, son, he told himself sternly. This is only a single, outward aspect of a very confusing woman. And it's the things you *don't* know about her that bother you.

"How did Eldridge's private séance go last night?" he asked, stirring sugar into the steaming, dark coffee.

Lauren wiped her hands on a towel before putting the big iron griddle on the stove. "Well, he seems to have made some progress," she said dryly, setting several slices of ham on to cook. "He didn't actually contact Mr. Danforth, but he spoke to a 'spirit close to him,' who implied that Thaddeus was upset because he owed a debt that had never been paid."

"That old saw!" Stephen shook his head. "I thought Eldridge was more original than that. How much did he want?"

"Ten thousand dollars."

"Ten thousand!" Stephen gave a low whistle. "She didn't agree to give it to him, did she?"

"Of course not—at least not without some sign of Thaddeus's approval." Lauren checked the biscuits again. Finding them a rich golden-brown, she whisked them out of the oven, slid them onto a plate, and placed them on the table in front of Stephen. "But she was most impressed with his efforts, original or not. You've lost ground, Mr. Hawkes."

324

"You sound pleased," he said, spooning a scarlet gobbet of jam onto a fragrant biscuit. "But I'll make up for it tonight."

"Oh, yes, your little . . . performance. Well, it better be good enough to convince Mr. Stanton, or I fear you'll be out of this house posthaste."

"You sound even more pleased than you did a moment ago." He added butter to the jam on his biscuit, then held it up to admire the mingling of gold and scarlet. "Are you really so anxious to be rid of me?"

"Yes, indeed, Mr. Hawkes." Lauren picked up a fork and turned the sizzling meat over.

"Even if it leaves you ladies alone with Eldridge?"

She poked savagely at an unoffending piece of ham. "I can handle Mr. Eldridge."

"But not me?" he asked.

Lauren whirled to point the fork at him. "I —" she broke off, as someone knocked loudly at the front door. "Who could it be at this hour?" she asked.

"I'll answer it," Stephen said.

He strode towards the front of the house, and Lauren could hear him open the door, speak briefly, then slam the door closed again with a force that echoed through the house.

A moment later he returned, scowling like a brigand, with a huge bouquet of red roses clasped between white-knuckled hands. Lauren stared at him, openmouthed in surprise at his anger. Then she recovered, reminding herself that *she* was the one who had the right to be angry just now.

"What's the matter with you?" she asked.

"What do you think?" he growled, squeezing the stems even tighter. "Do you always get red roses from your simpering sweetheart first thing in the

325

morning?"

Oh, Good heavens! she thought in exasperation. First the pearls, then these roses—red for love, a blatant declaration that would have made her uncomfortable even if Stephen weren't here to see. And Richard had promised not to pursue her like this! Truly, it was time she did something about him once and for all.

Infuriated by the absentminded look on her face, Stephen glared at her over the profusion of crimson blooms. "Now this is the end," he snarled, keeping his voice down with an effort. "I've reached the limit of my patience."

"*Your* patience!" Lauren cried. "*Your* patience! Who do you think you are?"

He strode across the kitchen to the back door, wrenched it open, and hurled the roses out into the snow. Lauren stood with her hand clasping her throat, stunned by his sudden, unexpected violence.

"What are you doing?" she demanded. "Have you gone mad?"

He turned to face her. "For a while, perhaps I had. But now I've regained my sanity." His face set in determination, he began walking towards her.

Lauren, fork still in hand, began to back up. "What . . . what are you doing?"

He only smiled, and his continued silence was unnerving. She glanced over her shoulder to gauge the distance to the hallway. There was no possible chance that she'd make it. Refusing to be dragged down from behind—final ignominy!—she stood her ground. He closed the distance between them, stopping only when his chest was a scant few inches from hers. She was truly frightened now, of him, and of herself. He was too near, too vitally handsome, and she knew he was going to kiss her. Her heart felt as though it was going to pound right out of her chest. She couldn't let him do this to her!

"Stay away from me," she warned, raising the fork. "I'll stab you."

His smile broadened. "Stab away."

"I will, I swear I will!"

He took her hand, the one holding the fork, and pulled it towards him until the tines were touching the starched front of his shirt. "Go ahead."

She stared into his storm-colored eyes, knowing she was beaten. No matter what he had done to her, no matter how angry and frightened she might be, she could no more poke that fork into his flesh than she could into her own. And he knew it. With a little sob of indrawn breath, she flung the fork aside and tried to turn away.

His hands came down on her shoulders, holding her in place. "No," he said, his voice gentle now. "This has been coming all week, love. There's no point in fighting it any longer."

"Leave me alone," she said, trembling under his hands.

"I can't." His fingers tightened and relaxed, tightened and relaxed. "I've tried my damndest, but I can't."

His right hand moved from her shoulder to the nape of her neck, then slid into the thick knot of hair at the back of her head. A vortex of desire went through her, sweet, hot, and oh, so dangerous. She tried to will it away, but it was stronger than she was, more tempting than the devil himself.

"I'll hate you," she whispered. She'd hate herself more.

His left arm encircled her waist, drawing her inexorably against him. "I'll have to take the chance," he said, his breath warm against her lips.

Lauren watched his face come closer and closer, until she could see the variegations of gray in his irises. It was going to happen now. She tried to turn her face aside, but his long fingers cupped the back of her head, anchoring her firmly.

She watched as his eyes closed, the thick, black fringe of lashes dark against his skin. Then his lips settled on hers, gently at first, then with increasing pressure as he tried to urge her mouth open. Stubbornly, she locked her teeth. Despite the heat raging through her body, she was determined to give him nothing.

"Let me in," he muttered against her lips. He opened his eyes to find her staring at him, and the corners of his mouth quirked upward in a rueful smile. "You're supposed to close your eyes when I kiss you."

"Really?" she asked. "But I've learned not to turn my back on you for a moment, Mr. Hawkes."

"Let's try it again," he murmured, ignoring her sarcasm.

"Let's not." But there was no conviction in her voice, and she knew it.

He kissed her brows, her temples, each tender corner of her mouth, then nibbled playfully at the full, ripe curve of her lower lip. He gently tipped her head back, so he could trace the graceful line of her throat with his tongue. Lauren's arms ached to clasp him to her, and it was all she could do to repress a moan at the exquisite sensations his caresses created in her. This volcanic attraction between them was wrong, so wrong, but so incredibly powerful! No amount of self-control would withstand it.

Lauren fought her own arousal, but her body ignored her mind to respond to him with fiery passion. And he took swift advantage, returning to claim her mouth once again. Of their own volition, her lips parted to allow him access. He explored her expertly and leisurely, tracing the edges of her teeth, teasing the sensitive insides of her lips, then delving deep to play with her tongue. He coaxed her tongue forward, then gently drew it into his mouth. Lauren was lost. She could feel the muscular length of his legs pressed tightly to hers, even feel the frantic beating of his heart.

He raised his head a fraction of an inch to stare into her dark, desire-glazed eyes. What a woman she was! Even given reluctantly, her passion was a wonderful thing. "Do you see?" he asked. "Do you see how good we are together? *That's* why I can't leave you alone."

"Let go of me," she snapped, reality crashing in on her like a cold tide. Reality, and self-disgust.

He released her. "Damn it, can't you even be honest about your own feelings?"

"Those aren't *feelings,* Mr. Hawkes." At least on your part, she added silently.

"Well, I'll take them, whatever you want to call them," he said.

Her hands clenched into fists. "You're despicable."

"Perhaps. But I'm also your lover."

"You must have taken leave of your senses," she retorted.

He smiled. "Perhaps that, too. But I'm still your lover. No matter what you may think in that pretty head of yours, your heart knows that, Lauren."

The truth of his words was unbearable. Without

thinking, she slapped him across the face with all her strength. Afterward, appalled by her mindless action, she took a step backward, her hand going up to clasp her throat.

"I'll give you that one," he said, his eyes darkening to the color of charcoal. "But we're even now. Don't try it again, unless you're willing to take the consequences."

She was appalled by her action. Why had she allowed him to goad her to violence? "I didn't mean to strike you," she said.

"Yes, you did." He reached up to touch the still-stinging skin of his cheek. "You're not as goddamned cool as you'd like to think. I've always known it, but you've insisted on fooling yourself. The truth hurts, doesn't it, Lauren?"

She took a deep, calming breath. Every word he'd said was true. She *had* fooled herself. But not about her nature—about his. "If you really want to be honest about . . . Oh, no! The ham!" she cried, suddenly becoming aware of the acrid smell of scorching meat.

She whirled and rushed to the stove. Wrapping a cloth around the handle of the griddle, she carried it to the back door and flung its blackened contents out into the snow with the roses.

When she turned around again, she saw that Stephen was gone. A tear escaped her to make a hot trail down her cheek. Whisking it away impatiently, she began cutting more ham.

Lauren walked up the steps to her mother's apartment, trying to think of a gentle way to break the news of Caldwell Stanton's return.

As soon as she reached the landing, the door to Alanna's apartment opened. "I saw you from the window," Alanna cried, rushing to embrace her daughter. "Oh, Lauren! I missed you so!"

Lauren hugged her, tears coming into her eyes as a sharp rush of happiness caught her chest. "It *has* been ages, Mother. It's so good to see you."

"Come in, come in! Mary is out visiting some friends, so we've got plenty of time to ourselves." Alanna took Lauren's hand and tugged her into the apartment. "I've been so worried since I got your note about Mrs. Danforth being ill. She's better, isn't she?"

"Much." Lauren removed her cloak and hung it on a hook beside the door. "But it was nip-and-tuck for a while. I was terribly worried about her."

"You look tired, dear. Come sit down." Alanna took her own advice and took a seat on the sofa.

Lauren obeyed. "Well, *you* look radiant. Being in love agrees with you." If only I could say the same! she thought.

"Lauren, about Martin—"

"Not another word." Lauren took the older woman's hands in hers. "You don't owe me any explanations about Martin."

"But—"

"I understand. For the first time in my life, I truly understand." Tears stung Lauren's eyes again. "I'm sorry for ever thinking of your ability to love again and again as weakness. *I* was the one who was weak, for not daring to face life as it really was."

"Oh!" Alanna looked deeply into her daughter's eyes. "But that has changed now, hasn't it? You fell in love."

Lauren nodded, glad for her mother's perception.

331

"I gave him everything, Mother, and he threw it away."

"And he's gone now?"

"Yes. Well, no, not exactly. He came back, but not for me. He wants Mrs. Danforth's money." Lauren glanced out the window, unable to bear the sadness in her mother's eyes.

Alanna stood up, smoothing the front of her dress with hands that trembled. "Then he's a fool." She studied her daughter's face, then sighed in resignation. "You still love him."

"I'm an even bigger fool than he is," Lauren said. "I made a mistake, and I hope to accept it with as much grace as you've faced *your* burdens." Forcing herself to smile, she tugged Alanna back down to the sofa. "But enough of that. I've got something very important to tell you."

"Yes, dear?"

Lauren took a deep breath. "Caldwell Stanton is here in New York."

Alanna's steady gaze faltered for a moment. "Yes. I . . . I saw it in the newspaper."

"Mother, he wants to see you." Lauren took her mother's hands and held them tightly. "He wants your forgiveness."

"How do you know?" Alanna demanded.

"I met him." Lauren shook her head in response to the unspoken question in her mother's eyes. "He doesn't know who I am. But somehow, we came to talk about you."

"Oh . . . well . . ." Alanna took a shuddering breath. "What do you think of him?"

"I've never met anyone more infuriating." Except for Stephen Hawkes, she added silently. "But I believe he sincerely wants to make peace with you."

332

"What do *you* want me to do?" Alanna asked.

A month or two ago, Lauren would have been quick to give her opinion. No longer. "It's *your* decision, Mother."

"Not completely," Alanna pointed out. "If I come forward, then your identity will be revealed as well. Anything Caldwell Stanton does is news, and our names and faces will be blazoned across the front page of every newspaper in the state. Not only that, my . . . my earlier indiscretions will be brought out again to titilate public interest. How will you feel about that?"

Lauren hesitated before answering, searching deep within her heart for her true feelings. To her surprise, she found that she feared nothing but being hurt by Stephen again. "I don't care," she said honestly. "Whatever happens, we'll face it together, as we always have."

Alanna smiled tremulously. "What about Mrs. Danforth?"

"I love her dearly. If she truly loves me in return, she loves what's here," Lauren tapped the center of her chest, "and not my name. If she orders me out of her home, I'll just find some other way to help her."

Alanna sighed. "I was hoping you'd object, so I wouldn't have to take the responsibility for this decision. But I suppose it's time I stopped leaning on you." She raised her hand to prevent Lauren's protest. "Even as a little girl, you were my support and my protection from the world. Don't deny it, Lauren. I denied it long enough, and I'm proud to be able to admit it at last."

Lauren ducked her head, embarrassed. "Your father is coming out to the house tonight. If you want, I'll arrange a meeting—"

"No. First, I must discuss it with Martin, for he, too, will be thrust into the limelight if I come forward."

"Why?" Lauren asked. "Why involve him at all?"

Alanna reached out and caressed her daughter's cheek. "He and I are going to be married."

"But he's already married!"

"No, dear. His wife died nearly three months ago. As you know, she had been ill for a long time."

"But I thought he was devoted to her. Surely his grief—"

"No, dear. Although his marriage was one of convenience and quite loveless, Martin was far too honorable to reveal that he had come to care for me while she was still living. But once he was free . . ." She tightened her grasp on Lauren's hands. "Oh, Lauren, sometimes I feel so guilty, but sometimes . . . Am I so terrible to reach for happiness even though that poor woman is barely cold in her grave?"

"No!" Lauren said fiercely. "No! You deserve any joy that comes your way!"

"And what about you? Can you deal with this man after he hurt you so badly?"

"Yes. Yes, I can," Lauren said, wishing she felt as certain as she sounded. "Come, Mother, let's get back to this wedding of yours. We'll have to make you a gown . . ."

The next few hours were spent in a pleasant discussion of colors, styles, and the contents of Alanna's trousseau. Lauren was beset by a mixture of emotions: joy for her mother, regret that she would never be doing this for herself, and most important of all, vindication for the lie she had lived these past two years. If she hadn't taken her post with Mrs. Danforth, Alanna and Martin would never have met. But then she wouldn't have met Stephen Hawkes, and she wouldn't have been hurt. But, seeing her mother's face glow, Lauren decided that even that price was worth paying.

She left the apartment refreshed in her soul, ready to face whatever challenges life—and Stephen—presented her. Smiling, she walked rapidly towards the nearest streetcar stop.

Bianca, who had followed Lauren from Mrs. Danforth's house, stepped out of a nearby alley and peered after that swiftly retreating figure. Now what business did refined Miss Wakefield have down here in Bleeker Street? she wondered.

Bianca's brow furrowed as she remembered how Lauren had jumped to her defense when Clarissa Farleigh had called her a stupid cow. No woman had ever come to her defense before.

"I'll find out her little secret, Dickie, don' you worry," Bianca said to herself. But she wasn't sure if she was going to tell him about it—yet.

Chapter Twenty-three

Portia, excited by the prospect of Stephen's séance, fidgeted restlessly as Lauren tried to brush her fine, white hair.

"Do sit still, Portia," Lauren scolded gently.

The old woman held herself motionless long enough for her hair to be wound into a smooth chignon. Lauren tucked the last pin in, then stood back to admire her handiwork.

"Thank you, dear," Portia said, pinning a jet brooch to the bodice of her black silk dress.

Lauren smiled at the widow's reflection in the mirror. "I think you'd look lovely in pink, or perhaps a pale blue."

"But I'm a widow, Lauren. Widows wear black." A wistful expression crossed her face. "Thaddeus especially liked to see me in pink. He always said . . . Oh, pay no mind to an old woman's maunderings!" She clapped her hands together, returning to her agitated state. "Oh, I'm looking forward to this séance *so* much! Think of it! We might actually contact Thaddeus tonight!"

Lauren dropped the brush. "Portia—"

"I know what you're going to say," the widow interrupted. "You've told me often enough that it's all bunk, and both Stephen and Mr. Eldridge are frauds."

Lauren opened her mouth to reply, but Portia raised her hand. "No, dear, let me have my say. We were very close, Thaddeus and I. We expected to grow old together, but he died suddenly and very quickly, and I never had the chance to say goodbye." She heaved a deep sigh of regret. "Many times I've felt that he was near, so very near, and that all I had to do was reach far enough, believe hard enough, and I would finally be able to say farewell. That's all I want, Lauren. If I can do that, then I can let him go."

Lauren's breath caught in her throat. "Why didn't you tell me?" she asked softly. "Didn't you think I would understand?"

"Actually, I was afraid you would *really* think I'd gone soft in the head." Portia gazed pleadingly at Lauren's reflection in the mirror. "You're always so practical, dear. And you see, I *must* believe in these two spiritualists, or I must give up all hope of contacting Thaddeus one last time."

"And what if neither can help you?" Lauren asked. "What then?"

"I . . . don't know." For a moment Portia's lip quivered, then she brightened. "But with Stephen, I've felt closer than ever before."

Lauren bent to pick up the brush, using the opportunity to wipe away the tears that had suddenly begun to flow down her cheeks. All Portia wanted was to say goodbye to the man she loved! And for that she'd been hounded by those two . . . *Thieves* was much too good a word for what they were! Biting the inside of her lip to keep any more tears from escaping, she straightened and tucked a few stray wisps of hair into Portia's chignon.

"There," she said at last, giving the old woman's hair a final pat. "You look lovely."

"Thank you, dear." Portia tucked a black lace handkerchief into her pocket. "It's nearly eight o'clock, time for our guests to be arriving. Would you mind terribly answering the door when they do? Bianca is not, well . . . you know."

Yes, Lauren knew. "I'll be glad to," she said, smoothing a wrinkle from the front of her deep green woolen dress as she turned away.

Closing the widow's door behind her softly, she turned and walked rapidly down the hall. As she passed the corner, she found Stephen waiting for her. She faltered to a stop, wishing she could become invisible. She really wasn't up to dealing with him now, and particularly since he was wearing the look of a predatory male.

"I've been waiting for you," he said.

"Mr. Hawkes, I'm really very busy just now—"

"You're beautiful." He made a leisurely survey of her from head to toe and back again. The rich green fabric of her dress made her skin look like translucent silk, and her hair like molten bronze. "You should wear that color more often."

"Gray suits me," she replied, wishing she hadn't let the widow talk her into wearing this dress tonight.

"Only because you think you can hide behind it," he said.

"Nonsense," she scoffed. "Now, if you're finished—"

"I'm not." He grinned, crossing his arms over his chest. "You've been avoiding me all day, Lauren."

"I have not."

His smile widened. "Was it the kiss, or the slap?"

She gave him a frosty glance, but knew better than to try to walk past him. He'd only stop her, and she had the awful feeling that if he touched her now, she'd shatter like glass. Thaddeus might be long gone, she reflected, but there were many ghosts in this house tonight: her hopes, her dreams, her innocent giving of her deepest love to a man who hadn't wanted anything but the use of her body. Illusions all.

"When will you realize that this false reserve with which you've bound yourself is too costly?" Reaching out, he traced the fatigue shadows beneath her eyes, then brushed his fingertip over her still damp eyelashes. "Something's wrong. Why don't you tell me about it?"

She trembled, for this gentleness was far more dangerous than even the powerful attraction she felt for him. "You would be the last person I would choose to confide in, Mr. Hawkes."

"Then I'll have to guess," he said, smiling. She looked like a rabbit that was ready to bolt, but didn't quite dare lest the cat pull her down from behind. "Is it the séance that put you in such a grim mood?"

"I'd hardly call my mood grim," she retorted drily. "Let's just describe it as unfriendly. And as for the séance, well, if I thought there was any hope at all that you might contact Thaddeus, I'd look forward to it."

Stephen was surprised in his turn. "You would? What brought about this sudden change of heart?" he asked, leaning his shoulder against the wall beside him.

"All Portia wants is to say goodbye to her husband." Tears stung Lauren's eyes and she looked away, towards the shadows at the end of the hall. "Just goodbye. Such a simple thing, and so completely out of her reach." Suddenly she met his gaze with fierce determination. "Portia likes you. For some unfathomable reason, she values your opinion. If you had any compassion at all, you'd help her!"

Stephen studied her closely, noting how tight-strung her nerves were beneath her brave front. He ached to fold her in his arms. "I'm doing my best," he said.

"Oh, yes, your best," she snapped contemptuously. "Your best to take her money." She started to turn away, intending to take the back stairs to get away from this conversation, but he lunged forward and grabbed her arm.

"Have I once asked her for money?" he asked sharply, swinging her around to face him again.

"Not *yet*. But I'm sure you plan to as soon as the time is right." She tried unsuccessfully to pull away. "It would be worth attending your séance just to find out how much you're going to try for. Will you beat Mr. Eldridge's ten thousand, just to prove yourself the better man?"

He jerked her against him, his eyes darkening to the color of a winter sky. "I'm not for sale," he growled.

She gasped, shocked at the savagery in his voice, but forced herself to face his anger calmly. "Then why are you here?"

He let her go, raking his hand through his silver-flecked hair in frustration. Stung by her contempt, he'd made a serious slip. Once again he'd let his emotions cloud his purpose, and damn it, he just couldn't trust her! "I don't have to justify myself to you."

She tilted her head back to look at him. "I don't understand you. You seem to like Portia, to care about her welfare. And then you do something like this séance. Why? Are people's feelings nothing to you that you reduce them to . . . to mere counters in some sort of game?"

Ah, games, he thought. Truly, she was the expert about that. Games within games within games. It was a shame it couldn't be otherwise with her.

"Perhaps another kiss might help you to understand me better," he asked, intending to distract her.

She gaped at him in astonishment. "It certainly would not!"

"Just a small one?"

"Absolutely not."

"I think we should try it." He raised her hand to his mouth and brushed his lips over the back, then turned it over and kissed her palm. Yes, he'd managed to distract her. But he'd distracted himself even more, for the faint violet scent of her skin brought his need for her into knife-sharp focus. Looking up to gauge her reaction, his lips moved to her wrist.

"See how nice it feels?" he whispered against her skin.

Lauren stood still, her heartbeat hammering in her ears. His mouth felt like hot velvet against her wrist, and the memory of how he had kissed her—every inch of her—rose in her mind and brought an aching flood of warmth to her body. Her own lips were suddenly dry, and she licked them.

He put her hands on his chest. When she pulled

them away, he brought them back. She could feel his heartbeat, strong against her palms.

"One more kiss, for understanding's sake?" he asked.

"No," she said, but her heart cried yes, yes, yes. As his head lowered to hers, her eyelids drifted closed. Desire had taken control of her body, stealing her will, making her do things she never would have done if her senses had been working properly. She ought to protest. She ought to push him away. But as he brushed his lips over hers, testing, she found herself unable to move. He fitted his mouth to hers slowly but completely, then sought a deeper union. Mindlessly, she parted her lips to accomodate him.

"Ah, Lauren! How can you deny me when we have *this?*" he whispered into her mouth.

His voice shattered her bemusement, and she pulled out of his grasp. Not again! He'd done it to her again! "I hope your dratted séance fails miserably. I hope you make a complete fool of yourself."

He chuckled. "How can I fail, with my fair lady watching?"

"You expect me to attend? I wouldn't participate in your nasty little scheme—" She took a deep, shuddering breath. Why was she unable to abandon her feelings for him, as he had abandoned her? Always the fool, to love him despite everything he had done. She clenched her fists at her sides, wishing she had the courage to slap his face again.

That would only incite him to touch her again, she knew. So instead, she turned on her heel and walked away.

"Lauren." His voice was a tether, dragging her to a halt. "Where do you think you're going?"

"To my room, Mr. Hawkes. I've had about as much of your company as I can bear."

Stephen lost patience completely. A few long strides, and he was beside her again. Taking a gentle but firm grip on her upper arm, he urged her toward the stairway.

"What are you doing?" she demanded breathlessly.

"You *will* attend the séance," he growled. "And you *will* behave yourself."

"I will not!"

"For Portia's sake, you will. I won't have you ruin this for her."

Lauren tossed her head in defiance. "For your sake, you mean."

"Damn it, for *yours!* I'm about half an inch from turning you over my knee and teaching you some manners."

"I'll make you regret this," she said through clenched teeth. She marched down the steps beside him, holding herself as stiffly as a wooden doll. If only she could *be* wood, so that his touch would not affect her so.

When they reached the foyer, he stopped so that the light of the chandelier fell upon her. Rainbow sworls swung lazily across her face; they were pale compared to the auburn glory of her hair. At that moment, he regretted every harsh word he'd spoken. But damn it to hell, it was her own fault. That stubborn defiance of hers was completely infuriating. She'd challenged him, goaded him, and made him determined to have his way. Intertwined with his anger, however, was a tenderness he'd give much to shake.

But it was there, and it was much too powerful to

resist. He cupped her face in his hands, turning it more fully into the light. Such beauty, such strength, he mused. Her eyes were so sad, and yet so defiant. Deep brown pools full of secrets he would give his right arm to know. They drew him down, drew him closer. His thumbs stroked the satin curve of her cheeks, and he saw a delicate pink flush follow his touch.

Lauren saw the line of his mouth soften. He was going to kiss her again. With her face imprisoned between his hands, she couldn't even shake her head no. As she watched his mouth come closer and closer, she realized that she couldn't have moved if she'd been free to do so.

A knock at the door shattered the moment. Stephen raised his head, and his jaw went forward pugnaciously. "Who the hell is that?" he asked.

Lauren reached up and took his hands from her cheeks. "You haven't forgotten your audience, surely."

"Audience?" His dark brows contracted.

"No performance is complete without an audience." She hated the sharp sarcasm in her voice, but couldn't help herself. It was her only defense, the only way to create the distance she needed to protect herself. She had to keep him from touching her again, or she was surely lost.

"Damn it, Lauren . . ." He grasped her by the shoulders and pulled her closer.

"Don't touch me!" She held herself stiffly, willing herself not to react to the closeness of his broad chest. Willing herself not to *feel*.

The visitor knocked again, peremptorily. With a

muffled curse, Stephen let go of her and stepped back.

"I'll answer it," she said.

"We'll go together," he said, taking hold of her elbow.

Perhaps he thought she'd run shrieking into the night and never return, Lauren mused. Perhaps he was right. It certainly would be easier than taking part in the séance.

He swung the door open to reveal Caldwell Stanton's scowling countenance. As always, the sight of the old man's granite face stiffened Lauren's spine. She'd *never* show fear in front of her grandfather, *never!*

Stanton growled, "Well, are you going to invite me in or not?"

There were a number of things Lauren would have liked to say, but he was an invited guest in this house. With an effort, she forced herself to answer politely. "Do come in, Mr. Stanton. Let me take your coat and hat."

The old man stepped inside, turning his icy glare from Lauren to Stephen and back again. "So, you two are still going 'round and 'round?"

"Whatever do you mean, Mr. Stanton?" Lauren asked, retreating into dignity. Good heavens, did the man read minds?

The old man gave a bark of laughter, short and sharp. "When you opened that door, you looked as though you wanted to strangle one another."

"I'm sure you were mistaken," she said, hoping the frost in her voice would discourage him.

Perhaps it did, for he grunted, then turned his sharp glare to Stephen. "So, you're going to entertain

345

us with some of your little tricks, eh?"

One corner of Stephen's mouth went up. "My plan is to contact Thaddeus Danforth, I'll have you know."

"Hah!" Stanton bared his teeth in a sardonic smile. "I've got a bad effect on ghosts, Mr. Hawkes. Better not let them get too close to me."

Lauren stared at the old man, aghast, as she realized he was in high good spirits. "You're enjoying yourself," she said. "You're actually looking forward to this!"

Stanton snorted. "Pshaw! I only came to drink Thaddeus's Napolean brandy. If I have to put up with some of this young rogue's psychical twaddle to do so, well, so be it."

There was another knock at the door, punctuated by a shrill giggle.

"That will be Clarissa," Stephen said, moving to open it.

It was indeed Clarissa. She swept into the house, a vision in fur-trimmed velvet, and took immediate possession of Stephen's arm. He noticed the withering glare Lauren bestowed on Clarissa—jealousy, he hoped. At least, that was what he'd counted on. Before he had a chance to appreciate what he'd wrought, he saw Richard appear in the doorway, holding a bouquet of red roses in one hand.

"Hello, everyone!" Richard called, doffing his hat as he came into the house. He bowed to Lauren and presented the flowers, with a flourish that would have done a courtier proud. "For you, my sweet."

"Richard, I . . . Thank you." Lauren took the roses from him. There was nothing else she could do or say, lest she shame him. It was hard not to smile at

346

he expression on Stephen's face, however. The look
e gave those innocent flowers should have withered
em right off their stems.

"Better put them in something, darling," Richard
aid cheerily, earning an even more baleful glare for
imself.

"Yes, I-I will." It was amazing, Lauren thought,
ow the color of Stephen's eyes seemed to change
ith his emotions. Passion made them look dark and
ot, like molten steel. Just then, however, they were
lear, crystalline gray, as cold as ice.

Clarissa pressed close against Stephen's side. "I
ope you don't mind one additional participant,
tephen darling. When Dickie heard about your sé-
nce, he simply begged to come."

Stephen's gaze did not warm. Lauren quailed in-
ardly, thinking of what the evening was sure to be
ke with the two men constantly at odds. And Stan-
n observing them all with that too-knowing gaze of
is.

"Richard can have my place," she offered.

"No," Stephen said.

"Oh, why not let her, Stephen?" Clarissa tossed her
ead, making her blond fringe bounce. "That will
ake seven of us. Seven is a lucky number, isn't it?"

He didn't answer. His gaze was fixed on Lauren's
ce, and there was no yielding in it. She knew he'd
ade up his mind, and would see that she obeyed.
he roses shook in her hand, betraying her own
embling. With an effort, she controlled it, and even
anaged to make her voice bright. "I don't mind,
uly. I have a great many things to do—"

"No," Stephen said again. "Go take care of the
owers, Lauren, then come back here immediately."

347

His eyes promised that he'd come fetch her if she dis obeyed.

Lauren saw her grandfather looking from her to Stephen. The old man was smiling, and his eyes danced with malicious humor. "Go on, girl," he growled. "Do as he says."

She was tempted to defy them both. But Stephen had the look of a man who was one step from reck lessness, and she had the feeling she wouldn't care for the consequences. So she merely gave them each a withering glance from beneath her lashes, then stalked toward the kitchen.

Stephen watched the graceful — and indignant — sway of her bustle. Defiant, and beautiful with it, he thought. Someone else knocked at the door. "That will be the Talmadges," he said. Disengaging himself from Clarissa, he went to answer the door.

Stanton grabbed his sleeve as he went past. "Lauren Wakefield is a hell of a woman," the old man said softly. "She's going to take this out of your hide."

Stephen laughed. "There are some prices a man is willing to pay."

Chapter Twenty-four

When Lauren returned to the foyer, she heard voices sifting through the closed door of the drawing room. Perhaps they'd started without her, she thought hopefully. Perhaps Stephen would be so engrossed — a small, treacherous voice in her mind added, *With Clarissa* — that he wouldn't notice her absence.

Then the door opened, and Stephen's broad-shouldered figure filled the opening. "You weren't thinking of sneaking upstairs, were you?" he asked.

"Of course not."

He chuckled. "Of course not." Striding forward, he took her by the elbow. "Come, my sweet. It's going to be an interesting party, don't you think?"

"No, I don't. I think it's going to be beastly."

"You wound me," he murmured, urging her forward.

She stopped in the doorway and surveyed the room. A table had been brought into the room for the séance. Jane Talmadge was holding court at the far end of the table, with her son and Caldwell Stanton in attendance. The old woman was trading verbal barbs with Stanton, punctuating her words from time to time with her cane.

Portia, a tiny glass of sherry in her hand, was sitting to the right of the head of the table, where Stephen's place would be. Clarissa had taken the seat directly across from her, which, Lauren noted with a bit of asperity, would put her as close as possible to Stephen. Richard, evidently waiting to see where Lauren would sit, hadn't chosen a place yet. Both brother and sister looked angry, and Lauren guessed for the same reason: Stephen's possessive grip on her arm.

Portia waved her handkerchief. "Lauren, my dear, you've come back at last! Now that we're all here, let's get started, shan't we? I'm fairly bursting with impatience."

Richard came forward to take's Lauren's free hand in his. "Come, sit next to me, my dear."

Stephen's eyes narrowed. If he weren't working, he'd teach the prancing dandy some badly needed manners. "The seating of the participants is *my* job, Mr. Farleigh. Unless you'd like to take over the séance, that is."

"I just wanted to make sure of the lady's safety." With a smile, Richard raised Lauren's hand to his lips. "Surely you don't claim *that* perquisite as well, Mr. Hawkes."

"Stop it, both of you," Lauren hissed before Stephen could reply. She was conscious of Clarissa's malevolent stare. Please, she prayed, keep Stephen from making a scene. The woman's got the tongue of a magpie. Thank God they were too far away for Clarissa to hear the men's exchange.

Pulling her hand away from Richard and her elbow away from Stephen, Lauren went to sit between

350

Portia and Martin Talmadge. There, she was safe! She gave Stephen a defiant look from beneath her lashes, knowing he couldn't do a thing about it.

Stephen smiled. She looked like the proverbial cat with cream on its whiskers. So, she thought she'd maneuvered him, did she? Well, he'd faced greater challenges than this, and won. And for much less reward. He glanced at Richard. "Mr. Farleigh, if you would be so kind as to take the seat beside your sister's, we can get started."

Once Richard was seated, Stephen turned the gaslights off and moved surefootedly through the darkness to his place at the head of the table. "Will everyone hold hands, please? Excellent."

Silence fell, oppressive in the darkened room. Portia clutched Lauren's hand tightly, her plump fingers squeezing with surprising strength. Lauren squeezed back, trying to reassure the old woman.

Then Stephen said, "This isn't right. The arrangement of auras . . . Mrs. Danforth, I think it would be better if you sat here, at the head of the table."

"Do you really?" the widow asked breathlessly. "Then, of course, we should change."

"Auras?" Stanton asked. "What the hell is an aura?"

"Don't worry about it, Mr. Stanton," Stephen said, considerable amusement in his voice. "One wouldn't dare get near you."

"Do you see them or feel them?" the old man demanded. "Should I hold onto my wallet?"

"Caldwell," Portia said with some asperity, "Do be quiet."

Lauren closed her eyes as Stephen sat down beside

351

her, then opened them again when Stanton chuckled. Oh, they were providing the old rogue with a great deal of entertainment! She jerked as Stephen's hand closed over hers, warm and strong. He began speaking, his deep voice flowing over her like honey.

"I want you all to relax," he said. "Empty your minds of all thought. Open yourself to the world around you, then open yourself to the world beyond—that of the spirits."

Lauren heard the others' breathing and the minute shiftings of their bodies. Above all, she sensed Stephen beside her, the faint scent of his cologne, the almost overwhelming awareness of his desire for her. She held her breath as his thumb stroked over the skin of her palm, brushing over the pad of flesh at the base of her thumb, then moving lower to skim her pulse point. For all its feather-lightness, his touch was as intimate as a kiss. Heat followed his caress, then spread outward through her body. For a moment, she was grateful for the darkness.

"Miss Wakefield, you're shaking," Martin said softly.

"Oh, dear!" Portia's voice was overly excited. "Lauren, please, don't be afraid. Thaddeus was the gentlest, kindest man I ever met. He would never hurt you."

"I-I'm all right," Lauren said. With an effort, she controlled her trembling. "Please, continue."

As Stephen began speaking again, she tried very hard to empty her mind. If she could, perhaps she would actually get through this without screaming.

"Yes," Stephen murmured. "I feel the spirit world coming closer. A moment, and then we will have contact. Mrs. Danforth, you are our key. Call your husband. Softly with your voice. But with your heart, use every bit of strength you possess."

Portia's voice sounded low and dreamy. "Thaddeus. Thaddeus, beloved, it's Portia. I must speak with you. Come to us."

The darkness was complete, enveloping. Lauren stared into it so hard that her vision began playing tricks on her. A wisp of a glow there, a streak there, always at the edge of her field of view.

"Thaddeus, I'm calling to you!" Portia's voice was urgent now, throbbing with suppressed excitement.

Again, Lauren saw the light. And this time she realized that it was no illusion, but some glowing . . . thing darting around the table. Then Stephen truly meant to do it tonight. He was going to give Portia her husband—or rather, what *Stephen* wanted to give her of Thaddeus. She didn't know how he managed it, still holding onto her hand as he was, nor did she care. What mattered was that he would do it at all.

Lauren squeezed her eyes shut, praying for the strength to continue. It was a travesty. A mockery of Portia's very real grief for her husband. To have to sit here and listen to it . . . worse, to watch Stephen use the old woman's feelings to his own advantage, was more than she could bear. He'd take the widow's money, then move on, oblivious to the damage he'd done. Suddenly the darkness became a smothering blanket, choking her.

"Stop!" she cried. "Stop it this instant!" She jumped to her feet, sending her chair crashing backward to the floor. Her breath coming in harsh rasps,

353

she stumbled through the darkness to the door and groped blindly along the smooth wood for the knob.

There was a babble of confused voices behind her. She heard Stephen call her name once, and then the scrape of chairs being pushed back. Finally her searching hand found the knob. Wrenching the door open, she ran out into the foyer.

Stephen caught her just before she reached the stairway. "Where are you going?" he rasped, his voice harsh with concern.

"I can't do this. I can't." Tears were right beneath the surface, tears she refused to let him see. "Don't you understand? Dear God in heaven, I thought it was awful when Eldridge did this to her. But to sit there and listen to *you* . . . It's like a knife in my chest. I can't bear it." She stopped, not able to trust her voice any longer.

He pulled her closer, his gaze searching her face, probing her eyes as though to pull her heart out through them. She seemed to be telling the truth. But time and again he'd thought the same thing and learned to his sorrow that he'd been wrong.

She turned her face aside, but he grasped her chin and brought her back. "Why does it matter so much that I not be the one to do it?" he asked.

"I don't know." Yes, she did. But she would have died on the spot than admit it to him now.

For a brief moment, Stephen would have done almost anything to take that shattered look from her face. But the moment passed. He had a job to do, and that must take precedence over her feelings. Or his.

"Go on upstairs," he said. At least he could give

her that much. "I'll make your excuses."

She gazed into his eyes, seeing the softness that had come into them. Was it possible that he truly cared? That there was a conscience somewhere in him? "Thank you." She turned away. Suddenly she turned back and put her hand on his arm. "Stephen . . . Will you consider stopping this madness?"

"I can't."

She sighed; the softness had drained from his eyes, leaving only a weary cynicism. In her own foolish need to find compassion in him, she had misinterpreted what she'd seen. Taking her hand from his arm, she turned her back on him. "Then good night, Mr. Hawkes."

With Nero purring in her lap, Lauren sat in her window seat watching the wind chase whorls of powdery snow across Gramercy Park. The séance had been going on for more than an hour now. It seemed to be progressing smoothly; even Caldwell Stanton, after a few ascerbic observations she'd heard all the way up here, appeared to be behaving himself.

She'd thought to find refuge here, but there was none. She felt beset from every quarter: Stephen, Richard, Eldridge, Caldwell Stanton, even Portia was making demands on her emotions—demands she wasn't sure she had the capacity to meet.

"Oh, Mother, please make up your mind soon!" Lauren whispered, pressing her forehead against the cold glass of the window. "I don't care what price I have to pay. I just want this horrible mess to end."

Suddenly there was a crash from downstairs, and she jumped to her feet. Nero, dislodged from his comfortable nest, miaowed in loud protest.

"Shhh, Nero," she hissed. Had the noise just been part of the séance, or had something gone wrong? Then she heard Portia's voice, raised high in agitation, and that sound propelled her into motion. She rushed across the room, flung her door open, then picked up her skirts and ran down the hall towards the stairs.

Even in her haste she noticed that someone had turned out the gaslight in the foyer, leaving only the faint illumination from the far end of the hall to light her way. The marble stairs gleamed eerily in the dimness, a milky blur leading into a pool of murky shadow. Nero bounded ahead of her, his white fur making him almost invisible against the pale stone.

Lauren followed him as fast as she could, her shoes making the barest whisper-sound on the steps. Reaching the landing, she grabbed the bannister to steady herself as she made the turn. As her foot touched the stair below, something caught her ankle, pitching her headfirst towards the floor below.

She screamed in fright, clutching desperately at the bannister. Her fingers slipped and slid, then found purchase on one of the posts. She cried out again, this time in pain, as her knees slammed against the hard edge of a stair. The force of the impact tore her hands from the post, and she bumped painfully down the rest of the stairs before sprawling upon the marble floor below. The world spun dizzily around her.

The parlor door opened. A flood of yellow light speared through the dark foyer, and Lauren saw Stephen's broad-shouldered figure silhouetted in the opening. She rolled onto her side and tried to push up on one elbow, but her arm refused to support her weight.

Stephen saw Lauren lying in the wedge of light, a small, crumpled figure like that of a moth singed by a candle flame, and hurtled into motion. He went down on his knees beside her, almost afraid to breathe. "Lauren?" he whispered urgently. "Lauren!"

She reached out to him, and he clasped her hand tightly. "Easy, honey," he murmured. "I'll take care of you."

Martin Talmadge was the next to reach her, and the rest of the guests arrived a few moments after. Portia, her normally rosy cheeks ashen with fright, bent over Lauren solicitiously.

"What happened, dear?" the old woman asked.

"I fell . . . down the stairs," Lauren said shakily. Stephen's grip on her hand tightened.

Martin Talmadge glanced up the steep stairway and uttered a wordless exclamation of dismay. The others crowded around, staring down at Lauren.

"Don't move," Stephen ordered, gently holding her down with one hand. "Does anything hurt? Talk to me, Lauren!"

Still a bit dazed, Lauren stared up at the circle of staring faces, her mind vaguely registering their expressions: Portia's fear, the concern shown by the Talmadges, Richard, and Caldwell Stanton, and Clarissa's bored petulance. It was the latter that jolted Lauren out of her shock. She was *not* going to

357

lie on the floor at Clarissa Farleigh's feet!

"I'm all right," she said. "Please, Stephen, just help me sit up."

"I don't think that's wise just now," he said.

"I'm fine, really. Everything works perfectly, see?" she wiggled her arms and legs, hiding a wince of pain.

Stephen grunted, unconvinced, but slipped his arm behind her shoulders and levered her to a sitting position. "Does anything hurt?" he asked again.

Lauren shook her head. "Help me up."

Frowning, he obeyed, keeping his hand on the small of her back to support her. Something wet and warm crawled slowly down her shin, but she wasn't about to say anything about it. The awful vision of Stephen pulling her skirts up in front of everyone would have kept her silent, even if both her legs had been broken. Just let me get upstairs without a scene, she prayed. She forced herself to take a step, then another. "See?" she said. "Nothing is wrong with me at all."

"No?" Caldwell Stanton growled. "Then why the hell are you bleeding?" He pointed to the floor where she had been standing a moment ago. A splotch of blood, startlingly vivid against the white marble, stained the floor.

With a curse, Stephen bent and scooped Lauren into his arms.

Richard moved smoothly to block his path to the stairs. "Here, let me take her," he said.

Stephen didn't even pause, but brushed the smaller man out of the way and headed upstairs, Portia at his heels. Hearing Caldwell Stanton bark a curt order, Lauren glanced back at the others in time to see him leading the group back to the parlor. Jane Talmadge brought up the rear, herding a protesting Clarissa ahead of her with the tip of her cane.

"Dear Jane, always so resourceful," Portia murmured. "Here, Stephen, let me pass. I'll open the door for you."

"Hurry," he urged, feeling a trickle of wetness course down the hand that was supporting Lauren's legs. "She's bleeding badly."

"Oh, this is ridiculous!" Lauren protested. "Really, it's nothing."

He ignored her, striding purposefully after Portia's scurrying figure. The widow flung Lauren's door open and rushed to light the lamps. "I'll get the medicine chest," the old woman said as she hurried out again. "See to her, Stephen."

He laid Lauren on the bed and began pulling her skirts up. She pushed his hands away frantically. "Don't!" she cried. "I'll wait for Portia. Really, Stephen, you can't—"

"Shut up," he growled. Impatient with her interference and the layers of fabric, he simply tore her skirt from hem to waist. A scarlet stain was spreading across her outer petticoat, and his breath went out in a hiss.

"Stephen, no!" she cried, knowing what was going to happen next. "Don't!"

He ignored her, and her petticoats soon went the way of her skirt. Lauren clutched the tumbled heap of torn fabric around her hips in an attempt to preserve her modesty, but her legs, from garters to toes, were exposed to his view. She had nothing but her drawers covering the entire lower part of her body! Panic—sheer, gasping panic—took hold of her. She had to get away before he took even those!

"Damn it, Lauren, stop squirming and let me look!"

Portia came into the room and stopped, staring wide-eyed at the two young people. Then a dimple creased her cheek, and she closed the door behind her. "Make her behave, Stephen."

"I'm trying," he growled. "But this stupid modesty of hers . . . All right, damn it to hell, you've forced my hand." With that, he grabbed Lauren's ankles and pinned her feet to the bed.

"Make him go away, Portia!" Lauren sat up and pushed the remnants of her skirt as far down her legs as she could.

"I'll strip you naked, if I have to," he promised, half-hoping she'd push him that far.

Lauren froze, staring at him in horror. He'd do it. He would really do it, and right in front of Portia. Closing her eyes, she lifted the fabric away from her knees. After a moment, his hands left her ankles.

"It's not as bad as it looks, Stephen," Portia said, dabbing at the blood on Lauren's shin with a clean cloth. "Truly, I don't think we'll even need the doctor."

Pushing her embarrassment aside, Lauren looked down at her knees. They were beginning to swell, and huge bruises were already darkening beneath each one. A cut, perhaps two inches long, crossed her right shin. Even as she watched, the bleeding began to slow.

"Do you hurt anywhere else?" Portia asked.

Lauren shook her head, ignoring the twinge on her hip and the one on her shoulder. Mention them now, with Stephen in his present mood? Oh, no, no, no!

Stephen sat on the bed to watch Portia sponge the cut with cool water. Seeing that his attention was on the widow, Lauren took the opportunity to study his face. A muscle jumped spasmodically in his jaw, and his eyes were nearly black with emotion. Why, he was actually frightened for me! she thought in astonishment. He *does* care!

As though divining her thought, his gaze moved up to meet hers. There was such passionate tenderness in it that her heart felt as though it was going to leap right out of her body. For a moment—a single precious moment—it seemed as if she could see right through to his soul. Then his eyes changed, and it was as though a shutter had dropped down over them, leaving her on the outside. But she had seen enough. Joy filled her, and it was all she could do to contain it. There was one thing she needed to know.

"Tell me," she asked, hardly daring to breathe. "Was the séance successful?"

"The séance?" Portia frowned. "Oh, that. Well, we weren't able to contact Thaddeus, I'm afraid. Stephen said he just didn't have the proper concentration."

Lauren closed her eyes. He hadn't done it! She knew it had been his gift to her, and it was more precious than diamonds. There were many issues yet unresolved between them, but the simple fact that he had put her above his own ambition stood out like a

361

beacon. There was hope, then. Hope that somehow, someday, there might be a chance for them.

Stephen touched her cheek lightly, and she opened her eyes again. "How did you fall?" he asked.

"I don't quite know," she said. "I was running, and not paying attention to where I was going." She frowned, remembering that light touch on her ankle just before she fell. Had it really been there, or had it been her imagination? Looking back on it now, she couldn't tell. "And Nero was on the stairs with me. I suppose I tripped over him."

Stephen reached out to touch a scrape that marred the smooth skin of her wrist, and his hand shook with reaction. That had been a dangerous fall. If she'd hit her head instead of her knees, she could very easily have been killed. The thought of it brought him off the bed, his fists clenched. "If Eldridge had anything to do with this, I'll strangle him!"

Shocked by the violence on his face, Lauren scrambled from the bed and grabbed his arm. "He couldn't have. He wasn't even in the house!"

"That's right, Stephen," Portia said. "Don't you remember him leaving? He certainly made enough noise slamming the door."

"I remember." But that didn't mean he hadn't come back in, Stephen thought, bringing his temper under control with an effort. He made a mental note to check the stairs for any evidence of tampering, but he was sure he wouldn't find anything. Whatever else Eldridge might be, he wasn't stupid.

"Sit down, Stephen," Lauren said, tugging on his arm. "It was my own fault. I should have known

362

better than to go rushing down those stairs like that."

His gaze raked over her, taking in the shredded dress, the bruised knees, the concern in her eyes. The cut, aggravated by her movement, had begun to bleed again. With infinite gentleness, he bent and lifted her into his arms.

"Now," he said, laying her on the bed again, "let's see to your injuries."

"Portia will tend me," she said, wrapping the remains of her skirts around her legs again.

"Don't argue with me, Lauren."

"Stephen, dear." The widow tapped him on the shoulder. "You're embarrassing her, and you're interfering with me," she said. "Why don't you go make yourself useful downstairs?"

He hesitated, wanting to make sure for himself that Lauren was truly all right. Then, seeing the deep blush on her face, he took pity on her. "Very well, I'll go for now," he growled. He leaned over Lauren, propping himself with braced arms. "You are to rest. If you get up from this bed tonight, I'll tie you to the bedposts. Do you understand?"

"Yes, Stephen," Lauren murmured. *He cares, he cares!* was a triumphant paean in her heart.

He straightened, then stalked across the room and flung the door open. His footsteps faded as he moved down the hall.

"Such a forceful young man," Portia breathed. "Did you see how deftly he dealt with young Mr. Farleigh downstairs?"

"He has his faults, too," Lauren protested. "Arrogant, much too curious for his own good—"

363

"And handsome," Portia continued blithely. "If I were forty years younger, even thirty, I'd marry him right now." Ignoring Lauren's wide-eyed surprise, she plumped down on the bed and began bandaging the cut.

"There," she said, tying off the bandage neatly. "Now let me see the other ones." The dimple reappeared in her cheek. "Whatever else you told *Stephen,* I know there are more. Not that I blame you for lying to him about them. Goodness knows what he would have done!"

"*I* know what he would have done," Lauren said, unbuttoning her bodice to reveal a large, purpling bruise on her shoulder.

The widow drew in her breath with a hiss. "Are you sure you don't need the doctor?"

"Quite." Lauren raised and lowered her arm. "See? Everything works perfectly. Believe me, if I thought anything were broken, I'd be the first to call for the doctor."

"Very well." Portia helped Lauren pull her arm out of the sleeve. "Are you sure, very sure, that your fall wasn't caused by one of Mr. Eldridge's spirits?"

Lauren let her breath out in a sigh of exasperation. "I'm positive it wasn't a spirit, Portia."

"Stephen seemed to think so."

"I'm sure Stephen doesn't think spirits caused it, either," Lauren said firmly. "And I think this whole incident is best forgotten."

"If you insist, dear." The dimple reappeared in Portia's cheek. "But I don't think Stephen ever will. Why, the man was beside himself. You're a very lucky young woman, you know."

Lauren sat bolt upright. "What do you mean by that?"

"Good heavens, child!" The widow laughed. "I may be a bit silly at times, but I'm not blind."

"Oh." Heat rushed into Lauren's face. "I-I didn't know it was so obvious."

"It always is—at least to those not involved." Portia reached over to take Lauren's hand in both of hers. "Let me tell you something, dear. If you sit back and let Clarissa Farleigh steal him away from you, you're a terrible fool."

Lauren met the old woman's gaze for a moment, then nodded and settled back into the pillows. Yes, indeed, she mused, thinking of Stephen's planned outing with Clarissa tomorrow night. I *would* be a fool to give him up without a fight.

Chapter Twenty-five

Lauren woke to a soft knock on her door. "Yes?" she called sleepily.

"I've brought you some breakfast," Portia said.

"Oh, please come in." Lauren rolled over, wincing from the pain of sore, stiff muscles and bruised flesh.

The door opened and Portia bustled in, a tray balanced in her arms. "How are you feeling this morning, dear?" she asked cheerily.

"A little sore, but quite able to come down to eat." Stifling a gasp of indrawn breath, Lauren pushed herself into a sitting position. "Now don't fuss, Portia. You're not strong enough to be cooking and carrying trays around like this."

"Of course, I am. Never felt better, if you must know." Portia placed the tray across Lauren's lap and began arranging the silverware. "There. I was going to put one of Richard's roses on the tray for color, but they seem to have disappeared mysteriously during the night. I wonder how."

Lauren smiled. "Perhaps it was one of Mr. Eldridge's spirits."

"Perhaps." The widow smoothed a stray lock of hair back into her chignon. "I for one think roses should never be wasted in winter—no matter what the source. Now, dear, why don't you eat while the food is hot?"

Lauren obeyed. As she ate, she studied the old woman's face, noting that the color was beginning to come back into her cheeks. She was obviously enjoying this reversal of roles. Perhaps I've been selfish, Lauren thought. Perhaps she needs to be needed as much as I do.

"Portia, would you mind putting another pillow behind me?" she asked.

"Certainly, dear."

Lauren smiled at Portia as she happily plumped pillows. Then something drew her gaze to the doorway.

Stephen was standing there watching them both. He looked tired, and more than a little grim. Instinctively, she pulled the covers up to her chin.

His gaze raked over her, taking in her bright, tumbled hair, her startled eyes, and the hands that were holding the blankets tightly against her chest. She looked sleep-mussed and beautiful, and he wished he'd awakened in that bed beside her. If he had, she wouldn't be eating breakfast just now. He'd be kissing her, taking that damned girlish, high-necked nightgown off her, to reveal the sensual woman beneath. He took a deep breath, forcing his straying thoughts into other channels before he did something he'd regret later.

"How do you feel?" he asked.

"Fine." Lauren's hands trembled slightly as she saw the taut look of desire on his face. If Portia hadn't been here, he would have walked across the room to pull the covers from her hands. She closed her eyes, blocking out the delicious vision of what would come later. Until certain issues were resolved between them, she couldn't allow herself to weaken.

Stephen saw the passion come into the sable depths of her eyes, and also saw her denial of it. Although he burned to stride across the room to her and brush her protests aside with his lips and hands, he pushed his instincts aside. Crossing his arms over his chest, he leaned his shoulder against the doorjamb.

He stared broodingly at her, wishing he had more control over his emotions. The memory of her lying crumpled on the floor had haunted his sleep, and he'd awakened feeling savage and off balance.

"How are your knees?" he asked.

Lauren pulled the covers up another fraction of an inch. "Fine."

He looked at Portia. The widow picked up the teapot and headed for the door. "I'll just run down to the kitchen and warm this."

Astonished by her defection, Lauren could only stare after her. Then Stephen straightened, dropping all pretense of a casual air. He closed the door, locked it, and came to stand beside the bed.

"Let me see your knees," he said.

Realizing he wasn't in any mood to be thwarted, she set the tray aside and pulled the covers away. Her cheeks burning, she lifted her nightgown up above her knees.

Stephen drew in his breath with a hiss at the sight of her bruised flesh. Lightly, he brushed his fingertips over her knees, wishing he could heal her with his touch. She was going to be sore for a few days, but he could see that the injuries were only minor.

Seething with mingled relief and fury that such a thing could happen to her, he wrapped his arms around her waist and buried his face against her thighs.

Lauren was stunned by his action, and even more surprised by the strength of her reaction to it. Desire swept through her like a storm, making her weak, making her want to bring him closer. She fought it, fought the urgings of her heart and body. Last night they had made a tentative beginning, but there was still too much pain and too little trust between them.

There was also heat, always the heat. She felt his hands move restlessly on her hips, pulling her nightgown up farther. Sweet, sweet temptation, she thought as another, stronger wave of passion went through her.

"Stephen, let me go," she said softly.

He raised his head, looking like a man who'd been dragged unwilling from a wonderful dream. His eyes were heavy-lidded with desire.

"Don't tell me no," he said, his voice hoarse with emotion.

"I have to," she whispered.

He wanted to change her mind. He knew he could do it. But he could hear Portia's voice from the stairway, and realized there was no more time for them. Sighing, he levered himself off the bed. When Lauren reached to push her nightgown down, however, he stopped her.

"Just let me look at you for a moment," he murmured.

God help her, she didn't have the strength to deny him. So she dropped her hands to her sides and let him look. His gaze devoured her, hot and hungry, all but stripping her in its intensity. Her body responded with a rush of liquid warmth, and she felt her nipples rise up in taut peaks beneath the gown.

Stephen clenched his fists, struggling not to touch her. If he did, he knew they were both lost. He could see it in her eyes, in the actions of her body. All he had to do was reach out . . .

A knock at the door shattered the mood. "Damn!" he growled.

Lauren frantically pulled the covers over herself, both relieved and regretful that the decision had been taken from her.

"Stephen, dear," Portia called. "Open the door."

He winked at Lauren, then went to obey. The widow bustled in, teapot in hand, and plumped down on the bed beside Lauren. "Here we go, dear. Nice, hot tea. Stephen, would you like a cup?"

He shook his head. Sitting in this room just now, drinking tea with Lauren when he was burning to make love to her, was more torment than any man could bear. And he still had a job to do, which had grown more imperative than ever. Although the two women hadn't realized it, he knew that trap on the stairs hadn't been meant for Lauren. It had been meant for Portia, and he had to see that it didn't happen again.

He took out his watch and opened it. "I'm afraid I've got to go. I'll send the doctor back to take a look at you."

"Really, that isn't necessary," Lauren protested.

He ignored her. Pinning the widow with a forbidding stare, he said, "Make sure she rests, Portia."

"Certainly, Stephen," she said meekly. A dimple appeared in her cheek.

370

"And Lauren," his brows contracted in a scowl. "You're canceling your evening with Richard Farleigh."

"What evening?" she asked in bewilderment.

His brows went even lower. "You didn't plan to go to a party with Richard Farleigh?"

She shook her head. Damn it to hell, he thought, Clarissa manipulated me neatly by making me think Lauren was going to that party! Well, he'd tend to Miss Farleigh later. Right now he was late for an appointment with Commissioner Padgett.

"Stephen, what on earth is this all about?" Lauren asked in confusion.

"I can't explain now." Without another word, he turned on his heel and walked out of the room.

"My goodness," the widow murmured, fanning herself with her handkerchief.

"Goodness," Lauren said, "has nothing to do with it."

"I do believe he's in love with you, dear. Did you see the look on his face when he ordered you not to see Richard tonight?" The widow fanned herself. "So incredibly possessive!"

But Lauren could only think of one thing: Although he'd demanded that she stay home, he hadn't made the same promise in return. Later, when she was dressed and prepared beforehand, she planned to have a long talk with him.

But the morning passed, then lunch, then the afternoon, and still he didn't return. Her dread grew with each passing hour. Had she misjudged him? In her love for him, had she fooled herself into seeing something that was not really there? Had she once again mistaken lust for love, passion for true emotion?

As darkness fell, she began to panic. Was he going to go directly to Clarissa without coming home at all? He couldn't, he just couldn't!

Seven o'clock came and went, then eight, then eight-thirty. Lauren sat listlessly playing solitaire at the library desk. He wasn't going to come, she thought despairingly, and now he was with Clarissa.

"I can't stand this," Lauren whispered. Tears stung her eyes. The idea of that brazen baggage hanging on his arm, smiling at him, inviting him to do God knows what . . . Oh, it was infuriating! If only she knew where they were supposed to be, she'd almost dare going out by herself!

Portia peeked into the room. "I'm going to bed, dear. Don't stay up too late, now."

"No, I won't. Good night, Portia."

Lauren sat alone in the quiet room, flipping cards at random onto the desk. Nine o'clock. She sighed, pushing her chair back from the desk. A soft rap at the window caught her attention, and she went to look out.

Richard stood outside, his breath fogging in the cold air. Lauren tugged the window upward a few inches. "Richard, what on earth—"

"Are you feeling well enough to go out?" he whispered.

"Out? Now?" She stared at him in bewilderment.

"There's a grand party going on," he said. "You really ought to come." A chuckle threatened to bubble up, and he was forced to repress it. With Clarissa's help, he'd planned this evening so carefully that nothing could go wrong. And he had the perfect lure to bring Lauren to him: Stephen Hawkes.

"I couldn't possibly," Lauren said. "It's late, and more than that, we haven't a chaperone—"

"Clarissa and Hawkes will be there." That's got' her! he thought, seeing her expression change at the mention of her lover's name.

Lauren hesitated, tempted almost beyond good sense. Oh, how she wanted to go! But not with Richard. She had already hurt him terribly, and even her soul-searing jealousy was not enough to make her use him that way. "I'm sorry, Richard, but I can't go."

"But you must!" he whispered urgently. "I thought, well . . . that perhaps . . . no, I can't go against Clarissa!" Then he took a deep breath and added, "Truly, darling, you just *have* to trust me. It's very important that you come."

"What is it?" Lauren asked breathlessly. "Is something wrong?"

"Nothing . . . Oh, damn, I suppose I have to tell you!" He looked down at the polished tips of his shoes. "Even if my sister hates me for the rest of her life, it's the right thing to do."

"What?" Lauren repeated. Stephen. It had to be something about Stephen. And from Richard's manner, it wasn't good.

Richard came closer to the window. "I know you'll never love me. It's been hard to accept, but I have. I still love you, and want you to be happy. Even if that means giving you up to another man."

Tears of distress rose up in her eyes at his pain, but her concern for Stephen overrode her sympathy for the man before her. Later, she would deal with Richard and her own guilt. "Richard, please, about Clarissa—"

"I know, I'm digressing." Be humble, he told himself. You'll extract full revenge later for everything. "Clarissa wants to marry your Mr. Hawkes, even if she has to trap him into it. The moment she's alone with him, she's going to scream defilement. Father will see to it that he either marries her, or rots in prison for the rest of his life."

"No!" Lauren gasped.

He reached out to her. "So come with me, and we'll stop it."

"Just let me get my cloak. I'll meet you out front." She turned and limped from the room, ignoring the pain of her bruised knees in her haste.

Richard showed the edges of his teeth in a snarl. Oh, didn't she jump when she thought her precious lover was in danger! "By this time tomorrow, my lovely Miss Stanton, we'll be man and wife," he said.

But he soon regained his good humor. Truly, things were working out perfectly, just perfectly, for Lauren had just put herself — and Stanton's fortune — into his hands. And sweetest retribution of all, it was Stephen Hawkes who had made it all possible. Someday he'd have to thank the man.

Lauren grabbed her warm woolen cloak and threw it on hastily, then quietly opened the front door and slipped outside. Richard was waiting for her, his elegant black coat and top hat gleaming in the streetlight.

"Hurry," he whispered. "My carriage is just a few yards down the street."

He took her elbow and urged her towards the vehicle. A quiver of unease went through her as they reached it. She should have told Portia where she was going, or even left a note. Perhaps she should go back . . . no, Stephen needed her. Any delay might put him right into Clarissa's grasping hands. So Lauren pushed her disquiet aside, and let Richard lift her into the carriage.

He spoke briefly to the driver, then sank into the seat beside her. "Here's the blanket, darling. Shall we share?"

Lauren shook her head, bracing herself as the carriage swung into motion. "How long will it take to get there?" she asked.

"Not long, darling. Not long at all."

"Where are we going?" She leaned forward to peer out the window.

"It's just a few streets away," Richard said, patting the blanket over his legs. "Are you sure you don't want to share my blanket? It's cozy under here, very cozy."

She shook her head and clasped her hands in her lap, once again beset by nervous doubt. Had she made a mistake coming? Outside, Richard had been earnest and generous. Now, there was a strange kind of sly humor beneath everything he said, and his eyes were lascivious, and strangest of all, gloating. The carriage, despite the luxury of its leather-covered seats, gilt fittings, and plush velvet curtains, suddenly seemed as claustrophobic as a prison cell.

"So, how are we going to go about this?" she asked, anxious to break the thick silence.

"As easily and painlessly as we can, my sweet."

Her heart began to pound. "That's an odd way of putting it, Richard," she said with false calmness.

"Oh?" His eyebrows went up. "Are you referring to the easy part or the painless part?"

Lauren studied him, alarm greatly sharpening her

375

perceptions. This was not the sweet, attentive suitor she thought she knew, but a shrewd, calculating man who had cunningly used her own emotions to get her into this carriage. Whatever his purpose might be, she was sure she wouldn't like it. "We're not going to meet Clarissa and Stephen, are we?" she asked, keeping her voice steady with an effort.

"Ah, brains as well as beauty. Truly, I'm a lucky man." He took her hand and raised it to his lips. "So cool and refined, even though you're afraid. I'm going to enjoy warming you, my love."

Lauren pulled her hand away, disgust coursing through her at the wet, greedy touch of his mouth. "What are you planning to do?"

"Why, only what we've planned all along. I'm going to marry you. But first we'll spend a delightful night together. Then tomorrow, when my mother and sister come to visit, they'll find us abed. Oh, the gossip *that* will cause!"

She gasped. "You and Clarissa planned this whole thing, didn't you?"

"Oh, yes, indeed." He ran his finger down the curve of her cheek, laughing when she recoiled. "You'll be well and truly compromised in the eyes of all New York, darling." He chuckled again, pleased at the thought of Hawkes turning from her in disdain, after finding out she'd bedded another man. "But if we visit the clergyman first thing in the morning and make an honest woman out of you, I'm sure I can convince my mother and sister to keep the news of our little tryst to themselves."

"You must be mad!"

"Yes, mad for you." He laid his arm across the back of the seat and leaned closer. Oh, how he

376

wished he could reveal his knowledge of her identity! Softly, a small corner of his mind urged. After you're married. Then you can do whatever you please with her.

She stared at him, wide-eyed with astonishment and the beginnings of terror. "You can't force me to marry you!"

"Force you? Perish the thought, darling girl. But I *am* taking extraordinary means to convince you," he said. Then he grinned. "You ought to see the horrified look on your face. I'm not so terrible, really. I'm just a desperate man, one who wants to claim his love before she is lost to him again. Someday a poet will probably compose an ode to my unswerving devotion."

For one wild moment, she thought that perhaps this wasn't Richard at all, but some changeling that had taken over his body. Shock held her motionless as the carriage pulled to a halt at the back stoop of an imposing brick house. This was horrible, too horrible to be real!

The coachman opened the carriage door, and the blast of frigid air jolted her out of her shock. She opened her mouth, intending to scream, but Richard moved with astonishing swiftness to smother her cry with his hand.

"No, that won't do at all," he said. "Now come along, darling.

She shook her head imploringly, but he merely lifted her out of the coach.

Stephen left the hired carriage waiting at the step and went up to knock on the Farleighs' door. His expression was grim, for he had sent three notes here, explaining that he couldn't keep his appointment with Clarissa, and all three had been returned unopened. Damn the woman for making him come all the way out here like this! By rights, he shouldn't bother. But he wanted to be certain she realized that it wasn't only tonight he was canceling, but any further contact with her. Neither she nor her brother were going to be welcome at the Danforth House any longer.

To his surprise, Clarissa herself answered. She was wearing a blue silk dressing gown and oddly, an elaborate pearl necklace.

"Come in, Stephen," she said. "You're not wearing evening clothes."

"Neither are you." He stepped into the huge gilt and marble foyer, glancing around at the costly, garish furnishings within.

"You're very observant." She closed the door and leaned her back against it. "I thought we might stay in. Mother and Father are out, and I've given the servants the night off. I guarantee you'll have *much* more fun here."

"Sorry, but no," he said. "Didn't you get my note?"

"No, I didn't." She smoothed the fabric of her dressing gown over her hips. "What did they say?"

Liar! he thought. "If you didn't get them, how do you know there was more than one?"

Instead of answering, she untied her dressing gown and let it fall to the floor. Beneath it, she was wearing nothing but the pearl necklace.

His brows went up in sardonic surprise. "Do you greet everyone like this?"

378

"No," she murmured. "Only you, Stephen."

"How flattering," he said drily. "Actually, I'm not in the mood just now."

She took a deep breath to show off her breasts to advantage. "Are you sure?"

He grinned, his ill humor evaporating as he realized the complete absurdity of the situation. "Quite sure."

"Quite, quite sure?" she breathed, walking slowly towards him. Teasingly, she ran her finger down the line of buttons on his overcoat. "Do I frighten you? I know I'm terribly bold, but I'm a woman who knows what she wants and isn't afraid to go after it."

"Sorry, Clarissa, but you don't frighten me a bit." He picked her up and set her to one side. "I'm just not interested in what you have to offer." Still smiling, he picked her dressing gown up and held it out to her. "Oh!" She snatched the garment from him and threw it on with furious motions. "I suppose you prefer redheads, is that it?"

He adjusted his derby at a jaunty angle. "Yes, as a matter of fact, I do." A certain redhead, he amended silently. With a nod, he opened the door and strode out into the cold.

Clarissa ran after him, her face twisted with hate. "Well, you won't have her, you arrogant bastard! She and Richard—" she broke off, her hand going up to cover her mouth.

"What?" Stephen whirled, taking one long stride that put him directly in front of her. "What about Richard?"

"Go to hell!" she spat.

Stephen grabbed her by the shoulders, lifting her feet clear off the ground. "Tell me!" he growled.

"You're already too late," she taunted. "He's probably in bed with the little bitch right now!"

"Where is he taking her?" His quiet, controlled voice was so at odds with the violence in his eyes that Clarissa became frightened for the first time. "Tell me *now!*"

"His house," she quavered. "I was supposed to keep you occupied—" She cried out as he thrust her from him with such force that she staggered. "Stephen!"

He whirled, leaping into the waiting carriage. At his curt order, the driver whipped the horse into a gallop.

Chapter Twenty-six

Lauren struggled wildly against Richard's pinioning arms. If only she could scream! She clawed at the back of his hand, trying to free her mouth.

Richard cursed. He'd never expected this much fight from her, and with having to keep one hand over her mouth, he was having a hard time controlling her. "Harris!" he panted. "Get over here, damn you!"

The coachman hastened to obey, bending to grab Lauren's flailing feet. They lifted her between them and carried her up the steps, still struggling.

Richard tightened his hold on her mouth. "Don't let go, Harris!" he hissed. "We're almost there!"

Lauren arched her back, but with her head pinned against Richard's chest and her legs tightly held by the coachman, she was helpless to do more. As Richard fumbled with the door, Lauren sagged in despair. This was the end. Once she was inside, she'd be totally in his power. Oh, Stephen, she wailed inwardly, if only you had come home tonight!

Suddenly a dark shape materialized beside her. There was the dull, sickening thud of a fist on flesh, and then the coachman went flying through the wood rail to land in a crumpled heap on the bricks below. A hard arm went around her waist, tearing her from Richard's grasp.

A deep, incredibly welcome voice growled, "Bastards!"

"Stephen!" she cried. "Oh, thank God!"

With a bleat of terror, Richard lunged for the doorknob. Stephen put Lauren behind him, then moved forward with leonine swiftness to grab Richard by the shoulder and spin him around. "Damn you, Farleigh!" he snarled, smashing his fist into the smaller man's face.

Richard reeled back from the blow, blood flowing from his nose. His groping hand closed upon one of the fragments of the broken railing. He hefted the wood, then, with a vicious oath, hurled it at his opponent.

Stephen knocked the flying wood aside with his forearm. Taking a smooth stride forward, he buried his fist in Richard's midsection, bringing him down in a heap. Richard curled around his pain, gasping for air in great, openmouthed sobs.

Stephen stood over him, his deep chest heaving with fury and exertion. "Get up," he said hoarsely. "Damn you, get up! I'll rip your heart out with my bare hands!"

Terrified of the violence in him, Lauren gripped his arm with both hands, feeling the rock-hard tension in his muscles. "No, Stephen! Enough!"

He spared her the briefest glance, and the cold fury she read in his eyes terrified her. "I have a carriage waiting at the end of the alley," he said.

"Wait for me there."

"No. Not unless you come with me."

"Do as I say!" His voice, for all its softness, was a lash.

Richard gasped air into his lungs at last. He laughed, his face a ghastly mask of dark blood. "Your lover doesn't want any witnesses, darling," he wheezed.

Stephen grabbed the front of Richard's coat. With a heave of his powerful shoulders, he hauled the smaller man upright. "You've called her darling for the last time, Farleigh."

"Lauren is mine, Hawkes. Mine!" Richard sneered. "*I* have the rights here, not you!"

Stephen growled low in his throat. Lauren pressed herself tightly against his side and wrapped her arms around his waist. "Don't," she said. "Please."

He looked down at her, his chest heaving with rage. "Why shouldn't I?"

"Because he's not worth the trouble," she said, willing him to listen. "And as for the other, well, I broke the engagement a long time ago."

"When?" Stephen demanded.

"The day you left me."

Stephen's breath went out in a long sigh. "Even then?"

"Even then," she said softly. "Now come away."

Slowly, he relaxed his grip on the other man. Richard fell to his knees again, folding his arms over his stomach.

"If you bother her again, I'll make you wish you'd never been born," Stephen growled.

He swept Lauren into his arms and carried her down the steps, ignoring the coachman's unconscious form. She leaned her cheek against his shoulder, reveling in the hard strength of him. His arms felt so good around her, so safe and secure, that she was almost disappointed when they reached the carriage.

"Open the door," he murmured in her ear.

She obeyed, and he put her gently upon the seat. After speaking briefly to the driver, he settled into the cushions beside her.

"Are you all right?" he asked as the vehicle swung out into the street.

"Yes, I'm fine." Lauren clasped her hands tightly in her lap, intensely aware of the muscular length of his thigh pressed against hers. She glanced at him, then quickly away. "How did you come to be there just then? I—I thought you were with Clarissa."

"I was." He grinned, remembering the look on Clarissa's face when he hadn't taken the offer of her body. "She was the one who told me where you were."

Lauren's eyes narrowed at the sight of that smile. Jealousy twisted in her heart like a white-hot knife, and she couldn't stop herself from saying, "I'm surprised you could tear yourself away."

"Why don't you just say 'thank you, Stephen'?" When she remained stubbornly silent, he raked his hand through his hair in frustration. "You're the most maddening woman I've ever had the misfortune to know. After the fright you just had—"

"Stop it! Just stop." Lauren took a deep, shuddering breath. The incident had been so bizarre, so frightening, that even now the memory of it nearly made her ill. Her eyes stung with sudden tears, and she turned her back on him hurriedly.

He touched her shoulder, grimacing when she flinched away. With a grunt of exasperation, he turned her and lifted her into his lap. "Can't you accept comfort from me even now?"

Surprise banished her tears, and she put her hands flat against his chest in an effort to create some space between them. She *wanted* to be comforted. She *wanted* to sob her fear away in his arms. But more than anything, she wanted to be secure in his love, and that was the one thing he hadn't offered her.

"Let me go, Stephen," she said softly.

He shook his head. "Not until you talk to me."

"What do you want to hear?" she demanded. "That I was wrong about Richard? That I prayed you'd come for me?"

"That will do, for a start."

Her bottom lip quivered as all her plans for a gentle discussion about love and their future together vanished. He was insufferable! Her hands closed into fists. "All right, it's true. I was wrong and you were right. I was terrified, and I'm grateful to you for saving me! Now, is that enough?"

"Well . . ."

"What more do you want from me?" she cried, trying unsuccessfully to push free of him.

He chuckled. "Right now, I just want to check that cut on your shin to make sure it isn't bleeding again."

Her anger deflated, to be replaced by dread. "It's fine."

"Let me see," he growled.

"No."

His voice changed, deepening, taking on a beguiling note. "Please."

Lauren stared up at him with frightened eyes. His face was illuminated in garish flashes as the carriage passed under the streetlights, casting intermittent shadows beneath his brows and cheekbones. Her breath came in rapid pants, partly fear and partly something else—a familiar, coiling warmth that made her limbs feel heavy and slumbrous.

Her fists opened, her fingers spreading out over his chest. He reached up to tuck a stray curl behind her ear, and his eyes were so full of concern and such a deep measure of caring that she couldn't deny him. Slowly, she lifted her skirt and petticoats up to her knees.

His gaze swept the bandages, finding them unmarked. "That's a relief," he murmured. "I was afraid all that movement might have broken them open again."

She started to push her skirts back down, but he grasped her wrist to stop her.

"Why did you go with him?" he asked.

She glanced away, unable to bear the raw emotion in his eyes. "Because he said Clarissa planned to trap you by naming you her seducer."

"So you rushed to my rescue." His lips brushed the hair at her temple, then slid down her cheek. "Then you *do* care."

386

She tried to look away from him, but failed. He raised her hand to his mouth, kissed her palm, then teasingly nibbled at the pad of flesh beneath her thumb. Of its own volition, her other hand curved around the back of his neck. The inside of the coach suddenly seemed too warm, too intimate, a tiny, private world of sensuality.

"God, I missed you!" Stephen muttered hoarsely. He caressed her calves, then tickled the sensitive spot behind her knees he remembered so well. His fingertips traveled upward over her lace-trimmed drawers, and he would have given everything he owned just then to have the interfering fabric gone from between them. Already he was aching for her, his body clamoring to possess her again.

Her heart beat a frantic tattoo as desire rushed through her body in a molten tide. This was going too far, much too fast, and it was her own senses urging her along. There were so many things that needed to be said before she could allow this to happen again. "Your hand—"

"Mmmm?" He captured her mouth with his, pressing light kisses along the sweet curves of her lips.

Lauren gasped as his hand moved further up her thigh. She should stop this. She should . . . Her gasp became a sigh as his fingertips brushed the beginning swell of her buttock, then closed over the smooth curve. Scorching heat swirled through her body, making her forget everything but the incredible delight of his touch. His mouth settled over hers with possessive intent, claiming her. Her tongue moved forward to meet his, accepting his claim. They kissed and clung, their breaths mingling, their lips joined in a searing dance of passion.

"I want you," he moaned into her mouth. "It's been so long since I've touched you."

His lips left hers to taste the smooth skin of her throat. He could feel her pulse thudding in rapid counterpoint to his, and exulted in her fiery response. So it was still there, that unique passion that would have drawn him back from hell to claim her again.

"Stephen, I . . ." She broke off as he turned her, pressing her breasts against his hard chest. He kissed her again, thoroughly and skillfully, while his hand stroked slowly over her buttocks.

"Lauren," he murmured, nuzzling her hair aside to trace the curve of her ear with his tongue. "I'm on fire for you. Is it the same for you?"

"Yes," she moaned. Her head fell back helplessly against his arm, and he moved to press hot kisses down the graceful line of her throat.

His mouth traveled leisurely along the tiny buttons that held the front of her bodice closed. "I want to kiss your skin without — Damn!" he hissed as the carriage drew to a halt. "Damn it to hell!"

With a gasp of mingled surprise and embarrassment, Lauren bolted out of his lap, pulling her skirts down hastily. Stephen drew his fingertips down her flushed cheek, then helped her down from the vehicle.

While he paid the driver, she stood in the yellow glow of the streetlight, wrestling her wayward

388

emotions into some semblance of order. By the time he turned back to her, she was able to speak calmly. "Stephen, we have to talk," she said, stepping away when he would have put his arm around her.

"What's wrong?" he asked, wanting nothing more than to take her upstairs and make love to her.

She met his gaze levelly. "Why did you leave me?"

"I can't tell you," he said. With one finger, he tilted her face more fully into the light. His woman, good or bad. Beautiful, proud, infinitely desirable. "But tonight, I'll make it up to you."

His words evoked the delicious memory of the wonderful lovemaking they had shared. That, and the leaping flame of desire in his eyes, made her tremble with her need of him. But she also remembered the terrible heartache that had followed that brief interlude of passion, and she took a step backward, away from his hand.

"Why can't you trust me enough to tell me?" she asked.

Because I don't even know who you are, he thought. "Why can't you trust me enough not to ask?"

"Because I have to know," she said, searching his face for any clue as to his thoughts. But he was closed to her, his gray eyes as unreadable as fog. "Give me a reason I can understand. Give me a reason to take the risk again."

"Ah, I see," he murmured. "You want my assurance that I'll never leave again, is that it?"

She nodded. He thrust his hands deep into his pockets and cocked his head to one side, regarding her silently for several moments.

"I can't do that," he said at last.

She turned away, tears stinging the insides of her eyelids. There were too many secrets between them, too many lies. It would never work.

He grasped her arm, pulling her around to face him again. "Can't you accept me without that?"

"No." Disengaging her arm, she turned towards the house again.

He moved ahead of her to open the door. She went past him without a word and walked slowly upstairs to her room, feeling as though a great weight had settled on her shoulders.

She sat on the edge of her bed for a long time, shivering with cold and reaction. Tears kept slipping out, and she kept wiping them away. "Oh, Stephen, why didn't you just stay away?" she muttered, pulling off her shoes and stockings and hurling them across the room. "It would have been so easy then!"

Jumping up, she began pacing back and forth beside the bed. He wasn't being fair, expecting her to give him her trust when he hadn't done anything to deserve it. Truly, she should be proud of herself for having the strength to walk away from him, when she wanted so very much not to.

With a hiss of exasperation, she sat down at the dressing table and began brushing her hair with long, overly vigorous strokes. Yes, she should be proud of her self-control. Then why did she feel so bereft? Yes, loving him again would be a terrible risk, completely, utterly foolish. Then why did sitting here alone feel so completely, utterly wrong? Why did the prospect of spending the rest of her life without him seem to stretch before her like a burned-out landscape . . . desolate, empty, futile? Her tears began to flow in earnest. Disgusted by her weakness, she threw the brush down on the table before her and buried her face in her hands.

Something soft brushed across her feet, and she jumped up with a startled gasp. The cat stalked out from beneath the dressing table, his golden eyes narrowed in annoyance.

"Miaow!" he scolded.

"Nero! You startled me half out of my wits!" She bent to pick him up. "What are you doing sneaking in here like this, you naughty thing?"

Completely unrepentant, he ducked his head against her hand, purring loudly when she obediently began to scratch his ears. Lauren carried him towards the door, rubbing her wet cheeks against his soft fur. "Let's just take you back to Portia before she misses you."

She opened the door and came face to face with Stephen. His jaw was set, his hands clenched into fists at his sides. The moment her gaze met his, she knew she was lost. He'd come to claim her, and no power in the world would be enough to stop him. God help her, she didn't *want* to stop him.

Nero, having delivered her neatly to her fate, jumped down from her arms and scampered off down the hall. Lauren stood frozen, staring at

Stephen in dread and hope . . . and the warm re-awakening of desire. At this moment, she knew that nothing could be worse than not holding him again.

Stephen's gaze raked over her, in one swift, re-vealing moment taking in her tear-stained face and the forlorn pain in her dark eyes. So, her decision hadn't been any easier for her to accept than it had been for him. "I won't let you tear us apart," he said softly. "You belong to me, and it's time you faced it."

She drew in her breath, caught by the coiling desire in his eyes. This was the man she loved. The man to whom she had given herself, the man who had given her joy and laughter and incredible pleasure. Remember the pain! a small, lucid corner of her mind urged, but the molten heat in her veins overrode thought and swept away that last vestige of caution. She loved him. As much as she belonged to him, so did he belong to her. Trapped by his need, and hers, she could only watch help-lessly as he closed the few feet separating them. He looked down at her for one long, heart-clench-ing moment, and she swayed towards him.

He gathered her against him, lifting her into a brief, burning kiss. Then, still holding her, he strode into her room, closing the door behind him with his heel.

"It's cold in here," she whispered shakily. "Let me—"

"I'll warm you," he said, letting her legs slide down along his body until her feet reached the floor. "Our love will be the only fire you'll need."

He cupped her face between his hands and gazed down at her, as though he'd been starving and she was his sustenance. Her lips parted in invitation, and he slowly bent his head and fitted his mouth to hers. She welcomed him with a sigh, eagerly meeting his thrusting tongue. Their heads moved in unison as they sought a deeper joining. Her hands slid along the solid strength of his shoulders, then sank into the thick darkness of his hair.

"Sweet, so sweet," he muttered against her lips.

She felt cold air on her back, and realized that his hands had been as busy as his mouth. Without breaking the contact of their lips, he slid her dress down over her hips, then removed the layers of petticoats beneath. Her corset followed, leaving her clad only in chemise and drawers.

He stepped back to look at her, his gaze lingering for a moment on her bruised shoulder. Then he lifted her into his arms and carried her to the bed.

"It seems like a hundred years since I touched you," he said, his voice hoarse with desire. "Asleep, awake, I wanted only to love you again."

"There . . . was no other woman?" she asked, her throat tight with dread.

He let his breath out in a long sigh. "From the moment I met you, I haven't even looked at another woman." Fiercely, he said, "You've wound yourself into my very soul. Day and night, willing or unwilling, being away from you tears me apart."

He leaned down, claiming her mouth again.

Lauren was buffeted by his need and the force of her own love for him. Winding her arms around his neck, she clung to him as though she were drowning and he was her lifeline. Passion, sweet, liquid passion settled in the core of her.

Stephen moved slowly onto the bed, fitting his body to her warm, yielding curves. God, she was beautiful! He wanted to do everything at once—kiss her lips, her body, caress her, bury himself in her velvet depths.

Lauren gasped at the sensuous rasp of his trousers against her bare legs. The thin fabric of her drawers was scant barrier between them, and she could plainly feel the long, thick line of his erection as he settled between her legs. She gasped again, this time as his open mouth trailed down her throat to her collarbone.

He paused. "Am I hurting you? Your knees—"

"No," she said. "Don't stop. Please don't stop."

With a chuckle, he resumed his caresses. But a moment later he stopped again, bringing a murmur of protest to her lips. "Why didn't you tell me about this?" he asked, touching her bruised shoulder with gentle fingertips. "If Farleigh—"

"No," she soothed, putting her hand over his mouth. "It happened when I fell last night. I didn't tell you, because you would have insisted on seeing it."

"I threatened to strip you naked," he said. "I wanted to."

"I wanted you to."

His tongue darted out to taste her palm, then he took her hand from his mouth and rolled onto his side next to her. "Where else are you hurt?" he asked. "I want to see every injury, no matter how small."

"Honestly, Stephen. I don't think this is the time . . ." Her voice trailed off as she noticed the humor dancing in his eyes. Humor, and a leaping flame of arousal. Instantly understanding what he wanted, she pointed to the scrape on her wrist. "Here."

He kissed the tiny injury, then sat up and looked at her expectantly. "My hip," she said, caught up in his sensual game. He smiled, then bent to kiss the bruise she'd indicated.

"And here," she whispered, touching a spot on her ribs where there wasn't a bruise at all.

He smoothed her chemise, drawing it tightly across her breasts. Her swollen nipples were clearly visible through the fabric, and he drew in a sharp breath. "I can't see any bruise," he rasped.

"No," she said, loving the way his jaw tightened with passion. "I expect you can't. Perhaps you ought to take a closer look."

"Perhaps I should." With hands that trembled slightly, he removed her chemise. Although he burned to caress her breasts and taste the rosy, beckoning nipples that crowned them, he forced himself to touch only the spot she'd indicated. "Is this the spot?" he asked, kissing it.

"No, you've missed it," she murmured. "Try again."

He kissed another place, then another, feeling a tremendous surge of desire in his loins. She'd caught on to this play all too well, and he was having a difficult time keeping to the game he'd begun. He raised his head to look at her. Staring into his eyes with a boldness that both surprised and excited him, she wet her lips with the tip of her tongue.

"Do that again," he said hoarsely, his mouth poised a fraction of an inch from hers.

She obeyed, but it was his lips her tongue caressed, not her own. With a groan, he plundered her mouth, tasting the sweet, hot depths of her. Then he pulled away, holding himself over her with braced arms. He was nearly out of control, reeling from the force of his emotions. This went far beyond passion, far beyond possession.

"Let me pick a spot this time," he murmured.

"Yes . . . Oh!" She arched her back as his hands closed over her breasts at last.

He kissed his way down the smooth curve of her neck, pausing to dip his tongue into the depression at its base. Lauren gasped, savoring what he was doing even as she ached for yet more. Then his mouth reached her breasts, and a soft moan of delight escaped her. His tongue made teasing circles around one aching, turgid peak, then traced a moist path around the other. Wanting more, she held his head closer.

"Please," she said.

The trembling passion in her voice nearly made him groan. He could not deny that sweet plea. He began to suckle her, first one nipple, then the other.

Caught up in a tremendous surge of passion, Lauren moved her hips against him. He lifted himself off her to caress her mound through her drawers. She whimpered, her fingernails rasping across the back of his shirt.

"God, Lauren!" he groaned, finding her hot and ready even through the fabric. He stripped the interfering garment away, then explored her welcoming flesh with expert, seeking fingers.

"I want to touch your skin," she said urgently, fumbling at the buttons of his shirt.

He moved away, but only to remove his clothing with impatient haste. Magnificently naked, magnificently aroused, he came back to her. She ran her hands over the hard muscles of his chest, his taut waist, then clasped the swollen strength of his manhood. Yes, he's mine, she thought, watching his eyes close with pleasure.

He grasped her hands, pinning them above her head while he kissed her again. Lauren moaned softly, a wordless plea for him to claim her. He bit softly at her lips, nibbling, teasing, until she was whimpering with need. She was aware of him, so near and so powerfully aroused, and yet separate. She wanted them to become one, to merge together in love.

Feeling her hips move rhythmically beneath him, Stephen knew he wasn't going to be able to wait. It had been too long, and he wanted her so badly!

"Open for me," he murmured, releasing her hands.

Her legs slid apart, and he moved between them, shaking with the force of his long-restrained desire. He drove into her hot, eager flesh, and it was like coming home. "I want you too much,

397

love. I'm half-crazy with it. Can you take me?"

For answer, she wrapped her legs around his lean hips and her arms around his neck. With a deep groan, he held her to him and began to thrust into her with driving power. She met him boldly, moving her legs higher to take even more of him.

He murmured things in her ear, sensual, incredibly exciting things. She whimpered with pleasure, with need, and with the almost unbearable delight of being possessed by him again. He kissed her mouth, her throat, the tender flesh where her neck joined her shoulder, then sucked heat to the surface. And always his aroused body stroked hers, plunging deeply into her eagerly welcoming flesh, withdrawing, then driving deep again. He slid one hand beneath her buttocks to bring her just a little closer, and himself just a little deeper.

"Stephen, oh, Stephen!" she moaned as the first tiny tremors began. Like a tidal wave, they grew larger and stronger, and finally rolled over her in a tremendous wash of sensation.

Stephen, clasped within her throbbing body, was helpless to keep from following her into fulfillment. Burying his face in the curve of her neck, he gave himself up to his own climax. Shuddering, gasping with the force of it, he moaned her name against the fragrant silk of her skin.

When he could breathe again, he rolled over onto his back, bringing her with him. "Beautiful," he murmured, combing his fingers through her bright, coppery hair. "This is the most beautiful hair God has ever given a woman."

"You must be daft, sir," she said, laughing. "It's just plain, red hair, and sorely out of fashion."

"Not daft, besotted," he growled in mock ferocity, sliding her up a few inches to kiss her mouth.

Lauren ran her hands along the tautly flexed muscles of his arms and shoulders. Surely no woman had ever been loved with such strength and tenderness! He had claimed her, and in doing so, had given himself totally to her. Feeling his manhood rise up against her, she straightened her arms, breaking the kiss to look down at him with love-softened eyes. The affirmation of his desire kindled her own, and she moved against him, fully and boldly.

Stephen arched as her silken skin slid over him, loving the way her lips parted with renewed passion and the way the light turned her hair into a fiery aureole around her shoulders. "Come here," he said hoarsely.

She smiled. "Where?"

"Here." He lifted her, poising her just above his taut manhood. "Unless you're tired."

"No," she whispered, yearning towards the potent promise of him.

"Good." He eased her down, joining their bodies with exquisite slowness. "You *will* tell me if you tire?" he asked with a grin.

She braced her hands on his lean, hair-roughened chest and began to move. "You can be sure of it."

But she didn't think she would ever tire of loving him, or being loved by him.

Richard stood out in the street and stared up at Lauren's window. It was three in the morning, and her light was still on. *They* were together, and he knew what they were doing. Damn them both to hell!

Slipping around to the back door, he let himself in with the key he had filched from the widow's reticule the night before. He waited a moment to let his eyes adjust to the darkness, then moved stealthily to the drawing room. Going directly to the sideboard, he opened the decanter of brandy and the one of whiskey, wishing he could remember which Hawkes preferred. Shrugging, he took a small bottle of clear liquid out of his pocket and poured some into both liquors. After a moment's hesitation, he added some to the bourbon, as well. Might as well be sure.

He touched his bruised and swollen nose with light fingers, then replaced the decanters. "Take what is mine, will you?" he muttered under his breath. A giggle threatened, and he repressed it sternly.

"Dickie!" Bianca whispered from the doorway behind him. "What are you doin' here?"

He whirled, his face twisting in surprise. Recovering his composure, he walked quickly to her, taking her by the arm and pulling her farther into the room. "Bianca, my sweet! I came to see you."

"What're you messin' with in here?"

"Just getting myself a drink." He let go of her arm, only to wind his hand in the hair at her temple.

She pried at his clutching fingers to no avail.

400

"You're hurtin' me!"

"This is nothing, compared to what I *could* do to you. You've been disobedient, Bianca. I told you to get me a key, and you didn't." He punctuated each phrase with a jerk on her hair. "I told you to follow Lauren wherever she went —"

"Ow! I did, I did!" she whispered frantically. "I know where she been sneakin' off to."

His fingers twisted cruelly, forcing her to her knees in front of him. "Why didn't you tell me?"

"I was goin' to," she sobbed. "I was."

"Tell me now." When she did, he laughed softly. "That's a good little whore. And now, for your reward, I'm going to let you service me." He twisted her hair even more. "With your mouth, Bianca. Isn't that what you like best?"

"Yes, Dickie," she whimpered, fumbling hastily with the buttons on his trousers.

A few minutes later he was finished. Leaving her sobbing on the drawing room floor, he let himself out.

Chapter Twenty-seven

Lauren woke just before dawn the next morning. Stephen's head lay on the pillow beside hers, his naked body sprawled out across the bed. Propping herself on one elbow, she watched him sleep. It was hard not to touch him. But she just wanted to study him, to watch his broad, muscular chest rise and fall with his breathing. What a man he was!

Her lover. She'd taken an irrevocable step by allowing Stephen into her bed again; never again would he let her go. She waited to feel the guilt at what she'd done. But there was none. Having him here beside her, being able to touch him, was more important than anything else in the world. Perhaps later she'd regret making love to him again. But for now he was hers. For now, she would grasp the joy and hold it to her.

She gave in to her need to touch him. Resting her hand on his chest, she felt the steady beat of his heart. She loved him. And he loved her. Fascinated by his hair-roughened strength, she slid her hand lower to the taut ridges of his belly.

There were still things to be worked out between them. But now she had hope. Their love was like a shining beacon, to lead them through the shoals and treacherous currents of their lives. A beacon to lead them into the future.

Suddenly Stephen's arms came around her, pinning her against him. With a quick twist of his body, he placed her beneath him.

"Break into a man's sleep, will you?" he growled, his gray eyes alight with passion. "You must pay the price for that, wench."

"What price is that?" she murmured. His naked skin was hot against hers, and oh, so welcome.

"Everything." He kissed her then, exploring all the secret recesses of her mouth. Slowly and leisurely, as though he had all the time in the world.

As always, Lauren lost herself in him. Passion, sweet and powerful, coiled deep in her belly. It was heightened by her love for him, stirred into a searing flame that threatened to consume her. She wanted to be consumed. Her body responded eagerly, a hot, liquid rush of desire.

Stephen felt the small, impassioned movements she made beneath him, and was inflamed by them. She was breathtaking—slim and curved and utterly responsive—and she was his. "Do you want me?" he asked. He knew she did; he just wanted to hear the words.

"Yes," she murmured. "I want you." And as he slid downward to reach her breasts with his mouth, she said, "Yes, yes, yes."

He suckled her, moving from one nipple to the other and back again. He slid lower, his tongue making hot, moist trails down her abdomen, while his hands caressed, explored, and incited. Sweet desire ran through her veins like fire. She reveled in it, arching her back to encourage him further.

With a muttered exclamation, he propped himself over her to look into her eyes. She felt as though he were drawing her soul out, claiming it along with her body. Then he lowered himself to her, rubbing his chest against her swollen nipples. Skin against skin, heat against heat.

"It's always like this, like being burned alive," he rasped. "I don't think I'll ever get enough of you."

Lauren gasped at the exquisite sensations he was giving her. She wanted more, much more. She wanted nothing less than for him to possess her completely, and to claim him in her turn. "Love me, Stephen. Love me!" Aching to hear the words.

"Yes, yes," he muttered thickly, moving down her body to taste her nipples again.

Her faint disappointment was drowned in an intense sweep of desire as he slid lower. Maybe he *hadn't* said the words. But with every movement, every caress, he was showing her how he felt. She gasped as his tongue dipped into her sensitive navel. He moved lower yet, pressing her thighs open as he did. And then he claimed the heart of her passion. With his mouth and hands, he brought her to the brink of release. Twisting, her breath coming in quick pants, she pulled at him, desperate to have him inside her.

"Please, Stephen!" she gasped. "Please, now!"

With a hiss of indrawn breath, he slid up her, and into her, pushing her over the edge in that instant. She buried her face against his chest and cried out, shuddering.

"You belong to me," he growled low in her ear.

His body kept moving, kept stroking. "Admit it."

"I belong to you. Already her body was responding, tightening around him in reawakened pleasure. "Forever, I belong to you."

"Forever." With rhythmic power, he brought her into ecstasy again. And this time, he followed her. They clung together, kissing, as though they'd never separate again.

When his breathing returned to normal, he propped himself on his elbows and looked down at her. So many things had happened to them, between them. He'd watched her change from a shy spinster into the responsive woman lying beneath him. Was it love that had made it happen? He hoped so. Perhaps love would also make her give up her damned secrets, to come to him honestly, so he wouldn't have to protect himself against her any longer.

"Portia will be waking soon," he said, brushing her tumbled hair back from her face. "You don't want her finding me here."

Lauren was glad of his care of her. She had come very far in the past few months, but not so far as to be comfortable with Portia finding her abed with a lover.

"Always the world intrudes," she murmured.

"It seems to." Reluctantly, he separated from her.

"Kiss me once more before you go," she said, holding out her arms.

He did, as tenderly as though it were the first time. Then he dressed and silently left the room. Feeling marvelously loved and cherished, Lauren went back to sleep.

A woman's full-throated shriek echoed through the house, bringing Lauren out of bed with a gasp. It was full light now, hours since Stephen had left. The woman screamed again, a terrified sound.

"Dear God, what's wrong? Portia!" Hastily, Lauren pulled her dressing gown over her nakedness and rushed out into the hall. "Portia!"

The widow's door opened. Portia hurried out, clad only in her nightdress and with her cap falling down over one ear. "Did you scream?" she asked in obvious confusion.

"No," Lauren said. "It came from downstairs!"

Whirling, she dashed towards the stairway. "Bianca!" she called. "Are you all right? Bianca!"

There was no answer. Lauren reached the foyer and flung open the door to the parlor. Finding it empty, she ran to the drawing room. There she found Bianca crouched on the rug, her face buried in her hands. Stephen was standing beside Eldridge's supine body.

"Prussic acid," Stephen muttered, sniffing the contents of a glass on a nearby table. "Damn!"

"Stephen, what happened?" Lauren cried.

He stalked across the room towards her, his jaw tight with fury. Grabbing her by the arm, he hauled her roughly over to Eldridge. *"This* is what happened!" he growled.

Lauren took a single, horrified glance at the man on the floor, but his grotesquely convulsed features and the violently pink skin of his face would haunt her forever. She turned her back on the awful sight, struggling to control her nausea. Tears of pity sprang into her eyes. "Oh, the poor man!" she gasped. "He's . . . he's dead?"

"Yes, he's dead!" Stephen shouted. "Damn it to hell, I *knew* better than to let you do this to me again!"

"Me?" she asked, bewildered by the unwarranted attack. "What did I—"

"You had to get to me one last time, didn't you?" He raked his hands through his hair, fighting for control. This was absolutely the worst time to lose his temper, but damn it to hell, a man had been killed right under his nose, and it was his fault! If he hadn't let his feelings for Lauren blind him to everything else, he might have been able to stop this.

"What are you trying to say?" Lauren asked quietly. Her hands were beginning to shake, so she clasped them in front of her.

"I'm saying that I've been stupid, incredibly stupid, and—"

"What happened?" Portia asked from the doorway. Then she saw the sprawled shape on the floor, and her eyes widened. "Good heavens, is Mr. Eldridge ill?"

"I'm afraid he's dead, Mrs. Danforth." Stephen said. "No, don't come in. You don't want to see him."

Portia groped for her handkerchief. "An accident?"

"No." A muscle jumped spasmodically in Stephen's jaw. "He's been murdered."

"Murdered!" Portia gasped. "Oh, dear. Oh, dear.

Then we must send for the police. Bianca, will you—"

With a cry, Bianca jumped to her feet and ran from the room, nearly knocking Portia down in her haste. A moment later the outer door slammed closed.

The widow cleared her throat. "Well, my goodness! Stephen, if you could—"

"I'm sorry," he said. "I can't leave this room unattended. Evidence."

"Oh." The widow gathered the folds of her dressing gown around her. "I'll run next door, then, and ask one of their servants to go for the police."

Stephen nodded. "Tell them Detective Hawkes is already here."

Portia gave a start of surprise. "Oh! Yes, very well." She turned and hurried away.

Lauren was numb with shock. "Detective Hawkes?" she asked, her voice almost inaudible. "You . . . you're a policeman?"

"Yes." He squatted beside Eldridge and began searching his pockets with quick efficiency. "I was sent here to find a way to pry Mrs. Danforth out of Eldridge's grasp." Swiveling on the balls of his feet to face her, he added, "But it seems as if someone beat me to it."

Understanding, horrible, *horrible* understanding burst upon her. She drew in a shuddering breath, sick to her very soul. "You think I did this?"

Stephen saw the innocence in her eyes. Saw it, and turned away from it. He didn't dare believe in her, because he wanted to believe so badly. He'd already believed too much, given too much. And lost too much. Sternly, he pushed his emotions aside, forcing himself to see her with a policeman's cynical perceptions.

"What possible reason could I have for doing such a thing?" she asked, her hand going up to clasp her throat.

"We know about the will."

"What will?" she cried.

His aloof calmness dissolved in a flood of outrage. "Don't play the innocent!" he shouted, rising with a lithe coiling of muscles. Before she could react, he stood before her, his hands coming down hard on her shoulders. "You ask for motive? I'll give you a quarter of a million dollars' worth of motive!"

She hung in his grip like a broken doll. "I don't know what you're talking about!"

"Don't lie to me," he snapped. "Just once, don't lie. You know as well as I do that Mrs. Danforth is leaving her entire estate to you."

"She isn't! She told me everything is going to charity!"

He shook his head. "Sorry, but we've seen the will."

"Oh, no!" Lauren whispered. "Oh, no! And you think I pois—" she took a deep breath before forcing the word out, "poisoned Mr. Eldridge, because I was afraid he'd convince her to change it?"

"Do you think I *want* to think that?" he raged, his voice hoarse with anger and pain. And even now, in the depths of his rage and betrayal, the sight of her made his heart turn over in his chest. He shook her, wishing he could shake the truth from her, wishing even more that it could be a truth that would let him stay with her. "What are you hiding? Give me a reason to think otherwise, damn you! Give me *something!*"

Lauren studied his face closely, surprised by the agony in his voice. With sudden clarity, she understood how deeply he had been hurt by what had happened here, and how very much he wanted to be given an excuse to put those suspicions aside. Logic dictated that she tell him everything. But it was her heart, not logic, that prompted her response.

"After what we shared, do you really believe me capable of this?" she asked, reaching up to touch his mouth with her fingertips. "In your heart, can you really believe that?"

He grasped her wrist with one hand, then slid his other arm around her waist to pull her against him. "Faith, Lauren? Is that what you're asking from me?"

"Yes." Hope began to burgeon in her breast.

"Sorry, but I can't give you that." He turned her around, still keeping her pinned against him, and forced her to look at Eldridge's contorted body. "See that?" Stephen said in her ear. "Dead bodies bother me, Lauren. They bother me a lot. And this one got here right under my nose, when I was all befuddled with love for you."

"Don't," she whispered, squeezing her eyes closed.

He spun her around again, shaking her to make her look at him. "It's my job to find out who killed that man, and I can't do it with my heart.

410

Facts solve murders—not faith, not blind belief, or thoughtless acceptance. Only facts."

"Then I'll give you a fact, *Detective* Hawkes." She straightened, meeting his gaze levelly. "If you think that I would ever harm another human being, then you don't know me at all."

"You're right," he said harshly, letting go of her. "I don't know you at all."

She turned on her heel and walked away.

"Don't leave the house," he called after her. "We'll want to question you further, Miss *Wakefield*."

She hesitated in mid-step, caught by his bitter emphasis on the last word, then forced herself to continue walking. As soon as she was sure he couldn't see her, she broke into a run, barely reaching her room before the tears started.

She slammed the door closed and flung herself across her bed, crying for herself, for her lost happiness, and for poor, doomed Edward Eldridge.

"Oh, Stephen!" she whispered, blotting her streaming eyes with her sleeve. "How did things get so jumbled up?"

That seemingly simple lie she had told more than two years ago—one small change, Stanton to Wakefield—had blown up into a grotesque horror. And now a man was dead. Perhaps if she had told the truth long ago, Eldridge would be alive now. And perhaps Stephen would not be down there thinking that she'd had something to do with his murder.

In sudden decision, she scrambled off the bed and began to dress. It was time to correct the wrong she had done—for all the right reasons, but a wrong nonetheless. No matter what price she had to pay later, the time had come for Lauren Stanton to come into the open. Her mother would never want her to keep the secret under these circumstances.

As carefully as a knight donning his armor before a battle, she washed all traces of crying from her face and coiled her hair into a knot at the back of her head. "So, Detective Hawkes, you'll get your wish," she said to her reflection in the mirror. "The true Lauren will be revealed to you in all her tarnished Stanton glory. What will you think, I wonder? Will the child of illegitimacy be more palatable to you than the possible murderess?" Would he turn away from her in disgust, or would he accept her?

She turned away from the mirror, unable to bear the flash of hope that brightened her eyes for a moment. Still the fool, she thought, wishing for what will never be. She squared her shoulders, hiding her nervousness behind her accustomed mask of composure, then went downstairs again.

As Lauren passed through the foyer, Portia came hurrying back in, bringing a flurry of wind-driven snow into the house with her. Lauren ran to close the door against the gusting breeze.

"It's awful out there," the widow said breathlessly. "Good heavens, child! You're as pale as though you'd seen . . . Oh!"

"A ghost, Portia?" Lauren asked gently, taking the widow's cloak and shaking the snow from it. She hung the garment up to dry, then touched the old woman's cold-reddened cheek with her fingers. "You're shivering, dear. Why don't you go upstairs and get in bed, and I'll bring you a cup of tea?"

"That sounds wonderful." Portia started upstairs, but paused to look over her shoulder at Lauren. "Perhaps I should stay to greet the police . . ."

"Stephen seems to have everything well in hand," Lauren said. "Go on, before you get pneumonia all over again." As soon as she got Portia settled, she promised herself, she'd go in to talk to Stephen.

She watched the old woman walk upstairs, then hurried to the kitchen to set water on to boil. She hovered beside the warmth of the stove, for the steadily worsening wind seemed to seep through the very walls. Heavy, wet snow lashed against the window, coating the glass with a thick, obscuring film of white.

The water began to boil, and Lauren turned to place the tea things on a tray. Her hands began to shake, rattling the delicate Limoges china dangerously, but it wasn't because of the chill.

Why are you trembling? she asked herself. *It's only a matter of saying a few simple words, after all.*

Sternly repressing her nervous shaking, she finished making the tea and carried the tray upstairs to Portia's room. Once the old woman was settled in bed, Lauren went downstairs to the drawing room. Finding it locked, she knocked softly.

"Stephen, may I come in?" she called.

The door opened and Stephen stood framed in the doorway, looking inordinately tired and grim. There were deep grooves bracketing his mouth, and

413

his eyes were chillier than the weather outside.

"What do you want?" he asked.

She clasped her hands in front of her. "I have something to say to you."

"If you've come here to ask for faith again, you're wasting your time."

"No, I didn't come here to ask for that," she said. Her voice was almost too soft to be heard, so she cleared her throat and tried again. Her gaze skittered from object to object, never daring to meet his. "I . . . I . . . came to tell you . . ." A lump rose in her throat, sealing the words within.

Stephen knew she was ready to tell him the truth at last, but strangely, he dreaded hearing it almost as much as he desired to know her secret. But just the fact that she had come to him eased some of the grinding pain in his heart. Caressing her cheek gently with the back of his hand, he said, "You can tell me, love. I won't let you face this alone. Just tell me the truth, and I'll stand beside you all the way."

She looked up at him, startled. "You think I came to confess to Mr. Eldridge's murder! Oh, Stephen, you couldn't be more wrong!"

With a muttered curse, he turned away. She ran to block his path, grasping his arms to bring him to a halt. "Listen to me," she said urgently, silently begging him for understanding. "I had nothing to do with poisoning that man. You *know* me. If you look into your heart, you'll know I couldn't have done it."

He raked his hands through his hair, irritated by the imperative urging of his heart to believe her.

414

"You're asking for faith again."

"No! Not faith," she whispered. "Understanding."

"That's even more to ask than faith," he said wearily. "I don't even understand myself any longer."

There was an imperative knock at the front door. Stephen ignored it. "What did you come down here to tell me?"

"Hawkes!" a voice bellowed from outside.

"Padgett," Stephen growled. Raising his voice, he called, "In a moment, Commissioner."

"The Police Commissioner?" Lauren turned away hurriedly. "I'd better let them in."

Stephen reached out and took her by the arm. "Wait. Tell me first."

"Hawkes!" the voice shouted again. "We're freezing out here!"

Lauren shook her head, rejecting the idea of revealing her secret like this. She wanted time to assess his reaction, time to grieve alone if it wasn't what she hoped. If he turned from her in disdain, she'd be too shattered to deal with anything else. "I can't now. Later. When . . . when we're alone."

He released her reluctantly, his brows contracting in a black scowl as he watched her hasten towards the door. What the hell had she wanted to say? He felt a tingle at the back of his neck, his instincts telling him he had missed something damned important. He took a step forward, intending to pull her back and make her talk to him again, but she had already opened the door. Padgett and two other policemen came in with a gust of windblown snow, and he knew he'd lost his chance. He'd have to wait until later.

Lauren took the visitors' hats and coats and hung them to dry, overly conscious of the Commissioner's piercing regard. "There's hot water on the stove. I'll make you gentlemen some tea," she said, then fled towards the kitchen.

"Mighty upset, isn't she?" Padgett observed.

"So am I." Stephen led the way into the drawing room, giving the others a quick summary of what he'd discovered so far.

Padgett examined the corpse, then sniffed the decanter of brandy, wrinking his nose at the smell of bitter almonds. "Whew! Enough in there to kill twenty men, if I have my guess!"

"It's in the whiskey and bourbon, too," Stephen said.

Padgett grunted and bent to inspect Eldridge's body at closer range. Then he straightened. "Well, what do you think, Hawkes? Did the girl do it?"

Stephen tried to imagine Lauren slipping into this room to pour virulent poison into the liquor, and then to lie in his arms upstairs, making sweet, abandoned love to him while she waited for a man to die. No! Every fibre in his body rejected that image—body, mind, heart, and soul. The facts be damned, he just couldn't believe it of her.

He met the Commissioner's gaze levelly. "No, I don't think she did."

"Evidence?" Padgett demanded.

Stephen shook his head, thumping his chest with his fist. "Instinct," he said, his mouth twisting with a self-deprecating smile.

The Commissioner grunted again. "Some of the best police work is done on instinct," he growled.

"And some of the worst," Stephen said. He propped one hip on the arm of the sofa and stared gloomily at the floor. So, he'd made the leap of faith Lauren had asked for. He ought to feel like a fool. But the hard-edged anger that had been gnawing at his guts was gone, replaced by a sense of rightness.

There was a knock at the door. "Enter! " Padgett barked.

Lauren came in, pushing the tea cart ahead of her. Padgett took it from her and pushed it to one side. "Miss Wakefield, I'd like to ask you a few questions."

She shot a glance at Stephen, finding his face set and unresponsive. He had withdrawn from her, her tender lover hidden behind those cynical policeman's eyes that could see only facts. She'd never felt so alone, or so vulnerable. She returned her attention to the Commissioner, schooling herself to calmness. "Yes, sir?"

"What kind of liquor did Eldridge drink?"

"Liquor?" she asked in surprise. "Why, he always drinks—drank brandy."

"Not whiskey or bourbon?"

She shook her head. "Never. He hated them both."

"Thank you, Miss Wakefield," Padgett said. "We'll call you if there's anything else."

"That's all?" she asked in surprise.

The Commissioner nodded. "I'm sure we'll have a great many things to ask you, but later."

Lauren glanced at Stephen again. He was looking at his feet, a frown upon his face. She retreated from the room in confusion. Why had the Commissioner asked that particular question? She'd expected him to ask her about her identity or Portia's will, anything but what liquor Eldridge drank. Shaking her head, she started up the stairs, intending to check on Portia.

Before she reached the landing, however, a knock sounded at the front door. She hurried down and opened it, expecting to see more policemen, but there was only a young, raggedly dressed boy standing upon the stoop.

"Are you lost?" she asked. "Come in out of the weather, and we'll see—"

"I ain't lost," he said, holding out a folded piece of paper. "I got a message here for Miss Stanton."

Lauren hesitated for an instant, then said, "I'm Miss Stanton."

The boy thrust the paper into her hands, then dashed off down the street. Lauren closed the door and leaned her back against it as she opened the note. It was from Richard.

Lauren, darling, she read. *I'm here at Alanna's, apartment, and we're having such fun. I want you to join us. Be quick about it, and be sure you're alone, or you won't like what happens.* He had signed it with his usual elaborate flourish.

"Oh, dear God!" Lauren whispered, her heart fluttering wildly in panic. "He's got Mother!"

Grabbing her cloak hastily, she rushed out into the storm.

418

Padgett stared out the window, gloomily watching the snow fall while Stephen paced the confines of the drawing room.

"You know, Commissioner, it's damned odd that there was prussic acid in three decanters," Stephen said, watching the other policemen cover Eldridge's body with a blanket.

Without turning, the Commissioner said, "I'm beginning to think you're right about Miss Wakefield. Hell, she was doing all the cooking! If she wanted to poison Eldridge, a few weeks' judicious application of arsenic would have done the trick and left no one the wiser. This way," he thrust his thumb at the shrouded corpse, attracts too much attention."

"Besides, she knew he drank only brandy," Stephen murmured. "Why spike the other decanters and take the risk of killing someone else?"

Padgett gave an explosive snort. "A person can only hang once. But I agree that this doesn't feel right for her. From what you've told me, she's too damn smart to make such a messy business out of murder. No, neat and tidy and quiet fits our pretty Miss Wakefield."

Stephen sighed and rubbed the back of his neck. Something was nagging insistently at the corner of his mind. Damn, but this whole thing smelled wrong! The wrong poison, the wrong decanters, the wrong . . . Suddenly he stiffened, realization bursting upon him like a bolt of lightning. The wrong man. *The wrong man!* "*I* drink whiskey," he said.

Padgett whirled to stare at him. "So you do. Haw! Then maybe it was you she was trying to kill."

"No," Stephen said with absolute certainty.

"Then it could be any number of people," the Commissioner growled peevishly. "There must be dozens of criminals who'd like to see you buried."

And one rejected suitor, Stephen thought grimly. I wouldn't put anything past that young man, even murder. He opened his mouth to say something about Richard, but he was prevented by an urgent rapping at the door. One of the policemen went to answer it, and Bianca came into the room, twisting her hands in front of her nervously. She had obviously come in from outside, for her hair was wet, as was the bottom third of her skirt.

"Mr. Hawkes, I got to talk to you," she said. "Alone."

"All right, Bianca," he said, taking her arm and leading her into the foyer.

"What is it?" he asked when they were alone. "Why did you run away like that?"

"I hate police." She pushed a lock of wet hair back from her face. "Look, I wouldn't have come back a'tall if it wasn't for Miss Wakefield. She been decent to me. Now somethin's up, somethin' bad, and I think she's in trouble."

Every muscle in his body tensed. "What do you mean?" he demanded.

"Just go to Bleeker Street. There's a brick house in the middle of the block that's been divided up into apartments. Number Four, that's where you need to go." She gave him an impatient push.

"Now, go on! Trust me, she needs you!"

He crossed his arms over his chest and stared at her suspiciously. "Bianca, Miss Wakefield is perfectly safe. She's upstairs with Mrs. Danforth."

"That's what I been tryin' to tell you! She ain't upstairs!" Bianca shoved him again, harder. "I passed her on my way here. She was gettin' on a stage on Broadway."

"Damn it to hell!" he shouted, grabbing the first coat he saw. A moment later he hurtled out of the house, leaving the door open behind him.

Chapter Twenty-eight

Lauren peered out the frost-blurred window as the stage moved slowly down Broadway. The buildings looming four storeys above her head wore a thick coating of snow on their cornices and window ledges, and the normally crowded street was nearly empty of vehicles. A few pedestrians hurried along the walkways, their shoulders hunched against the gusting wind.

The driver opened the small trapdoor in the roof. "Miss, it's blowin' somethin' fierce out here. I'd like to get off the road soon."

"Please, just take me as near Bleeker Street as you can," she begged.

"I'll do my best," he said, banging the trapdoor closed.

"Hurry, oh, please hurry!" Lauren whispered. If only she were a bird to fly to her mother's side! How had Richard found Alanna, and why? What did he hope to gain by this seemingly mad scheme? But after last night, she no longer felt able to predict Richard's actions, or even understand them. She didn't have any idea what she'd do once she got to the apartment; the only thing she was certain of was that he would do something terrible to her mother if she didn't.

The stage tilted abruptly, and she grabbed the edge of her seat to keep from being flung to the floor. She heard the driver's startled curse, and then the crack of his whip. The vehicle lurched forward, then sank back again.

The driver opened the door. "We're stuck, Miss. If you'll just stay inside, I'll —"

"Help me down, please," she said.

He obeyed, then gaped in astonishment when she hurried away. "But Miss! You can't go on foot in this weather!" Realizing that she couldn't hear him, he shrugged and began unhitching the horse. A moment later he lost sight of her in the storm.

Lauren trudged down the street, struggling against the wind that tore at her cloak and hair and sent snow slashing into her face like thousands of stinging needles. Her skirt and petticoats were soon soaked through, their clammy weight dragging heavily at her legs. She was nearly sobbing with exhaustion by the time she reached Bleeker Street.

"Just a little farther," she told herself, forcing her way through snow that was halfway to her knees. "I'm coming, Mother. I'm coming!"

The storm howled around her savagely. Several times the visibility was so poor that she was forced to creep slowly along the wall of a house, to keep from losing her way completely. After what seemed like hours, she spied the looming, red-brick front of her mother's apartment house. She staggered into the welcome shelter inside, then leaned against the wall to catch her breath.

After a moment she straightened and peered up

the dark stairway. Save for the wind shrieking angrily outside, all was silent. It was time. Feeling uncomfortably like a sheep going to slaughter, she squared her shoulders and walked up the creaking stairs to knock at the door of Number 4.

The door swung open, and Richard came out to take her by the arm in a grip that had no gentleness in it. "Come in, darling," he said. "So nice of you to come out in such foul weather."

Lauren saw Alanna lying on the sofa, gagged, her wrists and ankles tied with strips of cloth. "Mother!" she cried, lunging against Richard's restraining hand.

"Now, now, sweetheart. Don't get in a dither," he said, holding her with one hand, closing and bolting the door with the other.

"Let me go to her!" she hissed.

"Oh, very well. But keep your voice down, or I'll have to gag you, too." He pulled her over to the sofa. "See? She's perfectly fine."

Alanna nodded in reassurance, her eyes eloquent over the muffling bandage. Lauren reached to pull the gag down, but Richard's hand came down on her wrist with numbing force. He pulled her away, forcing her to sit in a chair near the fireplace.

"Let me take your cloak," he said, divesting her of her outer garment. "Goodness, you're soaked to the skin! Wouldn't you like to change into dry clothes?" His voice dropped to a sly whisper. "I'll help. I'm very good with buttons."

Lauren lifted her chin, hiding her panic behind the small show of defiance. She knew he wanted to see her fear—to savor it—and she wasn't about to

424

give him the satisfaction. "I'll stay as I am, thank you."

He chuckled and moved away. "Such a modest little home for a Stanton," he said, sweeping his arm to indicate the inexpensive furnishings, the clean but shabby room that served as both living and dining quarters. "Old Caldwell would have a fit."

Lauren ignored his supercilious grin. "Where's Mary?" she demanded. "What have you done with her?"

"The maid, you mean?" He waved his hand negligently. "Your mother was ever so cooperative, sending her on an errand so we could talk alone. You two . . . ladies were *so* easy to manipulate." Taking a flask from his pocket, he drank deeply from it and sighed. "Ahh, absinthe. Warms the cockles of the heart."

Lauren clasped her hands in her lap to hide their trembling. All the while, Richard had been the true villain. How could she have let herself be so completely fooled by his elegant manners and seemingly ardent pursuit? Her stomach writhed as she remembered how she had thought the worst of Stephen, ignoring all evidence of the true nobility of his character.

"You don't love me," she said. "You never did."

"Love!" He uttered a weird, high-pitched sound that was more a giggle than a man's laugh. "You must be a holdover from the last century, darling! Such romantic notions in that pretty little head of yours!"

"Then what do you want with me . . . us?"

"Oh, many things, my dear Miss Stanton. Many, many things." He began to pace the room, his arms swinging with frenetic energy, and his voice turned petulant. "You haven't been very nice to me, you know. Bedding Hawkes right under my nose, then cheating me out of my twenty thousand—"

"What twenty thousand?" Lauren asked.

"Your dowry. Do you think I would have considered marrying you if the old woman hadn't offered some incentive? As Miss Wakefield, you didn't have the social standing to wipe my shoes."

Anger flowed into her with a rush, stiffening her spine. "And I suppose Lauren Stanton would be more palatable?"

"Why, yes, darling." His pale eyes danced with malicious humor. "Even the bastard of a whore is acceptable, if the whore happens to be Caldwell Stanton's daughter. There's such a thing as being so wealthy that people don't care about your morals."

"Ask my mother if that's true," Lauren retorted bitterly.

"But, darling, *she* didn't have the money. If Stanton had wanted to, he could have crushed the gossips."

"So it's Stanton's money you want," Lauren said.

"Not entirely," he said. "I *will* have to modify my plans somewhat; judging from your behavior last night, marriage no longer seems to be an option." He took his flask again, bringing it to his nose to savor the biting, heady aroma of the absinthe. "But I pride myself on being a flexible man. If marriage won't work, then we'll just have to think of something else. You would make a charming mistress, charming. Either way, I'll get what I want." Tilting his head back, he let the fiery liqueur slide down his throat.

Lauren sat motionless, watching his prominent Adam's apple bob up and down as he drank, and knew with utter certainty that he was insane. Insane and vicious. The wind rattled the window behind her, howling like some hungry beast. But even more bestial was the man before her, and much more frightening. For a moment she struggled for breath, as the walls seemed to close in on her.

Almost at the edge of panic, she glanced at her mother. Alanna pointed to the door with her bound hands. *Run,* her eyes pleaded. *"Save yourself!*

That selfless gesture gave Lauren strength she never expected to have. A smile crossed her lips briefly, and she gazed lovingly into her mother's eyes as she shook her head in refusal. Whatever happened here, they'd face it together.

Richard lowered the flask, then pulled out his handkerchief, and patted his lips daintily. His pale, unutterably cold gaze fell on Alanna, and Lauren's heart began to pound in terror. "Just what do you plan to do, Richard?" she asked, hoping to draw his attention back to her.

Swiftly, he crossed the room to her, putting his hands on the arms of her chair and thrusting his face close to hers. "Many things, darling. Many, many things. But first, I want you to write a letter to your grandfather."

Lauren recoiled from the strong licorice smell of

427

his breath. "A ransom note, you mean? You're wasting your time," she said. "He doesn't care what happens to me."

"Perhaps not." He whirled away from her and began to pace the room again. "But if you mention his long-lost daughter, I'm sure you'll get a reaction from him."

She shook her head. "You can't—"

"I'm tired of people telling me what I can and cannot do!" he shouted. "All my life, that's all I've heard." His voice went up shrilly. "Well, it's time you learned that I can do anything I want with either of you!" He pulled a knife out of his pocket as he stalked towards the sofa where Alanna lay.

"Mother!" Lauren gasped, jumping to her feet. "No!" She ran forward, but knew with sick horror that she would be far too late.

Richard grasped a handful of Alanna's hair and pulled her head back, exposing her vulnerable throat, then pressed the tip of the knife just above the rapidly throbbing pulse point. He looked up at Lauren.

"I wouldn't scream, if I were you," he said.

She stopped, holding her hands up in a placatory gesture. "I'm not going to scream. Please, Richard, let her go."

"Are you going to write the letter for me?" The knifepoint sank a fraction of an inch into Alanna's skin, bringing a tiny drop of crimson to the surface.

"I'll do whatever you want!" Lauren cried. "Just don't hurt her!"

Nodding towards the writing desk, he said, "Now

428

write what I tell you. Ah, let's begin it with a salutation that is bound to get his attention: My dearest Grandfather. For the rest, let's see . . ." he began dictating a rambling message in which threats to Alanna's safety figured heavily. He ended with a demand for two million dollars.

"Two million dollars?" Lauren repeated, sure she hadn't heard him correctly.

"A pittance, at least for him." He chuckled. "One million dollars for each Stanton woman."

Lauren finished writing the note, then blotted it, and brought it over to him. She moved slowly, carefully, her gaze never leaving that threatening knife. Oh, Stephen! she thought. If only my heart could somehow call directly to yours and bring you here to me!

"Thank you, darling." Richard lifted the locket Alanna wore around her neck. "This looks old. Is it a family heirloom, something your father will recognize?"

Alanna nodded, her eyes wide and frightened. With a flick of his knife, Richard cut the delicate chain. The blade moved up, hovering over her face for a moment, then slipped downward to cut a lock of her honey gold hair.

"Just so he knows this isn't a hoax," Richard said. A wild light came into his eyes. "What a truly marvelous day this is turning out to be!"

Lauren knew he hadn't the slightest intention of letting either of them go, even if he got the money. She closed her eyes for a moment, wrestling with an almost uncontrollable urge to scream. Somehow she had to put her own fear aside and speak calmly, to try and reach whatever spark of rationality remained to him. "Richard, why don't you stop this before it's too late? You're only going to get yourself into a great deal of trouble."

"Too late?" He uttered another of those blood-chilling giggles. "Lauren, my sweet, it's already much too late." Lifting the knife, he advanced on her.

She took a step backward, her heart beating a frantic tattoo of terror. "What are you going to do?" she whispered.

"I just want a token to send your grandfather. Now stand still, darling, or someone's going to get hurt."

Lauren obeyed, trying to ignore the shudder of fear and distaste that went through her as he reached behind her to pull the pins out of her chignon. Her hair fell about her shoulders in a coppery flood, and he lifted a handful of it admiringly.

"Lovely," he murmured.

Mesmerized by the glittering blade, she watched helplessly as he cut a single lock from the bright mass of hair. When the knife withdrew, she let her breath out in an inaudible sigh of relief. But suddenly he grabbed the neckline of her dress and yanked it brutally, making a foot-long tear in the fabric, and her terror returned in a crashing flood.

He pointed to the small love-mark Stephen had made on her neck the night before. "Did you and Hawkes have fun, darling?" he rasped, his face twisting into a terrible mask of rage and hatred.

"Did you open your legs eagerly for him? Did you like it when he—"

"Stop it!" she cried, pulling her dress together with hands that trembled with shock and outrage. How dare he speak that way about a lovemaking that had been tender and generous and right? "You're disgusting!"

"I'm disgusting?" he screamed. *I'm* disgusting?" Grabbing her arm, he jerked her against him with a wrench that made her cry out in pain. "I'll take you right here in front of your whore of a mother, and then I'll cut her—"

The door exploded inward with a force that took it right off its hinges. Stephen, his coat covered with snow and splinters of wood, came hurtling into the room.

"Stay back, or I'll kill her!" Richard shrieked, raising the knife.

Without hesitation, Stephen leaped upon the struggling pair just as the weapon flashed downward towards Lauren's face. His left hand closed around Richard's knife arm, stopping the blow in mid-strike. With his free hand, he flung Lauren away from danger. Then his struggle for possession of the knife began. Richard was like a mad cat, biting, scratching, kicking, and Stephen was hard-pressed just to keep his grip on the man's wrist. They lunged from one end of the room to the other, overturning tables, smashing glassware, and knocking into walls with enough force to send the pictures crashing to the floor.

Lauren ran to the sofa and began plucking at Alanna's bonds, but the knots had been tied so

431

tightly that she couldn't loosen them. "Oh, Mother, I can't do it!" she cried in frustration. At least she did manage to drag the gag down.

Putting her arms protectively around the older woman, Lauren sat helplessly and watched Stephen fight for his life—and theirs. She wanted to rush into the fray and help him somehow, but realized she would only put him in greater danger. Please, God! she prayed. Don't let anything happen to him!

Stephen managed to overbalance Richard, coming down on top of his opponent with his knee in his stomach. Richard's head hit the floor with a loud crack. He went limp, and Stephen took the knife out of his hand and rolled him over.

"Is he dead?" Lauren asked shakily.

"No, just unconscious," Stephen panted. Glancing over his shoulder at her, he added, "I don't know how long he'll stay this way. Give me something to tie him up with, will you?"

Lauren looked around at the shambles of the room, then bent to remove her stockings. She handed them to Stephen and stood watching as he trussed Richard's hands tightly.

"That should hold him." Stephen discarded the coat that had been sadly torn and battered during the fight, then rose to his feet and held out his arms. "Come here."

Lauren walked into his embrace. As those strong arms closed around her, the tears she had been holding back for so long began to flow. "I was so afraid," she sobbed, burying her face against the front of his shirt.

432

"Shhh. Everything's all right now," he murmured.

"He was going to—"

"I know. He won't hurt you, honey. I won't let anyone hurt you." He stroked her hair comfortingly, his hands gentle and possessive.

Lauren savored his warm strength and the solid beat of his heart against her cheek. He'd come for her! She didn't know how or why, but for this moment she gave herself up to the wonder of the miracle that had brought him here. Then she pushed away from him. He looked down at her, and his eyes were so full of love that she trembled. She had to tell him now. No matter what the cost, there would be no more secrets between them. "Stephen, there's something I have to tell you."

"Let me say something first." He framed her face with his hands, his thumbs gently wiping the tears from her cheeks. "I know you didn't have anything to do with Eldridge's death."

"How?" she asked, trembling even more.

"Faith," he said. "Faith in what you are. I love you, Lauren."

Her hands slid around his neck. With a tiny sob of happiness, she pulled his head down to hers. He lifted her against him, his mouth claiming hers with gentle tenderness.

"Ahem!" Alanna cleared her throat meaningfully.

Stephen raised his head, reluctant to break the kiss for an instant. But as his gaze fell on the older woman, he sighed and set Lauren back on her feet. "I suppose we ought to untie her," he said.

"Mother!" Lauren gasped, rushing to the sofa. "Oh, I'm sorry."

433

Stephen followed her, his brows contracting in a frown. Using Richard's knife, he cut Alanna free, then turned to Lauren. "Sit down," he growled.

Lauren obeyed hastily, warned by the harsh note in his voice. Crossing his arms over his chest, he looked from her to Alanna. "I want an explanation, and I want it now."

"I'm . . . I'm . . ." Lauren faltered for a moment, then lifted her head proudly. No longer would she make excuses for who or what she was. "My name is Lauren Stanton. And this is my mother, Alanna."

"Stanton's granddaughter, by God!" He raked his hands through his hair. "You've been playing one hell of a game, Lauren. With me, with everyone."

Alanna raised her hand, forestalling Lauren's reply. "Let me tell him why," she said. "You see, Mr. ah . . ."

"Hawkes. Stephen Hawkes."

Alanna folded her hands in her lap. "I was ill for a very long time, and Lauren took the position with Mrs. Danforth in order to support me—or rather, my doctors."

"So?" he asked impatiently. "Why the lie?"

"I've never been married, Mr. Hawkes. Because of . . . the life I've led, Lauren could not obtain respectable employment without that lie."

Understanding came to Stephen in a rush. "And she—"

"Let me finish," Alanna said imperiously, lifting her chin in a gesture Stephen knew well in her daughter. "Because I was a kept woman, Lauren grew up friendless. There were people who crossed

434

the street to avoid passing close to her."

"Mother," Lauren protested. "Please don't. You don't have to justify your life to anyone."

"Yes, I do, Lauren. Because of what he means to you, I want this man to understand." Taking a deep breath, Alanna continued, "Lauren was taunted, reviled, spit upon. Why? Because of me, Mr. Hawkes! During the past two years, she has swallowed her pride, and put her principles aside to live a lie. Not for herself, Mr. Hawkes. To pay for medical care for me! Me, me, me!"

With each word, her fist beat the sofa. Lauren wrapped her arms around Alanna and held her tightly. Stephen glared at them both, jamming his fists against his lean hips.

"Are you quite finished?" he asked.

They looked up with identical expressions of astonishment. He towered over them, his jaw thrust forward belligerently. "And you thought I'd recoil in disgust from your daughter because she's illegitimate?"

Lauren flinched. Illegitimate. It sounded so ugly, so final. She studied his face closely, but it was iron-hard, closed even to her.

"Or perhaps you believe I'd deem her unfit to be anything but my mistress?" He took a deep breath. "What kind of man do you think I am?" he shouted, furious at the implied insult, but even more furious at the unfeeling cruelty of the people who had hurt Lauren so badly that she couldn't trust him. He pointed at her. "And you! Do you know what you've put me through with your goddamned foolishness?"

435

Lauren and Alanna clung together, staring wide-eyed at him. He turned his back on them, too angry to speak any longer. Then Lauren's brain began to work again, and hope blossomed in her heart. She disengaged herself from Alanna and went to stand behind him.

"You don't care?" she whispered, putting her hand tentatively on his shoulder. "You really don't care?"

He whirled, pulling her against him so suddenly that she cried out in surprise. Cradling her head in one hand, he looked down at her with blazing eyes, and kissed her. His lips slanted across hers with fierce possession, and she clung to him, meeting him with equal fierceness, equal joy.

"Ahem!" Alanna cleared her throat again.

Reluctantly, he lifted his head to look at her.

"What are your intentions towards my daughter, Mr. Hawkes?" she asked.

"I'm going to marry her as soon as I possibly can," he growled. He lowered his head, intending to renew the kiss, then met Alanna's gaze again. "Will I do?"

She nodded. "Yes, Mr. Hawkes, you'll do." Her lips curved upward in a smile as she watched him kiss her daughter again.

A high-pitched giggle came from the bound figure on the floor, and the lovers sprang apart.

"How sweet," Richard said, rolling over onto his back.

Lauren looked down at him, surprised that she felt no hatred for him, only pity. He'd been given everything a young man could want, but still

436

hadn't been satisfied. And saddest of all, no matter how much he had, it would never have been enough. "I'm sorry for you, Richard," she said. "Truly sorry."

"I don't want your pity, you slut." His gaze moved to Stephen. "You're supposed to be dead." His voice went up in a scream, and spittle ran out of the corner of his mouth. "Dead, dead, dead!"

"You killed Eldridge instead, I'm afraid," Stephen said.

Richard began to laugh, a shrill cackle that made Lauren put her hands over her ears and turn away. The laughter went on and on, insane, horrible. And then it stopped as suddenly as it began, to be replaced by whimpers.

With a sigh, Stephen bent to move the captive into a more comfortable position. "It has almost stopped snowing. In an hour or so, I ought to be able to get through. Until then, however, I'm afraid we're stuck with him."

Alanna smiled. "I've had worse company than a madman, Stephen."

"Do you mean your father?" he asked.

This time, she laughed. "Perhaps."

Stephen glanced around the wrecked room. "We'd better spend the night at Mrs. Danforth's house."

"Yes." Alanna folded her hands in her lap. "We . . . we should send for my father to meet us there. I have some things to discuss with him."

"Are you sure, Mother?" Lauren asked.

"I'm sure. It's time to forget the past. Time to forgive, time to forge a future." She picked a book

437

up from the floor and opened it. "Lauren, dear, my sewing kit is in the corner behind you. Why don't you take Mr. Hawkes into the other room and mend his sleeve?"

The only other room in the apartment was the bedroom, which her mother knew. She also knew that Stephen would never be content to merely have his sleeve sewn. Completely astonished, Lauren gasped, *"Now,* Mother?"

Alanna turned to Stephen. "If you stand there and do nothing, Stephen, I'll have to think you're a fool. And you don't strike me as a fool."

"I have been, many times, but I've mended my ways," he said.

"You're both mad," Lauren said, backing away from him. "This is impossible. It's—" She broke off as Stephen swept her into his arms.

"Your mother approves," he growled. "And we're married in every way that matters."

Lauren put her hand flat against his chest. "You said you love me."

"I did. Do you want me to say it again? Very well. I love you. I will love you until the end of my life. And if it's allowed, I will love you through all eternity." His storm-colored eyes blazed with impatience. "Now, Madam, will that do?"

She wound her arms around his neck. "It will do."

Chapter Twenty-nine

Lauren stood at the front window of the apartment, watching the street for any sign of Stephen. The city had become a fairyland, its dirt and smoke and sharp edges buried in a pristine white blanket of snow. The magic wouldn't last long, she knew. People and carriages were beginning to move about; in a few short hours, the snow would be churned into dingy brown slush.

She smiled, banishing that thought. She had learned to take joy as it came. For now, she would enjoy the snow.

"Is there any sign of him?" Alanna asked from her seat on the sofa. "It's been hours!"

Lauren let the curtain fall and turned to her mother. "I expect he had a great deal of explaining to do — not the least of which is what he was doing with the Commissioner's horse."

"You love him very much, don't you?" Alanna murmured.

"With all my heart." Lauren sat beside her mother and took her hands. "I'm so happy I don't know if I can contain it all."

A door opened and closed downstairs, and Lauren jumped to her feet. "That must be him!"

She ran out to the landing to wait for him. Stephen came up the stairs, looking tired and grim, but his face brightened when he saw her.

He took the last several steps two at a time and pulled her into his arms. "Did you miss me?" he asked. "No, don't tell me. Show me!"

She wound her arms around his neck and kissed him until they were both breathless. He broke the embrace first, his mouth poised a fraction of an inch above hers. "That will do," he said. "For now."

Keeping his arm around her waist, he drew her into the apartment. Alanna rose from the sofa. "What happened to Mr. Farleigh?" she asked, twisting her hands nervously.

"He's been arrested for the murder of Edward Eldridge."

Alanna heaved a sigh of relief. "I thought that perhaps his family . . ."

"Not even the Farleighs can help him now," Stephen said. "Even if we hadn't found an almost-empty bottle of prussic acid in his bedroom, he's been babbling his guilt to anyone who would listen."

Lauren closed her eyes, thinking about how close it had been. If Stephen had been the one to take that drink . . . She shuddered, pushing the unbearable thought aside.

Stephen's arm tightened on her waist. "Richard won't hang. But he'll spend the rest of his life in Bloomingdale Asylum, where he belongs." He nearly told them about Richard's ravings about Biance Cavalli being Lauren's half sister, but de-

440

cided that tomorrow would be soon enough. Lauren and her mother had faced enough for one day, and still had Stanton to deal with.

"Get your cloaks, ladies." He grinned at their identical expressions of apprehension. "Your destiny awaits you."

Quickly, so as not to give them a chance to think, he ushered them down to the carriage that was waiting outside. Although he kept up a constant flow of conversation in an attempt to distract them, Alanna grew increasingly more nervous as they neared their destination. When the vehicle pulled to a halt in front of the house, she began to cry softly into her handkerchief.

"I'm sorry, I'm sorry," she sobbed. "But I'm so terribly frightened."

"You don't have to do this," Lauren said.

Alanna took a deep breath and wiped her eyes. "It's just that Father has always been so, so difficult."

Lauren thought difficult was an extremely polite way of describing Caldwell Stanton. "Remember, Mother, he wants *your* forgiveness."

"I don't suppose you were intimidated by him at all," Alanna said.

Stephen laughed. "She very nearly gave him apoplexy." He reached over to pat Alanna's hand comfortingly. "What shall we do? Do you want to go or stay?"

Alanna's chin lifted in determination. "We stay."

"Good for you." Stephen jumped down from the carriage, then turned to lift them down in turn.

"Thank you," Alanna murmured, taking his

proffered arm. "So gallant, even when I'm such a coward."

"No coward could have raised a daughter like Lauren," he said.

Alanna stopped, turning around to look full into his eyes. "You know, Stephen, I believe you're right." Holding her head regally, she said, "Come, Lauren. Take your fiancé's arm and let us go in."

Lauren wanted to kiss him for his understanding and compassion. Her love shining out of her eyes, she tucked her hand into the crook of his arm and led him escort her to the door.

No one answered his first knock, or the second. His brows raised, he tried the door and found it unlocked.

Lauren hurried past him. "Portia? Portia!" she called.

A faint answer came from upstairs, and she looked at Stephen over her shoulder. "Please take Mother into the parlor. I want to talk with Portia alone."

Lifting her skirt, she ran upstairs to the widow's room and tapped softly at the door. "May I come in?" she called.

"Of course, dear."

The old woman, still clad in her voluminous black dressing gown, was sitting before the mirror, fussing with her hair. "I can't seem to get it right," she complained. "And Mr. Stanton is due any minute now."

"Here, let me." Lauren began coiling Portia's hair into a chignon. "I have something to tell you—"

"Your name is Lauren Stanton," the widow said, offering the box of hairpins.

The efficient movements of Lauren's hands faltered briefly. "You know?"

"Commissioner Padgett told me not a half hour ago. My goodness, but he was upset! Not only at discovering that the Stantons were involved in this, but to have Stephen bring the scion of the Farleighs down to the station trussed like a Christmas goose . . ." Portia giggled. "Did he really?"

"Yes, he did." Lauren stared at the old woman's reflection in the mirror. "Portia, don't you have anything to say about my deceit?"

The widow turned to face her. "What choice did you have, dear? You thought me a silly, prudish old woman—"

"Never silly."

"Prudish, then." Portia held out her arms. "Oh, Lauren, I don't care what your name is!"

Lauren went down on her knees to enter that embrace, not caring that tears were flowing down her cheeks in a hot flood. The two women clung to one another for a long time, not needing to speak to understand one another.

"Well," Portia said at last, "has Stephen proposed yet?"

"Yes—in his own inimitable way, of course."

"At least you'll never be bored." Portia dabbed at her eyes with her handkerchief. "A detective! And he seemed to be such an excellent spiritualist. I had such hopes that he could reach Thaddeus . . ." She sighed.

Lauren took the old woman's hands in hers. "I'm sorry, Portia."

"So am I," Portia murmured. "So am I." Gently, she disengaged her hands and stood up. "Have you brought your mother with you?"

"Yes, she's downstairs. I hope you don't mind us taking over your house this way—"

"I wouldn't have it otherwise." In a tenderly maternal gesture, the old woman wiped the tears from Lauren's cheeks with her own rather damp handkerchief. "Well, here I am dithering again! I'd better get dressed. You go downstairs and try to, well, smooth things along when Mr. Stanton arrives."

Lauren glanced at the black bombazine dress that was lying on the bed. "I'll help you," she said, rising to her feet. "It will only take a moment."

"No, I've changed my mind. I believe I'll pick another dress. Go on, dear, your mother needs you just now."

Lauren turned to blow a kiss at the widow, then hurried downstairs. As she reached the foyer, there was an imperious knock on the door.

"Old devil," she muttered under her breath, opening the door to let her grandfather in.

His granite stare pinned her. "Well, you said she'd come. It took long enough."

"It took *you* twenty-two years," she pointed out.

"Where is she?" he growled, throwing his hat and coat carelessly onto a nearby bench.

Her back stiff with indignation, Lauren led him to the parlor. Alanna jumped up from her chair and came to stand beside her daughter. Reassuringly, Lauren put her arm around her mother's

444

waist and held her tightly. "Don't be afraid, Mother. He's not nearly as awful as he pretends to be."

Stanton looked from one to the other of them incredulously, then turned to Stephen. "Is this to be my punishment for my sins?" he demanded.

"It seems so," Stephen replied with a chuckle.

The old man's gaze locked with Lauren's. The corners of his mouth twitched with mingled outrage and humor. "Snookered me well and good, by damn! I should have known. In your own way, you're just like me."

It was her turn to be outraged. "I certainly am not!"

Stanton grunted. "Are you going to marry her, Hawkes?"

"Yes, indeed."

"You have my deepest sympathy," the old man said fervently.

Finally, he spoke to his daughter. His voice was as harsh and peremptory as ever, but there was a new softness in his eyes. "Well, Alanna, what do you say? Can you forgive me for being a cold, sanctimonious bastard? Can you let me share your life again—just a little?"

Lauren gave her mother an encouraging squeeze, then stepped back to let her face this decision alone. Alanna hesitated for a moment, then walked forward and put her arms around Stanton's waist. He hugged her tightly, and Lauren had to turn away from the look on his face.

She sat down beside Stephen, trembling with suppressed emotion. He put his arm around her,

445

his other hand caressing her cheek tenderly. "While they're occupied . . ." he murmured, tilting her face up to his.

Lauren held him away with braced arms. "Don't you dare!" she hissed, torn between amusement and exasperation. Then her voice softened. "Can't you wait until we're alone?"

"No," he said, closing the distance between them. "I'll never get enough of you."

Lauren's gaze fell to his mouth, and the protest died in her throat. This was the man she loved, the man she was going to marry, the man who would give her beautiful children with eyes that changed from mist to storm-gray. The thought was unbearably stirring. Her world narrowed until it contained only him.

"I love you," she murmured. Her lips parted, anticipating the possessive touch of his.

"Hawkes!" Stanton's harsh voice rudely startled them both out of their bemusement. "Am I interrupting your tryst?"

Stephen looked up. "As a matter of fact, you are."

"Sorry," the old man said with patent insincerity. "So, *Detective* Hawkes. Tell me how the hell you expect to support my granddaughter on a policeman's salary."

"That's none of your goddamned business," Stephen said cheerfully.

"Haw!" Stanton put his arm around Alanna's shoulders. "What do you think, Alanna? Will he be able to handle her?"

"Yes," she said. Giving Stephen a wink, she

446

added. "Most of the time."

"Excuse me," Portia said from the doorway.

Lauren gasped; for the first time since she'd met the widow, Portia wasn't dressed in black. Instead, she was wearing a gown of pale lavender that made her skin glow and her hair look like spun moonlight. She was soft and feminine and very pretty, and Lauren caught a glimpse of the girl she had been so many years ago.

"I know this is a family gathering," Portia murmured. "But would any of you mind very much if I joined?"

Stanton, smiling with open admiration, extended his free hand to her. "Not at all, dear lady. Not at all."

Lauren let her breath out in a long sigh. Turning to look at Stephen again, she found him very close, his mouth just a few inches from hers. His eyes were the color of the morning mist, but there was a little leaping flame in those gray depths she'd come to know—and love—so well.

"While they're occupied . . ." he murmured again, leaning close.

As his lips settled over hers, she welcomed him eagerly, not caring in the least if the others saw her kissing him. After all, they were family.

HEART STOPPING ROMANCE BY ZEBRA BOOKS

MIDNIGHT BRIDE (3265, $4.50)
by Kathleen Drymon

With her youth, beauty, and sizable dowry, Kellie McBride had her share of ardent suitors, but the headstrong miss was bewitched by the mysterious man called The Falcon, a dashing highwayman who risked life and limb for the American Colonies. Twice the Falcon had saved her from the hands of the British, then set her blood afire with a moonlit kiss.

No one knew the dangerous life The Falcon led—or of his secret identity as a British lord with a vengeful score to settle with the Crown. There was no way Kellie would discover his deception, so he would woo her by day as the foppish Lord Blakely Savage . . . and ravish her by night as The Falcon! But each kiss made him want more, until he vowed to make her his *Midnight Bride*.

SOUTHERN SEDUCTION (3266, $4.50)
by Thea Devine

Cassandra knew her husband's will required her to hire a man to run her Georgia plantation, but the beautiful redhead was determined to handle her own affairs. To satisfy her lawyers, she invented Trane Taggart, her imaginary step-son. But her plans go awry when a handsome adventurer shows up and claims to *be* Trane Taggart!

After twenty years of roaming free, Trane was ready to come home and face the father who always treated him with such contempt. Instead he found a black wreath and a bewitching, sharp-tongued temptress trying to cheat him out of his inheritance. But he had no qualms about kissing that silken body into languid submission to get what he wanted. But he never dreamed that *he* would be the one to succumb to *her* charms.

SWEET OBSESSION (3233, $4.50)
by Kathy Jones

From the moment rancher Jack Corbett kept her from capturing the wild white stallion, Kayley Ryan detested the man. That animal had almost killed her father, and since the accident Kayley had been in charge of the ranch. But with the tall, lean Corbett, it seemed she was *never* the boss. He made her blood run cold with rage one minute, and hot with desire the next.

Jack Corbett had only one thing on his mind: revenge against the man who had stolen his freedom, his ranch, and almost his very life. And what better way to get revenge than to ruin his mortal enemy's fiery red-haired daughter. He never expected to be captured by her charms, to long for her silken caresses and to thirst for her never ending kisses.

Available wherever paperbacks are sold, or order direct from the Publisher. Send cover price plus 50¢ per copy for mailing and handling to Zebra Books, Dept. 3660, 475 Park Avenue South, New York, N.Y. 10016. Residents of New York and Tennessee must include sales tax. DO NOT SEND CASH. For a free Zebra Pinnacle catalog please write to the above address.